CRITICAL PRAIS

"Hot pick of the week."
—*US Magazine*

"Isenberg's delightful debut tells the tale of a woman trying to break into Hollywood screenwriting...making for a hilarious comedy of love and fulfillment in unexpected places."
—*Booklist*

"Chick lit fans will enjoy Lynn Isenberg's ironic homage to the movies..."
—*The Best Reviews*

"Isenberg's funny, debut novel about a porn writer with a heart, a conscience, and a soul...is bringing her some much-deserved success."
—*California Literary Review*

LYNN ISENBERG
graduated with a degree in English language &
literature and a minor in film studies from the University
of Michigan. Since racking up credits on a number
of Hollywood mainstream films, she's gone on to
write, produce and market programming for cable
television networks, live events and the Internet.
And write her first novel, *My Life Uncovered.* Isenberg
resides in Marina del Rey, California. Reach her at
www.lynnisenberg.com.

the funeral planner

Lynn Isenberg

**RED
DRESS
INK**™

THE FUNERAL PLANNER

A Red Dress Ink novel

ISBN 0-373-89533-X

© 2005 by Lynn Isenberg.

This book is a work of fiction. The names, characters, incidents and places are the products of the author's imagination, and are not to be construed as real. While the author was inspired in part by actual events, none of the characters in the book is based on an actual person. Any resemblance to persons living or dead is entirely coincidental and unintentional.

*Dedicated to the continuing spirits of
my father, Gerald W. Isenberg,
my brother, Steven Isenberg,
and my dear friend John Laurence*

*To my mother, whose laughter and courage
light up the path of life.*

I wish to thank my wonderful, supportive friends
and family, who provided me with idyllic places
throughout the United States and Canada in which
to write this novel. Thank you to Eileen Isenberg; Bobby
and Laurie LaZebnik; Adam Taylor, Leah Solo Taylor,
Alain Cohen, Evelyn Baran, Lea and John Sloan,
Steve Wright, Laura Banks, Ellen Binstock,
Virginia Herndon, Cynthia Gibb and Suzy Borson.

With extraspecial appreciation to those who have
inspired and supported this work: Lori Helman Pogoda,
whose offhanded comment inspired the kernel for
the idea; Mary Hanlon Stone, who readily offers those
early and necessary second opinions; Corie Brown,
whose every word is a cherished pearl of wisdom;
Lawrence Mandel, who shined the light; Jack Susser,
who listens with steadfast encouragement; Chelsea Low,
for her intuitive astute insights; my agent, Irene Goodman,
who really gets me and champions me; and to my truly
talented, highly perceptive and trusted editor, Kathryn Lye.

I'd also like to pay special tribute to Bill Bates, founder
of the Life Appreciation Training Seminars for sharing
his deep wisdom in the most encouraging manner; to
Fay Spano of the NFDA who generously opened doors to
new vistas; and Professor Timothy Fort at the University of
Michigan for his groundbreaking insights in the world of
leadership training.

•

In writing this novel, it is my goal that *The Funeral Planner* helps demystify social fears associated with bereavement and provides a shift in perception for enhanced experiences to ease the burden of grief. Therefore, I invite you all to share your life celebration stories by visiting "The Funeral Planner" at www.lynnisenberg.com.

I also hope this story provides some insight and appreciation for the unsung heroes of the caregiving profession as well as leadership skills for dedicated individuals who wish to start their own independent business within the balance of life.

Note: This novel is fictional and takes creative license with respect to rules and regulations within the funeral industry. Any likeness to real people, real organizations, companies, or funeral homes is purely coincidental.

Appendix A: Personnel Profile or
Reflections of a Failed but Still Determined Entrepreneur

The closet is dark all right.

Claustrophobic-dark. Suffocating-dark. And, well...casket-dark.

I plunge through racks of limp, hanging clothes, riffling for one particular outfit, wondering why all closets symbolize darkness.

Doesn't the very word itself—*closet*—connote a sense of obscurity, a feeling of entrapment, or a space for concealment? And furthermore, why don't closets have automatic lights? Closets with instant lighting would completely do away with their negative connotations. Think about it.

If you grew up with closets that blasted light every time you opened them, you might have a completely different association. One related to openness, illumination and optimism. On that note I ponder, why can't caskets have power-generated lights inside so the dead don't have to feel so alone in the dark? Okay, so they're dead, they might not know the difference, but still…it might make their afterlife adventure less intimidating if they could see, metaphorically speaking, where they were going. It's not such a far-fetched notion. I've heard stories of family members placing battery-powered cell phones inside the caskets of their loved ones. So why not internally-lit caskets for eternity?

Theories on darkness and light free fall in my mind as I stand solo in the narrow closet of my one-bedroom apartment in Los Angeles, unable to prepare for a task that I must prepare for: packing appropriate clothes to wear for a funeral in the dead of winter in Ann Arbor, Michigan.

I lift a wrinkled black linen skirt off a hanger and place it against my five-foot-three-inch frame. I stare at myself in the mirror. "Madison Banks, what are you doing? Linen in winter? Highly impractical." I lower the skirt and face myself in mismatched underwear and bra that have both seen better days. I'm still in great shape. Lissome and toned, with dark brown hair and eyes, and oh, yes…a brain that never stops.

The whole experience of packing is one big déjà vu. It was only one year ago to the day that my cousin, Smitty, passed away. And now on my dresser sit two *yahrzeit* candles; both purchased last night at a local grocery store.

You're probably wondering, what's a *yahrzeit* candle? Wax and wick minijars that represent a Jewish custom for honoring the dead. The immediate family of the deceased lights one Y-candle on the anniversary of a loved one's death and recites a prayer called *kaddish*. The candle burns for twenty-four hours in memory of the departed.

Granted, I am not a member of Smitty's immediate family, but Smitty left a mark on me, and though I'm not a practicing religious Jew, I do have a great affinity for ritual.

Every day of every summer when I was a kid I went sailing on Clark Lake with my uncle Sam. I'd sail the Sunfish to shore, place a daisy in the bow, and thank it out loud for bringing us safely home. Rituals are what give me a sense of stability. They're the only thing.

So when the one-year anniversary of Smitty's date of death faithfully appeared on my computer calendar, I bought a Y-candle for him. The reason I bought two candles? Well, one was for Smitty. One was an afterthought. I had never purchased a *Yahrzeit* candle before and was surprised to discover how incredibly inexpensive they are. I never expected to receive another call with the same message of death: last year my cousin Smitty; this year my former classmate and friend, Tara Pintock. I couldn't help but admonish myself for buying two candles. What if I hadn't? Would Tara still be alive? I knew it was a silly thought. But still…what if?

I glance at the Y-candles, blanching at the thought of picking up the phone on this very day next year, fearful an unwanted pattern may have begun. Neither Smitty nor Tara was supposed to have died. Smitty was a vibrant forty-two-year-old artist whose oil paintings were getting recognized in major museums. And Tara—Tara was only thirty-one years old, with a whole life ahead of her. A freak strike of lightning got Smitty. A faulty inhaler for an asthma attack took Tara. I fume with anger. Even more so because Tara had just taken the painful and liberating step of leaving her father's multimillion-dollar business in mortgage-lending to pursue her true life's passion: music.

My knees wobble at the thought of reliving the funeral scene all over again in the same cold winter, at the same funeral home, on the same Sunday, at the same time, only with a different cast of characters. Last year, the ensemble was comprised of family; this year it would surely include my fellow graduates from U of M's Entrepreneurial Studies Program, whom I hadn't seen in over nine years. Never mind running into people you really don't care to see at this stage of your perennially budding career, but ugh, the very thought of attending a funeral, let alone sitting through one of those interminably long, canned eulogies that rarely do justice to the deceased.

I am beginning to realize that I have no clue how to cope with death. It is full of…grief! And that is one department I have little if no experience in. Yet, it's a natural part of the life cycle. So how come in junior high or college, they don't have courses on how to deal with it? How was algebra, home economics, biology or entrepreneurial studies supposed to help me deal with bereavement?

I stop the outfit search and stand quietly among the hanging layers of dated pantsuits, sundresses, shirts and Dockers jeans. I feel numb. I know the feeling is temporary and that in due time it will fade to make way for the grief that is inevitable, but I wish it would linger forever.

Loss of any kind is something I prefer to avoid. Of course, loss is part of growth, which is part of change, and that is something I fully embrace—or at least try to…I think.

I sink to the bottom of my closet. Branches of loose fabric drape around me, forming a jungle of uninhabited human parts. I'm thirty-one, like Tara. I live alone in L.A., far from family. And I haven't had a lucky break career-wise in a really long time. I know deep in my soul that I was born an entrepreneur. Even before I knew the definition of the word *entrepreneur*—an individual who can rapidly identify an opportunity and act upon it—I knew who I was. Someone who's willing to take risks through experimentation, willing to learn by trial, willing to fail by error, and then start all over again. You have to be tenacious, unwilling to accept "no," and capable of discovering and connecting dots others miss. And that's what I do all the time: connect the dots between the most unlikely marriages of elements and then pursue them—relentlessly.

I grind my teeth as I sift through the dated textiles, brushing aside any hangers that drip with color. "Orange will never do. Where's that black wool top and matching skirt?" I ask aloud. But it's too dark in the closet. I redirect the reading light attached to the bed frame toward the innards of the closet, where I continue to search like a surgeon seeking the right nerve ending to cut. Okay, so it had been a while since I purchased new clothes. Money to buy…well, anything, had not been an option for, okay…years. But what was more important, a wardrobe or honoring investors? I can do without. The trouble is that I have been *doing without* for so long that I no longer know how to do *with. What a novel concept that is,* I think. *Doing with.* I look forward to that day. All I have to do is create one successful business and I will be "there," I think.

My wardrobe smells musty, laden with cedar and stale air. I find the black wool skirt and matching top. Would it be so horrible to do a wardrobe repeat? Not that I have choices. I check to make sure no moths have bored holes in the fabric then pack it in the black Tumi suitcase that Uncle Sam gave me for college graduation.

Uncle Sam is my best friend and the only one in my whole family who knows anything about business. He used to own a small fishing-lure company because fishing is his passion. As a kid, he carved a fishing lure from a fallen tree branch, caught a bass and started a company. He hired his younger brother, Charlie, my dad, at the age of five to paint the lures for him.

If you talk to Uncle Sam, he'll tell you that by the 1940s quality fishing lures had become an American art form, the quality of the craftsmanship began to diminish once plastics came on to the market. He developed his own brand of baits known as Banks Baits with the slogan "Baits you can bank on." Banks Baits produced ten thousand lures a day. Eventually, he sold the company and retired at the age of fifty.

Uncle Sam says, "Fishing is like living. It requires patience and persistence. The joy of the journey over the joy of a catch." He often reminds me, "Do the right thing in all of your affairs, conduct yourself in business as you would with family and friends, because it makes no sense to have different codes to live by for different facets of life." When I ask for examples, he follows our family's teaching traditions with a story.

"It was during the war," he begins, "before American manufacturing was exported to Third World countries—which has depleted America of its pride, but that's another story, Maddy. Now where was I? Oh, yes. I would drive to a tiny remote village in the upper peninsula of Michigan to buy caseloads of handcrafted ice-fishing lures. One day, I asked a Potawatimi Indian named Fisherman Joe, 'How much for a caseload of lures?' And Fisherman Joe said, 'Thirty-five dollars.' That didn't sound right to me. So I turned to him and I said, 'Why, Fisherman Joe, don't you know there's a war going on? I'll give you fifty dollars per caseload and three dollars for shipping.'"

I proudly relayed that story to a visiting professor of business marketing, who told me that Uncle Sam had been an idiot. An idiot? For not taking advantage of the ignorance of others? Incensed, I dropped out of the class, swapping it for a course in ethics but not before telling the greedy professor-meister that he was in dire need of a humanity injection.

Maybe my business ethics are one reason why I'm still playing the results? I chose to put my career first and then focus on a relationship that would include marriage and children. The only problem is, nine years out of college I am still trying to put my professional life in order.

I finish packing my suitcase, a sore reminder of my exodus from Ann Arbor to L.A.—where I intended to create my own American dream…one day.

"Maddy…you there?" shouts a thick male voice from behind the front door.

I glance at my watch—one of those bare-all watches where the Lucite encasement reveals the naked ticks and tocks of its internal mechanisms. I wear no other kind. I like to know how things work.

"Coming!" I call out. I zip up the suitcase and dash through the narrow hallway to open the door for my sort-of current boyfriend.

I've been hanging out with Seth Wickham, a twenty-six-year-old, extremely good-looking, out-of-work stuntman, for four months, during which time I've realized I can't fully commit to him. Yes, he is amazing in bed. But I've learned that aside from incredible endurance in the bedroom, stuntmen tend to enjoy putting themselves in harm's way, whether they're on the job or not.

I open the door. Seth takes me in his tattooed arms and kisses me. That part is lovely. Too lovely. I feel myself getting lost in him, lost in the comfort. And I fear that too much comfort will compromise me.

He halts the kiss and throws me a wink. "How ya doing, Bulston?"

Bulston is one of his nicknames for me because he thinks I possess looks and manners reminiscent of Sandra Bullock, Jennifer Aniston, Drew Barrymore and Reese Witherspoon.

His monikers range from Anilock and Bulston to Withermore and Barryspoon. At the moment, he's in a Bulston mood.

I scrunch my face and look at him. "It's Banks. Madison Banks."

"When you do that serious and funny thing at the same time…turns me on." He grins.

Before I know it, he's kissing me again. All thoughts pleasantly evaporate until his voice lulls me back to the present.

"Like my new tattoo?" He lifts his shirt in one sweeping motion, displaying a back laced with intricate designs.

"It's stunning, Seth. Incredibly artistic." What else can I say except that all those tattoos, as beautiful as they are, will prohibit him from ever being buried in a Jewish cemetery. If he was Jewish, that is.

His eyes glint with lust and he dives in for a French kiss. When it comes to Seth, I find myself overly preoccupied with sex, which distracts me from my *professional* goals, which delays me from accomplishing my *personal* goals.

"Where are your bags?" he asks.

"In the bedroom," I reply, softly rubbing the base of my neck where he unwittingly grasped a thick mound of locks.

Seth saunters into the bedroom and picks up the suitcase. "That's it?"

I nod, then glance at a week's worth of *Financial Street Journals* stacked in the corner. "Oh, and the *FSJs*. Can't forget those."

"You pack light," he says, grabbing the papers with his free hand.

"Actually, I pack efficiently. I don't like to take anything I don't have use for." As I utter these words, I can see a certain metaphorical truth with regard to Seth and me, and know that somehow, sometime soon, I will need to do something about it.

★ ★ ★

The long stretch of road on the way to the airport is void of other vehicles. Seth turns to me with a wily smile. "How about a three-sixty?"

"I prefer not." I quiver.

He offers a salacious grin, then swiftly jams his foot against the brakes of his Jeep Wrangler. He dramatically twists the wheel like a conductor orchestrating a sudden flourish of symphonic sounds. I find myself jammed against the passenger door, my heart thumping. The car swerves and weaves in a circle, then pulls out of a fishtale and veers into a straight arrow. We rock back into place.

Seth grins at me. I smile back, trying to be a good sport, realizing that impromptu three-sixties are not something I wish to include in my repertoire of experiences.

"Did you like that?" He smiles.

"Not particularly. I just established a corporation, registered the URL for a new Web site and finalized a Power-Point presentation. I'd like to stick around to finish what I started."

"Wow. Busy Barryspoon. Is that that Artist Showcase you've been working on?"

"Artists International," I reply. "I'm about to shop it to investors. I've got professional artists and designers lined up to have their bios videotaped with a licensing plan in place to capitalize on cross-promotional applications. I just have to be the first to bring it to market."

"How the hell do you do…all that?" he asks, dubiously lifting a brow.

My voice elevates in pitch as it always does when I get excited. "I secure financing. I stabilize strategic partnerships with globally recognized museums. I get the media jazzed about it so they'll write articles. I create an online catalogue for curators to download artist bios for prospective clients. I design a companion convention for art dealers with sponsors—who've given me verbal commitments. Oh, and I include a new emerging market called Outsider Art. It's raw, unaffected, unsophisticated and people are paying millions for it."

"Yeah, but how does this thing make money?" asks Seth.

"I license private collections of major art and design museums around the world to advertisers. Museums love it because the extra income helps them stay afloat. I want to do it with anime, comic-book art and video-game art, too. Anyway, it's all in the business plan that I gave to Jonny Bright."

"Who's that?"

"A venture capitalist." I pause, feeling my brow furrow.

"What's that face for, Withermore?"

"I should've had him sign an NDA. Last time I shared my idea with venture capitalists and strategic partners, someone leaked it to Derek Rogers."

"Derek Rogers? The dude who burned you in college?" asks Seth.

I nod. It still gives me a bad feeling. Forgiveness is not my strong suit. And when you consider that Seth and I have only known each other for four months and he already knows the history of an incident that occurred ten years ago, well, it's pretty obvious that I haven't let that one go.

Seth cocks his head toward me. "Can I ask you something? How can you even think about business when you're off to a funeral?"

"Simple. If I don't, I'll fall apart." Then, to keep the pain at bay, I force a smile, adding, "Though I am getting to be pretty good at interment these days. Black dress on hand, there's nothing to it."

We reach the airport departure terminal. Seth parks curbside and handles my bags for me. He leans in for another kiss when I remember the envelope and hand it to him. "I totally forgot. Could you please pop this in the mail for me? It's for Ryanna in South Africa. I promised her a sample business plan as a template for the business she wants to start."

"Who's Ryanna?" he asks, taking the envelope from me.

"She's in my e-chapter of Start-up Entrepreneurs."

"You're always doing that—helping other people, then getting taken advantage of or getting ripped off. Why do you do that?"

"I…I don't know how not to," I say, never having thought of it like that before.

"That's why I dig you." He slips me a deep-throated kiss, then probes, "So…can I borrow some money?"

I freeze. How can he ask me that when he knows I don't have it to give? Besides, he stills owes me seven hundred and fifty for his trip to Portland to visit his six-year-old son. I can give him anything else…like my apartment or my entire library of books on corporate marketing, demographic trends and strategies on how to generate income. But actual cash dollars—I don't have those to give. And anyway, it's a line I can't cross. Since I have less experience in relationships than in failed business ventures, I proceed in the following fashion.

"You know, Seth. I really like you and you are the *most* amazing kisser. But this, uh, merger that's in development is turning into a high-risk position and it's affecting my bottom line. Actually, I don't have a bottom line anymore because I went under it a long time ago. What I mean is, the proof of concept just isn't there right now because—well, because there are too many essential barriers to entry and I think that the value proposition has been, well, exhausted, and, uh…"

Seth interrupts. "Whoa. Can you pull back the reins and say that in English?"

I have to really think about it for a minute. "I propose we table the merger until our financial positions stabilize." It's the best I can do.

"So…you want to say goodbye."

"No. I did not say that word. Please, don't say…that word. I'd rather we just say, 'see ya later,' and see what happens. How's that?"

"Cool," he says. He pauses to squeeze my hand. "See ya later, Maddy." Then he throws me a wink loaded with goodbye.

On the escalator toward security I take a deep breath, holding back my tears—unborn tears that represent the loss of Smitty, Tara, past failures, disappointments and now Seth. Even though I knew I had to do it, it didn't lessen the hurt any.

I board the plane for Detroit only to get immobilized in the aisle, waist-to-face with a gentleman in first class. I recognize him: the iconic singer-songwriter Maurice LeSarde, whose melodic music and happy lyrics I worshipped as a kid. Uncle Sam introduced me to his music when I was six. It turned out that Tara was a huge fan, too. It was in fact LeSarde's songs that bonded Tara and me together as friends.

This must be a sign from Tara, I think, a message of some sort. He sits quietly next to me, his face inches from my waist. Not knowing what else to say, I whisper, "Are you Maurice LeSarde?"

He whispers back, "Yes, I am."

"I'm such a big fan of yours!" I say like a silly starstruck child. "I kept your signed photo on my wall all through junior high, and high school…and college…and, well, it's still up on my office wall, in the corner of my, uh, kitchen."

"Why, thank you," he says. There's a humble smile on his face.

"So, um, what will you be doing in Detroit?" I ask, timidity taking over.

"I've got a concert there."

"You're performing? Wow. You haven't given a concert in twenty years."

He looks at me, my fandom clearly validated now. "Well, it's a twenty-year anniversary."

"Then it's at the Fisher Theater."

"That's right." He nods. His interest seems to pique.

"That's a great concert venue." The bottleneck in the aisle breaks up. I move forward, guided by a herd of travelers behind me. "Well, um, see ya later, Mr. LeSarde," I say.

Once seated, I compose a letter to Mr. LeSarde and include $3.46 which I figure I owe him for unlawfully licensing his music at the age of six to put on a roller-skating show in the basement for which I had charged admission tickets. That was my very first business. The product was "entertainment," which I created and advertised by going door to door in the neighborhood and guaranteeing proceeds for a neighborhood compost site. All in all, I proudly produced two performances and raised $176, enough to build a small compost bin behind the local grocery store.

I include a few suggestions for restaurants for Mr. LeSarde to go to while in the Detroit area, then neatly fold the note up and ask a stewardess to give it to him. Okay, well, that took approximately twenty minutes, which now leaves me with the rest of the plane ride—an unwanted three hours and forty minutes to think about Tara and Smitty, the only two people I have ever known who died. I don't like the feeling at all. I intensely dislike goodbyes.

I flash back to memories of Smitty and my schoolgirl

crush on the divine older cousin who played drums and sketched pictures of naked people in cool shades of charcoal.

I think of Tara, recalling late-night study sessions where we created our own language called *e-o-nay,* which consisted of dropping the first consonant of each word. Our attempt to speak *e-o-nay* was a surefire way to provoke laughter. Tara was fun. She found humor in everything and had an uncanny ability to lighten any given moment with her infectious smile. She was driven to succeed, like the rest of us. And upon graduation, she entered the family's mortgage-lending business.

But a year ago, Tara summoned the courage to pursue her real dream of becoming a lyricist. When she was in school she used to make up songs in class or at the library, inspired by just about everything, even the tabloids. Her songs often made us laugh, and sometimes made us cry.

Tara had, like so many of us, replaced her desires with those of her father…for a while. How many of us do that? How many of us abandon our instincts and passions to acquiesce to another's vision for us, one that fits into *their* overall plans? Tara's father had reacted badly to her decision, yet how lucky was Tara to have the courage to do something about it before she died. It's an achievement most of us never make, I think, as I gaze out the window into the celestial midnight sky.

I had promised to visit her last year, but my business venture went bust, leaving my checkbook empty again. Why hadn't I visited? So what if I had accumulated debt—I could have seen Tara one more time. My thoughts fill with regret, so I quickly focus again on business.

I pull out my reading materials: *Business Week, Entrepreneur* and the *Financial Street Journal.* I start with the *FSJ,* my business bible. I zero in on the front-page article and gasp.

The article details the successful launch of a new company called Palette Enterprises, specializing in digital bios of artists for the worldwide fine-art connoisseur and novices offline and online. The company is targeting Outsider Art and has deals with art museums for corporate branded licensing. Palette has taken the lead in this marketplace by affiliating with a consortium of galleries and producing a sponsor-driven annual convention catering to art connoisseurs. The sponsors and museums are identical to the ones I approached, none of whom mentioned a conflict of interest to me.

I am shocked. My current dreams swiftly shatter. It's near-perfect plagiarism of my business plan. To make matters worse, it's spearheaded by "entrepreneur on the rise" Derek Rogers, with quotes for annual profits expected to be in the hundreds of millions.

I shake my head in denial. Tears stream down my cheeks. "I don't believe it." Grief, from every source, converges upon me, finding its outlet in this moment. Had my idea been leaked, or were all good ideas simply in the ethers waiting to be plucked and implemented by the person who committed to it the fastest.

In Baggage Claim, I watch stuffed luggage hypnotically thump and bump along the moving catwalk.

Maurice LeSarde taps me on the shoulder. "Hey, Madison Banks. I loved your note," he says with a warm smile.

I barely manage a grin. "Really? I'm glad." Even a one-on-one conversation with Maurice LeSarde does little to lift my spirits.

"But I can't possibly keep your money. I'm really flattered. I'd like to offer you a pair of tickets to my concert in Detroit tonight."

"That's really nice of you, but you don't have to do that."

"I want to," he replies. He turns to a young woman nearby. "Hey, Dawn, give Ms. Madison Banks here two tickets for tonight."

Dawn manages to smile and hand me two tickets while coordinating logistics on a cell phone. "I don't see the chauffeur yet," she says into the phone, "and Mr. LeSarde wants to make sure his room is ready for an early check-in…"

I stare at the tickets, truly touched. "Thanks so much. There's really nothing more I'd like to do, but I'm afraid I have to decline on account of a funeral and other family commitments."

"I'm sorry to hear that. Well, take them anyway. Just in case. If you don't use them, take my business card and consider it a rain check." He hands me his card with his personal e-mail address on it. "And thanks for being such a loyal fan."

"You're welcome."

Dawn interrupts. "I see our chauffeur now, Mr. LeSarde."

He nods. "G'bye." They turn and head toward the exit.

"See ya later," I say to the space left behind, slipping his card in my back pocket.

I drive a rental car through light snowfall and arrive at a large brownstone church. In an attempt to be inconspicuous, I don a pair of large dark sunglasses because I'm here for Tara, not to run into anyone I know, especially my college ethics professor, Mr. Osaka, who thought I showed the most promise of anyone in class. The last thing I want is to see any of them and have to tell the truth—that I'm a loser.

Inside it feels cold and looks plain. A few floral arrangements dot the sides of the aisle upon entry. Mourners coat the pews, creating a sea of black breathing fabrics.

I find a lone seat in the front, off to the side. A shiny mahogany casket displays Tara lying peacefully inside. Except that Tara's hair is all wrong. Her trademark bangs are swept off to the side revealing a bare forehead. Didn't anyone look at a picture of her, for God's sake? Tara loved her shaggy bangs. Reality sets in. Shit, she's dead. She's really dead.

"We gather here today for the death of Tara Pintock," bellows the minister. "Death comes to all, but such an untimely death as this one brings cause for unrequited redemption of the soul to heaven."

I later cringe at his performance of a canned eulogy. Squirming in my seat, I roll my eyes. Not once does he talk about Tara's hopes and aspirations. He never mentions her gift for songwriting or her insane ability to see the good in everything and everyone. I become more and more agitated. This is an injustice; I fume inside my head, wondering where Tara's parents are and how they can allow this to happen. Maybe grief has crippled them and they are simply not capable.

The minister flares his cape, preaching, "It is not just the memory of Tara we rejoice in today, but the power of grist in heaven and hell as a sacred religious symbol!"

I sweat with irritation and impatience. This is a travesty. I can't take it anymore. As the minister's about to wrap it up, I raise my hand to interrupt as politely as I can. "Excuse me, sir. I'm Madison Banks, and Tara was one of my best friends in school. Would it be okay if I added a few simple words?"

Stumped, he glances at an impeccably well-dressed man sitting in front of him. The man must be Tara's father—but how could anyone possibly deny a person the opportunity to express their grief? The man's nod to the minister is quickly transferred to me.

Standing behind the podium I remove my sunglasses to face the chapel of mourners. "Thank you. I would, uh, just like to add a few memories about Tara." I feel myself choke up. I pause to take stock and abort my tears. "Tara,"

I begin again, "was not only a loyal friend but a person who made every day shine. Her sense of humor was contagious. And she had the ability to forgive and move on. She loved words, and to merge phrases of cultures she visited into her everyday lexicon. When she returned from London all we heard for months was 'Blimey' this and 'blimey' that!"

Mourners laugh. Obviously the description revitalizes their memory of Tara.

"Tara was always making up songs. Remember the ones she wrote for our class? There was "IPO marries ROI," "The Adoption Rate Prayer Song" or "Oh, Lord, Please Grant Me a Front Bowling Pin Client." Classmates smile and chuckle. I sing the chorus and then turn to Tara in the casket. "Remember that one, Tara?" But only silence follows. I face the mourners again. "Her songs made the top of the chart on the university radio station. And she was a fierce advocate of justice, helping students obtain health insurance at fair and equitable rates. She even wrote a song and distributed it through the Internet. It worked like a charm—the students got the insurance. She flourished in everything she touched and I have no doubt that given just a little more time to execute her action plan, her path to profitability and personal accomplishment as a lyricist would have exceeded even her expectations. Tara was a great, trustworthy friend, and a proud daughter, who loved every moment."

I stare at the casket and, unable to say goodbye, simply whisper, "See ya later, Tara." Someone claps, then stops. Silence follows as I nervously return to my seat.

Tara's father, renowned Arthur Pintock who runs the world's largest international mortgage-lending business, stands up. He clears his throat. "Thank you, Madison. Thank you for honoring the life of my daughter." He nods at the minister and sits back down, squeezing his wife's hand in an act of solidarity.

The minister faces the crowd. "Thank you all for supporting the Pintock family in this time of need. Do remember to sign the guest book on your way to the reception line. God bless."

Now that I've blown my cover, I duck through the crowd for a fast exit. But suddenly, Sharon, from my leadership development class, blocks me on my left. I squeeze to the right, but Marcus from my ethics and corporate governance class appears along with Lani, president of the Venture Capital Club.

"Maddy! You look amazing! How are you doing?" asks Sharon.

"Did you write that speech?" asks Marcus. "It was beautiful."

Lani adds, "I'm sorry to see you here on this occasion, but you must tell us what you're up to and what kind of business you're in."

"Oh, um, well, I'm in L.A. and it's going great," I say, dodging the questions.

My ethics professor appears, smiling at me. "Madison Banks."

"Professor Osaka. How are you?"

"Great. I forgot you were in Los Angeles. That's perfect."

"It is?"

"Yes. I'm a visiting professor at UCLA. How would you like to do some mentoring for me? I've got some students who could really use your kind of influence. They can intern for you. You'll enjoy it. I'll send you the info."

Before I can utter a word, Osaka shakes my hand. No wonder he had a Guinness-like world record for deal closing— it was done before you knew what hit you. But how would he contact me without having my business card? Of course, at that moment, I wasn't thinking about the guest registry I had signed or Osaka's superb research methodologies. Clasping my hand, he does note a lack of jewelry. "What? No ring? A catch like you?"

"I'm practicing risk management. Besides, you're the one who taught me never to merge without the right value proposition," I quickly reply.

An unmistakable voice, sardonic tone and all, pipes in, "Nice way to get to the dad, Mad."

I turn to face my archenemy, the handsome, pretentiously charismatic Derek Rogers, as he cuts in to the reception line. I'm shocked he would be here. But of course he would— any opportunity to climb a corporate ladder and Derek Rogers is there. He would stop at nothing to find his success and do *whatever* it would take. The Tower of Babel had nothing on Derek Rogers. I'm mortified by the comment, remembering now why I lost respect for young, ambitious men, all because of Derek Rogers. But before I can counterpunch, he moves past me into the reception line to pay his respects to Arthur Pintock. I have no doubt that Derek Rogers will use this moment to insidiously work his way into Arthur's professional life, no doubt at all.

Outside, I'm about to climb into my rental car when I hear the familiar, soft, sweet voice of Sierra D'Asanti, a beautiful Polynesian mulatto girl and old flame from my first year of entrepreneurial studies. I turn to face her. She's beautiful and appears wiser and more mature than when we last saw each other seven years ago.

"Hey, Maddy…what you said about Tara was beautiful," says Sierra. "You made her memory a gift and we all needed it." She pauses, about to say something more but stops herself.

"Thanks," I reply. "You don't think I was out of line?"

"You're never out of line. You're Maddy."

"Guess I should take that as a compliment."

"Yes, you should."

"I'm going to miss her."

"I know…me, too." Sierra offers a hug.

I hug back for the loss of Tara's innocent life and for the grief I know I have yet to face. We break apart and she looks at me.

"I don't know what you're up to these days, but if you ever need my services, here's my card," she says, handing one over. "I've got a digital production studio and Web designing firm. You look…great, Maddy." She pauses, and then turns and leaves.

I watch the beautiful Sierra walk off, her colorful scarf floating in a whipping wind as it trails behind her. I remember how tumultuous our relationship was and how Tara was always there to lighten our load. Tara, Tara, Tara. I realize that I am going to miss Tara more than I could possibly have known from my small dark closet in the heart of L.A.

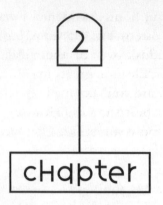

2

cHapter

Missions and Visions: The Genesis of an Entrepreneurial Idea

I drive to my brother Daniel's place on the outskirts of Ann Arbor, unable to stop fuming about impersonal funerals.

How many funerals employ ministers and rabbis and clergy who never even knew the deceased? How many people stop to think about how they want to be buried, let alone how they want to be remembered?

In an aging society where baby boomers dominate the demographics, I think I'm on to something. After all, the cost of a casket—who knows? The cost of a burial plot—not sure. The cost of the funeral experience itself—priceless. Like all businesses that sprout from the kernel of an idea, I know I just have to be patient and trust that it will reveal itself in time.

I park, but am considering the irony of the day—attending a funeral and bris hours apart. The former occasion represents the departure of a life, the latter the arrival of one.

Both capture a full house. Hardened snow crunches under the weight of my steps. I'm still stomping frozen ice off my boots in the muddy foyer of the small, quaint Victorian when my mother, Eleanor, greets me.

"Maddy! How are you? Let me help you with your coat." Without missing a beat, she asks, "How was the funeral, dear?"

"Can we talk about something else, Mom? Like, how was the bris?"

"A bris is a bris. One cuts, one cries," she says with a singsong delivery. My mother's a classical pianist, renowned as a woman of tremendous grace. "How would you like something to eat?"

Before I can answer, my debonair father, Charlie Banks, age sixty-two, and professor of mythology at the University of Michigan, arrives on the scene. "There she is! The red-eye girl. You must be exhausted. Do you want a big fluffy pillow or a glass of merlot?"

"I'll start with the merlot, thanks, Dad."

"You must be hungry, though," adds Eleanor. "I've got your favorite gourmet Neshama sausages."

I lift a brow. "You're serving sausages at a bris?"

"Well, *I* thought it was humorous. But Uncle Sam brought some bass, too. Can I get you some?"

"Uncle Sam is here?" My face brightens.

"He's at the park building a toboggan run with Andy," offers Charlie.

"Lucky Andy…where're Daniel and Rebecca?"

Before anyone can answer, my younger brother Daniel, age twenty-eight, a published poet whose entire wardrobe consists of nothing but black Levi's jeans and black T-shirts, saunters into the room holding his sleeping newborn son, Keating.

I walk over to my new nephew, cooing, "Wow. He's so little and so cute!"

"Thanks, we think so, too. You missed Keating's heroic display of exceptional strength and courage. Not a tear!" Daniel states proudly.

"I thought Mom said there was some cutting *and* crying."

"The crying was on the part of the less-heroic father," adds Rebecca, Daniel's wife and high-school drama teacher. She's simple and bright in her sweats, plaid flannel shirt and moccasins. "I've a good mind to put him in my students' next play where theatrics are needed," she adds, chuckling.

"Was I that bad?" inquires Daniel.

The entire group nods.

Rebecca laughs. "What marvelous timing! I should make you all part of the chorus!"

Laura Taylor strolls in and greets me with "Hey, cousin!" She's holding a glass of pinot grigio in one hand and an inconspicuous digital camera in the other. "I have to come all the way to Michigan to see you! You look awesome."

"So do you!" I reply, delighted to see her. Laura is a total inspiration for me. She knew nothing about business, yet through risk and determination capitalized on her acclaimed adult-entertainment writing career by transforming the experience into a novel and television series.

"Hey, come hither anon, quod ik, and bare thy teeth that I may capture your-e essence with my digital camera."

I give Laura an odd look.

"I've been hanging around your poet brother all afternoon learning Chaucer—what do you expect?" she says as she snaps a shot.

"Yes, but blending Middle English with modern poetry?" I ask. "Sounds like a bad merger to me…pun intended."

Charlie chuckles. Baby Keating lets out a wail as if to comment.

"So is Laura a good student of Chaucer?" I ask. "Which of the Tales did you teach, pray tell?"

"'The Reeve's Tale,'" answers Daniel. "What else?"

"I thought perhaps you might have strayed from the blanket." Rebecca winks.

"And, Laura, what did you learn?" asks Charlie.

"Well, after some serious word-tripping, I learned that the deceiver is finally deceived," she responds dutifully. Daniel smiles at his student's success.

Arrested by the implication of the words, I gulp my merlot. Language may change, but immoral behavior remains the same. I wonder if the deceiver knew he had been deceived. Because otherwise, what's the point? And if he did know, would he care? Or would he simply look for the next line of defense? Someone, say, like Derek... Before I can finish my thought, I am interrupted by my father.

"So, how was the funeral? Tara's parents must be beside themselves with grief."

"It was...the usual from what I can tell, Dad. Kind of a prefab funeral. They could have been talking about anybody. So I spoke about what Tara was like in school. It seemed like everyone appreciated it."

"That's beautiful. When I go, please sit around a campfire and tell stories about me," instructs Eleanor. "And for heaven's sake, have a good band."

"What about rugelah and Neshama sausages?" asks Charlie. "After all, Neshama does mean 'soul.'"

"That, too," Eleanor replies. "Oh. And make that a klezmer band," she laughs.

"Duly noted." Charlie grins.

"Well, since that's far off and Maddy's in town, tell us, what's the latest venture you've got going?" asks Daniel.

"I'm in between things," I mutter. Explaining that my latest venture had met an early death, as eulogized via the *FSJ* article, is something I don't have the energy to go into.

"Uh-oh. Something went bust," adds Rebecca.

"Honey, did you have another failure?" asks Eleanor.

"If you did, I hope it was as humorous as the laundry service debacle in college," quips Daniel.

"Right. After all, Daniel, you seemed to have benefited with a resulting lifetime supply of black T-shirts and black jeans, if I recall," says Rebecca. "In fact, I recall it every day you get dressed."

"Not to mention the financial benefit from a wardrobe savings, which supplements your children's college education, I might add," I say.

There's a long pause. "Well," Laura asks, "isn't anyone going to tell me the laundry service story?"

"It started with Maddy's first year of entrepreneurial studies," explains Eleanor. "Her class was given the challenge of actually starting a business."

How quickly the past catches up to the present. A barrage of memories resurface. The student who could create, implement and execute the most successful bottom line during the semester would win the "Challenge a Vision" prize of thirty-five thousand dollars to pay back their investors for seed capital, expand and/or begin another venture.

Deciphering a need for a convenient quality laundry service on campus that included pickup and delivery, I made it my business, and turned the desire for hygienic attire into an overnight success. My venture rapidly took off and soon I had multiple locations throughout Ann Arbor and investors wanting to talk to me about franchising the operation. This threatened Derek Rogers's success, so he blackballed me in order to win the competition. How did he do it? He snuck into my launderettes in the middle of the night and injected black dye into every load. The next day became a campus legend dubbed Black Tuesday.

Only later did the truth come out, and by then the prize money was long gone. And so was Derek, with his degree in hand and a stellar reputation as long as prospective employers didn't dig too deeply into his past. And they never did.

After that, I channeled my resentment into a successful campus prankster business. Students would spare no expense to have my company devise clever pranks to perform on friends, colleagues and professors. That worked out great—until liability insurance became a necessity and costs climbed too high to make the numbers work anymore—a classic case of market risk gone awry by greater margin pressures.

Following that I developed Dustin & Destiny Discover, a line of children's educational video packages combined with arts-and-crafts merchandise. The prototype consisted of two videotapes in the shape of a lunchbox. It included both a story on video and the parts to assemble a product organically integrated into the storyline, such as a homemade bird-feeder. I wrote and produced the story on videotape with the help of Sierra. Unfortunately, that failed due to an issue of real estate. It turned out that the video stores, art supply stores and children's bookstores didn't want the product because of "space." Two videocassette tapes packaged together as one at $19.95 cut down their profit margins as opposed to two single videocassette tapes each selling at $14.95. So in essence the space was worth $29.90 in sales instead of $19.95. That meant a loss of $9.85 in potential revenue to the retailer and subsequent brokers in between. Unfortunately, this was just before the adoption of the new DVD technology, which might have changed the outcome…but then, timing is everything.

It seemed that Derek Rogers and his black dye cursed

every subsequent effort I made at launching a successful business venture.

"So what was the name of the laundry business?"

The question floated in the air, riding on the smells of broiled bass, transporting me back to my brother's kitchen. Though I'm not sure who asked the question. "White Mondays," I say, finishing the last of my merlot.

"I always loved the metaphor," says Eleanor. "Top of the week hygiene."

"What was the result?" asks Laura.

"An endless supply of Black Tuesday remnants for me," chimes Daniel.

"For about two years it looked like the homeless population of Ann Arbor was in constant mourning," adds Charlie.

"So what happened to your latest venture, honey?" inquires Eleanor.

My entire family stares with expectant eyes, waiting for me to deliver the details. I take a breath. "For the past year I *was* commercializing an international-art business online."

"That's a multi-billion-dollar a year industry," pipes in Laura.

"A multi-billion-dollar industry? That is unfathomable," states Rebecca.

My family gets the "art" part, but their eyes glaze over when it's attached to the words *industry, business, capitalism,* or *commercialization*. But who can blame them? One relative made tenure in the Architecture department of NYU, another joined the Cleveland Symphony as a violinist, a third joined a modern ballet dance troupe, a fourth ventured into art therapy and there was talk of one cousin who lived on an island with a bunch of llamas from which she wove and sold scarves. My language of P&Ls, bottom lines and distribution channels is absolutely foreign to them.

"What happened?" asks Laura.

"Maddy didn't make it to market first," I say, trying to give myself a spot of distance.

"Sounds like a new line from 'The Three Little Pigs' in a revival twist," says Daniel, preferring to hear his own wit over how I might be feeling about the whole thing.

Go ahead, add another dent to my psyche, I think. These are my babies and they were constantly being aborted by outside forces. "You know what? I'm really tired. Where's that pillow, Dad?"

"On the couch in Daniel's office."

"If you'll all excuse me for a minute, I'm going to lie down."

I'm like a beloved black sheep, I think. Everyone else in my family is a writer, performer, artist or academic, following intellectual pursuits in art history, architecture, film theory and basket weaving. No one knows anything at all about business, nor do they care to, except for Uncle Sam.

But business was all I could think of from an early age. During art classes in kindergarten, other kids drew pictures of houses and birds. I drew pictures of one-hundred-dollar bills. When I turned eleven I begged my parents for a subscription to the *Financial Street Journal* and religiously read it every day thereafter. Meanwhile, my family members admire Van Gogh, Rodin and Stravinsky, while I desperately want to follow in the footsteps of the Rockefellers, the Warburgs and Jack Welch.

My family is also made up of storytellers. They *love* to tell stories, but I always wonder why none of them ever feature a tale of how to build a business. Instead they focus on how little Daniel got his foot caught in a jack-in-the-box and the firemen's rescue, or how Aunt Susie lost her paintbrushes in the fishpond and the fish took on rainbow hues.

Not that those stories aren't wonderfully witty and entertaining, but they don't provide the experience or knowledge I crave. The only family story revolving around business I have ever heard is the one Uncle Sam told about the fishing lures.

So when I enrolled in entrepreneurship studies, I had the passion but lacked the experience of most of my peers—born into families who lived and breathed business. I risked being a disappointment to my family as I entered a world they did not understand. In turn, it made me even more determined to succeed.

There's a knock on the door. "Maddy, you up?" asks Charlie.

"Yeah, come on in, Dad."

Charlie enters and sits on the couch beside me. "So how are you doing, hon?"

"A little wiped out actually. Dad, what are some of the myths around funerals?"

He takes a deep breath. "Tara," he says.

I nod. He takes a moment and pauses to consider his answer deeply before speaking like Gregory Peck in the role of Atticus Finch. "Well, let's see. Did you know most funeral homes' owners started out as furniture makers? People would ask them to build a wood casket, so they began to assume the role of the local funeral director, as well. They used to have professional mourners, too. I remember watching them when my grandmother passed away."

"Really? Women in black providing canned weeping on cue?"

"All day long, next to my grandmother's deathbed."

"How do people regard funerals today?"

"Well, there seems to be a trend away from funeral rituals. Symbols representing death in art and literature are diminishing, too. Used to be, people would wear armbands or hang wreaths on their doors to indicate that a loved one had passed on. Those kinds of rituals are fading."

"You think funeral services are important?"

"I do. Grief is a solitary, in fact, lonely experience. Without funeral services there would be no public place to express that kind of pain."

"That's interesting," I tell him.

"So is your state of mind. You're not thinking about doing anything…"

"Oh, like closing my own curtain?" I laugh. "Heavens, no, Dad!"

"I'd like you to find a job in a stable company and get some financial security—stick to one thing, Maddy, and work your way up."

I sit up. "But, Dad, that doesn't work in today's economy. For one thing, it's no longer a hierarchical path to the top. Old structures are crumbling because the flow of information can't be controlled, which puts meritocracy in vogue. But if you ask me, merit is based on being a diversified person the same way good investing is based on having a diversified portfolio. That means constant self-reinvention, without giving up your core integrity, of course."

Besides, I think, I don't want to function in "survival mode," I want to live in "thrival mode." But I leave that part out.

"I wonder if you should consider going to a doctor."

"Why?" I ask, surprised.

But before he can reply, Laura walks in wearing a warm down coat, offering her goodbyes.

My dad stands up and kisses Laura affectionately. "You have a safe flight home, Laura." And he exits the room.

"Don't worry, Maddy. You'll crack it yet. So many have had rounds of failure and then hit upon success."

"Thanks."

"Hey, what about the ol' love life? You never updated us on that. Care to tell me anything about your current *lovers* before I take off? Marriage has a way of stamping out first-hand experience. Generalizations will do."

"Generally speaking, I'd have to say that career goals have a way of stamping out any chance at true love," I say.

"On that I agree. But whenever you're ready to choose to be with someone, just remember freedom comes only *after* you surrender to the choice."

"Laura! Your cab is here!" yells Daniel from downstairs.

Laura hugs me goodbye and dashes downstairs. I walk to the chilled window and stare out at frozen fields of snow. Fat white flakes drift to the ground. I made a choice. I surrendered to a career, determined to get at least one successful company off the ground first. I'm not immune to relationships, on the contrary, I crave one—but I'm afraid it will get in my way. Deep down I'd rather play the results, or hedge my bets, because secretly I do believe a healthy happy relationship awaits me at the end of all this. It's just that I didn't expect the career phase to take so long. And now, everywhere I turn, all I see is constant rain—no, strike that…relentless hail.

A heavy drop falls on an owl sitting peacefully on a maple tree branch. The owl cocks its head, ever so slightly, unperturbed by the flake melting squarely between its eyes, accepting this as a natural part of everyday life. That is true freedom, I think as the sun casts muted shades of orange across the landscape.

"Have you seen my glove?" asks Laura.

I turn around to find her scrambling around the couch. "No," I reply. "But let me help you look." I spot it on the floor under a fallen black chenille blanket, another remnant of Black Tuesday. "Here you go."

credit card. Next, I need a Web site and a hip, cool logo to breathe life into Lights Out. There's only one person I trust for the job. I pull a business card from my wallet, remembering how White Mondays' logo sparked a legend.

I call and a young lady answers, "Candelabra Productions, may I help you?"

"Sierra D'Asanti," I say. "It's Madison Banks from Los Angeles."

In a moment, I hear a sweet, gentle voice ask, "Are you okay? Do you need to talk about Tara?" Concern dominates Sierra's tone.

"No, no, it's not that," I reply, touched by her immediate concern. "I'm okay. I want to know if I can talk to you about becoming a strategic partner on a new business venture."

"I'd be honored to."

"But I haven't even told you what it is."

"Anything you do, I want in on."

"Really?"

"You're so funny, Madison. You're the last one to see your potential. But I've always known it's just a matter of time before you pop into entrepreneurial stardom. I'd like to be there when it happens. So whatever you've got going, count me in. Now, what's the next step?"

"I need you to meet me in Vegas."

"For?"

"A funeral convention."

"When?" she asks, nonplussed by the topic.

"December first. I booked a room at the Hilton. I'm in major start-up mode, so are you okay sharing a room with me?"

"What do you think?"

"Okay. Can I reimburse you on your airfare in two months?"

"Of course. Just one question—are we paying homage to Tara with this new venture?"

"Let's just say the lack of meaning at her funeral was a catalyst."

A long pause follows as we both take a moment.

Sierra quietly adds, "I'm looking forward to this, Maddy."

"Me, too."

One hour later I'm standing in the empty lobby of a law firm in Santa Monica. I look at my watch. She's late again. Impatient, I pull out my *FSJ*. There's an article on gender-swapping roles in wedding parties. Apparently, the title of bridesmaid is expanding to bridesfriend and best man to best woman, making room for brides and grooms who wish to include close friends of opposite gender in the gig.

I hear a succession of clomping heels followed by the sulky voice of Eve. "This better be good. Sales at Nordstrom don't come around that often."

I put the paper down and look at her, decked out in a potpourri of the latest fashion brands. "Do you have your mission statement?"

"It took a back seat to *The Tempest*."

"Then let's start with a quiz, shall we? Inspired by today's *FSJ*."

Her face sours. "Since when do internships include tests?"

I ignore the minipout. "For two points, what would the analogous role of best man in a wedding ceremony be to a funeral ritual?"

She scrunches up her lip, stumped. "This is totally irrelevant."

"Come on, Eve, try to think in analogous terms."

She sighs. "The florist, no—the undertaker. I don't know, the pallbearer."

"Excellent. Now find out if pallbearers are traditionally men only or open to gender swaps." I hand her a manila folder. "And please proofread this and prepare the graphs and charts per my instructions inside. Thanks." I start heading toward the elevator.

"Where are you going?"

"My attorney's office. Todd Lake."

"Like that?"

I look at my army pants, vintage Nikes, white blouse and baseball hat. "What's wrong? I'm in L.A., the everything-goes place."

"Everything," she says. "Look, you may know content, but I know presentation. I'm sure you're going up there to engage in some form of tit-for-tat, so why not use appeal to do some of the work for you. At least let me fix your hair and makeup."

I did need something from Todd—legal advice on the cheap. I check out Eve; she has a point. "Okay."

"That will be for three points," she tells me, dangling her Prada makeup bag in front of me.

"Nice," I say.

Eve performs a quick makeover on me in the lobby restroom and I'm good to go.

Todd Lake, lawyer, husband, father of four, greets me in his office. He is handsome, kind, stable, and the only guy I trust in the city.

"You look great, Maddy. Really great. What's different? New hairdo?"

"More like new intern."

"So what can I do for you?"

"I need to register a trademark for my new company and find out if I should incorporate in California or elsewhere, since the business will operate on a national level."

"Your accountant can tell you the best place to incorporate and we have a division here that can take care of the trademark paperwork for you—"

"Can we do it on a percentage basis, Todd?" I nervously ask. "There's no way I can afford your hourly rate."

"Don't worry about it, Maddy. Just keep me posted on the details of your project every once in a while and we'll call it even."

"It's a deal." I hand over the paperwork for Lights Out Enterprises.

"Are you going to tell me what your new venture is about?"

"After I finalize the business plan in Vegas."

"Vegas? You're not opening a casino, are you?"

"Me? I've never touched a slot machine. Besides, you know me better than that—I gamble with concepts, not cash." I offer a wry smile. "By the way, what's the thing you like least about funerals?"

"No food. No water. And they're gloomy."

"And your positive slant? If there is one?"

"Connecting with friends and family…and it's a reminder to appreciate my family more." He pauses, suspiciously. "What are you up to, Maddy?"

My face is bright and eager. "I'll keep you posted…and, Todd, thanks."

I dash through traffic to my accountant's office. A tall, thin, intense Stephen Picard leans across his desk, addressing me in his thick Australian accent. "I advise you to set this up as an LLC, Maddy, in Nevada. But we can look after it from here." He stops and leans back in his chair, with a dubious expression on his face. "Maddy, what makes you so sure this is going to work?"

"I've got good instincts, Picard. So get ready. Because when it flies, I'm going to ask you to incorporate it into your clients' estate planning."

"I hadn't thought of that," he says, studying me. "I like your determination. I hope it really works out for you...this time."

I stare at him, frozen in place. I'm sick of trying so hard, sick of trying to convince others. "Please, drop the pity. I'm going to make it. Sometimes it takes longer for some of us than for others. If you don't believe in me, tell me now so I can find an accountant who does."

"I didn't mean it like that," he says softly. "I have great respect for you, Madison. I've never seen anyone persevere more. But I do hate seeing you get hurt."

"So do I, but I'll just have to practice better risk management." I gather my briefcase and notebook and walk out. Halfway down the hall, I stop to close my eyes, swallowing the tears of humiliation.

The funeral convention in Vegas resembles every other trade show with exhibitors displaying their wares from inside branded booths all crammed together in a large open space. Only, this one has a stable of high-end hearses and an endless variety of caskets ranging in color and price equivalent to the imagined distance between heaven and hell. If people are willing to spend twenty thousand on a casket, surely they'll be willing to spend that much or more on the funeral experience itself.

My phone rings, so I flip it open. "This is Madison Banks."

"Hi, my plane got in early. Where are you?"

I look over my surroundings. "Between a casket and a hearse."

"Cute. I can tell this is going to be fun. Okay, I'll find you in twenty."

I hang up and graze the aisles, soaking up all the knowledge I can and keeping my eyes peeled for opportunities to enhance Lights Out. I come across rows of booths selling urns in all shapes and colors. One booth has a brick wall on display.

"You look perplexed, young lady," says a thin, elderly gentleman standing behind a brochure-laden table.

"I'm not sure why you're exhibiting a wall," I remark.

He offers a knowing smile. "New to the funeral business?"

"Aside from limited funeral attendance, you're it."

"Let me guess. You're the prodigal daughter returning home to take over the family business but know nothing of it because you've been studying abroad in…Europe. Am I right?"

Eager to validate his assessment, I reply, "Close enough."

"Well, I'm glad to oblige you." He hands me brochures and a business card. "These are columbariums. They're pre-manufactured spaces inside of walls for standard-size urns."

I'm fascinated by the multitude of choices in the funeral market. Who knew? I think. Another customer stops by and I skip over to the next aisle, wondering what other surprises are in store. There's a booth displaying Memorial Comforters. A sweet salt-and-pepper-haired woman sits underneath the sign.

"Hi, I'm Madison Banks," I say, reaching out to shake the woman's hand. "These comforters are stunning."

"They're individually personalized, hand-woven ornamental cloths used during a ceremony of remembrance. They're for decorating a casket or an urn. Or they can be used as a memorial gift."

"Would you be interested in a strategic alliance with my company?" I ask her. "I'll need to know your product services and costs."

She beams back excitedly. "Why, yes. Please sit down."

We iron out a nonexclusive arrangement.

I walk the floor again, discovering a whole side market for pet funerals. Four aisles are solely designated for pet urns, pet caskets, different-size stones and rocks engraved with memorials to cats and dogs, and pet condolence cards.

Brilliant, I think, to capitalize on the thirty-billion-dollar pet industry.

I find a minibooth inside a larger booth arranged for the sole function of casket selling. Instead of showcasing full-length caskets, this company features multiple miniature caskets on show.

A vibrant sun-tanned man in his forties, dressed in a slick Armani suit, approaches me. "Can I help you?"

"Why is your casket display different from the others?"

"We want to minimize the discomfort and intimidation associated with average casket buying. Instead of offering customers a large room at a funeral home filled with imposing full-size caskets, we've strategically designed this booth. Here, the buyer is invited to explore the merchandise and know exactly what the cost options are. Go ahead, touch them all you want."

I touch the displays like a kid in Lego Land. The more expensive model clearly has the highest quality of combed cotton inside. All in all, they look like little toy coffins, shiny and rich in texture. I realize it's kind of fun and weird to stroke the finish and tug on the drawers where one's private items go, like medals, jewelry and cell phones.

"How does the pricing work in relation to the display?" I ask.

"Take a look at the wall," he explains. "Which quarter casket looks most expensive?"

I point to the one in the upper left corner.

"And which one looks least expensive?"

I point to the one in the lower right corner.

"That's retail 101," he explains. "Designing displays around the psychology of perception. We've integrated it into the casket-buying experience by offering funeral homes these movable casket display centers and movable gift shop centers where customers can buy condolence cards, guest book registries and memory boards. We also include a line of books and pamphlets on grieving and bereavement. Over here—"

He guides me to the movable gift shop before leaving to accommodate another prospective client.

"Hello, Maddy."

I turn. Sierra stands there in her reliable serene repose, bearing a sly smile. She cocks her head toward the displays. "Casket choosing by skin tone?"

"Very funny. But I believe skin tone has a tendency to fade when you, uh, go."

"Perhaps, but I believe the EnLighten Thee Makeup booth next door will fix that in a jiff. So what have you surmised so far?"

"That it won't be long before it's common practice to buy a casket at your local Costco or Wal-Mart. Only to be followed up with a line of designer caskets at Target. Can't you see it? Architects and designers like Frank Gehry and Philippe Starck designing caskets. And if you want to take it further, I don't think it's too far-fetched to imagine Michael Jordan designing a line of afterlife running shoes for Nike. Worn by the deceased when their metaphorically speaking 'soles' take flight. What do you think a shoe designed for encounters of the afterlife-kind might look like?"

Sierra cannot stop laughing.

"You know what you are, Maddy? You're a futurist. I'm

looking forward to seeing what happens when the future catches up with you."

"But then, wouldn't I be on to the next future?"

"Perhaps, but one day you're actually going to stop and enjoy it, which would put you in the present. I hope I'm there for it."

"What does that mean?"

"You'll see. Come on, let's go build your enterprise." She smiles.

We stumble upon a booth showing a series of CDs of original funeral scores.

I turn to her. "Know what I'm thinking? We make a strategic alliance with music production libraries and sound-effects libraries."

"How do sound effects fit in?"

"Say someone loves thunderstorms and rain."

"Like you."

"Yes, like me. So maybe I want those sounds at the closing of the service as people leave the premises. Or we use them in the biographical videos. Clapping sounds as a transition between the chapters in someone's life."

Sierra nods. "Okay, I'm starting to get this."

We pass a booth providing services for slide shows. One section features customized engraved casket lids, another displays fifteen varieties of leg hose. We share a look and smile. "Who's going to see the hose?" We move on.

Another area boasts headrests embroidered with phrases promoting peaceful rest. I think of Daniel. Maybe this could be a lucrative market for poets, offering their talents to the bereaved with personalized tributes to the departed. Moving on, we notice companies selling embalming paraphernalia.

"Shall we explore this?" asks Sierra.

"Let's skip this one if you don't mind." I discover my curiosity has its limits.

A company sells fabrics with beautiful wall-size tapestries hanging above caskets. A photo of the loved one is silkscreened onto a giant tapestry with overnight delivery guaranteed. I pocket a business card for future reference.

We find the heart of the organization that's behind the event. Their association commands a wide booth providing valuable educational information to its twenty-one thousand members, funeral home directors, including the latest information about their lobbying efforts in Washington, D.C., a monthly magazine on current funeral-related topics, public relations tips, programs plus information on everything from mortuary sciences to new compliance laws affecting safe, legal and compassionate operations of funeral homes and ways to help their members enhance quality of service.

I collect packets of their information, facts and figures gathered by organizations like the U.S. Census Bureau, the Cremation Association of North America and the Casket & Funeral Supply Association of America.

I turn to Sierra. "Think you've got enough visual stimuli here to come up with a great logo?"

"Oh, I'm buzzing with ideas…for the logo and the Web site."

"I can't wait, but we've got to hit the workshops now."

"Shall we divide and conquer?" asks Sierra.

"Good idea." I open my program and point. "Which one do you want?"

Sierra reads the options aloud. "'Business Transformation Trends,' 'Strategies for Independent Funeral Homes,' 'Civil Celebrants versus Traditional Clergy,' 'Everyday Ethics & Etiquette,' 'The Pre-Need Market,' and 'The Psychology of a Funeral.' I'll take 'Psychology of a Funeral.'"

"I'll skip between the 'Civil Celebrants' lecture and 'The Pre-Need Market.' See you back in the room at eighteen hundred hours." I smile.

"Aye, aye." She gives me a wink.

I slip in and out of workshops the rest of the afternoon, fascinated to learn about the growing number of "Civil Celebrants," a fairly new profession in the funeral field catering to clients without religious ties who want to ritualize the death of a loved one by hiring *not* your everyday clergy, but civil celebrants to conduct the rituals. Civil celebrants can be anyone from your local grocery store clerk to your neighborhood photographer to your personal trainer to your therapist.

I skip to the next workshop to learn more about the growing discussion on "pre-need" versus "time of need" markets. More funeral homes are using outside vendors to help with more complex funeral arrangements. I'm right on target.

Back to the room, I decide. I'm laden with brochures and pamphlets. The muscles in my arms have formed into complicated knots. Thoughts of Seth creep into my mind. One thing he excelled at was the soothing of twisted muscles. I miss his touch. I could call, but what for? We were not a good fit.

I take new action inside the hotel room and luxuriate inside a big bubble-filled hot tub. I leaf through the brochures to digest the information of the day. Sierra enters the room unloading her own accumulated handouts.

She eyes me enveloped in gyrating bubbles. "Now that looks relaxing," she says. "Would it be presumptuous of me to join you?"

"Only if you fail to bring a washcloth."

"Done deal," she replies, plucking a washcloth off the

towel rack and tossing it to me. She removes her clothes and slips inside the tub, releasing a sigh of relief. "Ah…the joy of the bath." She smiles. "So, what exactly is a civil celebrant? Sounds like someone stuck in 1865 on the side of the Union."

"You're ice cold."

"Then it sounds like a Miss Manners course on how to celebrate with civility."

"Getting warmer."

"Well, how about I wash your back while you enlighten me?"

"You're on." I turn and she glides a warm, wet, soapy washcloth across my back.

"You've got great skin. It hasn't changed at all, so silky and smooth—but these knots!"

I moan as Sierra kneads one out. "Wow. That feels great." And I actually relax for a moment. "What about you? Any revelations on the psychology of the funeral?"

"Plenty. Did you know an obituary is really a plea for help? A plea from the survivors to the community to be there and support their transition."

"I thought it was the deceased who was transiting."

"Nope. The result of their departure leaves the survivors to figure out a whole new social order. Funerals help survivors reconstruct a new social order inside their families and the community."

"I never thought of it that way." I turn around. "Here, let me do your back now." I take the washcloth from her.

Sierra releases a small noise of appreciation. I get the signal and drop the cloth to knead her muscles. "Hmm. That's the airplane ride, huh?"

"Mmm-hmm," she replies. "So are you seeing anyone right now?"

"Was…but I'm playing the results."

"Don't worry," she says, as if reading my mind. "The right person will fit naturally into your plans. And if it's any consolation, I think you're very hot, Madison Banks."

Her comment mollifies me. "Thanks, Sierra. Are you seeing anyone?"

"I lived with a woman but it didn't work. Lately, I've been dating men again."

"Anyone special?"

"Well…there is this one guy…Milton."

"Milton?"

"Yeah. What do you think? Could I marry a guy with the name Milton?"

"I would be suspect, unless he pleases you to no end." I smile.

"Not there yet… I'm taking it slow. But he does make me laugh."

"That's huge. Seth and I didn't laugh enough," I reflect.

"I'll make you laugh." A mischievous twinkle appears in her eye as she suddenly splashes water in my face. I reflexively splash back. A miniwater fight ensues.

"Okay, okay, you win," I say, my mouth filled with water and laughter.

We laugh some more and sink inside the water to rinse ourselves off.

Sierra gently runs her hand through wet hair. "It's pretty interesting, isn't it?" she asks rhetorically. "That the funeral, aside from being a socially acceptable place to weep and mourn in public, provides the last chance to learn."

"Learn what?" I ask, reaching for a towel.

"That the dead are really dead."

I freeze.

Sierra turns around. "What is it, Maddy?"

"I don't want the dead to be dead," I whisper.

She holds me in her arms. "Oh, Maddy…you know if it wasn't for Tara's death we wouldn't be sitting in a hot tub in the heart of Las Vegas right now."

"No, I don't imagine we would be."

"If Tara were here, what would she think?"

"She wouldn't be thinking at all. She would be out dancing."

"Then let's go dancing, Mad. For Tara. Let's keep her alive."

Couples and singles weave around the dance floor to a loud techno beat. Sierra's hair is down and wild, and she moves with fluidity and grace, hips shifting to the rhythm of the music as if the vibrations emanate from her bones, not the speakers.

I, on the other hand, can't hold a beat to save my life. My hips swing out in fierce gestures. I shake my head and roll my shoulders with pronounced vigor. I catch myself in the mirror fumbling to the beat, arms awkwardly gyrating, legs swinging out as if trying to land on undiscovered planets in the solar system. I watch Sierra's liquid-smooth moves. I stop dancing, shaking my head in defeat.

Sierra glides over. "What's wrong?"

"I suck. What happened to me? I used to win every single dance contest growing up. Now I can't even find the beat."

"That's because you're out of touch with the rhythm of life, from working too hard," says Sierra, through the din of the drums. "Keep your feet on the ground at all times," she instructs. "And switch your center of gravity from one hip to the other. Like this."

Her body moves fluidly. I attempt to duplicate her motions but to no avail. "I think I'm missing some vital hip coordination," I say.

"I can cure that," Sierra offers. Undeterred, she places my hands on the back of her hips. "Feel it and follow along."

I face her back, trying to own the beat. She patiently presses my hands on her hips, maintaining a slow, methodical pace until I start to catch on. In minutes, I'm moving to the music, mastering it.

Sierra leans close to my ear. "You want to take a break and get some water?"

I keep moving and shake my head. "Can't stop now. I may never get it back."

"I see." Sierra smiles. "Did you stop to think it might be like riding a bike?"

I shake my head again, still moving to the beat. "Oh, no. This is much harder."

"Okay, marathon woman. I'll get us both some water." She smiles.

Sierra heads toward the bar. A couple of guys approach her like magnets. Meanwhile, I keep moving, wondering yet again how long I can feed my ambition to pursue my goals in order to reach the life I think I ought to be living.

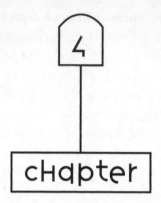

4

cHapter

Executive Summary: The Plan for Lights Out Enterprises

One week later in my apartment, I hit the print button and punch the sky with victory fists. "Yes!" I shout with glee. "By George, I think I've got it!" I stare at my hard work in its paper-form, with color coordinated graphs by Eve. I announce, "Lights Out Enterprises." I playfully turn the light on and off, screaming, "Lights Out! Lights Out! Okay, enough." I smile and dial a number. An answering machine picks up. Uncle Sam's prerecorded whistle of "Fishing Free" flows into my ear, followed by his trademark line "Have a beee-utiful day."

I hear the *beep* and take my cue. "Hi, Uncle Sam. I finished the business plan, with a mission statement, executive summary, company strategy, financial review, etcetera, etcetera. And I lined up a VC meeting. I'll keep you posted on the chain of results. Oh, and I promise to do those girlie things you insisted I do before my meeting. Love you! Mad."

I'm approaching the front doors of the famous Bali High Spa, known for its one-stop-shop spa circuit, when my cell rings. "Maddy Banks here."

"Hey, it's Sierra. I'm e-mailing you the final revisions on the logo today."

"Awesome! I can't wait…" I pant as I struggle to open the heavy mahogany doors while juggling the phone close to my ear.

"What are you doing?" asks Sierra.

"Oh, I have to get a manicure, pedicure, facial, massage, brow wax, bikini wax…"

"Have to? You make it sound like it's torture?"

"Believe me, I'd rather be putting together my advisory board."

"Maddy, you have issues. Do yourself a favor, will you?"

"What?"

"Enjoy it! Let go! Pamper yourself and—"

"Okay, okay," I say. "I, uh, promise to try to enjoy it." I take a deep breath and pass through the monster doors, which just added to the stress I'd come to erase.

I close in on the front desk and hand a woman my full-package gift certificate from Uncle Sam. "Hi, there, um, I'm here for all of this…stuff," I say, pointing to the list of pre-paid items on the certificate.

"Okay, let me see what you've got here," she says.

While she reads the list, I immediately rummage through ten different business magazines and newspapers in my brief-case. I find my trusty *Financial Street Journal* and pull it out, tapping my foot while reading. I can't help but laugh out loud when I spot a headline "Companionship in Prayer Extends to Four-legged Friends."

Traditional clergy are creating separate services for pet-owning congregants, so that together, they can attend religious ceremonies. I smile to myself and wonder what's next, doggie wafers and doggie wine? Then my eye lands on another article.

"It's scandalous! I can't take it anymore." I'm unaware I've spoken out loud.

The woman behind the desk offers an odd look and then politely interrupts me. "Excuse me, would you like your treatments in any particular order, Ms. Banks?"

Oblivious, the article about Derek Rogers's success has me engrossed. "This is unbelievable," I murmur. "Unbelievable."

The woman looks at me. "What's unbelievable?"

I toss my arms in the air. "Palette Enterprises stock just split. I just don't get it. How can someone so evil keep landing on top? I mean, really…"

"Do you ever unwind, sweetie?"

I squint at her. "Are you talking to me?"

"How long have you been carrying around these feelings?"

"What feelings?"

"Resentment and anger and betrayal. Those feelings."

"I don't have that," I say. "But I do have feelings of…desire…for, uh, retribution. That's right. Feelings of retribution."

"Honey, I think you need some serious unwinding. I'm starting you out with a massage first and I'm having Hans give it to you." Before I can utter a sound, she picks up an internal house phone and declares, "Hans, I need you big-time at the front desk, baby."

A hallway door breezes open and a brawny six-foot-five giant lumbers toward me. "Hello, my name is Hans," he says, with a distinct twang. "How can I help you?"

"This young lady needs to release some—how shall we say it?—emotional plaque that's clogging the pores of her soul."

I give her a look.

"Yes, it's that bad, honey. Go to it, Hans. Honey, when you're done today, you're going to be mush," she tells me, all the while maintaining her smile.

"Mush? I can't be mushy. That is so bad for business. I have to be strong!"

"Before strength, comes mush," pipes in Hans.

Hans flips me and spins me all over the massage table, releasing years of tension and frustration. I, in turn, release a continual stream of oohs, ahhs and ouches. By the time I get through the rest of the program, I am a complete mush-ball, euphorically melting in the hands of my pamperers.

Lying in a eucalyptus-scented steam shower for my finale, I smile, alas at peace with myself, though it is momentary. Uncle Sam was right. I feel great, and ready to put my plan into action. Well, almost ready. I need one more thing, something I can't do, but Eve Gardner can.

"Yuck. Those make your nose look like an elephant's," Eve tells my image in the mirror.

I remove the pair of sunglasses from my face only to swap them for another pair that she hands me.

"Here, try these," she says, refusing to give up after twenty tries. "Oliver Peoples has great lens colors. I think the lilac will complement your skin tone."

I begrudgingly put them on. "Why can't a simple pair of Ray-Bans do?" I ask.

"Oh, my God, what planet are you on?" she exclaims, then carefully looks me over. "That color's nice, but the shape is way too oval for your face."

"How about yellow frames? To go with my uncle's nickname for me—Sunshine."

"Rule number one, fashion never follows sentiment. Unless you have a perverse desire to look like a geek or you're intending to make a blatant statement. Otherwise, you just have to wait until yellow comes in—right now the rave is sage and lilac."

I take the glasses off as she hands me yet another pair. "You don't find this whole process exhausting, Eve?"

"Gee, I don't know." She smiles sarcastically. "You don't find the whole process of writing a business plan exhausting? Not to say borrr-ing! What's the difference?"

"The difference is that I create trends…or try to."

"And I live them. Without me, you don't exist," she argues, trying on a pair of sunglasses for herself now.

"You have a point there."

"Try the Guess glasses," she says, handing them to me. I slip them on. "Perfect, absolutely perfect." She confidently turns to the saleslady. "She'll take those."

"Hold it," I exclaim, seeing the price tag dangle in my peripheral view. "These are a hundred and twenty dollars!"

"That's a bargain. Besides, don't worry, it will balance out at the Shoe Pavilion." She checks *sunglasses* off a list, leaving *shoes, pantsuit, handbag, hair* and *makeup* to follow.

We hit the shoe store where I'm amazed to find discounted designer shoes on sale for the cost of a meal at Soup Plantation. Eve knows immediately where to go. I follow.

She abruptly pulls a pair off the shelf. "Let's see these on you."

"What do you have, Eve, a homing device for the perfect style and perfect fit?" I ask, as she hands me a sleek black pair of Anne Klein business pumps with a trace of white stitching across the top for a little flair.

"I scoped out locations and items after you called yester-day. It goes a lot faster this way."

"You're much better at research than I thought," I say.

"The process is not so bad if you know where to go and what you're doing."

"Same goes for a business plan, Eve." I try the shoes on. Even I'm impressed at how good they look. And the price is even better: a mere thirty-two dollars. "How does this place stay in business?"

"Volume. And do-it-yourself shoppers."

"What if you're not a do-it-yourself shopper?"

"You pay the premium," she quips.

Eve's black Audi TT transports us to Banana Repub-lic, where she immediately addresses a salesgirl, "Hi, I'm here for the size-two pantsuit I put on hold under 'Eve,' please."

I duck inside a dressing room to try it on while Eve stands outside the door lecturing me. "It's about following basic double-C guidelines. For example, a tight top goes with baggy pants, and a baggy top means tight pants. Oh, and al-ways have splashes of matching color. Like if you have blue flip-flops, wear a blue shirt or blue earrings."

"What are double-C guidelines?"

"Contrast and coordination," she replied. I step outside the dressing room in the pantsuit. Eve stares at me with pride. "Much easier on my eyes."

Ten minutes later, I walk out the door with another pur-chase at a modest price.

"What you need now is a really good handbag," she says as we climb inside her vehicle. "As long as you've got great shoes and a hot handbag, you're golden."

"Great. But I am not spending eight hundred dollars on a Prada bag."

"Who said you had to spend eight hundred?" She smiles, maneuvering the car up some steep hills into the canyons.

"There are stores up here?"

"I wouldn't say 'store,' but it's definitely a business."

Inside a small house neatly tucked away inside the Hollywood Hills, a young girl sells Prada. Eve insists I get a wallet and a slick matching purse. I insist that it be large enough for legal-size papers. She has me try several to make sure the proportions are right. They all look great, but I'm sweating to think how much it's going to cost.

"I think you should get that purse, the wallet and the sporty knapsack," concludes Eve. She turns to the girl and asks, "How much for all three, Denise?"

"I can give you a deal. Sixty-five dollars for them," she answers.

Eve smiles at me. "I told you."

Something's not right. "Why are they so inexpensive?"

"They're knock-offs, until you can afford the real deal."

"Knock-offs? I can't buy these," I say, putting the items back in place. Eve and Denise look at me astonished. "It's not right. How would you like it if you designed something and knock-offs came along to undermine your intellectual property?"

"It's not illegal to buy them," says Eve.

"It may not be. But it's not right. I wouldn't want someone ripping off my ideas and selling them for less."

Eve huffs out the door. "You're being silly."

"Think what you'd like, Eve. But sometimes, being true to one's moral compass isn't about convenience and money." I think about where Uncle Sam would be if there had been knock-off fishing lures, and stride outside.

Next to her car, Eve asks, "What are you going to take to the meeting?" I hold up my battered briefcase. "Over my dead body! You'll borrow my Prada bag instead."

I realize I've become Eve's personal makeover project. "Is it real?" I ask.

Her eyes narrow with indignation. "My father's high school graduation gift to me. It's as real as it gets."

"You don't have to take it personally. I can't tell the difference between the real one and the knock-off, anyway."

She stamps her foot in annoyance. "Then what difference does it make if you get the knock-off?"

"Because *I'll* know I undermined the designer."

"Then they shouldn't charge so much," complains Eve. "It's the same reason why everyone downloads music off the Net."

"Did you ever think that maybe it's because they charge so much that everyone wants it, Eve? They're investing in perceived value."

"Why does everything have to be a lesson with you?"

"Because life is one big internship. And by the way, you still owe me a mission statement."

The next morning, I'm fresh out of the shower doing my routine one hundred sit-ups and twenty-five push-ups when my doorbell rings. I check the clock: 7:00 a.m. "Not possible," I say. I throw a towel around myself and open the door, surprised to see Eve on time with her empty Prada bag and a case of makeup.

"Did we discuss bonus points for ungodly hours?" She yawns.

"Four points. And that includes your unexpected promptness."

"Okay. Let the games begin."

I laugh. "What is this? Trials for the Olympic Makeover Event?"

Eve enters, zeroing in on the coffeepot in the kitchen. "That's for amateurs. I'm a professional," she says, pouring herself a cup. She takes a sip and comes to life. "Ooooh, I think there's a reality TV show in that idea." She perks up at the thought. I look at her, and for a brief moment she reminds me of…me.

We sit down in front of my bathroom mirror as she pulls out her makeover accoutrements. "By the way, where's my mission statement?" I ask.

"You're looking at it." She lifts a comb and a tube of mascara. "Shall we?" And then she gets to work.

At Shepherd Venture Capital in the heart of Century City, I sit quietly in a large conference room that has a view extending to the ocean. I wear my new outfit, a classy pin-striped pantsuit with a button-down white silk blouse. My hair is pulled back to accentuate my features. My nails are perfect and my makeup just right, compliments of Eve Gardner. I anxiously lay my business plan on the table beside my laptop computer.

Jonny Bright, Bobby Garelik and Victor Winston saunter into the room with notepads and pens in hand. I nervously stand up to greet them. One look at me and Jonny and Bobby stumble in their tracks. My overall appearance and demeanor are undeniable. Victor remains poker-faced.

"You look amazing," offers Jonny.

"Thank you," I reply, trying to maintain my composure. "You're looking well yourself."

"Thanks. Hey, if it's okay, we invited Victor Winston into the meeting. He's got a first-look deal with Shepherd Venture Capital. Is that okay?"

"Of course." I turn to Victor. "Welcome."

He nods and the guys all sit down.

"Well, Maddy, I can't wait to hear what you've got," says Jonny.

"Me, too," I chime in. "But first, if you don't mind, I'd like you all to sign an NDA, and second, I'd like a cup of hot tea."

Victor releases the faintest hint of a smile.

Always request something to drink, even if you're not thirsty—it's a classic power play to command respect.

While Jonny and Bobby fumble over my looks, Victor calmly presses the intercom button. "Karina, could you please bring Madison Banks a cup of tea?" He turns to me and asks, "Milk and sugar?"

"No, thank you. Milk is too lactose oriented and sugar is too sweet, plus I could end up having a sugar high and then come crashing down in the middle of my pitch, which would really mess up the energy."

"So no milk and no sugar? Do you want herbal tea or black tea?"

"Depends on the kind of herbal, because if it's that sleepy-time kind or chamomile, it can cause fatigue due to relaxation and I'd prefer to keep my energy up, you know."

"Okay, so black tea, to play it safe," says Victor.

"Yep," I agree. "Black tea will be just fine."

"Just a regular cup of tea," adds Victor into the intercom.

"Yes, Mr. Winston," replies the voice of Karina.

I pass out the NDAs and focus on my PowerPoint presentation. "Okay. So, the business I propose for you to invest in today is called Lights Out Enterprises," I proudly announce. I clear my throat. "It's a design firm specializing in customized funeral experiences."

Jonny and Bobby look at me dumbfounded. Victor remains quiet.

"Excuse me, did you say *funerals?* Why on earth would anyone want that?" asks Jonny.

I confidently click to Important Facts & Figures. "I'll tell you why. Because the funeral industry generates 9.5 billion dollars in revenue and is expected to grow as the U.S. death rate is expected to rise…dramatically, by the way, in 2010, according to the U.S. Census Bureau." I pause, letting it sink in. "The other reason why—is that as baby boomers age, the desire to plan ahead for their funerals with personalized meaningful services continues to grow…to the tune of 21 billion dollars to date."

Bobby's mouth drops. Jonny's eyes pop open. Victor remains stone-faced.

"What's the value proposition to the consumer?" asks Bobby.

"It's a solution to a developing need," I reply. "Allow me to explain. You see, more and more people want a say in how they will be remembered, but typically, funeral directors deal with details associated with the burial process, and goods and services associated with that, such as caskets, urns, cemeteries, viewing rooms, death certificates and the location for these traditional services. So they rarely have the time or the skills required to prepare, plan and execute personalized memorial tributes. The solution I propose is Lights Out Enterprises, a company providing high-end preparation and planning for unique, memorable, personalized funeral experiences."

There's a long pause from the guys in the room.

"How much does an average funeral cost?" Jonny finally asks.

"Five thousand dollars," I quickly reply.

"And how many funeral homes are there? In the U.S.?" asks Bobby.

I feel Victor study me as I fire back with self-assuredness. "Twenty-eight thousand individually owned and operated for an average of sixty-nine years. Twenty-five hundred of those, which account for eleven percent, are owned by one of five publicly traded stock corporations. And each one produces an average of two hundred services per year."

The guys exchange glances as they do the math in their heads. I beat them to it. "That's an average of 5.6 million funerals a year multiplied by an average of five thousand per adult funeral. That equals 28 billion dollars…gentlemen."

Jonny's eyes nervously flicker. "So you think your consumer is…everyone?"

"Well, yes. Death is universal, it's not like you can opt out. And though our society has had a difficult time confronting death, baby boomers are beginning to embrace it, as far as preparation and planning goes. I'm not saying they're embracing death for death's sake, but they are getting better at approaching it from a different light, so to speak. Anyway, my focus is on the affluent pre-need client willing to spend an average of ten to twenty-five thousand on the manner in which they are remembered. Unless they want to be mummified, which alone costs on average sixty-seven grand."

"I thought mummification was an ancient Egyptian custom," says Jonny.

"It's having a revival."

Bobby looks at me. "Excuse me, but what's a pre-need client?"

"Pre-need clients are people who plan in advance for their time of need."

Bobby gives me a funny look, still not getting it. "And time of need is…?"

"As in time's up…you know…you're dead…lights out."

Bobby shudders, uncomfortable with the thought. "It all sounds very interesting, but what exactly is your product?"

"Customized funeral experiences," I reply.

"Doesn't customization make it labor intensive?"

"Not the way I propose to do it…which is all in the business plan."

"What's the competitive landscape?" inquires Jonny.

"A small percentage of funeral homes are doing this in-house, but as far as I know, there are no outside vendors doing what I'm proposing to do."

"And you are proposing to…?" asks Bobby.

"Create strategic alliances with all the funeral homes, vendors of funeral homes and the event-planning industry," I answer.

Victor remains still, keeping his eyes trained on me. I glance at him, refusing to allow myself to be unnerved by his composure. "You're awfully quiet, Mr. Winston."

"I'm too young for you to call me Mr. Winston."

"Okay. Do you have any questions…Victor?"

"Not one. Do you?"

"Yes. What happened to my tea?"

Victor smiles and hits the intercom button. "Karina?"

Before there's a reply Karina enters the conference room with a cup of hot tea.

"Thank you so much," I say. "That looks absolutely perfect." I set the tea down next to me but far from the computer, and address the guys again, "So where were we?"

"Do you have proof of concept? A prototype for this sort of thing?" asks Jonny.

"Well, um…no, no prototype at this time."

A pause follows. "Look, I think your presentation is excellent, Maddy," offers Bobby. "But I doubt it's going to fly. It seems way too trend-dependent. And it seems like a, forgive me, party-planning business."

Jonny, who appeared enthusiastic a moment before now appears to wuss out. "Yeah," adds Jonny. "It's really impressive, Maddy, but I don't envision securing customer acquisitions when the bottom line is, people don't want to face death."

Victor's eyes move back and forth as he takes everyone in.

"I think you guys are reacting to your own personal feelings about mortality. If you look at the numbers, you'll see that—"

"I'm sorry, Maddy, but I'm just not seeing it," interrupts Bobby. "I get the baby boomer angle, but when it comes to dying I think people's fears far outweigh their pocketbooks." He slides his signed NDA form across the table to me and then stands up to leave. "Thanks for the, uh, presentation," he says, and exits.

Karina's voice beckons through the intercom. "Jonny, you've got a call on line two."

"Excuse me, Maddy. I'll be right back," says Jonny. And he follows after Bobby.

Victor stands up and shakes my hand. "Excellent presentation. Not only efficient, but effective." He hands me his signed NDA form and adds, "By the way, you forgot to drink your tea."

"I'm not…thirsty anymore."

"You? Not thirsty? You know your value proposition on this stone-cold. Don't let a bunch of short-sighted fools become a barrier to entry for you."

I look at him, totally understanding his language but wondering why then he didn't say anything in the meeting. "So you see a path to profitability here with the right action plan and management team?"

"It's not what I see, it's what *you* see. Keep your eye on your vision."

I look at him, perplexed and contemplative. "I like that. Did Drucker say that?"

"No, Victor Winston. But it's yours to use free of charge. I haven't trademarked it…yet. Say, has there been any progress on the personal development front?"

"Um, not really. I just have to get this business off the ground and then I can focus on, you know, those kinds of things."

There's the hint of an awkward pause as he looks back at me. "Good luck. I hope Lights Out sees a lot of light." I watch him leave the room as Jonny re-enters.

Jonny faces me, staring at the dejection I'm sure is spread across my face. "Hey, I'm really sorry. You were so prepared and you look so, well, let's just say you look really, really impressive, Maddy. And for a minute you had me going there. I thought Garelik might even go for it."

"I don't get it, Jonny. I don't get what you guys don't get."

"Well, why don't you let me take you to dinner tonight and maybe you can get me to get what I'm not getting." I'm not sure but it sounds like there are traces of seduction in his voice. "And maybe I can help you get what you're not getting?"

"What do you mean?" I ask, perplexed.

"I mean, like, maybe I can help you iron out some of the kinks in your business plan. What do you say? How's Morton's at eight?"

"Okay." I nod.

At chichi Morton's, I sit with Jonny, not caring about the celebrities walking by, not caring about the five-star meal or the bottle of Chianti. I passionately make my case for Lights Out Enterprises as Jonny passionately pushes the wine. "Do you know what Margaret Mead said about death in America?"

"Who's Margaret Mead?" he asks.

"A famous cultural anthropologist. She said, 'When people are born, we rejoice, when they marry, we celebrate, yet when they die, we pretend nothing happened.'"

"That's because no one wants to deal with it, babe." He motions for a waiter to light the candle on our table.

Frustrated, I shake my head and carry on. "Don't you see the potential here? More and more people are becoming proactive about their funerals."

"Why?" he asks. "And don't you want to try this amazing wine?"

"Why? Didn't you read that article in the *Financial Street Journal* about couples renewing their wedding vows every year?" I ask, determined to make him see the potential.

Jonny takes a sip of wine. "Yeah…so what?"

I shake my head in exasperation. "Well? Weddings, funerals, memorial redos—it's the same thing, Jonny. People want a reason to celebrate. So why not funerals or tributes or whatever euphemism you want to give it, followed up with repeat memorials, which people might very well want to do given the money one spends on the annual maintenance of a memorial site. Why not original experiences and repeat performances where you're not mourning a death but celebrating a life? So you don't forget your loved ones, so you never have to say goodbye, just…see ya later." I sigh, spent on my pitch. "What don't you get?"

"I don't get why this lovely lady in front of me is not drinking her amazing, delicious, fruity, mature glass of one-hundred-and-fifty-dollar red wine, with an incredible aroma, I might add. That's what I don't get."

I whip my head around to look behind me. No one's there. "What lovely lady?" I ask, but then I spot a woman walking by with a martini in her hand. "Oh, you mean that woman that looks like Nicole Kidman. I think she's drinking a martini, Jonny."

"I meant you, Maddy."

"Me?" I look at my wine then back at him, suspicion growing.

"Yeah, you're pretty damn lovely, ya know. Not to mention amusing. And when you were in the meeting talking numbers, especially the billions, let me tell ya, I had a woody on me that wouldn't quit."

I look at him startled. "Is this supposed to be a date?"

Jonny nods.

"I don't want you to date me, I want you to invest in me."

"Oh, come on, Maddy. That's a dead-end business you're talking about. No pun intended."

"Excuse me, but I happen to think that death is alive and well, thank you very much. Think about it. Everyone has to go at one time or another."

"I'm sorry, Maddy. I don't think you're going to get traction on it because I don't believe people want to confront it. It's fucking morbid."

"Oh my God. That's the whole point. It's always been that way in the past. But baby boomers are going to change the perception. They're going to turn it into a celebration so they don't have to deal with the morbid aspect. You should be loving this idea, Jonny, you're the one with the celebration reputation. I've heard about the parties you threw at BU. Legendary to say the least."

He cocks his head arrogantly. "Yeah, they ripped all right."

"Think about it. How do you want to be remembered? What do you want said at your funeral?"

"I don't want to talk about it."

"Okay, okay. It's obviously a touchy situation for you. So let's give it a euphemism. What do you want said at your *trib-*

ute? And who do you want to say it? Do you want music? Do you want a band? Do you want the chef at Morton's to serve your favorite appetizer? Because funeral homes, I mean *tributary centers,* are starting to put kitchens on the premises."

Jonny looks at me, his interest piqued. "I could do that? Come on."

"Why not? You could preplan it. Pay for it up front. And get this. My plan is to invest the prepaid fees in secure bonds with double-A ratings, so by the time a pre-need becomes a time of need, it hasn't cost a dime. In fact, if enough pre-need time passes before time of need arrives, the heirs of the pre-need-turned-time-of-need will make money back on the funeral, so it will pay for itself *and* leave them with a profit."

For the first time all evening, Jonny stops filling his face with food and drink and looks at me with keen interest.

"Wow. I've got to hand it to you, Maddy. You got me. How much do you think you need to get it rolling?"

"Just give me a first round of three hundred thousand to get it off the ground."

"Okay, I'll see if I can talk Garelik into it. He's got the final word. But I need a copy of the business plan."

I whip out a business plan from Eve's bag and I hand it to him. Jonny's eyes start to do that funny flicker thing. "When can I get an answer?" I ask. "Because otherwise I have to move on to other VCs." I'm hoping potential competitive interest will spurn him to a quick green light.

"Give me a couple of weeks," he says. "Are you ever going to drink your wine?"

I notice Jonny nervously wipe his hands on his napkin like he did in the deli, and for an instant, I get that funny feeling again that something's amiss. I glance at my full wine glass. "I'm not…thirsty anymore."

Jonny leans in close to me. "Can I ask you something? Doesn't all this business talk make you…horny?"

I look at him, unbelieving, and lean toward him. "Can I ask you something? What is *wrong* with you?"

"Come on, Maddy, you've got that lust for the deal in your eyes. I can see it a mile away," he leers.

"So consummating a business deal for you is synonymous with a fuck?"

He nods excitedly at me.

"Well, just so we're clear, we're working off of two different dictionaries. I gotta go."

Jonny looks at me confused, then lifts my glass of wine and finishes it in one gulp.

While trudging up Inspiration Trail at Will Rogers State Park, dry air rushes to my lungs. I suck in the smells of nature, nostalgic for a different kind. These aren't the smells from my youth. Sycamore instead of maple, dry winds rather than humid breezes, parched beige paths as opposed to soggy black earth; I prefer the latter, perhaps because the familiarity of a happy youth brings with it a sense of groundedness I have never found in L.A., a sprawl of disenfranchised architecture sitting on earth that could be loosened at any given moment by a seismic sneeze.

My cell phone rings and I unhook it from my hip clip like a western gunslinger.

"Well, Sunshine?" asks Uncle Sam. "Did they go for it?"

"Hi, Uncle Sam. The presentation went…okay."

"But…?"

"Let's just say they're reconsidering…after a dinner date…which was not consummated."

"So the presentation lured them in. Did you wear chartreuse?" he chuckles.

"I'm not a fishing lure, Uncle Sam," I say, suddenly realizing that maybe I am. Maybe that's the metaphor, that every aspect of my presentation is synonymous with fishing, only I'm the bait and VC money is the catch. "Okay, maybe I am."

"What stopped them from biting?"

"A missing prototype. I think I can seal a deal with one."

"That's easy enough," he says cheerily. "*I'll* be your prototype."

"You will?" I'm shocked.

"Sure, why not?"

"Because it's going to mean more money to do it right."

"What doesn't? Besides, if you have proof of concept you can retain more assets in the company. Why do you sound so surprised?"

"I don't know. It sounds too easy."

"Well, enjoy this part of it, because the hard part will come. It always does."

"I'm already exhausted."

"That's from climbing a mountain, not a business plan."

I stare at my phone, and then put it back to my ear. "How did you know I just climbed a mountain?"

"Lucky guess," he answers. "Don't worry, Maddy. I'll be there to help you through the tough times. I promise. You just keep recharging those batteries with a good hike now and again. So what do we do besides send you a ticket back home?"

"I'll send you a list of questions for the life bio video and you think about the answers."

"You got it. Lights, camera, action."

I can see him clearly smiling across the distance. "See ya soon, Uncle Sam." I tuck my phone back inside its hip holster. An unexpected breeze packed with humidity swings by. I take in the momentary familiarity, and enthusiastically sprint down the mountain. "Yes! Thank you, Uncle Sam! Thank you, Inspiration Trail! Prototype, here I come!"

The red-eye to Ann Arbor is becoming a good friend. I sit in coach typing away on my computer to fine-tune the template for the Lights Out Video Tribute. I glance at the *Financial Street Journal* in my backpack, my incentive to finish. I hit the save button, put my computer screen down and pull out the paper.

I scan the front page and then flip to the Market section. A story with the headline "Palette Enterprises Commands Triple Valuations," detailing Derek Rogers's impending rise to fame, snags my attention. I sigh, and dare to read on, only to discover that the international art and design scene has become a hotbed of opportunity, now with Outsider Art catching on, and all at the hands of artistic business genius, Derek Rogers. The article goes on to mention that Mr. Rogers has been seen on more than several occasions milling about Washington, D.C., becoming buddies with a variety of lobbyists across a wide range of industries but that he declined to comment on whether it is Palette-related business or what his next entrepreneurial adventure might be.

I get that funny feeling again that something's not right in Derekville. But before I can get in touch with it, I spot a smaller headline at the bottom of the page: "Successor Speculation at Pintock International."

The article claims that president and CEO Arthur Pintock, of Pintock International, may step down from his thirty-year tenure position for personal reasons. "Some speculate a recent lack of leadership on Mr. Pintock's part on account of his daughter's death, and that scouting for a successor is something the board is advising the sixty-eight-year-old Mr. Pintock to consider sooner rather than later."

The article states that, "It was widely assumed that one day, Tara Pintock would take over the reins. But even after her departure to pursue her songwriting ambitions, and prior to her death, Mr. Pintock refused to comment on the subject. It is widely known that Mr. Pintock keeps close counsel with three key executives in London, New York and Shanghai, each of whom is considered by the board to be a potential candidate. Both Pintock's board of directors and analysts on Wall Street are eager to know who will eventually take over control and when, with respect to its affect on the direction of the company and its stock market value. But to date, the bench strength of the powerhouse board has failed to convince Mr. Pintock to utter the name of a single candidate, either in-house or out."

I close my eyes and think of Tara. I reach inside my bag, pull out a flashlight pen and hold it upright. I flick it on and quietly recite the *kaddish* prayer for Tara.

The last of winter begins to melt, making way for mud puddles and the smell of new foliage. A horn honks from the dirt road outside Uncle Sam's cottage on Clark Lake. Andy stands inside the cottage and turns to Uncle Sam, Sierra and me. "That's my dad. I've got to get to my piano lesson now."

"Hey, thanks, Andy, for giving us your time," I say, sharing a quick hug with him.

"Yeah, you were great," says Sierra from behind a high-end video camera.

Andy hugs Uncle Sam. "It was fun! See you guys later!" He scoots out the door.

"Let's see if we can get that magic hour of light," I say.

Uncle Sam, Sierra and I walk onto the backyard deck overlooking the lake at sunset. The ice begins to break apart, revealing baby ripples of water against the shoreline. Sierra places the camera on a tripod.

I turn to Uncle Sam. "Be yourself, and remember to re-phrase my question inside your answer, cuz no one's going to hear me when we finish cutting it together."

Sierra crosses over to Uncle Sam holding a small lavalier microphone in her hand. "Can I hook you up for sound?"

"Absolutely, I'll take a beautiful girl hooking me up for sound any day."

"Why thank you, Mr. Banks."

"You can call me Sam."

"Okay, Sam." Sierra smiles.

"Hey, are you flirting with my production crew?" I tease.

"Why not?" He smiles back as Sierra finishes. "You okay with it?" he asks her.

"Actually, I'm flattered," she says, and turns to me. "We're good to go."

"Uncle Sam, you ready?"

"Ready."

Sierra lines up a master shot with a wide-angle lens. I stand to the side of the camera.

"Keep your eyes on me, Uncle Sam. Not the lens. Warm-up question number one. What's your favorite hobby?"

"My favorite hobby is fishing on Clark Lake. It takes pa-tience, and, well, that's a metaphor for life…because without the joy of the journey, there's no joy of the catch."

"Hold it," says Sierra. "The breeze is blowing his hair in his face and there's a hot spot on him." She readjusts his hair and powders his forehead. He blushes under her cosmetic touch-up. She smiles at him and returns to the camera.

"Tell me about your other hobbies," I suggest. "Like whistling."

"I love to whistle. It's how I communicate with myself and

nature. Puts air in your lungs. Makes you feel alive. Just put your lips together and blow." He puckers up and whistles the tune of "Fishing Free." An obvious sense of contentment washes over him as he gestures toward the beauty around us.

Sierra and I watch, mesmerized by the ease with which he handles the art of living. He finishes the song, looks at the landscape and offers his trademark line, "It's a beee-utiful day!"

We break into a round of applause.

Uncle Sam blinks repeatedly several times, revealing shyness graced with humility. It's an endearing mannerism and I watch Sierra capture it on tape.

I glance at my guide sheet. "Okay, Uncle Sam, tell me what you are most proud of in your life."

He takes a moment, then replies, "I'm most proud of my love of life."

"Can you explain what you mean by that?" I ask.

"I wake up every day and appreciate every moment. It doesn't matter if it's raining or the sun is shining. It's all beautiful. I'm very proud of that."

"*That's* beautiful," says Sierra.

I feel a pain in my heart I can't define. Will I ever feel that way? I fumble through my papers to resume the questions. "What's made your life special to you? So far."

"My life is special because of the people in it. *They* make my life special. I hope I do the same for their lives," he concludes.

"And your favorite piece of music is?"

"My favorite song is 'Fishing Free.' The melody is both light and introspective. It feels fresh every time I hear it."

"What do you believe life is all about? A collapsible reply please."

"Life is about doing the best you can without hurting yourself or others along the way."

"What advice would you give your loved ones?"

"Love yourself so you can love others."

Sierra gives me a look.

"What? I don't love myself?" I ask.

"You could love yourself more." Uncle Sam smiles.

"Ditto," says Sierra.

"I like this girl," says Uncle Sam. "Where'd you find her?"

"I found *her,*" chimes in Sierra.

Uncle Sam says, "She's good for you, Maddy."

"I like your Uncle Sam. He's good for me," says Sierra.

"Do I get a word in?" I ask.

"No," they say in unison.

"Okay, let's break. Uncle Sam, did you pick out a bunch of photographs for us to go through?"

"I sure did. Let's go look at them over a good hearty shot of whiskey." He breaks out a bottle. The three of us drink and videotape as Uncle Sam relays the memories prompted by each photograph depicting the many chapters of his life.

"Who's that?" I ask, pointing to one particular photo of a Native American-looking fellow in a red-and-black flannel shirt.

"That's Fisherman Joe."

"I remember the story about him." I stare at the photo as if Fisherman Joe is a long-lost friend.

Sierra shoots close-ups of photos, zooming out now and again to capture us capturing memories.

Even at night, Sierra's office bustles with activity. A freelance Web designer in glasses and a wrinkled T-shirt works a late shift finalizing a Web site design for one of Sierra's local clients.

"How goes it, Z?" asks Sierra as we hurry inside.

"Almost done with Little Tony's," he says.

Sierra glances at his screen. "Looks great. Keep going. Don't mind us. We're digitizing footage we shot today."

"Cool," he says, keeping his eyes trained on his screen. Another employee packs up for the night and waves at us.

"I left all your messages on your desk," she says.

"Thanks, Julie," says Sierra. She turns to me. "What do you think?"

"I think you've got a great operation going here."

Sierra guides me into her private office with views of downtown Ann Arbor. Her office is packed with video equipment, monitors and a high-end compact editing bay. Sierra hooks up cables and wires and monitors, and punches a bunch of buttons.

"Mind if I make a couple of calls while you…do that?" I ask.

"Go right ahead."

I dial Shepherd Venture Capital. "Jonny Bright, please," I say.

"I'm sorry, but Mr. Bright is out of the office today. May I take a message?"

"Yes, please. Will you let him know that Madison Banks called again, for the third time?"

"Yes, Ms. Banks," says the receptionist.

I hang up.

"What's happening with that?" asks Sierra. "He won't return your calls?"

"Yeah, it's weird. He's supposed to give me a final answer on the business plan, but every time I call he's gone."

Sierra finishes matching wires and pushing buttons. "Want to see what we shot?"

I nod excitedly. We watch a replay of the day's shoot. "This is great. How soon can we have a rough cut?"

"Couple of days, if we pull an all-nighter." Her phone rings. She picks it up. I watch a gentle sweetness coat her inside and out. "Hi, Milton," she says mellifluously. "I'm great. How's Chicago?" She offers me a brief smile. "I'm working with Maddy. Late night." She listens, then says, "See you in a few days, sweetie," and hangs up.

"How's that going?" I ask.

"It's nice. So far, so good."

"Are you in love?"

"Not yet. Though I'm sure I could let myself fall in love with him. You know there's that moment when you let yourself fall. I believe *you* make love happen. It's a split-second decision. But it is a decision. Like the one we shared nine years ago."

"Do you think love is reversible?"

"Never reversible, Maddy. It just passes through to other realms of friendship." Her eyes twinkle. "I know you were looking for answers today."

I cast a glance at the ground. "I wonder if I'll ever love again."

"Oh, Maddy, ex the solo pity party, you're playing your results. Don't beat yourself up for that. It's your way. And I'm going to help you get there. Remember, 'How do you build a life of joy and contentment?' By living your passion—and you are, Maddy. Enjoy the journey which is built on experiences and experiences require energy, so if you ask me, the pressing question now is, 'What do you want to eat to replenish the energy?' because I'm starving."

We smile. Memories of all-night study binges with the best Mexican food Ann Arbor has to offer rush to the surface.

In unison we chant, "Big Ten Burrito!"

"To Tara," I say. "With extra guacamole." We order in a feast and work through the night.

I peek. The fresh light of dawn shines through a crack in the curtain of my childhood bedroom. I lie straight as an arrow, crossing my arms over my chest, resting my head on a pillow, staring at the ceiling. I take a deep breath and meditate on my goals for the day.

There's a knock on the door. It creaks open. Eleanor pops her head in. "Hi, honey...uh, what are you doing?"

"Meditating."

"Aren't you supposed to sit up for that?"

"I prefer reclining meditation. That way if I get tired, I can go back to sleep."

"Oh, I see, dear. Well, breakfast is on the table if you like. Dad's reading the *New York Times* but he went out and bought you a *Financial Street Journal*. I'm running off to a piano rehearsal for Rebecca's high-school drama class."

"What's the play?"

"A revival of *Purlie.*"

"Didn't I see that with you at the Fisher Theater when I was seven or eight?"

"Yes. And you came back home and made Purlie hats out of cardboard and felt. You started to sell them, then stopped when you found out it was illegal because you didn't have licensing or merchandising rights or something like that."

"I did?"

"Yes. So you created your own Broadway musical so you could have your own products to sell. You called it *Stansbury* after the street we lived on before we moved to Ann Arbor."

"How'd that go?"

"Not well. Singing wasn't your forte. But it was a gallant effort. I accompanied you on the piano and sewed the name *Stansbury* on top of your *Purlie* hats. I think you broke even."

"Humph," I reply, trying to remember the details. "What happened to the hats?"

"Uncle Sam cleaned you out. Have a good day, honey," she says, and disappears.

I smile to myself. What a great uncle. I must remember to ask him what he did with those hats.

I get dressed and join my dad downstairs for breakfast. He's reading the paper and drinking coffee. Across from him lies the *Financial Street Journal.* I kiss him lightly on the forehead. "Morning, Dad. Thanks for the *Journal.*" I head for the coffeemaker behind the kitchen counter.

"Morning, hon—you're welcome. How's your secret project with Uncle Sam going?"

"Great. Any new news?"

"Arthur and Grace Pintock are splitting up. They put their home up for sale."

"Why?" I ask, surprised. "You'd think they'd need each other more than ever right now." I carry a mug of hot coffee to the table and sit across from him.

Charlie puts the paper down. "Actually, Maddy, it's fairly common in couples who lose a child, especially when it's an only child like Tara was. There's a lot of guilt and self-blaming that goes on."

"Self-blaming? It's not their fault. If anyone's to blame, blame the pharmaceutical company for the faulty inhaler," I say indignantly.

"He is doing that. But it won't lessen the grief, and lawsuits don't bring back the dead."

"But Hercules can," I say, proud to bring the mythology lessons of my youth to the table, lessons my father taught me. But he looks at me perplexed. "Remember? You taught me the myth of Admetus and Alcestis. Admetus gets ill and Apollo asks the Fates to spare Admetus if someone else will die for him. Only no one steps up to the plate. Not Admetus's warriors, nor his aging parents. So his new bride Alcestis dies for him. And then it's Hercules who fights with Death to bring her back and save her."

Charlie sits still looking at me with a mixture of subtle compassion and benign disappointment. "I'm afraid you mistakenly altered the ending. Hercules fights Death off *before* Alcestis actually dies."

"Oh," I say, frustrated by the inability to skirt death, even in a mythological tale, and at myself for having gotten the facts wrong to begin with—or had I manipulated the facts all these years to allay my own fear of death?

"I've got to get to my class. The age of chivalry beckons. Have a good day," he says, and walks out the door.

I open up the *FSJ,* turning the page to dissolve my disappointment over mythological tales of the past with the small print of the present. There's an article on the Exceptional Event gala in New York tonight, where all the top event planners will be, including spokespeople for its allied industries in catering, lighting design, tent rentals and so forth. I call Sierra.

"Hey, Si. You up?"

"I'm already at the office in the editing bay."

"Can you edit without me? The event planning industry is gathering in New York. It's a good opportunity for me."

"No problem. But I need to see Sam again. There are a few takes I want to reshoot. I've got his number."

"I'll let him know."

"Have fun and be safe. I hear a snowstorm is coming," she says.

I hang up and dial Uncle Sam. "Hello, Sunshine," he says. "What are you up to?"

"I'm off to New York for research. I'll be back in a few days. Sierra's going to call you for some reshoots this morning. You okay with that?"

"Absolutely! I'll put on some coffee for her."

"How are you doing after your debut on camera?" I ask.

"Great. And now I'm looking at the lake and whistling to the geese. Even though it looks like snow, it's a beee-utiful day. When you get back I'll set up a meeting for you and my buddy, Richard Wright, who runs the Jackson funeral home."

"Sounds great. I have a feeling the video is going to be the thing that puts this over, Uncle Sam."

"It will certainly help, honey. Don't you worry. I'll be by your side to lend a hand whenever you need it. Have a good time in New York."

"Thanks, Uncle Sam. I love you."

"I love you, too, Maddy."

I'm sitting at the airport in the pre-boarding area, when I realize I forgot to ask Uncle Sam about the Stansbury hats. I must remember to ask next time. Meanwhile, I set up all my New York appointments via e-mail, and manage to get myself on the invitation list for the event. I send a pop quiz to Eve: "Define the difference between a good business and a good investment. Provide examples for both, due in a week." I send yet another e-mail to Jonny Bright reminding him that it's been two months now and to please reply so I can, if necessary, move on to other venture capitalists. An automatic e-mail reply bounces back saying he's out of the country for two weeks. I sigh, and log on to other Web sites to learn what I can from reading obituaries.

My first appointment in New York is with the head curator at the Museum & Gallery of International Sculptural

Design. A slender brunette named Toby Helman sits across from me at the museum-gallery's café, sipping a latte.

"I still can't believe your deal here was usurped by that guy Derek Rogers who started Palette Enterprises. You were so ahead of the curve."

"Thanks. But I've moved on."

"Well, just so you know, we can't stand that guy. The museum board wants him out."

"Why? Aren't the licensing deals bringing in revenue for the museum?"

"We call it sell-out revenue, deals with brands that cheapen the art. Derek Rogers doesn't care about maintaining the integrity of art with a product, as long as he gets his cut from the advertiser. Pairing up a Giacometti with Pucker Up toothpaste! Please! Believe me—it's just a matter of time before the rest of the art world catches on."

She sips her latte and I wonder how Derek's managed to last this long.

"So what can I do for you now, Maddy? What other great ideas have you got?"

"Well…I've got a new enterprise…and I'm going to need sculptors willing to take their talents into a whole new field."

"What kind of field?"

"Fields…with gravestones on them."

"Cemeteries?" asks Toby. She seems too shocked for words.

I nod with confidence. "I want high-end sculptors to create customized gravestones. I want to sign your gallery and museum in an exclusive deal with my company. And I'd like you to be on the advisory board. Most importantly, you need to keep this confidential until my product launch."

Toby studies me. "You're dead serious."

"Well…so to speak," I say.

She pauses, then nods. "I'm intrigued…keep going…"

I take another hour to go over the details, and then head for my next appointment.

I repeat a similar scenario with Adam Berman, president of Ubiquitous Music, the world's largest production music library in the world, whom I had met at my cousin Laura Taylor's wedding two years ago. As is my custom, I had hung on to his business card. He remembered me when I called.

I sit across from him now in his Midtown office. "So you see, Adam, I really believe this is one market that you have yet to tap into. Funeral homes, or tribute centers as they're now being called, need good music and better options to serve their communities. By creating a strategic alliance with Lights Out Enterprises, we can infiltrate that market for you. Our independent pre-need clients can log on to your online music library and select the music they want for the experience we design for them."

Adam carefully listens. Excitement grows in his eyes. "I'm very interested," he replies. "And here's something else. We haven't yet announced this, but we're starting a division for original customized music."

Now my eyes light up. "That's huge," I say.

"I know. We just had an order from Worldwide Sports Network for twenty hours of original music. Plus we're signing young emerging artists all the time."

"What about older artists? Artists who would connect with the baby boomer demographic? Musicians like…Maurice LeSarde."

Adam nods. He gets where I'm going. "That's a very smart idea, Maddy. I'm going to pursue that." He jots down a note. "And I'll give you the credit."

"Thanks." I smile.

By the time we're done, we're shaking hands and Adam Berman's on board.

Exhausted, I stop at Starbucks. I sit down at a window table to review my action plan and update the status of my advisory board.

<u>ADVISORY BOARD—in progress</u>

Sam Banks, Former President of Banks Baits

Richard Wright, Funeral Home Owner (rec. by Sam; have yet to meet)

Sierra D'Asanti, President of Candelabra (DVD & Web design firm)

Toby Helman, Curator, Museum-Gallery of International Sculptural Design

Adam Berman, President, Ubiquitous Music

To Be Determined—Event Industry

To Be Determined—Catering Industry

To Be Determined—Travel Industry

To Be Determined—Venture Capitalist

I pull out my laptop and check e-mail. A reminder message appears, alerting me of Palette Enterprises' Investor Relations Webinar. Curious, I log on to www.paletteenterprises.com's investor relations page to hear what Derek Rogers has to say live from the Waldorf Astoria, less than one mile from where I now sit.

A video window pops up on my screen. The smirking face of Derek Rogers materializes as he addresses investors, stock analysts, financial press and a Web camera.

"As Palette Enterprises enters its second fiscal quarter, I am pleased to announce several strategic partnerships are now in place. They're signed, sealed and delivered, ladies and gentlemen."

The audience of investors claps. Derek nods and continues, "Those partnerships include Relate Greeting Cards, Pucker Up toothpaste, and Arrow department stores for the licensing of Palette's private collections. In addition, fifteen major museums and galleries nationwide have signed on. Furthermore, the convention for the cross-application of art is under way and set for one year from today in New York at the Jacob Javits Center…because art rocks, ladies and gentlemen, art rocks!"

I've had enough. Those were my plans verbatim, with the exception of Pucker Up toothpaste. I'm about to hit the delete button when the camera angle on screen cuts away to reveal a glimpse of the audience cheering for Derek. There's a flash of a guy who looks like Jonny Bright. I do a double take, but the shot returns focus on Derek.

That couldn't possibly be Jonny, I think. Besides, Shepherd Venture Capital itself had nothing to do with Palette Enterprises and Jonny's e-mail said he was out of the country. I let the thought go and delete Derek with a click. I sigh and look out the window at the streets of New York. A woman and a man pass by, arms wrapped around each other as they kiss. I wonder when I might experience love again, when I might have time to love again. Compromising now, however, would be something I feared I would later regret.

I glance at my watch. A young man enters the café in a gray flannel beret. Right on time. I wave and he nods and saunters toward me with an easy gait.

"*Bonjour,* you must be Maddy. I'm Davide," he says with a French accent. "Pleased to meet you."

"You, too," I say, standing up to greet him. "Would you like a *café?*"

ployees standing under a sign that reads "Banks Baits—baits you can bank on." There's Sam horsing around with a young Charlie and young Eleanor on a pontoon boat on Clark Lake; Sam playing catch with Daniel and giving him his first book of poetry by Robert Frost; Sam wearing a tall felt hat that says *Stansbury* on it as he introduces me at the age of seven in my pseudo-Broadway debut of *Stansbury* on the lawn at the lake house.

I do a double take, wondering how Sierra found all this extra footage and managed to cut it all together. I glance at her. She relays a knowing nod of sweetness.

The Lights Out life bio video manages to capture life's rituals from birth to graduation ceremonies, from holiday cookouts and family weddings, to the pleasures of solitude and crowded spectator sports. Interspersed throughout the timeline of memories are Uncle Sam's comments about life and a lesson on how to whistle, ending with him in silhouette by the lake whistling "Fishing Free."

He winks at the camera. "Now I want you all to do something fun, make a memory, and don't waste another day feeling bad. It may look like the lights went out, but really, they're just getting turned on…in another room. Have a beee-utiful day!"

I cue a teenager backstage and as the video screen goes up, the old high school theater lights overhead fade up on stage with hues of bright yellow causing the urn and fishing paraphernalia to glitter like gold.

The congregation sways between tears of laughter and tears of sadness, not sure whether to applaud or not. Someone in the back starts clapping and shouts, "He'd want the applause, man!" And everyone joins in, applauding a life well lived. Sierra gives me the thumbs-up sign. I grin the way Uncle Sam would.

"That was beautiful," says Eleanor to me.

Charlie nods. "I think you just initiated a new ritual."

Daniel sobs. Andy turns to Rebecca. "Uncle Sam did all those things, Mom? Wow!"

"Yes, honey. He accomplished a lot and he enjoyed every moment of it."

I take the stage again. "Thank you, on behalf of Uncle Sam." I wait until they simmer down and continue. "People dear to us usually have a signature or trademark they carry or do. Sometimes it's a hat or the kind of cologne they wear. Uncle Sam's was whistling to the tune of "Fishing Free." Finding a recording was difficult because the LP is out of print and it has yet to be published on a CD. But my uncle wanted the song to be heard today and so, without further ado, I present to you...Mr. Maurice LeSarde."

Maurice LeSarde marches down the aisle and leaps onto the stage. He smiles quietly and politely addresses the crowd. "That is one great guy and one great fan." Everyone laughs. Maurice looks at the urn and says, "This is for you, Sam." He then belts out an unbelievably beautiful a ccapella rendition of "Fishing Free." The audience is in awe. Maurice concludes to a standing ovation.

Andy grins from ear to ear. "I'll never forget Uncle Sam, Mom."

Rebecca smiles at me and mouths, *Bravo.*

"Thank you, Maurice," I say. He steps to the side. I address the shell-shocked mourners. "In honor of Uncle Sam, we have, uh...funeral favors. Everyone gets a Moonglow jig fishing lure and a whistle. Moonglow jigs are specifically for ice fishing because they glow in the dark, which is a nice metaphor for keeping Uncle Sam's spirit glowing in our hearts and minds forever. And the whistle, well, anytime you want to recall his memory, just blow. Attached to each of your Moonglow jigs is an invitation with directions to join us in the continual celebration of Samuel Banks's life during shiva, which takes place now, at his cottage on Clark Lake. You're all invited to participate in some ice fishing, and afterward, we're going to cook the fish we catch and tell Uncle Sam stories…over shots of whiskey."

The congregation cheers. Maurice grins. "Well, I'm sticking around. I want to get to know my greatest fan, even if it is belatedly. The whiskey doesn't sound too bad, either."

I nod in appreciation. "Rabbi, back to you."

Rabbi Levin stands before the crowd. "Thank you, Maddy. I must say this is the most…unique funeral I've ever participated in. I'd like to conclude by reminding all of you that even as we gather here today to acknowledge the passing of Samuel Banks, I encourage you to reflect on his parting words of wisdom, to remember him in your hearts, and to know that you've been transformed into a better person for having known him. God bless."

As the crowd disperses, Daniel murmurs to Rebecca, "I think this is a blasphemous display of disrespect."

Rebecca rolls her eyes. "You would. You like to live in doom and gloom, but some of us like the idea of remembering the departed not just with a smile, but the ceremony around their passing with one, too. I know it's a novel idea for you, Daniel, but try."

Daniel huffs. "What do you think, Mom?"

"I agree with Rebecca. I told you, I want rugelah and a klezmer band when I go."

"I think it's…unusual," states Charlie. "But that's Maddy. Uncle Sam did say he wanted that song sung and she made it happen. She's definitely resourceful, your sister, definitely resourceful."

★ ★ ★

The cottage buzzes with mourners. I designate five small ice-fishing circles with Uncle Sam's jigging rods, augers and skimmers. People skim the ice from the holes. There are plenty of buckets to sit on and plenty of Coleman lanterns underneath to keep everyone warm. Ice tents will break the wind if it kicks up again, though for now, the sun shines low in the sky and the wind is on hiatus.

Sierra and I watch as roughly sixty people from the service take to the ice. Among them are Andy and Rebecca, Charlie and Eleanor, and even Maurice LeSarde, who has become chummy with Rabbi Levin.

Richard Wright approaches. "Beee-utiful tribute, Miss Madison Banks." I blink shyly back at him, the way Uncle Sam used to do.

"Thanks, Mr. Wright."

"Call me Richard," he says. "Think I can get me a copy of that video tribute to remember him by? I'm happy to pay for it."

"Sure, but you don't have to pay for it."

"I want to. Tell me what I owe you and I'll deduct it from the funeral bill, along with the cost of those bad jokes," he chortles. "Well, I know Sam would want me to get out on the ice and catch a couple of bass for him, so I'll see you in a few."

Sierra turns to me. "Gee, Maddy, you could make DVDs and give them away as funeral favors or sell them and donate the money to a charity in the name of the departed."

"You're starting to sound like me." I smile. "Come on, let's go fishing. Got the camera?"

The two of us capture the unfolding scene on ice. People laugh, trying to catch a fish or two, shooting back whiskey to keep warm, and all the while talking about the video tribute, the fishing lures lighting up on cue and seeing Maurice LeSarde in person! And most of all, how much Uncle Sam would have loved it, too.

Andy shouts with glee, "I caught one!" Richard Wright helps him haul in a large bass. Sierra catches the excitement on tape.

A medium-built dark-skinned man of sixty with thick jet-black hair approaches me. He looks familiar but I can't place him.

"Hi," he says. "That was a beautiful tribute. I came from up north to remember your uncle. I knew him when I first started out in the fishing lure business. I'm Joe."

"You're Joe—Fisherman Joe?" I ask, putting it all together. He nods.

"It's really great to meet you. Uncle Sam's story about you has been a morality compass for me my whole life."

Joe smiles. "Sam was a good man. He always kept his promises, even when they hurt. When he had financial troubles, he still paid me what he promised—"

Maurice LeSarde interrupts, "Madison, excuse me, but I have to go now. When my time's up, I want you to do my memorial service. And thanks again for putting me together with Ubiquitous Music and for the opportunity to really get to know your uncle, even though it was, you know, after the fact."

"Thank you so much for making it. I know Uncle Sam is smiling."

"Goodbye," he says.

"No. No 'goodbye.' 'See ya later' will do."

"Okay." He pauses, and then says, "See ya later."

Rabbi Levin interrupts the life celebration by cupping his hands to his mouth. "Let's all please gather round!"

I watch everyone huddle over one of the holes in the ice

as the Rabbi leads the prayer for the burial of the dead. "As per the wishes of Sam Banks, we lay him to rest in the place he was most comfortable, here on Clark Lake."

Rabbi Levin hands the urn to Charlie, who gets ready to pour Uncle Sam into the lake. I duck out of sight, slipping behind the crowd. This is one ritual I don't want to acknowledge.

The burial ends and everyone gathers inside the cottage around the fireplace to eat fresh-cooked bass seasoned with a little cayenne pepper, the way Uncle Sam liked it.

I lead a circle of people sitting Indian-style around the fireplace in the living room. I blow a whistle. "Okay, Rebecca's turn." A bottle of whiskey is passed to her.

She swallows the now-ritualized shot before speaking. "Well, I remember when Uncle Sam took me fishing for the first time. He taught me how to stick a worm on a lure…and I fainted." Everyone laughs. "Ever since then, he would tease me about worms. One day he bought me a big stuffed animal shaped like a worm. I was thirty-two!"

The whistle blows and the bottle is passed to a small, stocky gentleman in wire-rimmed glasses. "I'm George. I was Sam's accountant. I'll never forget how he put all his advisers together in a room to come up with creative tax incentives that would save money. He paid us each for our time—his lawyer, his investor and me. It worked. We made history, saving him money and paving the way for other small business owners to do the same."

So the stories go, until someone says, "Maddy's turn to tell an Uncle Sam story."

"Me?" I ask. "Oh, um, you know what? I have to go to the, uh, the bathroom. Yep, all those shots of whiskey, whew!

It's running right through me. You guys keep going. I'll be right, uh, back." I make a move to escape.

Sierra puts the camera down. Everyone looks awkwardly at each other. Rebecca nudges Daniel. He looks at her as if that hurt. She nudges him again, harder.

This time he gets it. "I, uh, I remember the first poem I ever wrote for Uncle Sam, 'Sam. He is a fisher man.' That was it." Everyone laughs, dispelling the weight around my abrupt exit.

Richard says to him, "You owe me ten for that one."

"I thought that rule only applied to jokes, not poems," replies Daniel.

As I listen from inside the bathroom, I rock back and forth curled over on the edge of the bathtub, tightly hanging on to the Ziploc bag with Uncle Sam inside.

The next morning, I wake up in my childhood room again. I stretch in bed and stare out the window at the morning light. I whisper, "It's a beee-utiful day!" The words do nothing for me, and instead of practicing my reclining meditation and writing up an action plan for the day, I curl up in a fetal position and go back to sleep.

Hours later, Eleanor gently knocks on the door and peeks inside. "Maddy?"

I murmur from within a dream.

"Honey, would you like to come down and have some breakfast?"

Exhausted, I somehow manage to join my parents at the kitchen table. Charlie looks sad and drained. And yet, there's a *Financial Street Journal* on the table next to my plate. I glance at it and then do a double take.

"Um…what happened to yesterday?" I ask, bewildered and sleepy-eyed.

"You slept through it, honey," says Eleanor.

"I did?"

"After all the planning you did for Uncle Sam, it's no wonder," says Charlie.

"So what's going to happen to all of Uncle Sam's stuff at the cottage?" I ask.

"Nothing, right now," says Eleanor, sipping from a cup of hot tea.

"I'm not ready to go through it just yet," says Charlie, staring at his food, hanging on to the ritual of breakfast for some comfort.

"When are you going back to L.A.?" asks Eleanor.

I take a moment to compute the lost day into my schedule. "That would be this evening. But I have to see Sierra. We were supposed to work yesterday."

"I told her you were sleeping," says Eleanor.

"What you did was quite extraordinary, Maddy," says Charlie. "Uncle Sam would have been very proud."

I nod, grateful for my father's sentiments.

"I come bearing gifts," I say, knocking on Sierra's office door with two caffe lattes in hand. I've splurged, but then she deserves it. I hear Sierra editing; sounds of online music samples from Ubiquitous Music play back as I knock on the door. There's a swiveling sound on a hardwood floor as a chair rolls toward the hallway. I hear a kick and the door pops open. I watch Sierra swivel back to her desk. I enter, noting the clutter of multiple digital videotapes. She keeps her eyes on a surgical editing job.

As the coffee's aroma wafts over to her, she murmurs, "Mmm, smells good. Hang on, let me just finish this cut." She hits a few buttons and then, satisfied, turns to face me. "How's Sleeping Beauty?"

"Fine. Really. Fine. Except that I loathe losing time I can't account for. And you?"

"Excited to show you what I've got. Three prototypes for you."

"Three?"

"One is pre-need, one is time-of-need, the third is a combo deal. So you have options depending on the circumstances."

"Okay, let the screening begin," I say, taking a seat next to her.

"First we need to order some fuel. And since Uncle Sam talked about creating memories…how about revitalizing one in particular?" She pauses and gives me a knowing look. "You thinking what I'm thinking?"

I nod and place the order to Big Ten Burrito. Then Sierra reveals what she's done. I watch, making careful comments to adjust by cutting for tone and length. Hours of fine-tuning pass before I think to look at my watch.

"Oh, no! My flight to L.A. is taking off right now…without me."

"Let it go," she says. "Leave tomorrow morning and you'll have this ready to go."

We work until 3:00 a.m., when Sierra starts to peter out. Her head hits the table and she lets it stay there, too tired to lift it.

"You're exhausted. I'm driving you home. We'll finish in the morning and I'll take an afternoon flight," I insist.

Sierra mumbles from the table, "No argument here."

"It's too late for me to wake my folks. Is it okay if I crash at your place?" Sierra lifts a brow as if to say, *What do you think?*

"Thanks. Now shoot a gaze in the direction of your car keys. I'll handle the rest."

Sierra glances toward the couch. I pick up her purse and the videotapes.

★ ★ ★

I manage to maneuver Sierra into her house and to the bedroom, where she promptly crashes. I slip her boots off, find a blanket and cover her with it. I take an extra blanket with me. I'm about to walk out of the room, when Sierra comes to—well, sort of.

"You're letting me sleep in my clothes?" she murmurs.

I smile and by the time I pull her faded blue jeans off, she is fast asleep again. I give her a small kiss on the forehead and tuck her in. "Thanks," I whisper, "for everything."

Wide awake after thirty-six hours of sleep, I pop the rough cut into the VCR machine in Sierra's living room. I curl up on the couch under a blanket with pen and paper in hand to take more notes. But this time, watching in the stillness of the night, I am quickly transported to the grief I am desperately trying to avoid.

"Maddy."

Startled, I turn. Sierra stands tentatively behind me in a Michigan sweatshirt. "How come you never let yourself cry?"

I remain silent. To go there, to try, widens an already open wound.

She crosses over to me. "It's okay to cry, Mad. There're no heroics in stoicism. It takes more courage to be vulnerable."

"I know," I say.

She sits next to me. "Why don't you tell me an Uncle Sam story?"

"I—I can't." Because it's too hard. Her compassion shows in the lines around her eyes and mouth, begging to be addressed. I do it with a dollop of humor. "Got any more of those comfort cookies?" I grin, masking my pain.

"You demolished all of them, remember?" She smiles, the

most forgiving smile I've ever seen. "But I've got comfort in my arms. Can you let me comfort you, Maddy?"

The compassion in her eyes makes me nod. She takes me in her arms and holds me, soothing my emotions. Inside the safe circle of her arms, the unleashed tears pour out of me.

She tenderly dabs the tears away with the back of her hand, then with the slightest dab of her tongue. Feeling her warmth, I let my mouth find hers and succumb to a comfort kiss. She senses my needs and responds. Her hands slip lovingly inside my shirt, pulling me down on the couch. I release a murmur of sensual pleasure and then gaze up at her.

"What about that guy...Milton?" I ask.

"What about him?" she replies, and then passionately kisses me.

"Aren't you seeing him?"

She pauses and gently answers, "We don't live together. We've never discussed exclusivity. He's out of town. And... this has nothing to do with him."

In that moment, I decide to let love in. It is far easier to allow myself the comfort of Sierra than to succumb to the pain. I am good at avoidance, I think, and I plan to keep it that way. I will outrun grief like a marathon runner determined to win the race. I had no idea how many miles it would take or that I was racing against myself, instead, everything is quickly washed away by the oh-so-loving comfort of Sierra.

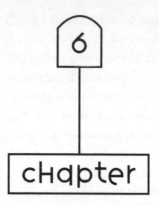

6

cHapter

Financial Strategy: The Venture Capitalist Reprise

Six a.m. My stark Los Angeles apartment. I stretch, recline and meditate for thirty seconds, then I do my sit-ups and push-ups, and jump into the shower. Water streams down my face as I repeat, "I am grateful for VC money coming to me, I am grateful for VC money coming to me."

No sooner do I turn the shower off than my doorbell rings. I leap out of the shower, wrapping a towel around me. I open the door and experience déjà vu as Eve Gardner stands in front of me in one of her perfect double-C outfits. Before I can say anything, she holds up a digital camera and snaps a shot of me with dripping wet hair.

I scrunch my face. "Hi, um, what's with the a.m. photo shoot? Did you miss me? Or did we schedule an appointment this morning?"

"No, but you did, which means I do," says Eve as she enters. "Is there coffee?"

"Yes. But I think I'm experiencing a disconnect here."

"You mentioned a meeting this morning in your e-mail. I'm here to help you accomplish your goal. As a vital part of your presentation team, that puts me here…now." She pours herself a cup of coffee and whips out her Prada makeup bag.

"That's awfully ambitious of you, Eve." I'm suspicious. "Might there be another reason?"

"Well, now that you mention it," she says, sipping coffee, "Professor Osaka wants a visual essay on the before and after effects of our internships, and I believe my contribution has a direct effect on the progress of your company."

"I should have known," I say. "He did this to my class. It's his way of helping students identify their strengths and weaknesses in business. Okay, well, let's get to it."

Eve smiles victoriously as she leads the way to my bedroom closet. I follow—wondering how that happened.

Eve quickly composes an outfit combining my new pantsuit with the new muted yellow sweater. She polishes me off with makeup and a stylized blow-dry. She admires my image in the mirror and remarks, "Ooh, I'm good. Now just transfer your stuff from that disgusting briefcase into my Prada bag and you're set."

I give her a look. "It's not disgusting, it's well loved. And while I do this, can you please bring me those letters of emancipation on my desk."

She brings a small stack of letters over to me. "What are you free of?"

"Debt. Remember, Eve, entrepreneurship is about taking risks, but you still have to be responsible and pay people back. Oops, I almost forgot." I lift my black ribbon to pin on me.

"Stop! What are you doing?" screams Eve. "You'll destroy the stitching."

"Eve, I have to wear this. It's part of the ritual. Mourners wear black ribbons for a month after shiva."

"Okay, but if you do that you're going to be mourning over your clothes next. At least let me turn it into a necklace." She takes off her Guess or Gap or Tiffany silver necklace and somehow blends the ribbon in so it almost looks like an art piece. I put it on. She smiles at my entire ensemble. "Okay, now you can go."

"Thanks, Eve."

"Oh, almost forgot," she says, and whips out the digital camera for the "after" shot.

I confidently walk through the large double glass doors of Shepherd Venture Capital. I reach the receptionist and offer a big smile. "Hi, I'm here to see Jonny Bright. I don't actually have an appointment, but I e-mailed him that I would be coming in today…at this time…and…"

"Oh. He no longer works here," says the receptionist. "Is there someone else I can put you in touch with?"

My cheerful countenance crashes and burns. "Excuse me? Did you say…he no longer works here?"

"Yes, as of last week," she replies.

I can't seem to make sense of it. "Well, um, where did he go?"

"He didn't leave us with any forwarding information. It was all very sudden…and very weird," she adds.

I stand there punctured and then repair myself with a shot of hope. "Okay…is Bobby Garelik in?"

"He's out of town."

My energy takes another deflated dive. I suck in a deep breath. "Well, um, is anyone here?"

"I'm here," says a calm, steady voice.

I turn around to face Victor Winston, who is standing across from me at the other end of the lobby.

"Oh. Hi. Do you know where Jonny Bright went?"

Victor shrugs. "Not a clue. But, if I can be so blunt, I don't think he's a mystery worth solving. Is there anything I can do for you?"

"I have proof of concept," I say, feebly holding up Eve's Prada bag.

"And I have some interesting statistics I've been gathering on the funeral industry," he replies. "A feasibility analysis, if you will."

I perk up as this kind of news and its implications sink in. "Really?"

"Let's just say you left me more intrigued than my counterparts," says Victor. He glances at my bag and smiles. "I'll show you mine if you show me yours."

"Um, sure. Okay," I say. I feel a grin emerge on my face. I follow Victor to the conference room and gently pat my purse. Glancing down at it I whisper, "Good going, Uncle Sam!"

Victor and I sit in the conference room. He reaches over to the intercom and hits the button. "Karina, can you please bring Ms. Banks a cup of hot black tea." He pauses to glance at me. "That is what you like, right?" I nod.

"Anything for you, Mr. Winston?" asks Karina.

"I'm fine, thanks."

I show Victor all three versions of the Uncle Sam Prototype for Lights Out Enterprises. My business plan lies open on the table in front of him. Victor watches intently, affected, and I realize I, too, am not immune to the emotional reactions the video elicits. Uncle Sam's death wallops me in the heart again.

As the final shot closes, Victor swivels in his chair to look directly at me. He remains quiet, contemplative, statuesque. I sit there watching him, not sure if I should speak. More time passes and I become more nervous. I clear my throat. This does nothing. Victor sits there in a deep trance. I begin fidgeting coyly. I cross my legs, uncross them, and then cross them again. I clear my throat again, louder this time. Still nothing. Finally, I wipe my hand in front of him like a window washer.

"Yoo-hoo? Anyone in there?"

Victor blinks. "Sorry. I was thinking."

"That's good cuz I thought maybe your lights went out."

He pauses. "First, let me say that I'm truly sorry about your uncle. He was…quite a man."

"Thank you," I say, realizing that I wish Victor had met Uncle Sam.

"What are you in it for?" Victor asks.

It's a key question, my answer a do-or-die one.

He continues, "You want to be a CEO? Or are you capable of seeing your idea evolve outside of your control and then let it go?"

I wait a beat. "I'm an entrepreneur," I say. "I give birth to ideas and guide them into becoming capital-producing entities and from there let them become what they're meant to. I just…for once…want one of my ideas to make it to adulthood—even puberty would be nice."

He smiles. "What's the exit strategy for Lights Out? So to speak," he adds, realizing the unintended pun.

"A private sale of the majority interest, a public offering or a leveraged buyout. I'm open to any of the above."

He stands, picks up a Magic Marker and starts writing on a white chalkboard. "Do you know how many people work in funeral homes in the United States?" he asks.

Before he can finish writing the number down, I beat him to it. "210,000," I say.

He stops and looks at me.

I continue. "And an increasing number are women and people of diversified ethnicities. Creating an opportunity flush for nontraditional funeral services."

He nods at me. "Exactly. And do you realize that cremation is rising annually by…" He turns back to the chalkboard to write the answer.

"Approximately ten percent," I say, beating him to it. "Creating a greater savings on funeral costs, which can then be leveraged into more dollars spent on more unique tributes."

"Yes. Precisely. And eighty percent of funerals use a casket," he adds, this time not turning around to face the chalkboard but keeping his eyes trained on me in anticipation of my interjection.

"Which invariably includes a ceremony or some form of ritual, which Lights Out will be primed and ready to offer," I say.

He drops the Magic Marker and faces me. "What makes you so sure baby boomers will go for this?"

"Because baby boomers want to validate the meaning of their lives by giving meaning to their death," I answer. "That…and my gut."

"Okay," says Victor. "I believe you. But…from a client's perspective, why would I hire *you?*"

"Because I'm not privy to the funeral paradigm."

"How is that a plus?" he asks, perplexed.

"Most of the 210,000 people who work in the funeral industry are generational to it. In fact, most go back three and four generations. Funeral home directors are used to thinking in very traditional terms. I haven't been raised in that world so I'm able to think…outside the box. And to create customized funeral experiences at the level that Lights Out intends to, I believe that coming from *outside* the box is rather an advantageous way to get it *in,* pardon the puns."

Victor's thinking again; he sits down and faces me. "How much do you need?" he asks laconically.

My mouth drops open. "You mean…you want to invest in Lights Out?"

"Would $250,000 be enough to get you started? In return for a twenty-five-percent ownership position and I'll take an active advisory role."

I feel my eyes widen. I catch myself and quickly feign a clearing of the throat, to play it cool. "Well, uh, what exactly does taking an active advisory role mean?"

"I want you to think big. Zero limitations. I'll help you articulate your vision. I'll advise you on the finances and administration so you can concentrate on creative content and business development."

Without Uncle Sam to guide me, I know I need someone like Victor, someone with a steady hand to counsel me through every phase of the process.

"What about Bobby Garelik?"

"I'm going solo on this one," he states. "And he's going to regret it."

"That's a lot of faith."

"Faith is what I'm good at," he says. "So what do you say? I'll keep the lights on while you turn the lights out?" He smiles.

"I think I can manage on $250,000 for a first round."

"Great. I'll draw up the paperwork for your attorney. In the meantime, you're going to need a front bowling-pin customer. Any ideas?"

"Some." I nod, camouflaging deep concern for this next crucial step. It was one thing to beta-test my product with Uncle Sam. It is quite another to acquire a high-profile client in the world of big business willing to have a cocktail party with the Grim Reaper.

Convincing corporate executives who often believe unequivocally in their immortality would be the key in flipping the lights on at Lights Out. I had hoped Uncle Sam would provide the finesse needed to effectively persuade that person to commit to a pre-need extravaganza. Now, suddenly, I had Victor Winston's faith. I feel validated, a long sought-after recognition I hadn't known in years, if ever. The unfamiliarity of it left me feeling unsure. I had become accustomed to relentlessly digging myself out of a hole (interesting and ironic metaphor for my new business, I think). Now I feel a mound of solid dirt beneath my feet, and because even an inkling of stability feels alien to me, it carries with it an element of fear. The stakes are climbing and I don't want to let one more investor down nor the greatest opportunity in years that at last, seems to bring me closer to my dreams.

I sit in my parked car on a street in Beverly Hills, taking in what I've just agreed to. I pull out my cell phone and dial Sierra.

"What's the verdict?" she asks.

"Jonny Bright is history, but Victor Winston gave me a green light for an initial round of $250,000!"

"Oh my God, Maddy! Congratulations! I knew you could do it!"

"I couldn't have done it without your help, Sierra."

"But it was your concept. Don't undermine what you've done. I am so proud of you! Keep me posted on the next step!"

We hang up. I call Eve, who asks for a photocopy of the check to add as proof to her visual essay. "The outfit didn't close the deal, Eve."

"No?" she says, on the phone. "It certainly played a part. I have marketing research that can prove that. Shall I e-mail it to you?"

"Okay, you don't have to play me anymore, Miss Academy Award-winning actress on the rise. Jeez, I'd hate to be on the other side of a negotiating table with you."

"Well, you are my mentor," she says, and clicks off.

I smile.

"So, we did it, Uncle Sam. Without you, I couldn't have made it this far." I sigh, engulfed by a hasty transition into sadness. I turn the ignition on. "I wish you could have seen this." I pull away from the curb and turn my attention to the traffic in front of me, trying hard to ignore a thick layer of dark cloud overhead.

Later, I'm sitting alone in the bar of the Bel Age Hotel on the Sunset Strip nursing a grapefruit juice. A rather handsome guy bedecked in gold jewelry tries to make eye contact. I pay no attention. I'm too busy strategizing on how to acquire a front bowling-pin customer.

Minutes pass, and the bartender brings me another tall glass of grapefruit juice. "Compliments of the gentleman at the other end," he says.

"Oh, no, thanks. Really, can you just take it…" I blunder, but the bartender's long gone. "…back," I finish, sighing. I don't have to wait long.

The gold guy swaggers over and begins, "Hi, there. Anyone ever tell you how beautiful you are?"

I quickly shake my head. "Um, sorry but I can't talk right now. I'm in mourning." I point to the black ribbon pinned to my shirt.

"Oh. Well, hey. Sorry about that. I've never had anyone close to me die," he says, still trying to make conversation. "Maybe I can comfort you. Was it someone very close to you?" he asks, inching closer in.

"Yes. He's still very close to me. In fact, he's right here." I pull the Ziploc bag out of my briefcase. "Uncle Sam."

The guy freaks, swallowing really hard. "That is…gross."

"No," I say matter-of-factly. "That is…dust…"

"Well. I, uh, have to go meet someone," he mumbles.

"Okay," I say, holding up the bag. "Say, bye-bye, Uncle Sam."

The guy sprints from the bar. I slip the bag back inside my briefcase.

Three grapefruit juices later, Todd Lake shows up. "I'm sorry I'm late and I'm sorry about your uncle. Are you all right?"

"Oh, yeah," I say, burying my pain. "I'm fine. How are you?"

"Never been busier. I'm handling two giant acquisition deals between four major entertainment companies. But I can't complain," he says. "So what's your new news?"

"Well, you can expect some paperwork on your desk this week because I just secured $250,000 in an initial round for Lights Out Enterprises."

"That's great!" exclaims Todd. "You deserve it." He pauses with a sly smile. "So are you going to tell me what the business is?"

I take a breath and let it rip. "Customized life celebration experiences for the affluent pre-need client."

Todd stares at me. "Like I said before, I have no imagination, so what exactly does that mean?"

"Basically, its pre-planning prepaid funeral services…with a twist, in that they're highly personalized and hence much more meaningful."

"And who's going to buy this product or service?"

"It's an experience. And affluent baby boomers in corporate America will want it…which is where you come in."

Todd looks dubiously at me.

"I need just one little, itsy-bitsy, tiny, weeny, eeny…front bowling-pin customer. Someone who's got a really high profile. I thought maybe you could introduce me to some of those clients of yours...."

"I don't think discussing expansion opportunities is the appropriate place to discuss...going under," he says.

"I was referring to your estate planning department. It could be an extra added value that—"

"Sorry, Maddy, but our firm has a strict policy not to solicit anything, for anyone, even our own clients. But it's a great place to start looking. What's the business called?"

"Lights Out Enter—" Before I can finish, Todd's cell phone interrupts. He answers, mouths *excuse me,* and I know my time's up with him. I'm going to have to find another way.

I begin the task of calling estate planning attorneys at one law firm after another to set up meetings to describe my offering. But they insist on knowing what it is before setting a meeting and then, well, once the topic is mentioned it becomes a dead issue.

The conversation usually ends thus: "No, sir. I was *not* suggesting that you're mortal. I said life celebration, not a cocktail party with the grim reaper!"

I meet with my cousin Laura, who thinks it's an awesome idea, but instead of helping me find high-profile entertainment people, she encourages me to develop the concept as a reality TV show. I try Adam Berman at Ubiquitous Music, but he declines claiming it's a conflict of interest. I cold-call high-profile corporations featured in the *Financial Street Journal,* but the young assistants who play gatekeeper to upper management simply don't get it, thinking I'm some sort of quack.

After ten days of nonstop dead-ends, I throw my pen and notepad down and head over to the Bel Age Hotel for a real drink.

I sit at the bar nursing a grapefruit juice, but this time with a shot of vodka in it.

"I've never seen you come in here for a *drink* drink before," says the bartender.

"Me, neither," I reply.

"What's got you so down?"

"The search for that which doth not exist," I say, slightly slurring my words.

"Maybe you're just looking in the wrong places. What are you seeking?"

"Oh, just a high-profile corporate executive willing to share his life in the context of death."

"That's easy," he says, cocking his head toward the bar. "People like that hang out right here, in bars. Traveling CEOs looking to share and connect. Bars are where they bide their time, trust me." He winks.

The guy with the gold enters. I glance at him, and then back at the bartender.

"Not him," says the bartender flatly.

Gold Guy sees me but I've got my black ribbon on, so he keeps his distance, every so often casting discreet glances my way.

Meanwhile, I sit there stumped. The *Financial Street Journal* lies by my side next to the *New York Times* obituary page. A large loquacious crowd of suits pass the bar on the way to what must be several ballrooms.

"What's up with crowd central?" I ask the bartender.

"Another convention, real estate or something," he replies.

I nod. "Hey, maybe I should hit the trade show industry," I tell him. "You know, traipse around the country going to conventions seeking clients looking to book their own funeral gigs."

I shake my head. When I glance up I notice Arthur Pintock standing alone at the end of the bar, rubbing his temples, looking tired and worn out. I get an idea.

Moments later, the bartender brings Arthur Pintock a hot cup of cappuccino, compliments of Madison Banks. Arthur looks up, recognizes me and nods thanks.

Mr. Pintock moves from his end of the bar to mine. "Hi, Mr. Pintock," I say. "Madison Banks. How are you?" I see the pain on his face that my connection brings, leaving him absent of words. "I'm sorry to hear about you and Mrs. Pintock," I say, providing discreet filler for him until he can regain his composure.

He nods, and then notices the black ribbon on my shirt. "What's that ribbon for?"

"My uncle Sam passed away last week," I say. "He was like a father to me."

"I'm sorry," he says. "May I join you?"

"Yes, of course," I say, moving my papers over and quickly stuffing the obit page in my briefcase. He sits next to me.

"And call me Arthur. How about a couple of martinis?"

"Sure," I say. "Arthur."

Arthur and I drink up. The more we drink, the more we cut loose about our feelings of loss.

"The thing about it," says Arthur, "is if people haven't experienced death, they have no idea what you're feeling. It makes them uncomfortable to be around you. They don't know what to say. You don't know what to say. So they ignore you, as if you were some stain that might rub off on them and…inflict them with your grief."

"Yeah, as if grief were contagious," I concur, swilling my drink. "I don't understand why schools and universities don't teach practical classes on dealing with grief and bereavement. It should be mandatory. Don't you think?" I bury the rest of my drink down the hatch and slur on. "Especially with an aging baby boomer population. How is a nation of grievers going to cope?"

"That's a good point," says Arthur. "I hadn't thought of that."

"You know what else I wonder? How come there are no eternally, internally-lit caskets?"

"Hadn't thought of that, either," says Arthur. "Interesting proposition, though." He pauses again. "So what are you doing now, Maddy? Why are you sitting alone in a bar?" he asks.

"I'm grieving."

"Oh, right."

Both of us are a little tipsy—okay, more than a little tipsy—okay, a lot tipsy.

"Actually, I'm grieving a death and a celebration."

"How's that work?" asks Arthur.

"I finally secured an initial round of VC money for my new business but without a front bowling-pin client, I'm afraid it's going to flat-line."

"What's the business? Maybe I can help you."

"I'd rather not say." He gives me an odd look. "I think it would be…inappropriate," I add. "Truly."

He guffaws. "You think I haven't heard the most outrageous ideas in my time? If you don't tell me, I'll be insulted."

I size him up, then slowly and apprehensively let it out. "Customized funeral experiences for the pre-need market, strategically targeting those who want to bring value to their lives by doing the same in preparation for their death." I finish my martini. "With all due respect, Arthur, I want to make those experiences about celebrating a life, as opposed to mourning a death. I just didn't think so many people would be so put off by it."

Arthur stares at me, coming to a slow realization. "I see. And when did you come up with this concept?"

I look at him, starting to sober up. "Well, sir, the idea-generation process was initiated at Tara's funeral."

He nods. Silence follows before he turns to me. "I'm not afraid. After what I've been through, I'm not afraid of anything. Especially death. I'll be your front bowling-pin customer, Madison Banks. Just tell me what I need to do and how much I need to pay."

I'm stunned. "But, Arthur, I'm not sure you realize what you would be getting into…" I say, protesting. "The process requires some introspection and…"

"And you think I haven't been doing that? Nonstop since Tara's death?"

Hanging on to the edge of the bar, I look him over. He's not fooling around. "It would require a serious time commitment," I whisper.

"Keeping busy to fill the void would be a, uh…welcome relief," he says quietly. "Please."

"Okay, okay," I say. "You're in. I'll tell you what you need to do."

He extends his hand and I shake it.

"Can I ask you a question?" he asks.

"Sure."

"Do you think Tara would have really made it as a songwriter?"

"I have no doubt, Arthur. No doubt at all."

He grins. "Me, too."

"Would you like to see some photos of her? I recently downloaded them."

"Yes," he says. "I would love that."

I pull out my PDA-cell phone-camera and bring Tara back to life. "See here—this is the time we were at the library studying for an Ethics test and Tara started creating lyrics out of random sentences in our text books…."

He recognizes the oh-so-mischievous smile of his daughter and lights up. "She made everything fun, didn't she."

"That was Tara," I say. "Oh, and check out this one." I click to another photo. "This was when Tara, Sierra and I…"

My words and sentiments seem to create solace we both desperately needed.

Arthur Pintock becomes my primary focus for the next month. I fly back and forth between Los Angeles and Ann Arbor coordinating pre-production of the life bio video, and finalizing the paperwork with Winston Capital. I coordinate with Sierra to take over the video. I have extensive conversations with Arthur Pintock about what he's gotten out of life to date, what he hopes for in the future, how he wants to be remembered, what he wants to say to those who survive him, what kind of music he likes, whom he would like to speak about him and what valuable wisdom he could impart to friends, family and colleagues.

In the midst of the Pintock Project, I receive an e-mail from Eve with an attached pdf file. It's her visual essay for Professor Osaka. I'm impressed, not so much with her content, but with her visual style. Eve clearly has a talent for graphic arts and research, information I neatly tuck away in my memory bank.

Sierra and I interview Arthur at work and in his hotel room where he now lives separated from his wife. Arthur realizes he has no hobbies in his life because he never made time for any; he realizes he has no musical preferences because he never took the time to listen to any; he realizes there are no clergy who he'd want to speak on his behalf because he never took the time to know any.

I interview his colleagues at the office, but no friends, because Arthur comes to realize he has no real friends since he never took the time to make any of those, either. His over-achieving, workaholic nature is what took him to the top CEO position of the world's most powerful mortgage-lending business, not a well-rounded, well-balanced social life, nor a well-rounded, well-balanced home life.

I interview Grace Pintock, who decides to take this opportunity to tell her husband on video all the feelings she's had to unwillingly hoard inside her heart because he was never willing, ready or able to hear them for the last thirty-two years of their marriage, highlighted and microscopically emphasized in the months following Tara's passing.

Arthur flies Sierra and me on the company's private jet to film him in action and continue the questionnaire process while he conducts business in New York, London and Shanghai.

I try to discover something about Arthur during these trips that might reflect a dimension other than his need to control, manage and expand the empire he's created. I hunt for anything that might resemble a hobby or a passion we can use. But aside from his staunch discipline for exercise—he jogs a ten-mile treadmill run every day at 5:00 a.m.—the closest I get is his undying interest in building companies.

"So…building…is a big thing for you. That's a good start," I coax. "You like the art of erecting and assembling. Did you ever want to be an architect?"

"No. The closest I've ever come to architecture is my desire to reconfigure commercial space so it's conducive to labor performing better."

"So have you done that?"

"No, but I placate that desire by making contributions on a smaller scale."

"Can you give me an example?" I ask, digging for more.

"Well, I suppose office chairs are a good example," he says. "I believe they're as valuable as good sleeping mattresses."

"How is that?"

"In order to have a good day you need to have a good night's rest, and in order to have a good night's rest, you need to have a good chair at the office. That's why I only use Aeron chairs by Herman Miller. The ergonomic features provide aeration and adjustable mobility—and they are top quality. Makes you feel invincible at work."

"Sort of a self-esteem booster for you."

"Not just for me. I know it's considered a luxury item for executives. But I consider it a necessity for high performance in the workplace, which is why every one of my employees has one."

"Any examples aside from the chair?"

"Office systems," he says. "How spatial configurations of office furniture affect productivity."

The closest thing I can find to a hobby for Arthur is his penchant for driving to the warehouses of Herman Miller's corporate headquarters in Zeeland, Michigan, to stay up-to-date with innovations in office systems.

I am beginning to think that to do justice to Arthur Pintock, his tribute should take place in an office with Aeron chairs for all to mourn in; only they wouldn't really be mourning, they would be celebrating his life in comfort with high-performance memory…thanks to the, er, chairs.

While Arthur Pintock's life bio video gets cut in the editing room, rumors spread that he's planning a video roast for himself in preparation of a tendered resignation. The board thinks the naming of a successor is imminent. They assume he's finally acquiesced to address the issue and they quit harping at him on the matter.

Eventually, however, the rumor finds its way to Arthur,

who immediately calls his board together and informs them once again, that he has no intention of resigning or naming a successor.

"The video is not a roast but a life bio video as part of my pre-need estate planning," he says.

A member of the board asks, "Does this mean you have a health issue?"

"I assure everyone that I am in excellent health and more than capable of steering the company toward its ongoing expansion plans. I advise everyone to stop spending their time scrutinizing me and focus on your own personal affairs, or I *will* have a health issue," he says, fuming under his breath.

While Sierra works on the post-production of the Pintock Project, I fly back to Los Angeles to work on the product offerings, finalize the advisory board and schedule a meeting with Victor Winston. He e-mails me an address where to meet him, but when I get there all I see is a run-down bowling alley.

I am standing next to my car, checking the address again on my PDA, when Victor swings into the parking lot driving a grey-green Saab convertible. His face is pleasantly tan and his cropped hair is slightly askew for the first time since I met him. It's nice to see him looking less than perfect, I think.

"Welcome back to the West Coast," he says, pulling up next to me.

"Thanks."

"You look tired," he says, noticing the bags under my eyes.

"Yes, well, globe-trotting across hemispheres might have something to do with it. So…why are we meeting at a bowling alley?"

"I thought it would be an appropriate place to celebrate the acquisition of your front bowling-pin client." He smiles. "Do you mind? They've got great burgers."

I shake my head. "I don't mind."

"Kind of goes with your whole raison d'être, don't you think?" he asks, sliding out of his car.

"I think I'm missing something," I say as we head toward the bowling alley.

"You know, customized funeral experiences. I thought I'd make it a customized meeting experience...to go along with the front bowling-pin client theme." He winks at me and opens the door to the entrance.

"Cute."

"You know what, Banks? You need to have more fun. I think we should bowl over lunch. You can show me how you nailed a kingpin like Arthur Pintock, and how you're going to hook all the other lucky pins to follow. Did you use a spinner release or a helicopter strike?" he asks playfully.

"Are you throwing bowling jargon at me?"

Victor nods.

"But I don't bowl."

"Sure you do. I'll teach you."

"I thought you were my adviser, not my teacher."

"What do you think an adviser is, Maddy?"

At the bowling alley, over burgers and lemonade, I fumble with my form, producing a series of slow-rolling gutter balls. Victor's form, on the other hand, is graceful, elegant, powerful and balanced, and he produces one strike after another.

"Good thing I'm on your team." He grins. "So tell me. What's been your greatest obstacle so far?"

I think about it, and then answer, "Finding a way to bundle the product offerings. It would help if I could categorize people and create life-celebration templates for the Workaholic, the Retiree, the Student, the Nomad, the Dreamer, the Musician, and so on and so forth...but then I would compromise the personalization aspect, and, well, that's not an option."

"Keep working on it," he says, grabbing the ball and readying himself for another shot down the alley.

I shrug and quip sarcastically, "Now that's some sound advice."

Victor approaches the lane with a five-step technique. He pushes away, releases and follows through to roll another strike. He looks back at me. "What's the status of the advisory board?"

"All done and gift-wrapped to go. I have domain expertise in all the designated categories I want representation in—music, catering, event planning, lighting, funeral homes…"

"And the Web site? Your turn."

I pick up my bowling ball. "Sierra's working on it, but she's also editing Arthur Pintock's life bio video. I'm hoping to launch in a month. We're including streaming media samples from both Uncle Sam and Arthur Pintock's videos."

"Is the logo done?"

"It's awesome. I'll show you on the PDA." I toss the ball right into the gutter.

Victor is oblivious to my gutter ball as his single-mindedness has him now solely focused on the topic of Lights Out. "Have you thought about your marketing campaign?"

"I'm doing it on the low-down. My strategy is to rely on buzz marketing and establish a sales pipeline as an exhibitor at the next funeral industry trade show."

He stares at me. "You just generated $35,000 in revenue from your first client. Why don't you want to spend a portion of it on marketing?"

"You never know what you might need reserves for," I say. "That and I believe buzz will tip it into early adoption."

"Maddy. Are you giving yourself a salary?" he asks pointedly.

I look away. "It's your turn."

"Hey. I want you to start giving yourself a salary," he says as he generates another strike. "It will make your job easier. Trust me on that one."

"Trust you? What happened to advising me on bowling?"

He picks up my ball and hands it to me. "Breathe. Keep your eye on the pin…not the ball. Or if it's easier, you can use the spot technique."

"What am I spotting?"

"Pick a spot. Focus on the middle of the lane a third of the way down."

"It's that simple, huh?"

"Remember to move your arm like a pendulum and follow through on your swing to eye level, keeping your focus in alignment."

"Anything else?"

"Try to hit as many pins as you can."

I grin, then stand before the ten pins and for once try to follow someone else's directions. I take in a deep breath, forcing myself to slow down. I line up the front bowling pin with a spot fifteen feet in front of me and roll the ball right toward it. Strike!

I look at Victor in disbelief. "Hey! I just got one!"

He shrugs and smiles. "Good thing you're on my team."

The balls roll back to me as the pins automatically realign. I wonder if that's been my problem all along. Had I always been looking at the ball, rather than the destination and the market it was supposed to serve? Was that all I needed to create a flow of success, a paradigm shift in my focus?

"Yoo-hoo… Anyone in there?" asks Victor.

I come out of my trance to see Victor waving his hands in front of me. I wonder how long he's been at it. "Sorry. I was thinking. Where were we?"

"You were going to unveil the first of your intellectual property to me?"

"Oh, the logo." I reach for my briefcase and my Ziploc bag with Uncle Sam inside falls to the floor. I quickly fetch it.

"Do you always carry bags of dirt in your purse?" asks Victor.

"It's not dirt. It's dust."

"Okay…do you always carry around bags of dust in your purse?"

"It's, um…magic dust," I say. "Uncle Sam left it for me."

Victor looks oddly at me. "Was he a magician? Because if he was, you missed that on the life bio video altogether."

"Well, that's because it was a sample video and we didn't have time to get everything in there. And besides, he was very private about his, uh, magic."

"Why do you carry it around with you?"

"It's for, um, ceremonies and rituals. Whenever I need to bless a situation, or a person, or an idea, I just, um, sprinkle a little…on my shoes," I say, trying to make it sound logical and perfectly sane.

Victor looks me over. "Your shoes?"

"Yes. Because it's your, um, feet that take you where you want to go and usually you have shoes on, so you sprinkle a little on your shoes and it, um, blesses the journey and the destination in one. It's some eastern philosophy thing. And I'm into rituals—not cults or anything, mind you, just rituals now and again that symbolize the interpretation of the…uh, hard-to-explain kind."

"Like the black ribbon on your shirt?"

"Exactly. Jewish custom. It symbolizes that I'm in mourning."

Victor leans closer to me. "Well, for integrity's sake, wouldn't you say now that you're in a state of extended celebration over your uncle's life?"

I stop, realizing the importance of his perspective. "That's really beautiful."

"How long are you supposed to wear it?"

"A month."

"It's been three, hasn't it?"

"Mmm." I nod. "So it has." My phone rings. I see it's my mother calling and answer. "Hey, Mom, I'm in a meeting. Can I call you back?" I listen, and then say, "What?… Why?… Yes. I'll be back soon." I hang up.

"Red flag on the home front?" asks Victor.

"I don't believe it. My brother and sister-in-law just decided to kick their personal merger in the bucket."

"Any speculations as to why?"

"My assessment would be poor financial management, creating a rut, and then a disbanding in order to create some sort of necessary action," I say, thinking out loud.

"Any solutions in sight?"

"Not according to my mom," I answer, reeling from the news. "It's unbelievable. Tara, Uncle Sam, now this." I look at him. "Do you have brothers or sisters?"

"No. No sibling rivalries here."

"What about your parents?"

"They're together in Boston." He pauses. "Look, why don't you take care of your family business, Maddy. You can e-mail me the logo later."

"Yeah. Okay. Thanks," I say, in a daze. "What do you do?" I ask, shaking my head.

"Sprinkle their shoes…and let them walk where they will," says Victor.

I have plenty of time to think on the red-eye back to Ann Arbor. I lean back in my seat fondling the black ribbon on my shirt. I think about Uncle Sam. I think about Tara. I think about the death of a marriage.

I pat my purse on my lap and murmur, "Oh, Uncle Sam, what are we going to do about Daniel and Rebecca?"

Death, I think, strikes not only living human beings but living entities like marriages, states of being, concepts, be-liefs, even prototypes. I shake the thought off, not wanting to feel grief, anguish or regret. Instead, I leaf through my newspaper.

Once again, Derek Rogers's name is in print. A brief blurb mentions his appearance in Washington, D.C., with the Senate Special Committee on Aging and the Federal Trade Commission. Why would Derek Rogers be concerned with that? What did aging have to do with art? Unlike other pro-fessions, didn't aging artists possess greater bodies of work giving them greater recognition and greater value in their senior years than that of young, struggling, unknown artists? But knowing Derek, there had to be a twist. Then I think about what Victor said: *Keep your eye on the pin.* Yes, I tell myself, stop looking at Derek and stay on your own track.

With that I put the paper down and write up my action plan for the rest of the week.

I sit around the kitchen table at my parents' house with Charlie, Eleanor and Daniel. We sip tea and nibble sliced oranges, except for Daniel, the perfect picture of misery with his all-black wardrobe and matching facial expression.

"What was her overriding reason?" asks Eleanor.

"I'm not proactive enough. Correction—at all," replies Daniel.

"What are you supposed to be proactive about?" asks Charlie.

"I'm supposed to have us counting dollars…not pennies. I'm supposed to find a way to provide a lifestyle with some modicum of security. She also says I don't do enough to help out with Keating, or play with Andy—that I'm too busy locked up in my *room*…creating *doom* and *gloom*, as she puts it."

"That rhymes," I say.

Daniel shoots me a look.

"Sorry."

"Has she filed for a divorce?" asks Eleanor.

"She wants a separation for now and probably a divorce later," says Daniel. "She wants us both to take time to think about what we want."

Eleanor and Charlie pause. They know how hard it is for Daniel to make money and how hard it is for Rebecca to raise a family without financial support.

"What about the money you're inheriting from Uncle Sam?" asks Charlie. "I would think that would be a big help."

Daniel sighs. "Oh, it is. But even with all of that going to pay off all of our bills, we're still in debt."

"How much debt are you talking about?" asks Eleanor.

"The loan officer at the bank said it was over a hundred thousand."

"How did that happen?" asks Charlie.

"That's the thing," says Daniel. "I have no idea."

"I do," I say, then suck on an orange.

They all look at me…waiting.

"Risk management," I say, as if it makes perfect sense.

"What are you talking about?" asks Daniel.

Charlie and Eleanor raise eyebrows, as well.

I put the orange down to answer. "Well, nowadays, the cost of raising a family includes accounting for risk management in everything you do, and that, on top of inflation, costs money. It's no longer just a bicycle, it's the bicycle helmet, and the protective knee pads and the wrist guards. It's no longer just a stroller, it's the top-of-the-line ultimate-safety stroller. It's no longer regular produce, it's organic produce. It's no longer public schools because they've gone to pot; its private schools that cost a fortune, not to mention the fund-raisers where they constantly hit you up for more contributions on top of the annual fee. And it's no longer a good ol' used car, it's the family van with all the safety features and the safety buckles required by law when it comes to driving around kids… It all adds up… Shall I go on?"

"How do you know all this if you don't have kids?" asks Daniel.

I lift up my trusty *Financial Street Journal*.

Charlie looks at Daniel. "So what are you going to do?"

"First I want to know if it's okay if I stay here for a while so I can save some money and be close to the kids."

"Of course," answers Eleanor.

"Take the time you need," adds Charlie.

"Thanks," says Daniel. "I've got a meeting with a publisher next week and I'm hoping that goes somewhere."

"Where do you want it to go?" I ask.

"I want it to go toward a publishing deal."

"What if you get published but they don't give you an advance?"

"What are you getting at?" asks Daniel defensively.

"Just trying to help you focus on what you really want," I say.

"I'll manage on my own, Maddy," says Daniel. "You're hardly the picture of success. Mocking the dead for a buck. Death is not a fucking party."

The comment stings. "That's what you think I'm doing? I raised $250,000 to start this business. Obviously, the idea has merit."

"Yeah, merit to your pocketbook," says Daniel.

"Please take your verbal abuse outside," says Eleanor. "I will not have it in this house." She turns to me and smiles with genuine happiness. "Did you really raise all that money for your business, honey?"

"The first VC I went to," I add, with bittersweet tears running down my face.

Charlie smiles. "That's fantastic, Madison. Congratulations."

Daniel gets up and leaves the room.

"Don't take it personally," says Charlie. "He's just going through a tough time right now and he's taking it out on you."

"So what am I supposed to do about it?"

"Practice compassion."

"Good answer," says Eleanor.

"I'm not staying here," I say. "I'll stay with Sierra while I'm in town."

Sierra opens the front door and I drag my luggage inside. "I can't thank you enough, Sierra," I say.

"Don't be silly. I love having you here. And you don't have to stay on the couch, you know."

"No. I insist."

Inside the foyer, I spot a beautifully framed black-and-white photograph of Sierra in the arms of a handsome man. "Is that Milton?" I ask.

Sierra nods. "That's Milton."

"He's handsome. You guys look good together. Happy." I take a deep breath. "Jeez, I feel like I'm hitting loss on every level."

"Please don't say that, Madison." She puts her arms around me. "I will never be a loss to you, ever."

"Look, I want you to be happy. I'm just ultra-sensitive about loss these days. Apparently, any kind."

"I know. It's okay. I'm always there for you."

"I know. Thanks." I put on a cheerful face. "So…how is he?"

"He's good. He's a good guy. And we have fun…when we see each other."

"He travels that much?"

"Yeah, but it's okay because I'm so busy working for you." She smiles.

"Speaking of which—" I pull out an envelope for her "—your first official paycheck… I included your reimbursement for the trip to Vegas."

"Thanks. Now that you're here, let me show you what I've done for Mr. Pintock."

Sierra pops the video in the machine and…

I sit with Arthur in front of a large flat-screen television inside his office showing him the rough cut of his life bio video. He watches intently.

On screen, an executive from Pintock International comments, "Arthur Pintock. He's a genius who knows how to turn a company around. A hell of a guy."

An executive from a furniture design firm speaks. "Arthur is a professional. He really understands how good design can enhance an environment, especially the workplace. He's a true visionary."

"You went to Zeeland?" asks Arthur.

"I like to be thorough," I reply.

A married couple appears on screen standing in front of their home, thanking Pintock International for the mortgage that helped them acquire their first house.

Three businessmen stand with pride in front of a giant shopping mall pointing to its expansiveness. They thank Pintock International for helping them make their dreams come true.

We cut to Arthur Pintock in his New York office. "When you're having a bad day, the best thing to do is simply...Aeron-it."

Grace Pintock appears on screen. She speaks of Arthur with disciplined emotion. "Arthur...well, I'd have to say...his *intentions* were always honorable."

"Intentions?" asks Arthur out loud. "What about my actions?"

"She didn't discuss those."

Grace continues on the video. "I believe his potential was...minimized by his grief over Tara. He knew how to work but he missed out on the chance to live. Most people work to live. But Arthur lives to work...."

There's a montage of photos of Arthur Pintock. Every photo is work-related, from his childhood where we see him on a scooter selling ice cream, to his higher education graduations, to his days in corporate America. There are photos of Tara and Grace, but few have Arthur in them. The music underneath is "The New World Symphony" by Dvorak, for its likeness to marching band music, with a full dynamic range and strong, hearty finish.

Arthur looks at me. "I believe the music has more range than me," he says quietly.

"You didn't specify a particular kind of music and I wanted to give the piece some…flavor that also reflects the complexity of running a huge corporation."

He looks disappointed. "Is that how people really perceive me?"

"They have the utmost respect for you."

He shakes his head, "Come on, Madison. I look more like a commercial product for an impervious CEO than a human being."

"I wouldn't say that, Arthur."

"I would, and I did." He pauses, thinking some more.

I show him the storyboards for when the pre-need becomes time of need. "Here's a sketch of the service. I removed the standard seating and replaced it with a variety of Herman Miller furniture. I thought funeral favors could be gift certificates to Herman Miller, or stock options, depending on how elaborate you want to go. And I thought you might want to designate charitable contributions to Detroit's Center for Creative Studies—in particular, their design division."

"These are impressive ideas, Madison. Impressive for a, uh, workaholic."

"I would say achiever."

"That's a euphemism for workaholic," he says, and stands up. "You've done an outstanding job. I want you to use what you need to for the purposes of launching your business. And I'll recommend your company to others. But with respect to my own pre-need requirements, I want to reshoot this entire piece. I'll let you know when I'm ready. I'll pay for it all over again."

"Are you sure? We can re-edit it."

"More sure than ever. But first, I need to have a long talk...with myself." He presses the intercom button on his phone and addresses his executive assistant, "Anita, what's the rest of my day like?"

"You have a conference call with Mr. Haggerty at noon, lunch with the corporate governance committee, a presentation from Herman Miller on their new office plan, updates from the senior executives in Tokyo and drinks with a Mr. Derek Rogers, sir."

I do a double take. The sound of Derek Rogers's name sends chills down my spine.

"Remind me who Mr. Rogers is again?" asks Arthur.

"You met him at...your daughter's funeral, sir."

What is Derek Rogers doing meeting with Mr. Pintock? I wonder. But then I remember his actions at Tara's funeral and I am no longer surprised by his means—it's the end that concerns me. If Arthur is looking for a successor, after all, Derek should be his last choice.

Mr. Pintock takes a moment and replies. "I'd like you to cancel everything for today. In fact, please cancel all my meetings for the rest of the month. Tell Mr. Rogers I'll have to reschedule. I'm going on sabbatical."

7

cHapter

Operational Strategy: A Power Surge for Lights Out

True to his word, Arthur promotes Lights Out to his colleagues and my phone begins to ring. One by one the jobs start flowing in.

Arnie Haggerty, Sr. Loan Officer, Chase Manhattan Bank

The first call I receive is from a retiring banker named Arnie Haggerty, who's done business with Arthur for over twenty years.

We meet for breakfast in Bloomfield Hills, Michigan. The first thing he asks me is if I like coffee. I nod. This pleases him. I order poached eggs, rye toast and coffee.

Mr. Haggerty orders egg whites and spinach, and then turns to the waitress. "Shirley, I'd like to try a new brand today. This one's from the Dominican Republic. Can you brew this for me? Thanks, dear." He hands her a fresh-ground bag of coffee. "For both of us." He winks at me. "You'll love this coffee." He turns to Shirley again. "By the way, did you like that nutmeg flavor I got you for Christmas?"

"I loved it!" says Shirley. "I finished it in a week!"

Arnie turns his attention back to me. "As you can see, I like to prepare for everything—that goes for death, too." He smiles magnanimously. "So, I don't look so bad for seventy-eight, eh?"

"You look great," I say. And he does. Fit and trim.

"I ran a six-mile marathon last week. I do it every year for charity in memory of my wife. So Arthur tells me I need to bare my soul to you. Did he tell you I was a semi-practicing Lutheran until my wife passed?"

"He didn't tell me anything, Mr. Haggerty."

"Call me Arnie. I've got three children who live across the country and no longer talk to each other. That's the only sad thing you'll hear from me. So where do we go from here?"

"My job is to find out what and who is important to you and then create a plan for the best way to celebrate your life. I have a questionnaire that will help." I hand it to him. "I'll need photos and a list of names and numbers of who you want interviewed for the life bio video. Do you have any hobbies, Arnie?"

"I love landscape photography. I do my own printing, too. My work is on display in several galleries in Michigan, has been for the past ten years. Oh, and I'm on the board of the Detroit Zoo, and let's see, I'm an animal rights activist."

I write that down. "Is there anything in particular you're known for at the office?"

He laughs. "Probably my annual holiday gifts. I always give gourmet coffee."

Arnie and I meet several more times and each time I experience a new kind of gourmet coffee. Once we meet in his offices and he offers me use of the videoconferencing room.

I compile my ideas and videoconference Eve Gardner on

the UCLA campus. "Since you're the queen of presentation, how would you like to stylize a client presentation for me?"

"What do I have to do?"

"Give it a graphic flair, you know, à la Eve."

She stares me down.

"For eight points," I add. "And I'll cover all the costs."

"How many points do I need for an A?"

"Fifty. That includes participation, not just pop quizzes here and there."

"What am I at now?"

"Twenty-three."

"I'll do it for fifteen."

"Man, you're tough, Eve. Ten, and you deliver on time."

She rolls her eyes. "Oh, all right," she says, sighing.

"And, Eve, a cheery countenance gets you a bonus point."

"Ha-ha." She quickly draws a happy face and tapes it to the lens.

Armed with my PDA-cell phone-camera, I do a little research, starting with the Detroit Zoo, where I meet with the administrator and take photos of specific locations. I visit galleries where Mr. Haggerty's work is on display and I stop in at one of those do-it-yourself ceramic shops. I e-mail the photos to Eve with instructions and one week later she delivers my ideas in a polished format.

The next time I meet Arnie, I offer a slick presentation of visual concepts on high-end poster boards. Each display represents a variety of ways to celebrate his life.

"Over here—" I point to a graphic display of coffee mugs "—we'll have funeral favors." The next poster board reveals samples of Mr. Haggerty's prized photographic work screened onto the coffee mugs. "To give it more meaning, I thought we could add your photographs to the mugs."

Mr. Haggerty nods. "I love these ideas."

"Now for location, I was thinking of this." I reveal a visual display of the Detroit Zoo. "I suggest a 'walking tribute' at the zoo, with stops in front of different animals for those who want an opportunity to speak about you."

He looks thoughtful, and takes a sip of coffee from somewhere in Brazil.

"In addition, we'll have a gourmet coffee stand at the zoo's entrance." I show the poster depicting the scenario. "We'll serve gourmet coffee and everyone will receive a digital camera to take photos of the animals. But what will make this an even more unique memento is a superimposed photograph of you, Arnie, alongside their favorite animal. We can either have that photo superimposed on the coffee mugs or use photos of your landscapes. Now for music, I'd like to suggest this." I hand him an iPod with all the samples I need from Ubiquitous Music. I hit Play so he can listen.

"That's fantastic. What is it?"

"Symphonic Sounds of Africa," I reply. "Well, what do you think, Arnie?"

"I love it, Madison. Tell me, what kind of numbers are we talking about?"

"Including the video tribute, digital cameras, coffee mugs and the day rental at the zoo with catering, valet parking and the gourmet coffee stand, for a hundred people, we're looking at approximately $54,000." I hand him a general breakdown list.

He looks it over, sips his coffee and smiles. "I'm in."

"Really?"

"Really."

Victor is more excited than I thought over the consummation of Arnie Haggerty's pre-need deal. His enthusiasm breaks through his usual cool, calm demeanor. For a minute,

I look at my phone, wondering if I'm talking to the same Victor.

"This is great, Maddy. I'm proud of you, and I'm proud of Lights Out," he says again. "This is real cause for celebration."

"And Arthur Pintock wasn't?"

"I wasn't sure if that was beginner's luck."

"What happened to 'faith'?"

"Faith is staying in the game when the luck wears thin."

"I'll have to remember that. In the meantime, he's wiring the money tomorrow. I think half should be allocated into an account never to be touched until his time of need. And the other half towards operating expenses. What do you think?"

"I'd like to invest his funds in General Obligation Bonds. They're safe, double-A rating, and exempt from state, federal and local tax. It will give you a leg up in case vendors retrade you by hiking their fees during a time of need."

"All that gobbledygook sounds good to me. I just want to make sure that any gains on the principal go to the estate of the client."

"Agreed and duly noted," says Victor.

We hang up, and I contact Sierra asking her to handle the life bio video for Project Haggerty. And I put a plan in place for her to train other videographers in case we get too busy for her to handle it all.

Norm Pearl, Commercial Developer-Entrepreneur

Famed commercial developer Norm Pearl calls upon my services. He's a visionary who twenty years ago built large loft-style work-live spaces throughout Manhattan and Chicago, which made him a wealthy sought-after urban developer.

To prepare for his pre-need tribute, Mr. Pearl pays extra

for me to meet with him in various urban dwellings such as Philadelphia and Cleveland, where he's considering his next mega-development. While checking out urban landscapes with Mr. Pearl, I learn that he is a very young sixty-five who gives all of his projects in development code names based on constellations. Besides loving his lifestyle as an entrepreneur and developer, the next and only thing Mr. Pearl loves is the game of golf.

Between teeing up and driving the ball from one hole to the next, Mr. Pearl does his most creative thinking, and the course is where he figures people out.

"Everything you need to know about a person can be summed up in one game of golf," Mr. Pearl tells me on more than one occasion. "It's how you play the game."

He also insists on teaching me to play. He buys me a Taylor Made golf package featuring their R500 series and Miscela club. I've never played golf before, but soon learn why the sport carries so much weight in corporate America. Where else can you take a stroll in the woods with your buddies and play a brain game that requires not only physical prowess but strategic thinking in terms of isolating the best weapons (i.e., clubs) for the particular situation (i.e., driving, putting, et cetera.). It's like playing chess on a giant, green canvas.

While playing one particular golf course in Philadelphia, I ask Mr. Pearl, "So what are your favorite charities?"

He steadily focuses on a putt and replies, "I don't believe in giving to charities."

"Really? Not even for tax write-offs?"

Mr. Pearl hits the ball. It drops in the hole. "I just tell my accountant to make donations where he sees I need to. But truthfully, I don't trust any of them because I have no idea where that money is really going."

"What if I could start a charitable organization for you? It would be part of your trust and it would activate upon…"

"Expiration?" laughs Mr. Pearl. "The trouble is, I don't see myself making a difference when it comes to big charitable organizations. And I'm about making a difference. But I'm open to hearing any ideas you come up with, Madison."

"What about food? What's your favorite food that you might like to have served at the tribute?"

Mr. Pearl thinks for a moment. "I want everything I can't have now. Donuts, Ding Dongs, corned beef sandwiches, apple martinis…the works."

I go to the drawing board and prepare a strategy for Mr. Pearl's life tribute. Once again, thanks to Eve's graphic design contribution and twelve points toward her internship, I present my ideas to him in storyboard format on a golf course in Cleveland.

"I suggest your tribute be held at a golf course for a night game but limited to nine holes due to time and for a…nine-lives metaphor. Your guests will each receive a package of glow-in-the-dark golf balls with your name engraved on them." I present the graphic depiction.

"I love that!" exclaims Mr. Pearl. "My spirit will fly on a golf ball soaring through the constellations!"

"Glad you got the metaphor," I say, pulling out the next concept's storyboard. I excitedly continue, pointing to the board, a graphic illustration of people huddling around a hole as if FDR is about to give a fireside chat. "At each hole, everyone will get an opportunity to tell a story about you and what you meant to them. Each hole will be named a constellation that matches one of your developments and what it meant to you and to them. When we get to the ninth hole we'll announce that your trust is creating nationwide golf camps for underprivileged urban kids who wouldn't normally have the opportunity to learn the sport and the ethics of the game that can be applied to everyday life." I pause to catch my breath. "So, what do you think?"

Mr. Pearl beams. "This is phenomenal! But why wait until I kick the bucket to get this noble idea off the ground? I want to start that camp today so I can see the results and be proud of it. In fact, why wait for my demise to enjoy this whole ordeal you've concocted? I want to do it twice, Ms. Banks. Once while I'm alive, like a dress rehearsal! So I can enjoy it, because it sounds like a heck of a lot of fun. Then you can do it again when I'm gone."

I stand there dumbfounded. "That's twice the cost."

"You worry too much about money."

I cock my head at him, wondering what that's supposed to mean.

"You're very pretty when you're trying to figure things out. I find it…endearing. Would you like to go out sometime?"

"Where did that come from?" I ask, surprised.

"I act on impulse."

"Well, I'm, uh, flattered. But I don't date my clients. Strict policy, especially when I'm just getting my company off the ground."

Mr. Pearl heckles. "You got the bug, don't ya?"

"What bug?"

"The 'I've gotta make a mark' bug," he says, putting his golf club in the bag.

"Well, that is what I went to school for. And it is part of human nature, to take steps toward accomplishing… something…worthwhile."

"The thing is, Madison, once you've got the bug, there's no going back. It's in your blood. It's who you are. It's your lifestyle for the rest of your life. It's like having an on button that never goes off."

"You have that, too?" I ask, feeling an instant kinship with him.

He nods. "Born with it. Nothing turns it off. To tell you the truth, I don't even think death can turn that sucker off."

I smile at him. "You know, I believe you. But how do you balance the professional button with the personal button?"

"I'm still trying to figure that one out. Whoever figures it out first has to promise to tell the other." He winks. "Deal?"

"Deal."

Kate and Henry Foster, General Contractors

Kate and Henry Foster learn about Lights Out from their good friend Norm Pearl, only they decide to call me about handling a different kind of demise.

Over a cup of coffee at a local diner in Ann Arbor, I meet with the couple, both in their mid-forties, young and full of life.

"Look, we don't want a pre-need tribute for the closing curtain on our lives," they tell me. "We want a time-of-need celebration for the death of our marriage."

"You want to celebrate…a divorce?" I ask, trying to make sense of their request. They nod. "This is a new one on me. What you're describing is not Lights Out's core business, so I'm not sure I get what you want us to do."

Kate begins. "We want to celebrate the life of our marriage…and its finale. But no one believes us that it's over."

"They think we're not serious about getting divorced because we don't fight," adds Henry. "In fact, we still love each other, and we have this great general contracting business together."

"But we both want to move on," clarifies Kate. "We're not growing with each other anymore the way we would like to. We don't have a problem with moving on, but everyone else around us seems to."

"We don't want to affect morale within the company, either," says Henry.

Kate chimes in. "We're afraid that if we get divorced, it's going to cause major rifts among our family, friends and business associates. And neither one of us wants that. So we think if we have a happy celebration, a tribute for what our marriage was, then we'll make everyone see it differently."

"So you want an exit ceremony for your marriage, not your life?" I ask. They nod in unison and an idea is born inside my head. "Okay. Tell me more about your marriage. What are the highlights? What are the low points?"

For the next hour, Kate and Henry share the joys of their marriage with me—how they met and created their business, and about their children, their personal passions, their love of adventure travel and their friends. I take notes and give them questionnaires and templates to fill out. We make a plan to meet again and finalize the details.

I'm about to leave the coffee shop when I spot my brother Daniel, in black jeans and a black T-shirt, sitting quietly in a corner, writing. I glide into the seat across from him and break the ice. "Hey. How's it going?"

He looks up, caught off guard, and offers a platitudinal grin. "It's going."

"Did you have your meeting with that publisher?"

He nods.

"And?"

"They offered me a publishing deal. They're going to print three thousand copies."

"That's great!"

"No advance," adds Daniel, meekly offering full disclosure.

"Oh. Well, it's still great. And you can use this one to get an advance on the next one. How's Andy doing?"

"Not too happy about the breakup. He's starting to sulk a lot. Like me."

"How is it living at Mom and Dad's?"

Daniel smirks. "I'm twelve again…only with two kids now."

I laugh. "You can be funny when you want to be."

He asks, "How's the death and dying business going?"

"Alive and well," I say, then feeling the awkwardness of the situation I stand up. "Well, I have to go." I turn to leave.

"Hey, Mad…when are you going to drop the black-ribbon act already?"

I glance at my black ribbon commemorating Uncle Sam's memory faithfully pinned on my shirt. "Maybe when you drop the doom-and-gloom act."

"That will never happen. You want to know why?"

"Why?"

"Because loss is way the fuck underrated," he softly says.

"I know." I nod. "I know."

I walk out thinking about Daniel. What made him so prone to misery? What made us both unable to let go of grief? It wasn't like we had bad childhoods. We had wonderful upbringings, good educations, overnight camp, parents who cared. What was his issue? Or mine? What compels me to play the results? Was it the era we grew up in? Society's pull? Do you shape yourself? Or your generation and its inherent environment? I think about what Norm Pearl said. Do the lights ever really go out? And where does the light, the soul, the mist go after it leaves the body? Is it liberated? Like a butterfly's metamorphosis? Do liberated souls continue to shape life on earth, becoming the unseen writers, directors and producers of earth's soap opera, manipulating drama on earth for some greater purpose than is visible to the eye of the earthling? Are there politics of the soul? Our souls have their own journeys unrelated to those of our parents. So how does attachment fit in—if everyone is an adopted soul? I stop myself. *Keep your eye on the pin,* I tell myself. *Keep your eye on the pin.*

I sit at a coffee shop on Main Street catching up with the *Financial Street Journal.* I learn that Arthur has taken an extended leave to travel around the world. He still refuses to name a successor, instead trusting all to do their jobs without him for the time being. Apparently his trust in his executives is greater than the market's, because the stock has dropped a significant point. Palette Enterprises, on the other hand, seems to pick up speed again with the announcement of an acquisition deal of a leading video-game publisher. Palette will license the video-game publisher's artwork. I shake my head and sigh.

Sierra joins me. "You know, I think reading that paper is a downer for you."

"Information is power," I say.

"Depending on how you use it. Otherwise it's a depressant."

"Duly noted," I say. "Did you find a shooter for South Carolina?"

"Yep. I sent him the video-production template to follow. I'll edit as soon as I get the footage."

"Awesome. Oh, that reminds me. I have to make sure my lawyer trademarks the production template." I shoot off a quick e-mail to Todd reminding him, and then look at Sierra. "Can you create a Lights Out banner?"

"Are we going on parade?"

"If you weren't so cute, I'd…"

"What?"

"I can't think that fast. Anyway, I need a banner for the funeral convention."

"Why don't you hire a company to build an exhibitor's booth for you?"

"That's not where I want my dollars to go."

"But that is what the business is about, no? Impressive exhibitions? And you do want to inform potential clients about what you're doing."

"Yes, but I don't want to go over the top. It's not an entertainment trade show. I want a simple, tasteful booth."

"Do you want me to set up the video projection and make sure it runs smoothly?"

"That would be great. Invite Milton if you want. I'd love to meet him."

"If he's not traveling."

Mr. Pearl's "rehearsal tribute" takes place at his favorite golf course in Hilton Head, South Carolina. Approximately one hundred friends, family and business associates arrive at dusk to pay tribute to him.

I stand offstage next to Norm, who wears a tuxedo with a Taylor Made golf hat and shoes. He looks out at the burgeoning crowd of would-be mourners. I glance around looking for a familiar face in the crowd.

"Not a bad turnout, huh?" Norm smiles. He looks down at his feet and murmurs, "I think I'm feeling kind of awkward about all this. I never thought so many people would come to celebrate my life."

"How can you say that? You are an amazing person," I say. "You have accomplished so much."

"I don't think I'm worthy of this kind of attention."

I notice the crowd is growing restless, waiting for Norm to speak. I look Norm in the eye. "Oh my God, you are soooo worthy. You're worthy of being praised, you're worthy of being loved, you're worthy of celebrating *you* with the ones you love," I say encouragingly. I flash on my liberal arts degree and wish I had added just one course in psychology to all those business classes.

"Really?"

I wing it. "Yes. Absolutely. Now go out there and…be a brilliant dead man. You can do it. Go on. They're all waiting. If you get nervous, just look at the TelePrompTer."

"We have a TelePrompTer?"

"Well, sort of…the old-fashioned kind."

"The old-fashioned kind?"

I point to my mouth. "Read my lips."

"But I won't be able to see your lips in the dark."

"Don't worry, I'll send the words telepathically. Go on, you've got great dead-man talent in you." I give him a big push and out he goes.

Norm Pearl stands on stage staring out at his family and friends. He takes a deep breath. "Everyone, thank you for coming here tonight to participate in this tribute to…well, to myself. This tribute is supposed to happen in the distant future, but Lights Out Enterprises made it look so good, I thought I'd have a dress rehearsal so I could partake in the fun with you! Only you guys get a reprise!"

The guests cheer.

"Okay, so the deal is, we're going to pretend I'm not here so I can hear all the nice things you guys are going to say about me when I'm gone. At least I hope they're nice. If not, don't expect an invite to the encore!" He laughs and the crowd laughs with him.

"By the way, if you do make it to the encore, there's one overriding rule, no crying! I've had a great life so don't waste any tissues on me.

"Okay, so first up is the life bio video, which will play on the wall of the country club building. If I missed anyone—sorry, but we can reshoot and add you into the video for the final playback!" He chuckles. "Okay, everyone, enjoy!"

I cue the projectionist while guests lie on blankets watching the video summation of Norm's life. It ends with a resounding applause. Afterward, people mill around the buffet featuring all the food and drink that Norm Pearl wishes he could eat without restraint and which he happily partakes in tonight. And off to the side, the Charleston Philharmonic plays Norm's favorite symphonies by Ravel and Stravinsky.

Everything goes according to plan. Guests receive glow-in-the-dark golf balls with Norm Pearl's name engraved on them. Norm Pearl stories are told at each hole. I shepherd the rounds making sure everyone has enough balls, making sure that the field lights are on, that the video crew is getting all the highlights, and that no one gets hurt, for which I have a registered nurse on the premises as backup.

In the middle of a Norm story on the fourth hole, also designated as the Orion hole after an urban development in Cleveland, my cell phone vibrates. I grab it and walk away from the hole. "Madison Banks," I whisper.

"Madison, Victor Winston. I'm sorry but I'm not going to make it."

"Oh. Well, that's okay," I say. But I'm disappointed. I didn't realize how much I wanted my round-A investor to see my first official Lights Out dress rehearsal send-off.

"I'm stuck in a board meeting in Houston and missed the flight. How's it going?"

"Great. It's going great. Mr. Pearl plays a wonderful dead man. My skills at dead-man therapy are growing, and the sky is all a-glow with golf balls."

"Good. Keep up the good work and we'll talk later. Bye," says Victor. He hangs up.

"Right. See ya later," I say, and hang up. I stare at the phone, sighing and return to the celebratory crowd.

We reach the ninth hole and I turn to a sweet blond woman in her mid-fifties. I hand her a wireless microphone. "Okay, Elizabeth, you're up."

"Oh, dear. I'm not very good speaking with large crowds," she says nervously. "I usually speak to small groups."

"You'll do great. Just think of this as, you know…groups of small groups. Here's your speech." I hand Elizabeth a piece of a paper.

She looks at the crowd. "Oh, dear. I can't."

"Yes, you can. Just look for the TelePrompTer. And don't forget to tie in the constellation." I check my notes. "This is Aquarius, a.k.a. Project Phily."

"Did you say there's a TelePrompTer?"

"Sort of. But don't worry. Think of all the good this will bring!"

Elizabeth stands there frozen…until I shove her into the center of the green. Norm watches as Elizabeth shyly lifts the microphone to her mouth.

"Hello, everyone. Welcome, um, to the ninth hole, I mean, the hole of Aquarius. My name is Elizabeth Thyme. I'm here to make an announcement on behalf of the Philanthropy Golf Society. I've never had the honor of meeting Mr. Pearl, but I am so touched by this man's generosity and goodwill. Tonight, in paying tribute to this fine man, I am pleased to announce the formation of the Norm Pearl Golf Camp Academy."

Everyone raises their fists to the sky and cheers. "Go, Norm! Go, Norm!"

Norm blushes. A good friend pats him on the back. I notice Norm no longer watches the crowd of family and friends, but is suddenly mesmerized by the shy, humble, sincere and forthright qualities of Elizabeth Thyme.

"Really," says Elizabeth. "This is truly something. The Norm Pearl Golf Camp Academy is going to help many children across the country. Children who wouldn't normally have this kind of opportunity…to learn the game of golf and the leadership and team skills that go with it and that will serve them on the green and off. I can't thank Mr. Pearl enough. He's a real water-bearer, and water is the bearer of life, so please, let's all bless this man and give him a round of applause!"

Everyone cheers some more.

A small elderly lady walks up to Norm and pinches his cheek. "You're a good son, Norm. A good son!"

Norm blushes some more.

Elizabeth turns to Norm in the crowd. There's a glitter in her eye. "I know you're supposed to be dead for the night, Mr. Pearl, but I'd like to resurrect you and ask you to say something to your guests, on behalf of this occasion."

I watch Mr. Pearl suddenly become quiet and soft-spoken as he approaches Elizabeth. She hands him the microphone.

He slowly raises the mic. "I thought my life was great… until I died tonight…and was reborn in this moment. Because who can turn down a resurrection from a beautiful blond?"

People laugh.

"Seriously, I gotta tell you, a dress rehearsal on death is the best way to play out life. I never knew how much I was loved. And I never knew how much I liked to give. Without this tribute, there would be no Golf Camp Academy. And for that I'd like to thank the woman who inspired the idea to begin with, Madison Banks."

He points to me. Everyone looks. I try not to show how shy I suddenly feel. I nod my thanks, not really wanting any of the attention. I mumble, "Thanks."

Norm continues. "Thanks, Madison. I gotta say that death has never made me feel more alive. What a life-enhancer this is. Okay, now, everyone, I want you all to honor the request of a resurrected man…and that is enjoy this moment!"

Everyone cheers again and I notice Norm takes the moment to enjoy Elizabeth Thyme.

The finale to the evening has approximately fifty people lined up ready to tee off their glow-in-the-dark golf balls simultaneously. Someone counts down: "Three… two…one…and tee!" Suddenly fifty glowing golf balls baring Norm Pearl's name hit the sky. I look up. The sky is indeed all a-glitter with small lights popping through the atmosphere in an improvisational theatrical free fall. I smile to myself and whistle the theme of "Fishing Free."

I return to Ann Arbor to put together Kate and Henry Foster's "death of a marriage" tribute. I expect a somewhat resistant crowd of attendees, so I hire JoAnna Myman from Event Ventures to help with the details. Because the Fosters are adventure travelers, the marriage tribute is held at a local summer camp where they first met. Everyone has an opportunity to go waterskiing, sailing and kayaking.

Sierra puts together a ten-minute life video bio of the Fosters' marriage for the finale in the camp theater. One red balloon with both Kate's and Henry's names on it is released into the sky before the video begins. The video includes a montage of photos and video depicting the life of their marriage and its happy ending. When the video ends, a set of balloons, both white, bearing each of their names sepa-

rately, is released into the sky. Kate and Henry assure everyone this is what they want, that they are fine with it, and they
want everyone else to be fine with it, too.

Finally, one of the attendees lifts his glass of champagne
and yells, "To the death of a marriage and the birth of new
beginnings!"

It's exactly what Kate and Henry had hoped for.

I'm in Los Angeles when Arthur calls to say he's in town
on his way home from Australia. He invites me to dinner at
the Bel Age Hotel.

I wait for Arthur at the bar, reading my *Financial Street Journal* and sipping grapefruit juice. I notice Gold Guy at the end
of the bar, leering at me. I smile politely, but then he cocks
his head and winks while flexing his body. He starts moving
toward me. I quickly drop my paper and grab the black ribbon on my shirt, pointing to it and shaking my head. He
shrugs and sits back down, glancing around to make sure no
one saw his rejection repeat.

Arthur arrives and we're seated for dinner overlooking the
glowing neon lights of Sunset Boulevard.

"How have all your travels been?" I ask.

"Good. No. Terrific," he says, placing his napkin on his lap.

I ditto his action, remembering one of the golden etiquette dining rules is to napkin-place only after your host.

"I've made some remarkable discoveries about myself…
and all because of Lights Out, Madison."

"Arthur, I believe you're smiling."

"Am I? Well, it's about time." He picks up the menu,
glances at it and puts it down. I barely have time to read the
first item. I wonder if Arthur took classes in speed-ordering.

A waitress appears, ready to take our order. "What would
you like this evening?"

I hesitate. Arthur looks at me, politely waiting for my answer.

"Um…you know what, I think I'll have whatever Mr. Pintock is having," I say, unless of course he orders something really difficult to eat.

"I'll have the chicken Caesar salad and a glass of Chianti," he says.

The waitress writes it down and leaves. I sigh, relieved, and then give my full attention back to Arthur.

"Confidentially speaking, I've decided to leave Pintock International."

I nearly cough up my drink. "Excuse me, did you say *leave?*"

"I did. I haven't told the board yet. Before I do, I want to implement a few changes in the company."

"Have you chosen a successor?"

"No. And frankly, I'm not convinced any of my in-house executives have the drive and the leadership skills required to fill my shoes. They're certainly competent. Drive and leadership is another matter."

"What will you do after you leave?"

"Learn to live, for starters. Grace was right. I never did that very well. You know who really knows how to live? The Australians. I've never seen such a commitment to having a good time. Remarkable. I also discovered the answers to some of those pre-need questions you had for me."

"Such as?"

"Such as what kind of music I like. Well, I found out." He pauses for effect—a long pause.

"Are you holding me hostage in suspense?"

He smiles. "Ready for this? I love acid jazz and techno."

"Acid jazz and techno. That's great, Arthur."

Our food arrives, but he continues sharing his self-discoveries with me, so I politely refrain from eating until he does, yet another dining etiquette rule. This leaves me to drink more Chianti without any solids in my stomach.

"Yes. And I discovered how much I enjoy architecture and industrial design. I visited the top design firms in France, Germany and Japan," he says with childlike wonder. "I went on architecture tours in Barcelona, Paris and Switzerland. You should see Frank Gehry's Guggenheim Bilbao museum in Spain. Breathtaking, Madison, absolutely breathtaking. And in Yverdon-les-Bains, Switzerland, architects Diller and Scofidio designed a building made of mist. Imagine that. They call it the Blur Building because its shape is made up of clouds and it changes depending on the wind."

"Wow, Arthur. You've really found yourself."

"I'm sharing this with you, Madison, because I'm ready to do the life bio video all over again."

"Okay, tell me when and we'll set it up. Oh, and I can't thank you enough for your referrals."

"It's my pleasure. It feels good to think about someone else. I think it helps ease the grief." He pauses a moment, thinking of Tara, and then continues. "Speaking of helping others, there's someone I think you should meet or perhaps I should say become acquainted with. Maybe he can help you." He finally begins to eat his meal.

I dig into mine, trying not to appear starved. "Really?" I ask between big bites of my Caesar salad. "How?"

"I can't say, since I did sign the young man's NDA, but he seems to be quite talented and exceptionally driven, though I've only met him once."

"Does he have a name?" I ask, placing a bite of salad in my mouth.

"Derek Rogers."

I choke, then cough and gag, until I'm able to grab a glass

of water and wash the shock away. This is chased by a short, intense bout of hyperventilating.

Arthur isn't sure what to do. Concerned, he stands up, about to call the waiter over. "Are you having an asthma attack?" he asks.

I wave my hands back and forth to signal no. "No, no, I'll be fine. I seem to have an allergic reaction to, uh, to people with the initials *D.R.*" I catch my breath.

"I see. You don't care for doctors. Who does?"

I guzzle my wine down between blurting unintelligible protests. "I'd say it's more like young scheming corporate pillagers who seek short-term incentives to bolster revenues until they can raid and exploit another unsuspecting sector, leaving their previous habitats in shambles."

"What are you talking about?" asks Arthur, trying to follow me.

"Nothing," I say, shaking my head, refusing to stoop so low as to bad-mouth or gossip about another person, even Derek Rogers. "Are you, uh, doing business with this, uh, person?"

"Derek Rogers? Not at this time. I just thought he might be able to help you."

"Help me?" I shake my head. "I don't think so." I say under my breath, "That's the last thing he would do for me."

"Is there something you don't like about this fellow?"

I shut my mouth and shake my head.

"Are you sure?"

"He's got black dye under his fingernails."

"What does that mean?"

"Nothing," I say. "It's the, uh, name of a song Tara once wrote. I just remembered it."

"Sometimes you baffle me, Madison. But I admire you, really."

"Really?" I ask, flattered and touched. "That is so

nice…Arthur." I get teary-eyed and, forgetting all business dining etiquette, use my cloth napkin to dab my eyes, mascara and all.

For the next few minutes I fill Arthur in on the latest developments of Lights Out. It feels good to share my goals and aspirations with him. And for a moment, I feel like I'm talking to Uncle Sam.

It's Friday morning. I'm hard at work in the Los Angeles apartment putting together my itemized "customized experience" package in preparation for my meeting with Victor Winston. I glance at the clock. I've got two hours and twenty-one minutes to go. I break down costs and services into levels of participation. I include all the other amenities plus the life bio video, talent, and services from outside vendors for customized lighting design, music and catering. I add a breakdown of costs for risk management, destination management and tribute security, not to mention specialized costs for technology management for holograms, 3-D virtual reality, sensory theater, hi-tech attractions, emotion simulators, sports simulators and storytelling prompters, as well as adventure tributes that include hot-air balloons or customized tribute video games.

I'm preoccupied with all of this when I hear the ring of the phone, buried under piles of paperwork. I dig through and finally grab it.

"Lights Out Enterprises," I say. "Experience designers for transitional states."

"Hey, there, it's Victor. I like the new tag line."

"Thanks. I thought I should expand the brand after the Fosters' dead marriage celebration. Are we still on?"

"Yes. But I've got to get to a meeting in Palm Springs earlier than I thought. So instead of meeting at the office, would it be all right if I drop by your place? It's on my way."

"Sure. When?"

"Now? I'm about to park on your street."

"How do you know where I live?"

"I do have your paperwork, remember? And I have a GPS. It isn't difficult."

"But I'm not done with the presentation."

"That's okay. Show me what you've got so far."

I look at myself and glance around my apartment, which no longer had any semblance of personal living space, but of a start-up company. It's 11:05 a.m. and I'm still in my two-piece flannel pajamas. My place is a mess. My suitcase lies open with clothes half in and half out from all the traveling. Paperwork, videotape cassettes and stacks of newspapers and business magazines lie all over the living room.

One wall is covered with a large hanging white board. On the board is a list of clients and underneath is the action plan and status of each one. Computers, laptops, fax machine, printer, scanner, PDA, digital camera, CD disks, boxes of software, PowerPoint presentations, reams of paper and other office supplies—everything a girl needs to run a company from home—fills my entire living space. I'd prefer Victor not see this state of affairs. On the other hand, getting a meeting with Victor has become increasingly difficult with all of his other obligations. I need his input now, and who knows when he'll be able to reschedule.

"Can you give me ten minutes?" I ask.

"Sure," says Victor. "And thanks for accommodating me."

"No problem, see you in ten." I hang up and move into overdrive. I hit the print button on my current work and rapidly organize everything into messy little piles on my desk, couch and floor so the place looks presentable—well, sort of.

I try hiding all the cables on the floor so he won't trip over them. Then I run into my bedroom, toss the duvet cover over the bed and throw on a pair of jeans and sneakers. The doorbell rings. My hair is a mess and I've forgotten that I'm still in my flannel pajama top when I answer the door.

Victor stands there, clean and dapper in a pink cotton shirt and Dockers. Everything about him is neatly put together.

He smiles and holds up a Starbucks cup and a newspaper. "I brought you some tea. Black, the way you like it…and a *Financial Street Journal*. That is your news carrier of choice, no?"

"Yes. Thanks," I say, opening the door and taking the paper from him like a junkie. "Come on in," I say as I scan the headlines.

Victor surveys the room. There's not an ounce of judgment in his eyes or in his voice, but I'm hardly paying attention because I've become engrossed in an article that outlines transaction trends based on culture in different regions of the country.

"So this is the headquarters of Lights Out Enterprises," I hear Victor say in the background. He places the cup of tea on the only bare spot left on the kitchen counter. He takes in the mess. "Now this is…"

"Chaos," I say, still skimming the paper.

"I was going to say this is exciting. There's more energy coming out of this room then out of all of Shepherd Venture Capital."

"Well, you're welcome to come here and work from the Lights Out pit anytime."

"The Lights Out pit. Was that pun intended?" he asks.

But I'm too engrossed in breaking news to respond. "Humph, look at this," I say. "Ubiquitous Music makes a pact with a cell-phone maker to license their music into phones. Could Lights Out broker a deal between Ubiquitous and the entire funeral industry? I mean, why not let funeral homes have the same access to music that cell phones do? What do you think?" I look up at Victor.

"Is part of your brand to work out of your pajamas? Quite clever, really. Will all of the Lights Out employees be following suit?"

I look down at my attire and realize Victor's comment is a gold mine. "That is a great idea, Victor. After we build the brand, we can have Lights Out merchandise, starting with Lights Out pajamas." Then I stop myself, concerned. "Hugh Hefner doesn't have a trademark on pajama attire at the office, does he?"

"I don't think that's something you can trademark." He studies my surroundings. "Do you have any hobbies?"

"Reading the *FSJ*," I reply as my focus shifts to another section of the paper.

"What do you do for fun?"

"Work," I say, as if it's a perfectly appropriate answer.

"You mean to tell me you haven't become a fan of bowling?" He grins.

"That's work."

"You should try kayaking sometime. Especially when there are rapids to negotiate and you can implement a series of Eskimo rolls."

"That's nice," I say, putting the newspaper down and fetching the printout for him.

"I've found that kayaking builds business acumen," says Victor.

"Really?" I ask, interested now. "Business acumen, huh? I should try that sometime." I hand him the printout. "Here's the breakdown."

Victor glances at it. Seeing nowhere to sit except the floor, he gracefully drops into a sitting position to review my work.

"This is really good. Thorough," he says. "But you need to itemize the general price list. And I would urge you to break down the cost of the actual experience design itself."

"Why so detailed?"

"The Federal Trade Commission is expected to revise the Funeral Rule regarding truth in price itemization."

"It's not enough information for the consumer the way it's currently listed?"

"You don't want to open yourself up to a bad rap based on a few others' unethical funeral practices out there."

I nod, then plop on the floor next to him. "How does my honor statement look?"

"You've written an honor statement?" asks Victor, surprised.

"Page twelve. I want to have a compliance program in place well before we go public."

Victor flips through some pages to my corporate code of conduct, corporate values with ethics training and a plan for self-reporting. He nods, impressed. "Looks great. You just need to modify the format."

"In what way?" I ask. But then the phone rings. I jump up to retrieve it. "Lights Out Enterprises, experience designers for transitional states," I say. A look of concern crosses my face. "Oh my God… I'm so sorry. Yes, yes, of course. It won't be a problem at all." I hang up, shellshocked. "Our first client, Mr. Haggerty…just left us."

Victor looks up at me. "He canceled his pre-need package?"

"No. He…skipped over to his time of need," I say, shaken. "I, uh, I have to execute his pre-need plan two days from now. I can't believe he's gone. He was in such great health." I take a moment to try to recover from the news.

"I'm sorry," says Victor. "Do you need me to do anything?"

"No, no. I just need to call the zoo and the caterer, and a million other people…" I scramble around the apartment opening drawers and looking around stacks of paper. "I'll be fine. Really," I say. "I just have to book a plane right now and get ready, Victor." I finally find the object I was looking for, a flashlight pen. I calm down enough to say, "I think we should finish this up another time."

"Do you need a ride to the airport?"

"No, you've got your meeting. I'll call a cab."

"Well. Call me if you need me," he says.

As soon as Victor walks out the door, I turn on the flashlight pen and hold it upright. I close my eyes and say a kaddish for Mr. Haggerty.

During the cab ride to the airport, I make phone calls and send e-mails putting my vendors and strategic partners into high gear.

Two days later, under sunny skies, Mr. Haggerty's tribute service takes place at the Detroit Zoo. Sierra is there, documenting the experience on camera for Lights Out's marketing and Web site samples, and for the family.

Mourners celebrate Mr. Haggerty's life in a walking tribute around the zoo with gourmet coffee and a vegetarian meal as the symphonic sounds of Africa play on the speaker system throughout the zoo. The zoo's president speaks eloquently about Mr. Haggerty, noting his commitment to animal rights and his substantial contributions over the past thirty-five years. The life bio video is projected against a flat rock wall inside the penguin gallery, since those were his favorite animals. A select group of Mr. Haggerty's friends and colleagues, as well as his three children, all interviewed in their respective hometown months before, now speak expressively about their father and friend on camera.

Mr. Haggerty appears throughout the video talking about the meaning of his life. He concludes, "I want to thank all of you—for being a part of my life—for making it a wonderful adventure—and I wish you all as successful a journey as I've had. Oh, and one last thing. To my kids, life is too short, so work out your differences already. Adieu!"

People are teary-eyed and everyone's loss seems collectively shared as they create fond memories of Mr. Haggerty with the digital photo experience. Everyone also receives a coffee mug with Mr. Haggerty's critically acclaimed photographs on them, eliciting an array of wonderful stories about him.

Next to the monkey cage is a professional grief counselor I've hired to spend time with mourners who are having a particularly difficult time of it. At one point, the grief counselor uses group grief therapy with Mr. Haggerty's three children.

I turn toward Sierra who has tears in her eyes. "Sierra, why are you crying?"

"It's so nice to see people come together to really remember, not just show up and go through the motions of being supportive, but really participate in the grieving process together."

I'm touched, but compliments make me uncomfortable. "Okay, um, thanks, Sierra." I find a diversion and point. "Oooh, look over there—I think we should get a shot of Mr. Haggerty's children bonding with their coffee mugs."

Sierra looks, then turns back to me. "Didn't you say that Mr. Haggerty's biggest regret was that his children didn't speak to one another?"

I nod. "Yeah, he did say that."

Sierra looks at me, clearly moved by the meaning of it all.

"Quick, you don't want to lose the shot," I say, squirming out of the moment.

Sierra captures the reunion on tape, and I recede into the background watching the event unfold.

A thin man in glasses approaches me. "Are you Madison Banks?"

"Yes. Is everything okay?"

"Oh, yeah. I'm George Toffler."

"Really? *The* George Toffler? I love your work."

"You know my work?"

"You cover real estate for the *Financial Street Journal*. I especially liked your article last month on the challenges of selling real estate across cultures."

He seems flattered. "Well, thank you. I know now is not the time, but Arnie was one of my sources and we got to be good friends. Look, I really like what you've done here and I'd like to know if I can interview you for a story on your business."

"You want to interview me about Lights Out? In the *FSJ?*"

"Yeah. I think you're on to something. In fact, I think it's a cover story."

"Um, sure, that would be fine," I say, trying to contain my excitement.

I join my family for dinner at Zingerman's Roadhouse Café that evening. Eleanor and Charlie lift their glasses of red wine.

"To Maddy," says Charlie. "Congratulations on the success of your new venture."

"And on your upcoming interview," exclaims Eleanor.

Daniel reluctantly toasts me. Andy excitedly lifts his glass of water to join the celebration. Rebecca and Keating are not there.

"I can't believe I'm going to be in the *Journal*," I say. "This is a major launch for Lights Out."

"Isn't there anything else you can talk about besides business?" quips Daniel.

I put my glass of wine down. "Okay, how's your poetry book coming along?"

"That's still business," he says.

"You know what? I'm going to take a little walk while we wait for our meals," I say, intent on avoiding a confrontation. "Andy, want to come with me?"

"Yeah!" Andy jumps up and follows me out the door.

The two of us pace the perimeter of the restaurant five times.

"So, how's it going, Andy?"

"I'm okay. But dad's weird. All he does is act moody."

"Isn't that typical?"

"Yeah, but now it's, like, triple moody!"

"What about his poetry? Have you seen what he's been writing about?"

"Loss, loss, loss, loss, loss. It's really boring!"

I think for a few moments as we make another circle. "What about your mom?"

"She pretends not to miss him, but I think she does. And she keeps talking to herself in the shower."

"She does? What does she say?" I ask as we finish another lap.

"She just says the same thing all the time. 'I am grateful for the happiness Danny and I share together. I am grateful for the happiness Danny and I share together. I am grateful for the happiness Danny and I share together. Over and over and over and over. It's kind of mo-not-onous."

I smile to myself at his use of big words. "Those are called affirmations," I explain. "I think your Mom is trying to invoke good things for your dad so they can be together again."

"Well, it's not working," says Andy.

"I've got an idea as to how we might be able to help push it along, just a little. You game?"

"Yeah!"

"You have to keep it a secret, Andy. Because it's kind of like industrial espionage, which I do not adhere to, by the way, but in this case, I guess it would be called familial espionage, which means you have to keep quiet and pretend a little. Sort of like if you had a part in a play."

"I was the lead in *Peter Pan* last year!"

"Great, then you know what I'm talking about. Okay, here's the plan. The first thing you have to do is to wait for the right moment...."

Two weeks later, as dawn hits the West Coast, I excitedly jump out of bed and run to the corner newsstand. I buy ten *Financial Street Journals* and bring them back to apartment-headquarters. I spread them on my desk over an assortment of other business magazines. The article appears on the front page with a headline that reads "Lights Out Enterprises Lights Up Funeral Industry."

The story is an-depth interview on how I came up with the concept and developed the business. There are quotes from my board member Adam Berman, and clients Norm Pearl, Arthur Pintock, the Fosters and the children of Arnie Haggerty, who also mention that when the tribute was all over their father's estate received a refund of $2,019.23 in interest and dividends from the investments made on their father's prepaid plan. Toffler notes that had more time passed between Haggerty's pre-need and time of need, that number would have grown exponentially. He also mentions Uncle Sam as my angel investor, and Winston Capital, a division of Shepherd Venture Capital, who invested the initial financing. Toffler concludes that the products and services offered by Lights Out Enterprises, in essence, its experience design expertise, captures a whole new marketplace in a business otherwise conceived of as dark and gloomy.

I barely have time to gloat before my phone starts ringing. CEOs at corporations across the country from the biotech sector to Silicon Valley to the world of telecom, all start calling to book pre-need experience design appointments.

The doorbell rings. A florist delivers a beautiful bouquet of yellow roses. The note reads "You're a star! But then I always knew that. Love, Sierra."

Congratulatory e-mails arrive from clients, my mother and father and sister-in-law Rebecca. There's nothing from Daniel, but then, I wasn't expecting anything. More e-mails appear, one from Ryanna in South Africa in her e-chapter of Start-up Entrepreneurs who read about it online, and another from Professor Osaka.

The phone rings and National Public Radio calls me for an interview. Another call comes from a Hollywood producer interested in my life story as a movie. Then my doorbell rings again and this time it's a package from Winston Capital with a pair of flannel pajamas inside. The top piece bears the silk-screened name "Lights Out." Next to that is a novelty item, a green bowling pin bank. I smile and look up toward the heavens. The note reads "To brand awareness. May your dreams continue to inspire Lights Out. VW, Winston Capital."

I reach into my briefcase and pull out the bag with Uncle Sam inside and address him. "Thanks for believing in me, Uncle Sam." I place him on top of my desk. "Here ya go. You can't miss this, because I couldn't have gotten this far without you."

The phone rings again. "Lights Out Enterprises. Experience designers for life celebrations."

"New tag line?" asks Victor.

"I know, I know," I say. "Brand consistency rules, but I'm still beta-testing the tag line."

"I like it. Meanwhile, congratulations. Bobby Garelik just walked into my office begging to come in on a second round of financing."

"Really? What did you tell him?"

"I told him at the rate you're going there won't be a second round. You're already starting to pull in enough revenue that you don't have to dilute your percentage anymore. But I told him we'd think about it. How'd you like the bowling pin bank?"

"I'm going to put ten cents on every dollar we make inside it for charity."

"And the sleepwear?"

"I love it. Do you think we should expand the line into rainbow colors or a midnight blue?"

"All of the above, and I think you should give a free pair to all of your clients."

"Noted and agreed upon," I say, writing it down. "Hey, you wouldn't believe the calls I'm getting—NPR, Hector Thornton from Thornton Pharmaceuticals and Roger Lincoln from Green Power Corp."

"With this kind of publicity, it's time you get a real office and hire an assistant. Now is the time to start delegating. And I e-mailed you the name of a media coach. As your adviser, I advise you to talk to her before you do any more interviews."

"After I meet with Thornton in New Haven and Lincoln in Houston. They're flying me in their private jets to meet with them."

We hang up and a breeze blows the *FSJ* papers around revealing a *Business Week* on my desk. The title is "Professional Jet-setter" and the cover art shows a slickly dressed corporate female. I stare at it. I need a presentation strategy, I think, and I pick up the phone and call Eve.

"Go away," says a sleepy voice.

"That's no way to greet an offer."

"Is it a part in a movie?"

"No, it's a part in the funeral industry."

"Oh…what's the part?"

"Fashion therapist. On location in stores you pick. For lots of credit. Preparation involves reading the front page of today's *FSJ* on a particular company called Lights Out Enterprises."

"Really?"

"Yes, and oh, the cover story of this week's *Business Week,* too."

I have one day to upgrade my wardrobe before jet-setting to New Haven and Houston. Since Eve is already intimate with my wardrobe, she knows exactly what I need for a Band-Aid job. Her choices are precise but not necessarily economical, since I still refuse to pay for knock-offs. We're in her Audi TT on the way to Brentwood.

"So how goes the MBA-husband hunt?" I ask.

"Temporarily on hold while I mack it with my co-star in this really bizarro student film. Besides, the MBAs in my class are all super-stiff, as in totally one-dimensional."

"Maybe you could un-stiff them, give them some dimension, invite them to a performance of yours or the screening for this bizarre short." I smile. "What's happening in Osaka's class?"

"The worst! We have to start a business for the final."

I remember when our class had the same challenge and I started White Mondays. "What business are you starting?"

"I have no clue. So I might drop out."

"I do. Be a fashion therapist. You already have one client, me."

She grins. "Really? What do I do?"

I roll my eyes. "Eve, haven't you been paying attention?" She shakes her head. For the rest of the day, I lecture her, adding more mission statements and executive summary homework to her endeavor.

My preliminary meeting with the fifty-seven-year-old Hector Thornton takes place at his headquarters in New Haven, Connecticut. We sit on cushy forest-green couches in his office drinking tea. I'm in my new Eve-packaged outfit, pretending to be a secret agent absorbing as many clues as possible from his environment. Numerous scientific awards and degrees decorate the walls. The rug is forest green. The paperweight is forest green. Even the coasters are forest green. I take copious notes.

"My goal is to cure the common cold," he tells me. "Trials on our new drug have been quite promising. I predict we're less than five years away."

"That's great. How long have you been working on it?"

"Twenty-three years. I started out as a lab technician, got my PhD from Yale in genetic biology and formed Thornton Pharmaceuticals."

"Do you drink, Mr. Thornton?"

"Well, I do love a good martini."

I write that down. "Do you have any hobbies?"

"Botany."

I write that down. "Favorite song?"

"I don't like music."

"Where do you go for vacations?"

"I like to take my children to arboretums around the world and teach them about plants. You can learn an awful lot about the world from plants."

"Really? Like what?"

"Well, their circadian rhythms for one thing, and their adaptability to the world around them." He pauses. "I believe there's a reason for the phrase 'the tree of knowledge.'"

I stare at him, thinking. "Would you be willing to tape-record your thoughts on this?"

"Yes, I think I can do that."

"Great. I'm going to send you a high-quality tape recorder to get started. And if you could fill out this questionnaire for me that would be great, and then we'll start on the life bio video."

Mr. Thornton accompanies me to a limousine waiting curbside to take me to his private jet. He shakes my hand. "It's been a pleasure meeting you, Madison. I feel good about this, almost like I'm in control of my afterlife."

I glide into the limousine and smile. "That's exactly the point, Mr. Thornton."

"Good. I'm looking forward to seeing your proposal and budget next week."

"Next week," I say. The limo takes off.

I study my notes from the meeting and begin a plan. I'll propose the funeral take place in a forest or arboretum. If he wants a funeral home, I'll suggest having a large hi-def video screen show the life of plants and trees with time-lapse photography. I'm sure I can get that from *National Geographic.* And of course, I'll suggest martinis served in test tubes. Everyone can receive a forest-green lab coat with Thornton Pharmaceuticals' name embroidered on it. There will be no music, only the amplified sounds of nature, and an audio recording of Thornton's personal views on the lessons to be gleaned from the life of plants and trees. If he's ambitious, I'll suggest we package the audio tapes and distribute them either for free through his Web site or in arboretums around the world with proceeds going toward the cure for the common cold.

My thoughts are interrupted by my ringing cell phone. "This is Madison Banks."

"Aunt Maddy! I did it! They're watching it right now," Andy fervently whispers.

"They are? How did you set it up?"

"I told them that for my birthday I wanted to watch the movie *The Kid,* ya know, the movie where Bruce Willis meets up with the kid he used to be."

"Yeah…"

"Well…I told Mom and Dad I wanted both of them to watch the movie with me at Grandma and Grandpa's house, like you told me to do."

"And?"

"And then I switched the tapes, just like you said," says Andy softly.

"So they're all watching it now?"

"Yeah," he whispers. "I told them I had to go to the bathroom—so I could call you."

"What happened when they realized it wasn't *The Kid?*"

"Grandma said it must be one of those life bio videos you were working on. I told them I wanted to see some of it. And Grandma, Grandpa and Mom wanted to see some of it, too. Then they figured out it was about the death of a marriage and now they're all glued to the tube," he says, still keeping his voice hushed.

"Your dad, too?"

"Riv-e-ted…gotta go. I'll make contact later," he whispers conspiratorially. "Over and out."

"Over and out," I whisper back, hoping Daniel and Rebecca find a way to value their union again.

I pull out my trusty *FSJ* from my briefcase. I scan the headlines and skip to the Market section. There's a small article about Derek Rogers.

"Now what?" I say to myself.

The article states that Derek Rogers, CEO of Palette Enterprises, has resigned to pursue other interests. Mr. Rogers tells *FSJ* that his success in leading Palette Enterprises to its meteoric rise now leaves him challenged to take on new opportunities. He leaves Palette with substantial stock options and an exit bonus of five million in cash. I predict Palette's stock will fall in a matter of weeks. The article goes on about who will succeed Derek. I look at the printed words, turn the page and whisper, "I'm not going to wonder what you're up to next, Mr. Rogers, not anymore."

I jet-set from New Haven to Houston for my meeting with Roger Lincoln of Green Power Corporation. Roger's office is lined with books on every subject you can think of, a private library of over ten thousand books. He's five-six, stocky and well-dressed in his early fifties.

I pull out my steno pad for notes while Roger fixes me a cup of hot tea. I discover that he collects signed first editions of American literature and has a penchant for historical novels about Vikings.

"Oh, I love to read," he tells me. "I find it incredibly helpful for business, too."

"How's that?" I ask.

"When authors write about their regions, I learn about their customs. It actually helps when I travel for business. Like in the South, they ask a lot about your family before they close a deal. In New York, they're slick as oil, and the faster they talk, the less they know. In the Midwest, they're straight and real. How do you like your tea?"

"Black is fine. Thanks. Do you have a favorite author?"

"Lynne Sharon Schwartz. She wrote *Disturbances in the Field*. A classic, if you ask me—should be mandatory reading for college literature courses."

He hands me my tea. "Thank you. Do you write, too?"

"I dabble in poetry. I love Robert Frost. 'Stopping by the Woods' is priceless. And Sylvia Plath, she was a genius. The new young poets are quite incredible, too."

I stop writing. "Roger, I've got an idea. What do you think of having a poetry slam of your favorite poems?"

"That is brilliant!"

"How would you like it if I could get one of your favorite authors to read your eulogy?"

"That would be amazing!"

"I know you're into the Vikings, so have you considered a Viking funeral?"

"What a great idea! I could have flaming arrows hit the sails of a wooden boat set to sea at dawn with me in it."

"Yes, and you could have your favorite music playing at the same time. By the way, what is your favorite music?"

"Anything by Herbie Hancock. In fact, if you could get him to play live while the ship sets sail, I would resurrect myself for the event."

"Just so you know, we'll have to work out burial details for the "viking funeral" with your local funeral home. In the meantime, I'll leave you with some paperwork and you can start selecting the poems you want read."

Back in Los Angeles, I'm swamped preparing Lights Out for a funeral industry trade show. I leaf through stacks of mail and find a fancy invitation to the wedding of Norm Pearl and Elizabeth Thyme. "Good going, Norm." I mark it in my calendar, not surprised, given the looks Norm and Elizabeth shared at his "death and dying" dress rehearsal, yet I wonder how he found the balance of the buttons.

My phone rings, interrupting my thoughts. The caller ID reads my parents' house where Andy's been for a few days. I answer. "Hey, Andy. What's the outcome report?"

"That was a clever ruse you pulled, dear," says Eleanor.

"Oh, hi, Mom. What ruse?" I ask, trying to cover my tracks.

"You know very well. Andy included me in on the plot— in which he was a superb actor, I might add. You realize that you're a storyteller, don't you, dear? Whether you like it or not."

"How's that, Mom? I thought I was an entrepreneur."

"Your bio video on the life and death of a marriage is a story—a powerful one, by the way. Personally, I think those two will end up back together sooner rather than later. But stories are powerful teachers. You and Andy managed to wield that power. Rebecca's decided to delay filing for a divorce."

"We did? What happened?"

"Well, Daniel cried like he did at the bris. What's new? And Rebecca, even though she wore her stoic look, was without question affected. Not one quip out of her during or after the video. So she's holding off, for now. And Andy feels as though he's won a Pyrrhic victory," explains Eleanor.

"So that's good. It gives Daniel more time to get his act together," I say. "Does he suspect any behind-the-scenes coercion?"

"Not a clue," says Eleanor. "And Andy's sworn me to secrecy. I guess that makes me an accomplice."

"How's it feel?"

"Oh, super. I can't wait until it's over so I'll have a great story to tell," she laughs.

My doorbell rings. "Hang on, Mom, and tell me what you think," I say, and hit the hold button. While I retrieve a large box from FedEx, I know Eleanor is listening to a humorously prerecorded "hold" message.

A light feminine voice says, "*While you're acting out on the stage of life, do you ever wonder what people might say about you when the show's over? You know, when the curtain drops? Well, you don't have to wonder anymore. Lights Out lets you light up the way you want to be remembered…*"

I pick up the phone. "What do you think?" I ask as I open a box stacked with pajama tops baring the name "Lights Out."

Eleanor can't stop laughing. "I love it, honey. I think you ought to give out those little novelty flashlights at the trade show with your company name on them."

"That's a good idea," I reply. "Thanks!"

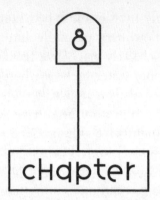

Competitive Landscape: The Past Reprised—
History Repeats Itself

The Funeral Trade Show in Las Vegas is filled with exhibitors displaying their wares. There are wall-to-wall items
related to one's time of need and the afterlife, and the room
is jam-packed with owners and employees of funeral homes
from across the country and its allied industries, as well.

My booth is in the low-rent district away from the main
thoroughfare, a cost-conscious move on my part. A large
banner boldly hangs above the booth baring the name Lights
Out Enterprises. I did, however, give in to Sierra's suggestions
and display a forty-five-inch television monitor playing clips
of the life bio videos in an ongoing loop, including scenes
of Maurice LeSarde singing live at Uncle Sam's tribute.

Pajama tops and novelty flashlights with the name Lights
Out on them are giveaway items. And on display is the cus-

tomized gravestone by the renowned French sculptor Da-vide. It is an extraordinary patina sculpture of Uncle Sam fishing. The artist cleverly placed the fishing line's hook and lure in a round empty watering hole where visitors can leave a memento. There's also an attachable video monitor inside a matching patina sculpture in the shape of a fishing tackle box. When you open the tackle box, the life bio video au-tomatically plays with sound. There's also a button to push on the sculpted fishing lure that plays the melody to "Fish-ing Free." At the base of the sculpture Uncle Sam's name is engraved along with his dates and a small inscription that reads "It's a beee-utiful day."

I also included samples of Andy's now-framed leaf art with poetic words about loss, loss and more loss written by Daniel Banks.

Crowds stand and gawk at the sculpture and the videos.

Sierra fiddles with the projector to make sure the image on screen is crystal clear. More and more people stop by. I conduct a series of miniseminars outlining the offerings of Lights Out with a PowerPoint presentation. And on two sep-arate monitors at either end of the booth the Web site is prominently displayed.

Sierra motions to me that she's going to check out the show. She signals that she'll be back in ten minutes. I nod and con-tinue my speech to the group in front of me. "And so you see…" I explain, "Lights Out Enterprises offers strategic part-nerships with funeral home directors so you can enhance your services to your communities. You supply the pre-need clients and we'll take care of all the details. Are there any questions?"

A man raises his hand. "How are you different from Trib-ute in a Box?"

"Tribute in a Box," I repeat. "I'm sorry. I'm not familiar with them. What do they do?"

"Seems like they do exactly what you do," a woman replies. "And they guarantee celebrities will perform at the funeral, I mean tribute."

I'm baffled.

"They're right around the corner," says another man. "And their price points are lower than yours."

On those words the crowd begins to disperse. Sierra returns wearing a concerned expression on her face as she shuffles through the exodus to me. She places a copy of the *Financial Street Journal* in my hands.

"Maddy. Today's journal," says Sierra. "Read and breathe. And whatever you do, don't go around the corner unless you want to short circuit your own lights."

I look down. There on the front page is a cover story:

Derek Rogers resurfaces with "Tribute in a Box." Derek Rogers's latest and greatest venture: prefab customized tributes for all. Since leaving Palette Enterprises, Mr. Rogers has quickly and quietly amassed ownership of 1,000 publicly traded funeral homes offering after-funeral services, estate planning, legal advice, grief counseling and now, Mr. Rogers's latest product, Tribute in a Box, specialized funeral services aimed at the baby-boomer generation. The consortium of funeral homes also offers accrued interest earned in prepaid plans. Tribute in a Box rolls out its offering at the Funeral Trade Show in Las Vegas with exceptionally low price points due to volume-based business incentives...

I throw down the paper and look at Sierra. "How is this possible? What does he do, have a chip in my brain that tracks novel business ideas? Even if he read the article on Lights

Out, he wouldn't be able to copycat me like this, and in such record time!"

Sierra shakes her head. "It's weird, Maddy. *Twilight Zone* weird."

"I have to go over there."

"I don't think that's a good idea."

But I've already begun my journey. I stomp toward the main aisle. As I turn the corner I stop in my tracks. My mouth drops open. The most extravagant exhibit on the whole floor is Tribute in a Box. Not only is there a slick life celebratory video on a giant eighty-foot HD plasma screen that bares an uncanny resemblance to my life bio video template cut-by-cut, but it seems like every concept of my business plan is on display in 3-D virtual hologram format, rotating at different points in the booth. On top of that, celebrity look-alikes for Billy Crystal, Whoopi Goldberg, Jennifer Aniston, Tom Cruise, Bob Dylan and Donald Trump wander the perimeters of the booth blurting out their trademark lines, shaking hands with all of the attendees, and promising to speak on their behalf at their time of need as long as it's arranged in advance via the Tribute in a Box Pre-need Celebrity Package.

I blink and take a step closer, only to discover none other than Jonny Bright animatedly propagating the business to a crowd of funeral-home owners.

I grab Sierra's arm. "That's…that's…that's Jonny Bright!"

Sierra shakes her head. "Holy shit. He never got back to you on your business plan. You've got one hell of a lawsuit if you ask me." I start heading toward Jonny. Sierra grabs my arm. "Don't go there, Maddy. Remember what Professor Osaka taught us. You'll just reveal weakness inside your anger. Besides, competition is good. Even your uncle Sam told you it keeps you on your toes. Remember?"

"I've got my anger under control," I mumble through tight lips. "I'm just going to do some competitive trolling, that's all. Can you please watch the booth?"

"Do I have a choice?" asks Sierra. "Maddy, if you're going to walk into the lions' den…take Uncle Sam with you." She hands me my purse.

I look awkwardly at her. "How did you know Uncle Sam was in here?"

"How long have I known you? I used to be your girl-friend, remember? It doesn't mean I stop knowing you."

I nod, pat my purse, walk right up to Jonny Bright and immediately unleash my anger. "Excuse me, but what the hell do you think you're doing?"

In the distance, Sierra shakes her head and covers her eyes.

"Maddy! Hi! Um…welcome…welcome to, uh, Tribute in a, uh, Box," Jonny stutters. He turns to the crowd. "And here's a, uh, sample video for all, uh, of you to look at." He hits Play on a DVD machine and moves to the side of the booth with me.

"Hey, you're looking really, uh, hot. So, how are you, Maddy?" he asks, nervously wiping his hands on his pants.

"How *am* I?" I ask, infuriated. "You hold on to my in-tellectual property, you don't return calls, you don't com-municate, you pull a Houdini—on everyone—and you turn up here, with *my* business plan on display, and you ask 'How am I?'"

"Look, Maddy. I think you're, uh, way, way overreacting."

"Don't you dare try to turn this around, Jonny."

He swallows hard. "Look, how do you know I'm not pro-tecting you? That Derek didn't come to me with the idea and I kept your plan away from him so there wouldn't be a conflict of interest?"

"Then why not return my calls? Why not return my business plan? What are you hiding from unless you've got something to hide?"

Jonny fidgets, nervously rubbing his hands together like he did at Morton's restaurant and like he did at the Beverly Hills Deli. And then it hits me. "You gave Derek my business plan for Artists International, didn't you." I am stunned by my realization.

Jonny squirms some more.

"You signed an NDA. I can sue you for this, Jonny."

"I never signed an NDA," he whines defensively.

I pull out my PDA to retrieve the legal docs I scanned in a long time ago.

"Really? I can prove it." I show him signed NDAs by Bobby Garelik and Victor Winston. But the third NDA is blank. Jonny never signed it. I falter.

He gloats and says, "See. I never signed an NDA."

"There are witnesses, Jonny."

"Only if you can get them to testify," he says cockily.

Before I can reply, Derek Rogers appears, immaculately dressed, and as usual, bearing an arrogant posture. "Well, look who's here. Madison Banks. I like your booth. It's got a nice quaint charm to it."

"Tell me something, Derek. Do you ever generate an original concept on your own?"

"Why should I? That's what I hire other people to do for me."

"Like Jonny?"

Jonny stands behind me, shaking his head in an attempt to signal Derek on his response. Derek remains calm and nonplussed as he replies, "Madison, you wouldn't want me to ask you to reveal your sources of inspiration, now, would you?"

"Why don't you try me?"

"Because frankly, I don't care where your inspiration

comes from. I care about results. And I have to say your Lights Out Enterprises is a nice little outfit. In fact, I'd be interested in acquiring it. What do you think, Maddy? Would a hundred thousand do it?"

"Is there anything you can do besides insult people, Derek? Or are your only abilities stealing, raping and pillaging other businesses?"

"What? My number's too low and you're hurt?" snickers Derek.

"You can't buy my business, Derek. It's an honorable business and it's not for sale to you, not for one hundred thousand or one hundred million, because no matter what, all you end up doing is leaving a black stain on whatever you touch!"

Derek laughs. "Still sore about that, eh, Maddy. Let it go. It's in the past."

"But this isn't, and neither is Artists International, which apparently became Palette Enterprises," I say, glancing between Derek and Jonny.

Derek looks at both of us and drops all of his pretenses, including his fake smile. He snaps, "This conversation is over. If you wish to reconsider my offer, Madison, you know where to reach me."

As Derek turns to address the attendees in his booth, the Donald Trump look-alike walks up to my face and blurts, "You're fired!"

I look at him, shocked and indignant, and then instinctively slap him in the face. He stands there, stunned. He looks at Jonny, who impotently shrugs.

Sierra stands at the corner of the aisle and has one eye on me and the other on the Lights Out booth. I see her gasp, "Oh, no" when my hand flies. I am marching toward the Lights Out booth, shaking, when I run right into Victor Winston.

Victor must see that I'm pale. "Madison?"

"What— I thought you had meetings in Phoenix."

"I saw the article in *FSJ* and got on the first plane here." He looks around and sees the Tribute in a Box booth with Jonny Bright standing on the stage proselytizing. In one instant he gets it. "Jonny Bright is here?"

"He never signed my NDA. Would you and Bobby Garelik testify if I sued him?"

"Maddy. Listen to me," says Victor. "Jonny Bright owes Bobby Garelik half a million dollars. It's unlikely Garelik would ever testify against Jonny if he ever wants to see his money. That would put me in a dead zone on the matter."

"Are you serious?"

Victor nods. "I would testify, but we wouldn't get any traction on it legally."

"Then what's the point of having an NDA?"

"The truth is, not much."

I shake my head and mutter, "There was a movie we watched in our Ethics class in college. It was a 1957 version of *The Brothers Karamazov*."

"Starring Yul Brenner and William Shatner," says Victor. "What about it?"

"There's a line where they talk about how business can contaminate you. That's how I feel now," I say, dropping my head.

Victor gently lifts my face up by my chin. "The point of that story, Maddy, is that anything is lawful, even crime, because everything…is not lawful."

"I really hate conundrums."

"Leave the conundrums to me and keep your vision on Lights Out. The game is far from over."

I try to pull myself together again. "Well, um, what's the next step?"

"Same as before, you just stick to the strategy. And expect there to be losing streaks in the short run. Remember, you're the one who envisioned a great opportunity. Your instincts for balancing risk against reward are spot-on. Don't forget that."

"Should we have an advisory board meeting?" I ask, trying hard to get back to business.

"Good idea. Let's set it up for next week."

Back at the Lights Out booth Sierra waits for me. "Sierra, this is Victor Winston, of Winston Capital. Victor, this is Sierra D'Asanti—she's the one…"

Victor extends a hand. "So you're the one who brilliantly puts the images together. It's a pleasure to meet you."

Sierra carefully looks him over, every inch, and then extends her hand. "It's a pleasure to meet you, too."

He looks around the booth. "You've both done a great job with this. The sculpture's likeness to your uncle Sam is remarkable." Then he sees samples of the framed leaf art. "What's this?"

"Maddy's attempt to promote homegrown art," says Sierra.

"The leaf art is my nephew's work. The poems are from his father, who doesn't know that we've matched his words to dead leaves," I explain.

"I like it," says Victor. "Have you sold any yet?"

Sierra shakes her head.

"Then I'll be the first," says Victor. And he buys two.

For the next two days, Sierra, Victor and I work the booth to make strategic alliances with funeral homes outside of Derek Rogers's domain. By the end of the trade show, we rack up partnerships with twelve independent funeral homes.

The second I return to Los Angeles, I contact everyone on the advisory board to set an urgent meeting for next week in New York, making it convenient for the three board members who live there. I offer to cover expenses to fly Richard Wright in from Michigan.

I receive e-mails from JoAnna Myman at Event Ventures and from Adam Berman at Ubiquitous Music, both saying that due to company pressures at this time they have to decline from being part of the Lights Out Enterprises advisory board. Completely baffled, I call Adam asking for an explanation.

"Derek offered me more money to be on his board, but I turned him down, Maddy. And then I realized that it's too politically risky for me to be on any board at all right now. But if you ever need me for anything at all, please don't hesitate to call. I think what you're doing is smart and courageous. I just can't personally be involved."

Then Richard Wright calls and tells me that he can't do it, either.

"Why?" I ask.

"I got bought out. My funeral home is part of a chain in a public company. It was the only way I could stay afloat. They used to let me do whatever I wanted. But they were taken over by another company. A thousand funeral homes are under new management now. And we've all been told we're not allowed on boards of any other companies."

I ask what I know I don't have to, but confirm it anyway. "What's the name of the corporation who took you over?"

"Tribute in a Box," says Richard.

Then Toby Helman calls from New York. "Maddy, you're not going to believe this, but I have to resign from your board."

"You, too? Why?"

"My boss has been asked to be on the board of directors of Derek Rogers's new venture, to do exactly what I was doing for you. He says it's a conflict of interest for me to be on your board if he's on Derek's, and told me I have to resign immediately."

"Wait a minute. You told me that your boss hated Derek Rogers for cheapening the value of the museum art with Palette Enterprises."

"Yes, he did," explains Toby. "But I did some digging, and well, opinions change when you get paid to change them."

I rub my eyes and shake my head. "Okay, thanks for letting me know, Toby."

"No problem. If I see anything funky, Maddy, I'll let you know."

I hang up and look at Uncle Sam in the Ziploc bag resting on my windowsill. "Are you hearing this? This must be the part you warned me about, Uncle Sam. Only you're not here to guide me through it. You broke your promise."

I meet with Victor at the offices of Shepherd Venture Capital. For the first time I sit in his office, which is as immaculate as he is. The entire room is sophisticated in design; there's a photo of his parents behind his desk, and another photo of Victor with a beautiful woman by his side.

I wonder if that's his girlfriend or perhaps his wife. For all I know, Victor could be the kind of guy who doesn't wear a wedding ring so as not to hamper business opportunities. I realize he knows a lot more about my personal life than I do about his. But then, I never wanted to know. I always believe it's best to keep personal and business separate, like church and state. But suddenly, I have this inexplicable desire to know who the woman in the photo might be.

Karina brings me a hot cup of black tea. I thank her and place it on the side table.

"Look, Victor, the entire advisory board has either been forced out or defected to Derek Rogers's camp. By the way, is that even legal?"

"It's sketchy. But I don't want you to worry about that. It's a ploy by Derek to psych you out. He's the kind of chronic liar who gets people to believe him even when they know he's lying."

"Should I counter? And offer the board more money to stay with Lights Out?"

"No," advises Victor. He leans closer to me. "No one gets a second chance to prove their loyalty. Once betrayed, it's forever gone. But don't dwell on that. We have other work to focus on."

"Like what?"

"Putting together an IPO."

"Now? List the company on the New York stock exchange with Derek Rogers sabotaging everything? Besides, I thought we were keeping it private for now. Didn't you tell Bobby Garelik we weren't opening it up?"

"With Derek in the picture, it's a new ball game. We need to think bigger. And I underestimated the potential here. Besides, competition is good, Maddy. It keeps you on your toes."

"Keeps you on your toes?" I repeat, remembering those were Uncle Sam's words.

"Believe it or not, it will help with an IPO," adds Victor. "I want to offer a Series B at five dollars a share. And I'd like to open it up to Garelik."

"Is that high?" I ask, trying hard to keep my eyes from shifting between Victor and the photo of him with the unknown woman.

"Not when you've been able to show revenue already."

"How many shares do you want to sell? And what will we use the money for?"

"Five million shares," Victor says confidently. "The money will go toward business development and marketing. I want you to hire full-time staff and start delegating some of your responsibilities."

"How much of the company will Garelik get? Assuming he buys the entire Series B round?"

"We'll give him fifteen percent. That gives us plenty for stock-option grants down the line. You good with all this?"

I nod.

"Okay. I want you in real offices now. There's an extra space at the end of the hall. If Bobby comes in on this I'd like to include those offices in the deal." He gets up from behind his desk. "Ready to take your baby into puberty?"

"If a Series B equals puberty, then what constitutes adulthood?"

"A successful IPO and a profitable business," answers Victor.

"And maturity?"

"A seminal exit strategy," he laughs. "Keep me posted on any hires."

He gets up from behind his desk and offers me a hug. I stare at the photo behind him, wondering but not wanting to intrude. I refrain from asking. Maybe I'm afraid to know the answer, but more importantly, why did I even care?

The UCLA cafeteria is charged with students, youthful energy and wireless laptops. I sit with Eve in a booth overlooking the campus. I've come prepared, dressed in one of my finest Eve concoctions and wearing the black ribbon, necklace version, specifically for her.

"I like your outfit," she says with a boastful smile.

"You taught me well. So how's the fashion therapy business coming along?"

"Here's my business plan. Will you be on my board of advisors?" she asks, handing me a pamphlet.

"Of course I will. I'm honored. Who's your target market?"

"Let's just say I've decided to give the MBAs here a second dimension through fashion. It's close to home, so my marketing comes down to direct word-of-mouth, as in *my* mouth."

"Well, you've got the right mouth for it." I smile as I sip a cappuccino.

"Thanks. I was hoping you would also mouth your praises as a guest speaker and lead generating client. All you have to do is come to class and sing my praises. You know, talk about how what you wore to the VC meeting landed you your capital. That should be rather easy, don't you think?"

"Confidence is something you definitely don't lack, Eve. Sure, I'd be glad to."

"Thanks," she says, and scans the crowd for some diva-dressed dudes. "See that guy over there? He's one of mine, and that girl, she's one of mine, too."

There's no question they're the best dressed in the cafeteria.

"How's Lights Out?" she asks.

"Great. I need to start hiring staff—one full-time and one part-time. Interested in the part-time?"

"You'd hire me? Really?"

"Well, only if you included designing my meeting wardrobe."

"Wow. I don't know what to say, except that I've got a full schedule. I wouldn't be able to until after spring break. But…you can hire one of my graduate makeovers for the full-time position. That would be good for my business. I'll send you only my best dressed."

"Gee…thanks, Eve."

"You're welcome. Shall we?" she asks, reaching for her Prada bag and getting up to go.

"Shall we what?" I ask, still working on my cappuccino.

"Go to my class, so you can talk to them. They're waiting."

"Now? You set this up for now and didn't tell me?"

"First of all, I knew you'd come dressed to impress me to make me feel good about my…work with you—or shall I say, on you—and second, they sprung me with today so…here we are."

"I'm not p-prepared," I stammer.

"Oh, please, like you can't improvise."

I shake my head. "Sometimes I wish Osaka never sent you."

She smiles at me. "You don't really mean that. Otherwise you'd have come in your torn Levi's. Come on, Osaka and twenty-two students are waiting."

I follow Eve, once again, wondering how that happened. We enter her classroom of first-year MBA students. Their eyes are filled with enthusiasm.

Professor Osaka immediately stops in mid-lecture and smiles. "Class, we have a very special visitor today, my former student, runner-up in the Challenge a Vision Prize, the most promising ethical entrepreneur I know, Eve Gardner's mentor and guest speaker, here to talk about Eve's new venture, let's welcome Ms. Madison Banks."

The class cheers as Professor Osaka relinquishes his lectern to Eve and me. Eve takes the microphone first like it's oxygen she swallows every second. Her entire demeanor suddenly lights up the room.

"Welcome, fellow students, to my business, FT 101, which stands for Fashion Therapy for beginners. And my first client is my mentor, Madison Banks, CEO of Lights Out Enterprises, a creative experience design firm specializing in preneed celebrations. It's imperative for Madison Banks to look good when it comes to attracting her clients….which is where my new venture, FT 101, takes the ordinary and turns it into the extraordinary. Allow me to show you some examples. Toni, hit it, please."

The lights go dim and a pull-down screen automatically drops from the ceiling. In moments, several photos appear, photos of me wet and naked behind a towel in my doorway, photos of me in mismatched outfits, and then photos of me looking smashing in my Eve-do's.

"While Madison Banks has been playing mentor to me," continues Eve on the microphone, "I have been playing fashion therapist to her. So you see, this has been an organic process. Here are some before and after shots. And here is the outfit that Madison Banks wore the day she secured her initial round of venture-capital funding for her new company called Lights Out Enterprises. A picture speaks a thousand words, but Madison is here to speak ten thousand more. Let's all welcome my amazing mentor and my successful lead generating client, Ms. Madison Banks!"

Eve joins in the round of applause and hands me the microphone.

"Hi, everyone. It's a pleasure to be here. First, I want to acknowledge Professor Osaka. He's truly the best when it comes to entrepreneurial studies. He's a master at closing deals, fair and square, even when you're not aware that you've been party to one, like me, in this mentorship program. But somehow, it always turns into a win-win for everyone, even if one party might not think so at the time. You just have to have faith." Everyone laughs. I smile at Osaka and at Eve, trying to contain my embarrassment at not being prepared, but then I realize, I am the one with the microphone now.

"So what can I say? I've been mentoring Eve, not an easy task. As you can see, she's quite strong-headed and determined to do things her way and on her terms. But that's what you want when you're looking for that perfect blend of fashion and therapy to guide you through the most delicate business opportunities. Let's face it, we live in a society that judges a cover first and so you have to make a good presentation, not just with your, uh, presentation in terms of your, uh, ideas, but the very presentation of yourself. The key is to remain authentic to yourself in the process. And that's what Eve does. She may challenge you along the way, testing your ethics when it comes to, say, wearing designer knock-offs, but isn't that what every good therapist does? So in the end, when you wear an Eve-do, you, uh, well, you're stronger for it, and you come to own it, so it's really, truly you, the best of you, and when you've got the best of you in sync with…you, you naturally win…even VC money."

As I come to the end of my improvised speech, I realize that Eve's very style of challenging and prodding, in the end, did just what I said. And my speech becomes an authentic description of her work. "So, with that said, I highly recommend Eve's FT 101 for all of you who wish to step out and represent the best of yourselves, the best of your ventures and the reclamation of angel money, VC money and customer satisfaction."

Everyone cheers. Students come up to me to talk and get my business card.

One handsome young guy gazes at me. "You are awesome, Ms. Banks, and so hot. If you ever go out with younger guys, here's my card." And he slips it to me. I blush. Eve sees and smiles.

I sit in front of my computer scrolling through resumes on Monster.com for MBA professionals seeking jobs. I am posting a description for staff hires at Lights Out when Richard Wright calls.

"I've left the business," he tells me.

"Why?" I ask. "It seems so unlike you." Hadn't he been in the funeral business his whole life? I swivel away from the computer screen.

"I don't care for the way Tribute conducts business. They want us to offer prepaid plans but with hitches. I can't do that."

"Well, what's the hitch?"

"For one thing, they neglect to mention that the interest earned goes to them, but taxes are paid for by the beneficiaries. And they won't honor state-to-state transfers unless it's one of their own funeral homes. So if someone buys a preneed plan from Tribute in Missouri and then moves to Arizona where the company doesn't own any funeral homes, that person forfeits his entire investment."

"You're kidding."

"Not even for a bad thousand-dollar joke, I'm not." There's a pause. "Since I'm the only certified mortician in town, the funeral home is now closed down."

"Will Tribute in a Box recruit someone else to take over?"

"They're so busy merging the bigger homes they acquired that they don't have time for a small-time operation like this one."

"What's the town going to do when someone dies?"

"They'll just have to call it in from Grass Lake or Ann Arbor until things turn around…if they turn around."

"What about you, Richard? What will you do?" I ask, concerned for him.

"My buddy owns the Eagle's Nest. He offered me the job of running the place while he takes off for Australia. So if you're back this way, stop in and have a beer on me. Good luck, Maddy."

"Thanks, Richard. Good luck to you, too."

I hang up. Curious about Derek's motives, I log on to his Web site to do some digging of my own. I drill down through the pages and find the small-print clause allowing Tribute in a Box a legal out on what is otherwise worded to imply full compensation if a prepaid client moves out of state. But nowhere can I find the details of their investment plan. They reserve the right to supply that information on a client basis—making their policies suspect to say the least.

I call Sierra. "I found a loophole in Derek's Web site. And we're going to use it to our advantage."

"How so?" she asks.

"By modifying our site. I want to highlight our offerings in comparison to what he neglects to reveal, that Lights Out—unlike Tribute in a Box—guarantees nothing less than one-hundred percent of consumer funds placed in interest-bearing trusts that give the client the right to a full refund of principal and interest if they cancel their pre-need pre-paid plan at any time and protects them from losses if they transfer from one funeral home to another."

"But we already offer that," says Sierra.

"I know. I want to make a bold statement and stress the comparison with Tribute. If competition is supposed to be good, then let's use it to our advantage. It's time for truth in advertising. Let's put our truth out front and center and stress that Lights Out lights up the benefits to consumers unlike Tribute in a Box, which keeps a lid on it."

"I see you've got your fire back," says Sierra. "I'm glad."

"Me, too."

"Send me the copy and I'll do it today. And, Mad, be careful whom you reveal your fire to."

"Why is that?"

"Well, what's with you and Victor?"

"Nothing," I say, surprised. "He's my VC. Should there be?"

"I thought I saw a flicker of something between you guys at the trade show. I think he's a really good guy, Maddy."

"You saw a good business relationship in play, and it will remain one. And besides, I'm playing my results, remember?"

"What about him? What's he playing?"

I'm stumped. I never thought of that. "I don't know. That's not my business. Besides, I think he's spoken for, so let's drop it."

We hang up. I set up interviews with candidates from Monster.com and one of Eve's top referrals when the Sullivan Funeral Home calls me. They're one of the funeral homes I created a strategic relationship with at the trade show. They contact me about a high-end, high-profile client. Before I know it, I'm on a plane to Little Rock, Arkansas, to put together a pre-need double header for the governor.

That evening in Little Rock, Arkansas, Governor Anderson sits in the parlor of his mansion drinking tea as I lay out the template for a pre-need plan. I'm quick to take note of all the details in the house, especially the items that point to the governor's love of motorcycles.

The governor's deaf mother, Willa Anderson, an elderly woman in her nineties, sits on a couch behind us meticulously knitting a pillow cover, chain-smoking cigarettes and drinking black coffee.

Governor Anderson shakes his head. "Understand that aside from my primary desire to represent the good people of Arkansas, my one and only other love is motorcycle ridin'."

"I see," I say, taking notes. "Then how about a hot-rod salute—a fleet of your friends and colleagues on motorcycles laying down some rubber immediately following the ceremony."

"I like that," he says, pacing the room. "Let's do more of that."

"Okay, well, tell me your favorite song you'd like to have played and if the musician's alive, we'll try to get him to sing it in person."

"In that case, I'd like to hear Neil Young sing, 'A Horse with no Name.'"

I write that down. "Tell me, Governor, do you watch movies, TV, go to clubs, play sports…?"

"I'll tell ya what I like. I like jokes. That comedy TV network keeps me sane after a long day in politics. Thing is, I can't remember jokes to save my life. So I started a little collection of jokes. See here?" He pulls an anthology of hand-written jokes out of his drawer.

"What if you could have a joke-telling festival? Who can tell the best jokes? Including some jokes about you, Governor."

"Yes! A joke-telling festival. I do believe I like that, Ms. Banks. Do you think we could get some famous comedians, too? Billy Crystal, Jerry Seinfeld, Ellen DeGeneres, Whoopi, and oh, that fellow Larry David! Maybe he could 'Curb My Funeral.'"

I chuckle. "We can certainly try," I say, but the governor can't hear me because he's laughing so hard. Finally, he sobers.

"Now what about my mother?" says the governor. "I want to prepare for her time of need, too."

"I can have a conversation with her, as well."

"No you can't," says the governor, flatly.

"How come?" I ask, and stop writing, surprised by his quick, stern reply.

"Because she'll pretend she's deaf."

I turn to look at his mother, who sits there as if she has no clue that we are talking about her.

"The truth is my mother is a first-class bitch," says the governor.

I cringe at the governor's choice of words, but I notice that Willa Anderson doesn't flinch at all. Instead, Willa takes a long drag on her cigarette and blows it in the direction of her son's face, then misses the ashtray, flicking her ashes on a white lace tablecloth. I wonder if it's on purpose.

"And proud of it," he adds.

"Oh," I say, trying to figure out how best to handle this situation.

"What do you do to honor a bitch?" asks the governor.

"Well, for starters," I say, thinking fast, "we could…pass out coffee and cigarettes and let everyone bitch…about the bitch. And we could supply knitted bitch pillows as funeral favors."

The governor points his finger at me. "I like the way you handle bitchin'!"

"Well, uh, thank you, Governor."

"You want more tea?"

I look at my untouched cup. "I'm good, thanks."

When I return to Los Angeles late in the evening, Victor insists on picking me up at the airport. I climb into his convertible as he drives me home northbound on the 405.

"How was Governor Anderson?" he asks.

"Great. He complimented me as someone who really knows how to bitch."

"Good, cuz you might want to do a lot of bitchin' right about now."

"So this is a bad-news pickup… What happened?"

"Bobby Garelik isn't investing in Lights Out Enterprises." He glances at me to see how I take it.

I pause to take a deep breath, preparing for the worst. "Why not?"

"Because he just put twenty million into Tribute in a Box."

"They gave him a deal to offset the half million Jonny owes him?" I ask, raising an eyebrow.

"Precisely," says Victor.

I let out a sigh, and then take stock. "Well, that's too bad, because it looks like Bobby Garelik just lost it all and more, then, doesn't it?"

Victor smiles at me. "That's my CEO!"

I notice Victor's eyes darken at the fire in my voice. Maybe Sierra was right. I must be careful where I toss my flames.

"I'm moving into new offices," he says. "I don't want to worry about competitive intelligence."

"You think Garelik would commit corporate espionage inside your office?"

"Garelik's okay, it's Jonny Bright I don't trust. He's got a hacker background and knows the server codes at the office. Who knows what he might have already stolen off my computer. And he may be visiting our offices more than I care to see him now. Besides, it's time I took some risks and put Winston Capital out there on my own."

"Wow, this is really big."

"Yeah, Lights Out is lighting up a new course of action for me." He turns toward me. "So how about it? Want to share office space with Winston Capital in a tiny furnished shack on Venice Beach for five hundred a month? My share is seven-fifty."

I look him over. He's serious. "Will you handle the office setup? I don't have time for that."

"Is that all?"

"Does it come with a teapot?"

"And the tea…" Victor smiles.

"Okay, deal," I say as Victor pulls up to my apartment building.

He parks the car and dangles a pair of extra keys in front of me. "The address is in your e-mail. Doors open at 6:00 a.m. tomorrow morning."

I take the keys and get out of the car. "Thanks. I'll be in at ten." I stop and turn just before he's about to take off. "How'd you know I'd go for this?"

"I'm the one with the faith, remember?"

"Right," I say, and watch Victor peel away into the night.

The next morning, I try to sleep in after my whirlwind travels but my internal clock objects. I find myself practicing reclining meditation at 6:00 a.m. as usual. I roll over, write up my action plan, then hear the *thud* against the front door. I'm quickly out of bed, hauling in my *Los Angeles Times, New York Times,* and *Financial Street Journal.* I scan all of them from the only free space in my apartment, my bed.

My cell phone rings. It's Sierra. "What's up?"

"Hector Thornton of Thornton Pharmaceuticals just cancelled the life bio video shoot."

"Why?" I ask, rising to a full sitting position.

"Are you sitting down?"

"Perched. Go ahead, spill it."

"He's opting out of the whole deal for a less expensive one with Tribute in a Box."

"He can't do that. We have a contract."

"He says he can, since he included his local funeral home in the contract. And since the local funeral home has a deal with you, he claims he can opt out."

"But we have a contract with the Baxter Funeral Home."

"Not anymore...they were just bought by Tribute."

"What!" I say, shocked, trying to assimilate this. "Okay, thanks. I've got to look into this right away. Bye." I hang up and immediately call the Baxter Funeral Home in New

Haven, Connecticut, only to discover that they have indeed been acquired by Derek Rogers's company.

"The deal was too good to pass up," explains Mr. Baxter.

"Why didn't you tell me?"

"I was going to, but they wanted everything kept secret until the papers were signed. It was conditional to the deal."

"But that's a breach of contract to Lights Out Enterprises," I explain. "Not to mention damages."

"Tribute said I had nothing to worry about. They're taking full responsibility for any legal actions you might take. I'm really sorry about this. But business is business."

"What about ethics is ethics?"

"Look, they said they would pay you for damages if you sued."

"And you believed them?" I ask, now pacing among the start-up obstacles in my apartment.

"Why shouldn't I?"

"So, basically, you think it's fair for me to have to file a lawsuit and incur legal fees over your actions?"

"Well, no," says Mr. Baxter. "I guess I didn't look at it like that. They did such a swell job selling me on this whole thing. They promised this was going to triple my business."

"How are they proposing to do that?" I ask, tripping over a ream of paper.

"Well, for starters, they're providing in-house training for nontraditional tributes in a box. The deal comes with a training video, production template, and they're even throwing in the video camera. And then there's the major discount for pre-need corporate executives…which is less than what Lights Out charges. Look, I shouldn't be telling you all this, but now I'm feeling badly for you."

"Me, too," I say, holding my tongue.

"I'm sorry," says Mr. Baxter. "I do wish you the best of luck."

I bite my lip, remembering that you never know how a ship can flip its sails, that one day I might need to do business with Mr. Baxter again. "Thanks," I mutter, and then swallow the rest of my unspoken anger.

I show up at the new offices of Lights Out Enterprises next door to Winston Capital at 8:00 a.m. sharp. Behind a glass door I can see Victor on a phone call. The furniture from his former office now looks out of place in the rustic Venice Beach digs. But there are also several new pieces of furniture, unlike any other furniture I've ever seen before— a round table with a top made of chalkboard and a center tray for multicolored chalk. It's all highly stylized, made of bright colors and strange materials. Yet it's simple and functional with clean lines. I notice a sign indicating an ocean view from the rooftop.

Victor sees me and motions for me to check out my new office across the hall, which he has taken the liberty of decorating with similar furniture. I enter, barely taking in my new surroundings. I immediately pull my wireless laptop computer out of my bag and place it on my desk, also made out of chalkboard material. What a paper saver—you can make notes and scribble ideas down on the desk as you work, I think, while searching for the nearest electrical outlet.

Victor wraps up his phone call and steps across the hall into my office. "How do you like it?"

"It's great, Victor. You and Arthur Pintock should start an office design company. Your tastes are identical. What do you have, an arsenal of high-end furniture design in storage somewhere?"

"Sort of." He points behind me to a changing-table posing as a credenza with a portable teapot and a box of black tea. "Your teapot…and tea."

I look and smile, but it doesn't last.

"What's wrong?"

"We have to talk," I say. "Thornton cancelled his deal because Derek bought out the Baxter Funeral Home and is offering pre-need deals at one-third the cost of those at Lights Out."

I quickly connect to the Internet. "Look at this." I log on to Derek Rogers's Web site and hop onto the member sub-site to show Victor the hyperlink to Tribute in a Box in-house training video and manual with sample production templates.

"Can you get in?"

"I'm trying," I say. Meanwhile, I call Toby Helman, who then quickly calls back.

"I've got the code for you," she says. "The username is Attila, and the password is The Hun, spelled out as one word."

"You're kidding, right?" I ask.

"No. The man is so full of his imperialist attitudes that I can't even comment anymore. Good luck."

"Thanks so much, Toby."

I start typing and click on the training-video link. Up streams a play-by-play version from my business plan and Web site on how to make efficacious life bio videos.

Victor squints in disgust at the screen. "It's a complete rip-off from your business plan… He's got balls."

It's the first time I've ever seen Victor show signs of irritation.

We both watch as the training video displays a large number of props to select from for use during a funeral service, and which they can supply—for a fee of course.

The props that fit onto the corner of a casket are known as "corner prop symbols," which the video shows, just as my business plan referred to them. Sample corner props include mini golf balls, guitars, horses, cars, fishing poles, chef's hat, bowling ball, soccer ball, football, baseball mitt, American Flag, rifle and ballerina shoes, to name a few.

Other kinds of prop symbols include cloth tapestries, known as "cloth props" which have the same symbols woven into the cloth. Cloth props are used to drape over a casket or around an urn, or to hang from behind the pulpit.

I recognize the suppliers listed in the selection. "I don't believe it, Victor," I say, disgustedly. "Derek's made deals with my vendors, too. But he's really pushing the props to define a life—no wonder why it's so cheap. It's so cookie-cutter and tacky the way he's doing it. Where's the tribute? Where's the personalization?"

"I certainly wouldn't want that at my funeral," comments Victor.

"Ditto."

I click on another link labeled "Interactive Funerals." I find the Tribute in a Box generalized interactive funeral maps for "types" of people, again verbatim from my business plan. But the way he's presenting it is everything I had tried to avoid for the very reason that Derek wants to achieve it: mass-marketed themed ceremonies in a box. Choices are broken down into a basic price list. There are also blatant directions to go to the Lights Out Enterprises Web site for more specific ideas and details on execution of nontraditional services that they should feel free to use and integrate into their own nontraditional community services.

"T-this is unbelievable," I stammer. "He's conducting virtual seminar trainings off of our Web site!"

Victor shakes his head. "I've never seen anything like this. He's bootlegging all your hard work."

There's another page offering lowball deals to corporate executives who sign up for pre-need packages through Trib-

ute, plus discount rates tied into their credit card mileage programs, another idea ripped straight from the pages of my
business plan.

"But he's got one huge hole in his plan," says Victor.
"There is no way he can provide quality assurance."

"Yes, but how long will it take for people to catch on? Or
who knows, Victor, maybe consumers will like this."

"Consumers, not clients. And if they do, my hunch is it
will be short-lived."

I continue through the site. "Let's check this out." I mouse
down to a list of member funeral homes. As we review it, a
new name suddenly pops up, Sullivan Funeral Home in Little Rock, Arkansas.

"Oh, great!" I toss my arms in the air. "I guess we can kiss
the governor goodbye now, too."

And right on cue, my cell phone rings. I grab it.

"I'm looking for Maddy Banks," says a young female voice.

"This is her," I answer.

"Oh, wonderful. I'm calling from Green Power. I'm Roger
Lincoln's executive assistant. Per Roger's request, I'm calling
to let you know that he won't be needing his pre-need package with you anymore and that you shouldn't worry about
flying out here for the life bio video. He's sorry if this causes
you any trouble. But he wanted to do you the courtesy of
calling before his local funeral home did. Oh, and he said that
he would be sending you a check for a thousand dollars for
your time."

I nod, trying hard to hold back the pain of defeat. "Right.
Okay. Thanks, anyway." I turn to Victor. "Roger Lincoln is
history now, too." I think about the domino effect now taking place. "Victor, at this rate, it's only a matter of time before the rest of our deals drop out, both the high-net-worth
individuals and the funeral homes."

Victor stands tall staring out the bay window, thinking.

"Is it possible to sue Derek and Jonny for plagiarizing Lights Out?" I ask.

"It will just turn into a three-year legal nightmare. The only winners in cases like these are the lawyers."

He turns to face me. "We just have to outsmart him." Victor looks at his watch. "Look, I've got an appointment with another client of mine right now. When I get back we'll brainstorm for a solution."

"Who's your client?" I ask. "If it's okay to ask?"

"Of course. They're called The Designer Tank. It's a virtual furniture design firm. We're launching the first product in two months."

"Virtual furniture?"

"Furniture designed to shape-shift for the wireless world." He motions to the furniture in the room. "As an investor, I get the old prototypes."

While Victor takes off for his meeting, I take off for the beach to think over a new plan of action. I walk along the ocean's edge, deep in my thoughts. If I want to save my current deals, I'll have to act fast or else come up with an entirely new business model.

I stop to scoop up a handful of sand. "Oh, Uncle Sam, I wish you were here. Does the battle ever end?" I let the sand sift through my fingers and keep walking.

I reach a little dive and stop for a grilled cheese sandwich and a bottle of water. I sit at an outside table watching an array of vendors share the boardwalk. They have virtual stores, I think, no walls and no leases to separate them. They just share the open space in search of a sale. I stop my thoughts from wandering any further, realizing the key word here is *share*. They *share*. That's it, I think.

I'll offer all the independent funeral-home owners a per-centage of Lights Out by presenting them with lucrative co-revenue sharing deals. If I can work out the numbers so I break even the first year in order to build market share, I bet I'll be able to do it. I pull out my PDA and imme-diately start working on the numbers, jotting notes on a napkin.

By the time Victor returns to the office, I've written up a template for the co-revenue sharing deal and am printing it out.

"Ready to take a meeting?" asks Victor.

"No need to. I figured out an open chute for us and a si-multaneous door-stopper for Derek Rogers." I hand him my paperwork. "With this plan, funeral homes won't have to sell out to Tribute and they'll still be able to increase their rev-enues. If we can delay any new hires and cut my salary in half for six months, I think it'll work."

"But if Derek's buying funeral homes at dollar-cap values what makes you think they wouldn't take the money and drop the hassle of running a business?"

"First, because most independent funeral homes are handed down from one generation to the next, so for one thing, they want to keep it in the family. Second, the younger generations taking over want to work for themselves. This is a way for them to do it. And third, there's a lot of pride that comes with owning your own business. Look at you."

Victor nods, and then takes a seat in the compressed card-board chair shaped like a Z with removable parts for one's cell phone, PDA, water bottle and a hook for a purse or back-pack. He carefully reads my documents and then goes into that frozen-thinking-stare phase.

I patiently watch him, but then I break his reverie. "Excuse me. Hello. Can you tell me which button do I push to put the lights back on?"

He comes to, looking straight at me. "Sorry. I was thinking."

"Yes, I see. I'm beginning to recognize what thought in its intangible form looks like. So, what do you...think?"

"This is a great solution," he says, pacing the room now. "It needs to be implemented immediately. And if it goes according to your projected schedule we can open a Series B round again in three to four months to pump up the cash flow and hire support staff."

I am relieved. "Thanks. It will be on our Web site and go out to all the national funeral homes by tomorrow... Derek Rogers would sooner do a life bio video with me, than opt for revenue sharing."

"In the meantime, you really do need to get someone to help you. Is there a college intern you can bring on board part-time?"

"Yes, I believe there is."

For the next four weeks, I see resurgence in Lights Out Enterprises. The word spreads about the new plan via the Lights Out Web site, phone calls, e-mails and viral marketing. Tons of independent funeral homes across the country contact me to sign up for the co-revenue sharing deal bringing with them a multitude of clients.

Not only does my plan bring in the strategic partners and client base I need to stay afloat, but it hampers Tribute's expansion plans, which I find out from Toby Helman, who is only too happy to share anything that rocks Derek Rogers's boat. Apparently, according to Toby who gets it from her boss, Derek Rogers is infuriated to be trumped by Madison Banks.

I move my home-office into the office-office. I place my green bowling pin bank on my desk and proudly pin the Lights Out pajama top on the wall.

I fly in and out of town to meet with clients for pre-need setups and with Victor's help begin interviewing for full-time staff.

Victor and I pass by each other in our office. He continues to advise me, as well as to oversee his other ventures in development.

I still wonder about the photo of him and the mysterious woman that sits on his desk, but I'm not sure what answer I would get, so I curb my curiosity. I've never seen the woman at the office or heard Victor mention anything at all about a girlfriend, a wife, or a boyfriend for that matter. These thoughts quickly fade away as I deal with more pressing matters. Happily everything seems to be falling into place. I even find myself gently fondling the black ribbon I still wear on my shirt and whistling "Fishing Free" at odd times of the day.

Eve joins Lights Out three mornings a week to help with organization, phones and presentations, including my wardrobe. She's been there three weeks before meeting Victor, who's constantly in and out of town.

Eve is making herself a cup of coffee when she turns to me. "I'm beginning to think this VC of yours doesn't really exist."

I keep writing at my desk. "Eve, he's busy. He travels. You see his office, don't you?"

"Could be a set design. You know, a whole made-up pretense to help you get business. If people think you have a VC they'll take you more seriously."

"You watch too many movies. Did you get the preliminary worksheets on Pullman and Brandeiss?"

"On your desk. But don't you think you should include what it is people want to wear in their life bio videos? After all, it does reflect on who they are…or were. Oh, while you're at it, why not have them plan what they want to wear when they split from earth? I mean, what if they think they're going to a party in heaven or if they want something more warrior-like, in case they think they need to battle ghosts or devils…or maybe they want wings. Wow, that's it, a line of clothing with wings. What do you think?"

I stop writing. "I never thought of that, but you're right, let's add that to the worksheets."

The door opens and Victor enters fresh from London. "Hey, Madison, how are you? I got back a day early." He sees Eve. "And you must be Eve Gardner. Pleasure to finally meet you." He extends his hand.

Eve stares up at him, and for the first time, I see she's speechless. She barely manages to smile back.

"I told you he's no ghost, Eve, so you can stop acting like you just saw one."

"Um, hi" is all she can say.

"Well, I'll let you guys get back to work." Victor leaves and walks over to his office.

Eve finds her tongue again and bursts out, "He's so hot! Talk about a poster-MBA dude! Never mind the Abercrombie & Fitch khakis, sage-green cotton T and Kenneth Cole black loafers."

I am just a little irked by how taken she is with Victor, and wonder, am I missing something here?

"How goes it?" Victor asks, standing in the doorway.

I smile and lift up *Live Wire Funeral Director Magazine* subtitled "The Funeral Planner" with a photo of me sitting on a casket holding a martini glass and a planner.

"Thanks to this business is good."

"Does this mean you're ready to implement phase two? Personal life missions?"

"Yes, I guess I, um, can actually start, uh, looking into that."

Victor makes himself at home and sits down.

"So tell me, what would your mission statement for meeting the right partner look like? I assume you would have a mission statement, a rollout strategy and a risk and mitigation action plan, no?"

"Yes, of course, I would. I mean, what if he became a drug addict or a hardened criminal?"

"Yes, you wouldn't want to get off course now would you? What exactly would your strategy be— Will you do Internet dating or leave it to chance encounters?"

"First, I have to identify the critical success factors—what needs to be in place to be successful."

"What would those be?"

"I haven't, uh, thought that through yet. I'm still wrapping up this life celebration of—"

"Well, have you considered your exit strategy? Will it be until death do you part? Or will you be going for a divorce settlement?"

"If I'd wanted marriage money I could have had that by now. I'm holding out for true love."

"I see. Good to know. Have you actually identified what true love looks like?"

"It's a work in progress. And in any case it's a feeling, not a visual."

A car honks outside. Victor looks. A cab is parked curbside.

"That's my ride. If you need an adviser for phase two, let me know. I'd be glad to be of service." He adds a wink as he heads out.

As Norm Pearl's wedding date nears, I realize it's a perfect trip to New York where I can attend the wedding, meet with clients and generate new business.

I stare at the invitation. It does say I can invite a guest. But I've been too busy to even think about it. Yet, in this moment, that feeling of isolation comes over me again. I'm tired of doing everything alone, going everywhere alone. True, I can get a lot more done on my own because I've never met anyone who can keep up with me, at least in business, though I have to admit that Victor Winston's accomplishments compared to his methodical slow pace are quite impressive. I scan the phonebook on my PDA and find the phone number for the sculptor Davide. What the hell, I think, it's worth a shot.

The wedding takes place at the top of Rockefeller Center and is about as extravagant an affair as his death dress rehearsal. The wedding ceremony is presided over by a female interfaith minister. She eloquently begins, "Welcome to the wedding of Norm Pearl and Elizabeth Thyme. This ceremony represents the power of love for one and for all…"

I sit alone in the pseudo-pews of the banquet hall watching both Norm and Elizabeth beam with pride and joy. I dab my eyes with a tissue as bride and groom place rings upon each other's fingers and together break the ritual glassware.

It is an elegant reception with tall exotic flowers and colorful bougainvillea decorating the walls. The band breaks out with renditions of old seventies disco and R&B. They start out with an upbeat song by the Spinners.

I stand by the bar where apple martinis are served with straws inside giant golf ball-shape glasses that say "Norm & Elizabeth" on them.

The bartender asks, "Would you like one?"

"Oh, no, thanks. That would put me on the floor."

"The floor could be a lot of fun," he teases.

"You look smashing," says a voice laced with a romantic French accent.

I turn around to see Davide standing next to me. I smile

nervously. "Thanks for coming. I'm so glad you could make it. I know it was last minute and all." I look him over in his debonair black suit. "You look…great."

"Thank you. How do the sculpture in de cemetery business do?"

"Great," I say. "It's finally picking up. And your gravestone sculpture of my uncle had a powerful effect at the funeral trade show." I realize I've forgotten how to date and small talk makes me more nervous. So I do what is naturally most comfortable for me, talk business. "So…I was thinking maybe we could start a whole line of themed gravestone sculptures…and…"

Davide glances at the band, which begins to play a slow song, then at me. "May I have this dance?"

"Okay, um, sure. If I can remember how to," I mumble.

Out on the dance floor, everything Sierra taught me in Vegas is a distant memory. I repeatedly stumble over Davide's feet as I try to let him lead.

He stops and offers a shallow grin. "I think I am thirsty. Do you wish a drink from the bar?"

"Sure. Uh, I'll have one of those apple martinis." At this point, I'm convinced on the floor would be more fun than trying to dance with a Frenchman.

Davide leaves and I stand there watching the celebrants.

Norm Pearl comes up from behind to give me a big hug. "Hey, you! You look awesome! How's your golf game?" he chides.

"Neglected." I smile. "Poorly neglected."

"We'll have to change that. Meanwhile, I am so glad you made it! You realize that without you, I wouldn't be here, either?"

"I wouldn't necessarily—"

"Come on, I'm taking you out on the dance floor," says Norm, cutting me off.

I try to resist, but Norm guides me to the floor, where he doesn't really dance, he just moves around in circles talking. "You're the one who came up with the Golf Camp Academy idea. Without that I never would have met Elizabeth. Did I tell you we're adopting a baby from China? I owe you big-time!"

I keep an eye out for Davide. "That's great, Norm. But um, actually, you owe me the answer to our unanswered question."

"I didn't forget. How do you find the balance between the work button that never goes off and the family love button that never seems to turn on? I'm going to tell you." He pauses. "It's sort of like golf. You get into your groove, then you let go and open up your best shot. You just keep driving and you just keep putting along and…"

"That is hardly an answer, Norm. How do you let go and open up?"

"Aha!" says Norm. "You're a wise woman, taking me all the way to the eighteenth hole on this one. The secret to that is that…there is no secret." He pumps his head up and down. "Huh? How's that?"

"I really hate conundrums," I say, standing still on the dance floor.

"Okay, okay. Look, here's the deal. It's a timing game and it's completely out of your control. It's like the buttons have their own internal timer. And there's nothing, I mean absolutely nothing you can do about it except live your life until they go off—so they can go on in a different kind of way."

As Norm finishes, I see Victor Winston enter the room with an exquisite woman by his side. I gasp, because for one thing, it's totally out of context.

"I know, I know," says Norm, misinterpreting my gasp. "It sounds dramatic, but the point is, it's really incredibly simple."

I immediately start moving to keep our circle dance in motion, swiveling behind Norm to get my bearings on Victor. I wonder what he's doing here and who the striking woman is who's with him.

The woman sees Norm and approaches with Victor proudly on her arm. Norm stops the circle walk with me and excitedly shouts in my ear, "Alyssa Ryan is here! Come on, Maddy, you have to meet this woman. She's absolutely remarkable. A lot like you!"

Before I can respond, Norm is pulling me off the dance floor.

As the two groups near, Victor recognizes me and cordially nods, as if this kind of chance meeting were an everyday occurrence. He may not be used to seeing me dressed up, let alone in glamorous attire and makeup, but from his calm, collected response, one would never know.

"Alyssa, you made it!" shouts Norm. He gives her a bear hug.

"Come on, Norm. I wouldn't miss my favorite client's wedding for the world," says the meticulously coiffed Alyssa, careful not to mess up her perfectly applied lipstick by avoiding his cheek altogether.

"Maddy. You look wonderful," says Victor. "What are you doing here?"

"What are *you* doing here?"

"Alyssa is my client."

"Norm is my client. Remember the golf game-death dress rehearsal?"

Victor puts it together now as Norm returns from his hug with Alyssa.

Norm jovially addresses our small crowd. "Alyssa, this is Maddy—Maddy, Alyssa. Two remarkable women! Alyssa is in charge of all the interior designs for me on my conversions of sixties office towers into apartment-lofts in Manhattan. And Maddy runs an outrageous business on customized pre-need funeral services."

"That sounds incredibly morbid," comments Alyssa, turning her nose up at me.

"Not the way Maddy does it. It's kick-ass. Not kickbucket!" laughs Norm.

I maintain my composure and extend a hand for a shake. "Nice to meet you."

Alyssa offers a limp handshake back, careful not to put any strength behind it, as if she were conserving her energy for more important people or perhaps reluctant to touch the hand of someone so close to a business predicated on death.

"And who's this handsome dude?" asks Norm.

"This is Victor Winston," says Alyssa. "One remarkable man." I pick up on Alyssa's subtext of *my* remarkable man. "He's the investor behind the Designer Tank."

"Terrific," says Norm. "You play golf, Victor?"

"I was on Yale University's golf team," replies Victor.

Norm pats Victor on the back. "Fantastic. We should definitely talk things over on the course sometime." He looks from Maddy to Victor. "So how do you two know each other?"

We answer simultaneously, crisscrossing over each other, "He's my venture capitalist." "She's my investment client."

"Speaking of which," adds Victor, "how did the meetings go today?"

"Great," I say, comfortable again in the saddle of business talk. "I lined up two more clients and—"

Alyssa turns to Victor and cuts me off. "Excuse me. But you invested in…death?"

"That's right," says Victor with humble pride. "I did. I believe it's going to be my best investment yet."

I grin as Alyssa raises her brows in mock disgust.

Norm punches Alyssa in the arm. "What's the matter, Alyssa? You can't mock death. You gotta make it your friend, like I did, then you get a whole other life to live. Speaking of which, I need to find my wife, compliments of Madison Banks."

Norm leaves as Davide shows up with two apple martinis in golf-ball glassware and hands one to me, catching me off guard. "Oh, Davide, um, thanks for the drink. This is, uh, Victor Winston, my venture capitalist in Lights Out Enterprises. And this is Alyssa Ryan, an interior designer. Everyone, this is Davide."

Alyssa seems to back off on her possessive-Victor energy upon Davide's arrival at my side. Victor, as usual, maintains his poker face.

"And Davide is…?" asks Victor.

"Oh, um, Davide is an extraordinary sculptor," I say, taking a big sip from my drink.

"Yes, and now I am also a gravestone sculptor," says Davide.

"Yes, of course," says Victor. "The piece you did on her uncle Sam was outstanding."

"Thank you," replies Davide.

"Wait a minute," says Alyssa, connecting some dots in her brain. "Are you Davide Davide? Famous Parisian sculptor?"

"I hope so," says Davide.

"Here's my card," she says, handing him one conveniently ready to be plucked from her purse. "I would love to talk to you in the next few days. Not now, obviously, as this is a social gathering."

"I don't mind if you want to talk business," offers Victor.

"Oh, but I do," she replies. "Come. Let's all dance."

I'm impressed. At least Alyssa knows how to turn her on button off. On the dance floor, I watch Alyssa let Victor lead.

They dance in elegant fashion together, while once again, I fail to let Davide guide me. It's simply out of my realm.

Davide shakes his head. "You do not know how to let a man guide you, no?"

"I'm trying," I say as I trip over him. Victor catches my fall.

Victor looks at Davide. "Do you mind? I need to talk to my business partner."

"Not at all," replies Davide, and we switch dancing partners.

Victor immediately shifts his energy, allowing me to take the lead, as if he's known all along how to dance with my kind. As long as techno stays out of the picture, I figure I'm fine, and suddenly I'm dancing in sync, as elegantly as Alyssa was with him. Davide happily leads Alyssa, yet I can see that he's quite surprised to see me working wonders on the dance floor with Victor.

Victor pulls me closer to him. "So, you were saying about those two clients…"

I smile with excitement as the old eighties tune "Eternal Flame" by the Bangles starts to play.

"I landed a professor of literature at NYU who wants to send e-mails after her death that reveal all the millions of secrets she's had to keep private for so long."

"I can see privacy issues are going to become a dead issue."

"Oh, Victor."

He smiles. "Sorry, that one just slipped out. Anything else?"

"I also landed a brand manager of Branded Entertainment. The brand manager offered to help brand Lights Out for a discount on her pre-need arrangements. What do you think?"

"Great idea, I'm all for barters, but both of you should give each other a list—"

"Of deliverables," I say, cutting him off. "We already did."

"Excellent," says Victor. "Does she know what she wants?"

"Yes, when she's not branding, she's a vocational actress, and for her life bio video…" Victor and I twirl around, then continue. "She wants to do a scene from *Heaven Can Wait* with any famous actor we can line up. Do you think that's possible?"

"If you're engineering it, I'd say it's a done deal." And he twirls me around again effortlessly.

Davide and Alyssa cut in, ready to switch partners again. Davide looks at Victor. "How did you do that?"

"Sometimes letting someone else lead is just another form of leading," says Victor with a sly grin.

Davide nods in acknowledgment.

I stare at Victor. "Oh, really?"

He grins at me. "It's just a conundrum, Maddy."

"Great," I say.

Alyssa pulls Victor away. "Come. It's time to meet the bride."

I watch Victor disappear in the throng. "Um, you know what?" I say to Davide. "I am exhausted from jet lag and I have all this work to do. So, um, why don't you stay and enjoy yourself. I'm going to catch a taxi back to my hotel."

"Are you sure?"

I nod. "Hmm. Yeah, I'll just, uh, you know, see you later."

I return to the Venice office, where Eve helps keep everything organized.

"How'd the outfit do?" she asks.

"I'd have to say it played a major part, Eve. Nice going. Another win-win deal negotiated. I want you to follow up for me, oh, and by the way, FT 101 will be handling any future costume design when needed for the bios."

Eve grins. "You rock, Madison!"

"Thanks, but it's a team effort. Anything I need to know?"

"Mrs. Nuzzo is expecting you at her home in Scottsdale.

Here's your itinerary and your mail. Your plane's on time and your cab will be here in ten minutes. I have to get to class now."

"Thanks, Eve."

She leaves as the mailman enters with a stack of envelopes. "This one needs to be signed for," he says.

"Thanks," I say, and quickly sign the certified registered mail slip. The mailman leaves and I open the certified letter. As I read, I slump into the prototype chair, unable to move. Devastated. The office phone rings. Then my cell phone rings. Still, I cannot move. I sit there for some time. Still. Very still. All energy stopped. I finally flip open my cell phone and dial a number to leave the following message. "This is Madison Banks calling. Please tell Mrs. Nuzzo that I'm sorry, but I…I have to cancel our meeting. And I won't be rescheduling."

I shuffle out of the office, passing the cab now parked at the curb, and get in my car. I somehow manage to drive home. I turn off my cell phone and shut down my computer. I look at the Ziploc bag with Uncle Sam inside. "I'm sorry, Uncle Sam. I'm so sorry." I close all the shades. I unplug the phones. I climb into bed with the clothes on my back and I cry myself to sleep.

An incessant knocking occurs on my door. I burrow my head under the covers but the knocking turns into a pounding. I reach for some earplugs.

"Maddy? Are you in there? Open up! It's Victor. I'm not leaving until you open up!" More pounding.

I shake my head and climb out of bed in my wrinkled work clothes and slowly drag myself to the door. I open it up, shielding my eyes from the fluorescent hallway lights. Victor looks me over, then picks up the two-foot-high pile of newspapers at the door and walks in.

"What's going on?" he demands, pacing the room, dropping the newspapers in a corner. "I've been trying to reach you for three days. No one's heard from you and you don't let anyone know where you are. Are you sick?"

I shake my head no.

"Did someone die?"

I think this one over for a moment. "Sort of," I say, mumbling under my breath.

"Who?" he asks, concerned.

"More like what," I say, shuffling back into my bedroom.

"What?" he asks, following me. I never knew how relentless Victor could be until now, but I'm beginning to get an inkling of his persuasive powers.

I hang my head and slowly utter, "They turned the Lights Out."

"What are you talking about?"

"The FTC and the Senate Special Committee on Aging—they revised the new Funeral Rule," I say, climbing under the covers again.

"We knew a revision was in the works. What is it?"

I pause, holding back the tears. "Under the new rule, Lights Out falls under the definition of 'Professional Civil Celebrant.'"

"I'm listening," says Victor, now sitting on the edge of my bed, clearly weighing the details of my body language against the words that tumble out of me.

"The difference between a professional civil celebrant and a nonprofessional one is that the professional has partnership agreements with funeral homes."

"Tell me more."

"To comply, professional civil celebrants have to go through a government-approved accreditation program…which requires one year of study…with tests that must be passed. And the head of this new accreditation task force is Derek Rogers. Effective immediately. Operating without accreditation results in closure of business, plus fines exceeding a quarter of a million dollars."

"This sounds a bit far-fetched, no?"

"Not to mention a conflict of interest."

"How can they pass a bill like this...and have Derek Rogers in charge?"

"The same way they can have a judge judge the friend he goes hunting with."

"What about any funeral organizations?"

"Well, if they tried to fight it, they failed. Or else they're part of it. Who knows? Derek must have been working on this for months. He probably slipped it in under some other legislation. Even if we follow this new law, we can't afford to lose a year without operating. We'll lose all market share, and by that time Derek's empire will have grown and the event industry will infiltrate and dilute whatever business opportunities remain. And besides all that, Derek Rogers will make it impossible for us to get accredited."

"We can fight this. It's a clear case of antitrust. We'll go to D.C. and meet with the FTC and the Senate Special Committee on Aging and tell them he can't build a monopoly."

"Oh, Victor. How do you know they're not all investing in Tribute? I'm sure Derek set it up that way to protect his interests."

"It would be a scandal to uncover."

"At what cost?" I whisper. "At what cost?"

"We can create another accreditation program. Why should there be only one?"

"Then what are we doing? Wagging the dog? Building

one business after another to chase Derek instead of sticking to the original game plan? I can't keep playing one-upmanship with him. That's not the business I want to be in."

Victor stands up, opens the shades and stares out the window. He knows I'm right. He turns around. I realize he's staring at my work clothes and the wrinkled black ribbon still pinned on my shirt. "Why don't you put on some pajamas and I'll make you some tea."

"Okay," I say.

By the time Victor returns from the kitchen, I'm in flannel pajamas, and propped against some pillows. He brings me a cup of hot tea and sits down next to me. "Thanks." I swallow hard and look straight at him. "I'm sorry, Victor. I've lost your investment. I failed. Lights Out is…dead."

"Look, Maddy. If you think you failed, it's crucial to understand why."

"Why? Derek Rogers is a better salesperson than me. He can sell someone their own car, for Pete's sake. He gets people to believe him even when they know he's lying. And he used those skills to plagiarize my business plan, obtain unlimited capital, destroy my board, acquire my clients and form an impenetrable lobby to create a monopoly. What's to analyze? I think it's pretty clear, don't you?"

"There's more to it than that. You're honest and he isn't. You've got morals and he doesn't."

I throw my arms in the air. "And where does that get us?"

"Look, Maddy…you have a critical mass of expertise in the funeral industry that Derek doesn't have. He may be efficient but you're effective. You want to know why Lights Out is in remission? Because you never applied your true strengths to the business."

"What does that mean?"

"It means you need to deal with your grief."

"My grief?" I ask, surprised and baffled.

"You never accepted the death of Uncle Sam...or your friend Tara...or your cousin Smitty...or Mr. Haggerty for that matter."

My eyes well up with tears. I know he's hit a raw nerve of truth. "What makes you an expert on grief?"

"I've had my share of it," he says. I want to know what lies beneath those words, but he swiftly moves the conversation back to me. "Look, Maddy. You need to go away, get out of town, go into the woods somewhere where there are no computers, no phones, no *Financial Street Journal,* no newspapers at all."

"What if there's a terrorist attack?"

"I'll call you.... But you need to find yourself again. You need to unclog your heart."

"But I need to work," I protest.

"You're not meant to work. You're meant to listen."

His words strike me because the tone in his voice suddenly shifts, as if it is someone else's voice, not his. His words seem a message channeled through him to me from some other entity, perhaps God, or Uncle Sam.

"Okay. I'll go," I say. "But what will I do with myself?"

"Just be," he says gently.

"What happens when I'm done *being?*"

"We'll find out when you get there. I'm the keeper of the faith, remember?"

"Faith? How am I supposed to trust that? And what is it anyway?"

"That's not a question to ask. 'Faith requires no proof.'"

"Did you trademark that line?"

"Dostoyevsky did...and faith, by the way, is believing without questioning."

"Believing in what?"

"That's for you to figure out. No one said it wasn't demanding." He smiles and looks at my untouched tea. "I'm beginning to think you don't really like tea."

"Yeah, you know, it's never really been my…cup of tea. But the idea of it is soothing. Sorry. So, um, what about the business?"

"Well, as one of your remaining advisory board members, I advise you to drop me a line and let me know how you're doing."

"What about Eve?"

"I'll handle that. I'll make sure she gets her credit and I'll see if she wants to stay on board one day a week to wrap things up. There's nothing for you to worry about."

"Okay," I say, nodding. "Then I guess I'll see you when I see you."

"Yes," says Victor.

And before he walks out the door, he adds, "See ya later, Maddy."

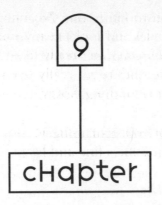

9

cHapter

Critical Success Factors: Diving into Grief

As dawn arrives, so, too, does my internal alarm clock. I practice my reclining meditation, and then by rote, reach for my daily action-plan page. But this time, I think twice, rip it up and get out of bed.

I address Uncle Sam in the Ziploc bag. "What would you do?" I wait a minute, and then nod. "Got it, thanks," I say.

Two hours later, I'm standing at the bottom of Mount Wilson in the San Gabriel Mountains near Pasadena in hiking attire. I stare up at the Observatory Tower, 6,171 feet above me, and announce, "Well, as Uncle Sam would say, 'Nothing like a good ascent to clear the cobwebs of the heart and mind.'" I take a deep breath and start climbing, focusing on one step at a time, forcing myself to hike at a slow pace so I can take in the scenery and foliage. That attempt soon fails as I find myself mumbling out loud and quickening my pace. "Go into the woods, he says. Go cold turkey on the *FSJ,* he says. Find yourself, he says. How do you find yourself? After all, I am where I'm at. Right? And how do you deal with grief? Just go be, he says. Doesn't being still require doing? After all, *to be* is a verb that means some sort of action is taking place…."

When I finally look up I realize I'm more than halfway up the mountain.

"Okay, take this in, Maddy," I tell myself. I scan the beautiful horizon and suck in the fresh mountain air. I'm about to continue when I hear a soft whimpering noise. I look around and under a cavelike rock formation is a skinny, mangy black puppy. The crying puppy awkwardly hops out from under the rock toward me.

"Oh my goodness," I exclaim. "Are you all right, little one?"

The puppy leaps into my arms. Its paw is injured and bleeding. I wash the blood off with water and tie my bandana around the paw to protect it. I look at the puppy's face.

"You are adorable. What am I going to do with you?" The puppy licks my face and a bond is sealed, forever, whether I want it to be or not. I look at the peak of the mountain approximately two thousand feet away and then at the puppy. "Well, this is a first. I've never abandoned a climb, but I'm certainly not going to abandon you, now, am I."

And with that, I turn around with the injured puppy in my arms and begin my descent. What I am about to discover is something not even the best business plan in the world could have predicted.

For the next five days, my sole focus is the puppy. I scour the newspapers' Lost and Found sections and place an ad in a dozen newspapers and on several Internet sites. I check with multiple dog pounds but there seems to be no owner in sight. I take the puppy to the vet and have her dewormed and defleaed.

The vet says, "She's a healthy puppy, mostly Border collie with some Lab. She was smart to find you."

I gladly pay for all the necessary shots and licenses and nurse the puppy back to health with the best puppy food my credit card can buy. I buy *Puppies for Dummies* and house-train her in one hour. She promptly pees on tabloid journals on my outside patio. Having her pee on the *FSJ* would be sacrilegious for me and is therefore simply not an option. I am impressed by her quick-study. I buy her toys and play with her while trying to think of a name, even if it's temporary. And yet, I realize I'm falling in love and that this puppy isn't going anywhere. At least that's what I think until my landlord tells me no pets are allowed in the building.

I fill Sierra in on all the details of the past week, including the puppy. "The puppy sounds adorable," says Sierra. "But do you want to give her away?"

I look at the black puppy rolling on her back with her head upside down, paws in the air, whimpering ever so slightly and staring at me.

"I can't. She's too cute. I'm puppy-whipped. You should see her right now, on her back with her paws in the air, pulling a Lassie and…"

"Is that all it takes to turn you into mush?" chuckles Sierra. "Look, there's a real easy solution here. Give up the apartment and move into Uncle Sam's cottage for a while, until you find yourself. If you get lost, call me. I'll come over and tell you where you are."

I can just see Sierra smiling on the other end of the line.

Once I make the decision, everything becomes quite easy. I give notice on my apartment lease. Eve helps me sell all of my possessions except for one duffel bag of clothes and one duffel bag of important paperwork. Then I take the puppy with me on my friend the red-eye to Michigan.

My father picks us up at the airport. Charlie gives me a big hug. "Welcome home, honey." He quickly loads my two duffel bags inside the car, then stands back and gives us the once-over. "You look good. Lighter, Maddy. And that puppy's a cutie-pie. What's her name?"

"I finally came up with the name on the plane," I say. "At first, I was going to call her Hepburn because inside the house she's like Audrey and outside she's like Katharine. But I finally settled on Siddhartha—Sid for short."

Charlie smiles. "Is that because you two are on a journey to find Buddha together?"

"I don't know about finding Buddha, Dad, but we're definitely on a journey together. What we'll find, I have no idea."

"Oh, almost forgot," he says. He reaches inside the car and pulls out a *Financial Street Journal.* "I brought you the paper."

As he starts to hand it over to me, I leap backward, waving my hands in the air, and immediately shut my eyes, as if the paper has cooties. "Ohmigod! Please keep that away from me. In fact, throw it away. Please! I'm trying to kick the habit."

Charlie cocks his head and then tosses the paper in a garbage can. "Okay," he says. "This is a first. Shall we go?"

We pile into the car and leave the airport.

I calm down as Siddhartha squirms a little in my lap. "So, how is everyone?"

"Everyone's fine. Your mother is telling stories at all the local schools and libraries now. Daniel still lives with us. He and Rebecca are still in limbo. Andy seems to be okay. Keating is getting bigger and bigger, and I convinced Daniel to get a teaching degree."

"Is he doing it?"

"Reluctantly. Oh, before I forget, I turned the electricity and water back on at Uncle Sam's cottage and had his car tuned up, so you'll have your own transportation."

"Thanks, Dad," I say as Siddhartha settles calmly into my lap now.

"I haven't cleaned out his place completely. I gave his clothes to Goodwill. That's all I've managed to do for now."

When we reach Jackson, Charlie helps me get settled into Uncle Sam's cottage on Clark Lake. We watch as Siddhartha frolics in the water. She runs endlessly back and forth between the water's edge and me, goading me into a game of tag.

"This is another first, someone with more energy than you," says Charlie. "When you get your bearings, let me know and Mom and I will drive out here and take you to dinner, okay, hon?"

"Thanks again, Dad. I really appreciate it. But Sid and I are going to hole up for a while, so don't expect to hear from me right away. Okay?"

"Take all the time you need." He gives me a hug, gets in the car and drives away.

While Siddhartha cocks her head and lifts her ears to contemplate the difference between butterflies and ladybugs, I wander around Uncle Sam's cottage, lightly touching the artifacts in the house and studying the books that line every wall. A faded red hardcover catches my eye. I pull it down off the shelf. It's a book on rituals published in 1932. I take the book with me to the outside deck and plop into a chaise longue. Under a warm sun, I leaf through the book's pages while keeping an eye on Sid.

The book identifies all kinds of rituals from the ordinary to the extraordinary, citing examples as involuntary as breathing or experiencing nature, to the more voluntary kind like creating a sacred space or private garden, making tea and conversation, to bathing, walking, writing, cooking, doing a chore, giving a gift and even making love. The book also lists the act of storytelling and honoring the past as rituals. There is a separate chapter on rituals as rites of passage that include religious confirmations such as bar mitzvahs, and the staples of birth, graduation, marriage, anniversaries and death.

The author points out a crucial common theme among all cultures—*"the need to create tradition and practice it over and over again…so that ritual is a reinforcement of memory, the memory of knowing who you are."*

I close the book. "Okay, so if I repeat a custom, I'll know who I am. But what is the definition of *custom?*" I look up. Siddhartha is gone. I leap up and wander the property calling out her name. I pass a faded white sailboat lying between the shed and the dock. Siddhartha's black head pops up from inside the boat. Curiosity and mischief shine in her eyes. I smile, relieved. The boat elicits a flash from my past. I lick a finger and hold it in the air, testing the wind like I did as a kid. I nod to myself, and then clap my hands. "Come on, Siddhartha! We're going sailing!"

Siddhartha practices walking the length of the boat while I clean it out, checking to make sure the mainsail and the rudder still work and that there is no damage to the hull. I change into my one-piece swimmer's suit, pack a lunch for Sid and me, include an emergency kit, life preserver, tackle box and fishing rod, and set sail. Siddhartha stands perched at the helm excitedly taking in the experience for the first time, while I take in the process of renewal.

The little Sunfish does well as we explore Clark Lake. I teach Siddhartha how to sail, explaining my actions and stressing the importance of safety. She stares at me and wags her tail. *What a good listener,* I think.

"Did you know that the Sunfish boat is the most widely sold sailboat in America?" I ask rhetorically. Siddhartha suddenly turns around, giving me her rear view while propping her front paws on the bow. "Sid, are you listening? This is important information," I say. Siddhartha growls. I spot the log in front of us and steer the boat in the opposite direction. "Good going, Sid. You're right. That was more important than knowing the market value of a Sunfish."

We sail back to shore and I tie the boat up to the dock. Siddhartha leaps to solid ground. I pluck a daisy and place it on the bow of the boat, repeating the tradition from childhood. Placing my hands together in prayer, I say out loud, "Thank you, Sunfish, for showing us an afternoon filled with nature and for bringing us home safely."

That evening, I make a fire in the living room's stone fireplace. Siddhartha sleeps on the floor near my feet. I lounge on big floor cushions staring at the fire, thinking about the demise of Uncle Sam, Tara, Smitty, Mr. Haggerty, and even Lights Out. I start journaling the thoughts that roll through my head, writing down my memories of each one of them. I write for hours and hours until the fire burns out and I crash on the cushion with Siddhartha at my side.

The next day, I head to the local market to stock up on groceries and canned foods. I return to the cottage and fill up all the cabinets. I take the overflow of canned goods into the basement where Uncle Sam kept a storage bin of food and batteries in case of a tornado. I'm loading the bin when there's a sudden loud commotion followed by Siddhartha's whimpering. I drop the canned soup in my hand and run to the other side of the basement. I find Sid awkwardly trying to pull herself out from among piles of fallen debris from an old, unstable cabinet that she had obviously tampered with.

I take her in my arms to make sure she's okay. She licks my face to say thanks. "What are you attempting to excavate, huh? Silly thing, you."

I let her go. She scrambles away, continuing her archaeological rounds. I stand to dust myself off when Siddhartha prances back into view proudly carrying a tall, felt top hat in her mouth with the name *Stansbury* sewed on it. My mouth drops. "You found my hats!"

In silhouette against a setting sun, Siddhartha and I walk along the water's edge. I wear the felt top hat and perform an odd combination of skips and hops for Siddhartha, who watches, bemused.

I match disjointed dancing with equally disjointed lyrics I created twenty-five years ago: *"Oh, Stansbury! I'm struttin' down the street! Feeling you with my feet! Oh, Stansbury, you got the beat! Of hometown love! Praise Stansbury forever!"*

Siddhartha jumps up on me, excited to join in. I hold her front paws in my hands as we pivot together. "Okay, so I'm not a lyricist like Tara, or a singer. Sorry, Sid." And I sing a reprise off-key again.

One day, I take Siddhartha on a walk along the outskirts of town. A row of newspaper machines startle me. I feel a compulsion to look, as if the *Financial Street Journal*s inside were beckoning. I backpedal, trying to control the urge to buy one. But then I shift directions and sneak toward the row of papers, peeking at the headlines, confusing Siddhartha as she unwillingly performs yet another about face. I back up again, feeling an urge to sink my teeth into the meat of a front-page article. I take a deep breath and with all my might, pull away from temptation once and for all. Siddhartha faithfully trails behind me. As Sid and I round a corner, I come face-to-face with the local bowling alley. I stop, stare through its large plate-glass window and wonder.

My routine provides continuity. Long morning walks in the woods with Siddhartha, followed by intensive dog-obedience training, bowling practice, cleaning up the cottage, documenting Uncle Sam's fishing lure collection, sailing in the afternoon with Siddhartha, fishing off the dock for dinner with Sid, and if that fails, heading to the cupboards for refueling. In the evenings, I follow all that up with readings from the works in the many bookcases, and writing in my own journal by the fireplace while Siddhartha sleeps.

One night during a thunderstorm, I'm reading and discover a passage where the author claims that only by caring for animals can man really know how to love himself and others. I look at Sid conked out on the couch next to me with her head upside down, front paws straight up in the air, back legs spread for that ever-desirable tummy rub. I gently rub her stomach.

I pull out my notebook and instead of recording my thoughts I start an old-fashioned handwritten letter to Victor.

Dear Adviser Winston,
I write to you from my native country of Michigan. The emotional armor I felt compelled to wear in the city has begun to evaporate here, allowing for a sense of perspective I have not had in years…if ever, where I can see that the quest for success has blinded me. I recognize a drive for approval, but from whom and why, I wonder. The addiction to work, compliments of a freelance life, has been replaced by a compulsion to find myself. Excavation is taking place on Clark Lake. I am, however, happy to tell you that I am determined to find my Self and have a good life, unlike a few of

the unhappy CEOs I came to know through Lights Out. I do have some help on my journey…her name is Siddhartha. And I'm in love. Is it okay to have help on this journey if the companionship is humane, but not human?
Sincerely,
Advisee Banks.
P.S. Have not picked up a newspaper in two months, with exception of puppy potty-training purposes.

Days later, I'm ready to start seeing people again. I invite my parents to the cottage for dinner and to meet Siddhartha.

One look at Sid, and Eleanor is smitten. The two take an instant liking to each other. Eleanor plays with Sid like a grandchild, cooing and tossing her a toy. I show my parents the results of Sid's recent education: sitting, lying down, rolling over and shaking on "hi five."

"I think you two should go to dinner and leave Sid and me together here," says Eleanor. "I'm sorry, but she's just too precious."

Charlie lifts a brow. "I think she's serious."

"Me, too. Come on, Mom. I promise to tell you Sid-dhartha stories on the way."

Eleanor finally pulls herself away from Sid. "Okay, but if you ever need a dog-sitter, call me."

I lock up the cottage and tell Sid we'll see her later. Then Charlie, Eleanor and I pile into the car.

"Where are we going, Dad?" I ask.

"I thought I'd take you to the Eagle's Nest."

"Why is that familiar?"

"It's where your dad and Sam went the night he passed away," says Eleanor.

"Oh, right, seems like I've heard about it since then, though," I say, realizing I left my black ribbon at the cottage.

Once seated inside the restaurant Charlie orders a merlot, Eleanor orders a pinot grigio and I order a cold local beer.

"So, dear," says Eleanor, "what are you doing out here all by yourself?"

"Licking my wounds and trusting that new bearings will arrive soon."

"I still think it was a good business," she adds.

"Mom…if you don't mind, I'm on a business diet."

"Well, this is a first. Honey, are you feeling all right?"

Charlie grins. "You sound like me now, Eleanor."

The waitress returns. "Drinks are on the house."

We all look surprised. "Why is that?" asks Charlie.

The waitress shrugs. "The bartender insisted."

We all turn our heads. Standing behind the long well-worn wooden bar, nodding a warm hello, is Richard Wright.

I recognize him immediately and wave back. "That's Richard Wright," I tell my parents. "Uncle Sam's friend who used to own the only local funeral home in town. He told me he was coming to work here but I forgot."

Richard Wright appears at our table. "Hello, Madison, Mr. and Mrs. Banks."

"Please, Charlie and Eleanor," says Charlie.

"Thanks for the drinks," I say.

"I always keep my promise, just like Sam did." He smiles. "So what brings you to town?"

"The business died…."

"I'm sorry to hear that. Real sorry."

I try to stay off the business track. "Thanks. I'm staying at Uncle Sam's for now."

"Well, if you need anything at all while you're up here, you call me. And if you need a job, or a reason to pass the time, I could use an extra hand behind the bar. Place gets pretty busy in the summers. You know how to pour?"

"Thanks, Richard. I'll keep that in mind."

We chitchat some more about local weather and how much we all miss Uncle Sam. I start to wonder if my chance meeting with Richard Wright is fortuitous and if his offer might be something I should seriously consider.

Sierra is the next person to arrive at the cottage a few days later. She gets out of her car and we hug each other, holding on tight. It is a long, heartfelt embrace until Siddhartha whines to get in on the action. Sierra sees the puppy and swiftly abandons our hug to kneel down next to Sid.

"Hey there, Siddhartha. You're quite the pretty one, aren't you." Siddhartha tenderly places her paw on Sierra's arm and licks her face.

"And smart, too." I smile.

Sierra laughs. She pets Sid and looks up at me. "She's got such a sweet disposition. You found a winner, Madison."

"I didn't find her. She found me."

"Know what I think?" says Sierra, standing up now. "I don't think she *found* you—I think she *rescued* you. Honestly, I've never seen you look better."

"Really? Well, maybe we rescued each other. You look pretty wonderful yourself."

"I brought you a present." She pulls a Ziploc bag from her purse. "Homemade chocolate chip cookies."

"Thanks," I laugh. "This time I promise to eat every last one of them. Come on. Let's go for a sail."

Sierra, Siddhartha and I set sail in the Sunfish, laughing and splashing each other. In the middle of the lake, we settle down for tuna fish sandwiches and cookies.

"So how are you doing without Lights Out?" asks Sierra.

"I'm not doing. I'm being. Or trying to. But I gotta tell

you, being gets boring." When she laughs I ask, "Sierra, how did you get your business to grow so fast?"

"First of all, my business is a much simpler one. But what I did do and still do is practice flexing the muscle of gratitude."

"The muscle of gratitude?" I say teasingly. "Sounds like the title of a sermon."

"Well, it is in some ways. It's about getting into clearly defined affirmations such as 'I am grateful for my happiness,' 'I am grateful for my successful business.' Say it enough times over and over and voilà, success and happiness appear."

"I've tried that. It doesn't work for me."

"That's because you get stuck in the past. Drop the regrets, sweetie. Just take a deep breath and exhale them."

I take a deep breath and exhale. Sierra applauds. Sid gently puts her paw on my hand. "The next step, Maddy, and this is crucial, is to keep moving."

"How do you know you're going in the right direction?"

"You *make* it the right direction…because the only wrong direction is no direction at all. That's getting stuck in a state of paralysis, and well…then you might as well turn the lights out."

"Was there something I did in college that made me successful? Like, did I practice a certain custom or ritual?"

Sierra laughs. "Unrelenting drive and passion. And when you hit an obstacle you found a way around it—no, through it. I have no doubt you'll find your way through this one, too."

"No, I mean was there something I did on a regular basis?"

Sierra thinks for a moment. "You used to take Tara and me out to dinner every week and tell us we were your most trusted friends, and then you'd ask us to advise you on all aspects of your business and give you feedback."

"Did I listen?"

"All the time," says Sierra. "A lot of times you still did it your way, but you made us feel such a part of your decisions that we always believed we were part of your success."

I ponder that, and then hesitantly reveal a deep insecurity. "Do you think I can still be successful as an entrepreneur?"

Sierra holds my hands in hers. "Yes. Your results have yet to play themselves out. I'm just waiting for the green light so I can be back on board. You can always count on me, Maddy."

"I know. That's why I love you. You can count on me, too."

"I know. That's why I'll always love you."

We reach over to each other and share a small kiss of gratitude.

"I am grateful for our enduring friendship and love," I say in a mock-affirmation monotone.

Sierra throws water on me and laughs. "Smarty-pants."

Siddhartha emits a small woof.

"Was that a bark?" asks Sierra. We laugh. "Let's sail back in."

We swing the sail around and head back to shore. "So, how's Milton?" I ask.

"Great. It's really nice having a different balance of energies."

"What about women?"

"Right now I'm happy with Milton, but he doesn't own my sexuality. I don't have an either/or conflict about it…and neither does he."

"Did you use affirmations to set it up that way?"

"Absolutely." Sierra grins.

We dock the boat and all three of us pile out. Sierra collects her things. "I wish I could stay longer but I've got an edit session tonight. Walk me to my car?"

Sid and I accompany Sierra to her car, where she gives Sid a loving cuddle. "Goodbye, precious." Then she offers me a deep hug. "Remember who you are," says Sierra. "Which is anything you want to be. Now just keep moving."

I watch her drive off as the setting sun casts colorful hues against the horizon. Sid and I stop at the mailbox. Inside is a letter from Victor. It's handwritten—with meticulous penmanship, of course. With Sid by my side, I read the letter aloud for both of us.

"Dear Advisee Banks,
Great to hear from you. Glad the excavation is going well. Sid sounds like a loyal friend and I'm sure will help you reach your potential, which always takes precedence over accomplishing a goal. Loving another (even a puppy), requires risk and intimacy, but the sense of mutual belonging is well worth it. Dogs are masters at teaching us how to recognize happiness in the simplest things. My happiness today consisted of three green lights in a row, two great parking spaces, an awesome steam shower and making contributions to Mothers Against Drunk Driving and pharmaceutical research (as I'm hoping to abate a future comprised of cubicle rats as leaders—i.e., students on Ritalin). If you ask me, happiness is about NOT being annoyed. It's as simple as having tea with a friend (who may never even drink the tea she orders). It's about being the best you can be without judging yourself by the standards of others but by the standards you choose to define yourself. It's about letting sunshine in and regrets out. Hope I don't sound pedantic; just know it comes from a place of genuine caring. Please keep me posted on any and all future archaeological findings.
Sincerely,
Your Adviser Winston"

I look at Sid. "What do think, Sid? *My* Adviser Winston. Good thing I'm not the possessive type like Alyssa Ryan." Siddhartha sits, staring at me. "Come on, let's go visit the bar."

I walk over to the Eagle's Nest with Siddhartha in tow. Richard greets me with a free beer.

"How goes it?" he asks, seeming genuinely happy to see me.

"It goes. But I was wondering if I might take you up on your offer to bartend. The only thing is, I don't know much about bartending."

"Oh, that's easy," he says. "You know how to pour?"

"Yes."

"You know how to listen?"

"I'm told I could use some improvement in that area," I say, remembering Victor's channeled message to me back in my Los Angeles apartment.

"No problem, I'll get you some Q-tips."

He signs me up for duty and tells me Sid can come, too, as the bar mascot.

My routine now includes working every night. While Siddhartha plays the role of adorable-but-distracted hostess, Richard teaches me the art of tending bar. In the hour before the bar opens I receive lessons on the stocking of beer and liquor.

"What about fancy drinks like a Pink Squirrel?" I ask.

"You don't have to worry about those. Most people around here like a good ale beer or fine glass of wine. All you have to be concerned with is listening. It's really a caregiving experience," he tells me while wiping the bar clean.

"What if they don't want to talk?"

"Oh, believe me, they want to talk, it's human instinct. And they want to be heard, which is where the art of paraphrasing comes in."

"Paraphrasing?"

"Yep," says Richard, topping off all the bottles of hard liquor. He points out, "I like to keep the whiskeys to the right and the vodkas to the left."

My curiosity is piqued. "What exactly is paraphrasing?"

"Rephrasing what someone says without repeating it word for word, so they know they've been heard. I tell ya, it's just like when a grieving family comes to see you in a time of need. Never ask for the stats first, though," he adds, getting agitated by a jogged memory, "which is what that Tribute in a Box wanted me do. They've got it all wrong, insisting I take notes, makin' the whole thing so damn clinical and uptight when it's supposed to ease the pain of a survivor. Ya never take notes at a first meeting. You use counseling skills to help people deal with loss." He shakes his head, clearly irritated.

"It's not worth getting so upset over," I say gently.

"You're right." He pours himself a shot of whiskey, kicks it back and settles down. "Anyway, I was saying, when a customer starts talking at the bar, you do like a funeral director—you ask them to tell you about what happened, to explain what the whole ordeal was like for them. Be a mirror. The trick...is to do it with compassion."

"Be a compassionate mirror, so to paraphrase," I say.

"Right." He smiles at me like I'm an A student. "You reflect back to them the meaning their words have for you." He looks at the clock, which reads five, walks to the door and flips the Open sign around. "Watch me." He winks. "I'm pretty good in action."

The first patron to walk in takes his regular seat at the bar. He's a sixty-year-old man named Guy, who wears long-sleeved thermal shirts under dark green overalls with heavy work boots. "Hey, Richard. You finally got some help," says Guy.

"That's right," says Richard. He introduces us. "This is Guy.

He's here every day at five, sharp. This is Maddy Banks, Sam's niece. So be nice to her."

"Is that so?" asks Guy. "Sam was a helluva guy. Best fisherman I ever met."

"Thanks," I say. "Can I take your order?"

"I'll have the usual." He winks.

"That's a tall ice-cold glass of draft ale," Richard tells me. I pour a glass for Guy and hand it to him.

"Sally's fences around her garden's come undone again," Guy says.

Richard gives me a look and turns to Guy. "What happened?"

"I suspect some deer jumped clear across them, except for one who took the whole damn fence down. I've been fixing it for a week now."

"What's that been like?" asks Richard.

"Hard work, especially in this heat, but Sally makes damn good lemonade and meaty sandwiches. And she plays her music in the house loud so I can hear it. Pretty symphony music…makes the day go by a lot quicker."

"Sounds like the deer's mishap with a fence is providing you with some work and keeping you well-fed and entertained while you're at it," says Richard.

"Yep. That's exactly what it is," says Guy, then he takes another sip of beer.

I smile at Richard, impressed. "That was good," I whisper.

"That was nothing," he says softly. "It's more challenging around grief, when you're trying to help someone resolve unresolved feelings."

Siddhartha sticks her nose into Guy's leg. He looks down and smiles. "Now who's this little fella?"

"That's Siddhartha," I say. "She's a girl, so it's Sid for short."

Guy reaches down and pets her. "Hello, Sid." He grabs a

bar towel and plays tug-of-war with Sid for a while. He looks at Richard and me. "I had a dog once. A golden retriever. She was a great dog."

"What was her name?" I ask.

"Dunlop, because I found her as a puppy in a pile of opened-up white paint cans. Took me a month and two cans of paint thinner to get all the paint off of her," he says, smiling at the memory.

"What happened to her?"

"Couple years later I took her to a groomer for a good washing. When I came back to get her, they said she'd died."

"What! How did that happen?" I ask, horrified.

"They never really told me," says Guy, getting a little teary-eyed.

"That's insane. Did you sue them?"

Richard jumps in. "So what I hear you saying, Guy, is that you took Dunlop for a grooming and when you returned she was gone."

Guy nods his head.

"What was that like?" asks Richard.

"Pretty bad. It didn't make any sense, ya know? For a long time I felt like it was my fault. What if I hadn't taken her there to begin with?" He takes a gulp of beer as if to swallow his painful memories.

"I imagine it must have been a painful way to lose her," says Richard.

"Yeah," says Guy. "I never talked about it before."

"Sounds like you needed to talk about it."

"Yeah. I think so. Thanks for listening."

"No problem," says Richard. "The next beer's on me…in memory of Dunlop."

Guy offers a nod of deep gratitude.

I'm amazed, and turn to Richard. "You're *good*."

The next six hours are a blur of activity as I learn the ropes of tending bar and meet the locals—carpenters, builders, painters, writers, doctors, manufacturers, husbands and wives, brothers and sisters. Eleven o'clock rolls around and Richard flips over the Open sign in the window to read Closed. I help him lock up for the night, but not without a few questions.

"What does Guy do, Richard?"

"Oh, he's sort of like the local handyman but deep down he's quite brilliant. He can invent whatever it takes to fix a problem. He's an unsung engineering hero," says Richard, locking up the liquor storage bin.

"Does he have family?"

"Only family I've ever heard him mention is that dog, Dunlop."

"He started to get upset about it."

"That's healthy. It's all part of the protocol of grief." He faces me. "That's *love*. Remember, Maddy, you can't love someone unless you're willing to grieve over that someone. Need a lift home?"

"No, thanks. Sid and I like the walk."

"See you tomorrow, then. And, Maddy, you did a great job. You're a hard worker, just like your uncle."

Sid and I walk along the shoreline under the moonlight to Uncle Sam's cottage. "Did you get that, Sid? The protocol to grief is love. To paraphrase with interpretation…that would mean that those who have grieved are also those who have loved. I would grieve you a lot—you know why, Sid? Because I love you a lot. Would you grieve for me?" Siddhartha jumps on me and whimpers. "I know…I'd miss you, too…like I miss Uncle Sam…and Tara."

For the next week, I endear myself to the customers at the bar, listening and paraphrasing, while Sid endears herself to them by nuzzling up to them for a loving stroke on the head.

I'm working the bar one night when the town's librarian, Mrs. Jones, shows me a series of her watercolor paintings.

"Sounds like you really enjoy painting from your car-studio during your lunch hour," I say.

"Yes," says Mrs. Jones. "I painted these over some twenty lunch hours."

There's an extraordinary painting of Guy working outdoors on a fence with strange-looking parts strategically placed on top of it. "That's an amazing painting. You're really talented." I try to squash my instinct to introduce Mrs. Jones to a handful of gallery owners I know from my failed Artists International venture, but I'm determined not to meddle with people's lives here. What if I helped and it backfired? Better not to tempt fate in this little town, I think to myself. I glance down the bar at Guy sipping his beer. I top off Mrs. Jones's iced tea and remember the story of D. J. Depree, the founder of Herman Miller.

The story goes that when D.J. went to pay his respects to the wife of a millwright who had died while working for him, she showed him her husband's book of poetry, and forever thereafter D.J. wondered—was her husband a millwright who wrote poems or a poet who worked as a millwright? That one persistent and prescient thought marked the start of a changing perception of the American worker from machine-centric widget-maker to employee with inalienable rights—rights that D. J. Depree recognized in the 1950s. In fact, his was one of the first companies to give employees participative ownership through stock. Years later D.J.'s son, Max, succeeded him as an equally good leader, maintaining the values his father had instilled in him. It was Max who went on to write the little, well-known book "*Leadership is an Art*," declaring that leaders should leave behind them assets and a legacy; that they are obligated to provide and maintain momentum; that they must be responsible for effectiveness; that they must take a role in developing, expressing and defending civility and values and implement management-sharing opportunities.

Derek Rogers must have skipped that class in college because he certainly eschews all those principles. But Victor doesn't. As far as I can tell, Victor is a man of great principle. I watch the people in the bar. Is Mrs. Jones a librarian who paints or a painter who works as a librarian? Is Guy a handyman who engineers or an engineer who is handy? "God, I hate conundrums," I mutter under my breath, and focus back on the present.

"What do you think of this one, Maddy?" asks Mrs. Jones.

I stare at another stellar painting. "It's remarkable," I comment. In this painting of Clark Lake at dawn, Mrs. Jones has captured its essence perfectly. My instincts win out and I say, "You know…I know a little bit about the art world. I could give you a list of names and numbers of some art gallery owners in New York to contact if you want."

"Really?" asks Mrs. Jones. "That would be very nice. Let me think about it."

"Sure. And I'd be happy to call in advance, if it helps."

I glance toward the other end of the bar to make sure all the customers are happy. Richard pours another patron a second shot of whiskey. I hear the soothing tones of Richard's voice as he asks, "What was that like for you, Wally?"

"It's rough," says Wally, mumbling. "I can't look at my own bed without thinking about her. I can't walk up the driveway or stand in the garden without thinking she's going to be there."

"Sounds like your home is filled with memories of her."

"Beautiful memories," says Wally. He kicks his drink back.

"You ever think about moving, Wally…maybe taking a vacation?"

"Without her? Can't bear the thought. I'll take another shot."

"I don't think that's a good idea right now, Wally. We don't want any accidents on the road."

Wally nods. Richard passes me to get a fresh rag.

"What happened to his wife?" I ask.

"Mary Beth? She passed away six years ago. Wally's never gotten over it. That's what long-term grief can do."

"Long-term grief?"

"It lowers your serotonin levels and triggers hard-core depression. Some people get sad like Wally. Some get agitated and keep superbusy to hide themselves from their own pain. You don't want to encourage them to grieve anymore, but just help them cope with it."

Guy overhears us. "That's what I'm trying to do with Sally. I keep trying to help her cope."

"What do you mean by that, Guy?" asks Richard.

"When she cries, which is all the time, I try to ease her pain by doing chores around the house, buying groceries for her and bringing them in the house. Sometimes I make her a pot of tea. And I let her cry for as long as she needs to. I know she's in a lot of pain…but it makes me feel good to be there for her. She doesn't have anyone else anymore. I just wish she'd be willing to go outside sometime. She lets me walk her to the porch, but she hasn't left the house for eight months now."

"Sounds like each of you is helping the other in your own way," suggests Richard.

"I think there's some truth to that," says Guy.

I can't help but ask, "What happened to Sally's husband?"

"Joe died a few months after I closed down the funeral home. All the bereavement counseling groups I used to offer got closed down, too. It's been tough on the locals. They have no social place to grieve anymore. Sally, along with everyone else, had to use funeral homes out in Grass Lake and Ann Arbor. They feel like they've been ripped off by the Tribute in a Box Corporation. They now own all the funeral homes within sixty miles of here. Company's no good, taking advantage of emotionally vulnerable people. Don't get me started—especially when funeral directors may be the very last stop for some to ever release their grief," Richard fumes.

I pour a shot of whiskey and hand it to him. "Here, maybe you shouldn't talk about this stuff for a while."

Richard drinks his shot. "Maybe you're right. I can't stand seeing people get taken advantage of."

I shake my head and pour myself a shot, as well. "Me, too—especially by Derek Rogers. Oh, you have no idea." I have the shot and we smile at one another, and for a moment, I flash on Uncle Sam and me sharing a shot and shooting the breeze.

The next day is my day off. Sid and I sail around the lake and catch a bass. I think of Uncle Sam. "I wish Uncle Sam was here, Sid. You guys would have really liked each other." I start to cry, and this time, I don't try to hold it in. I just let it flow, and I let Sid lick the tears.

That night, I sit in front of the fireplace and compose another letter to Victor.

Dear Victor,

I hope this letter finds you well and happy. Thanks for the happiness tips. I found happiness this week catching a bass in Clark Lake (which I put back in the water), taking walks with Sid and bartending at the Eagle's Nest, where I now listen to people's hopes, aspirations and process with grief. Without even reading a newspaper, I unhappily learned that Derek's empire has expanded and is unfortunately taking advantage of the locals around here. I try not to let it get to me. I'm also learning to listen…to myself. It's amazing how many epiphanies one can have when one is quiet enough to hear them. I think I know now who I've been seeking approval from…myself. And working in a bar turns out to be a pretty good place to practice self-acceptance. I don't know what the results of playing bartender will be, but for now, it keeps me engaged with life—and the tips aren't bad, either.

Yours truly,

Madison

P.S. Since I'm out of the "know" going on three months and no newspaper, how was the launch of your Designer Tank company? Sid says "Hi."

Using a pencil, I shade an empty spot at the bottom of the letter, then call Siddhartha over and point to it. "Okay, Sid, sign here." Sid places her paw in a dish of flour and then puts her paw on the spot, creating a defined paw mark.

"Good girl." Sid licks my face. I neatly fold the letter inside an envelope addressed to Winston Capital.

The next night at the bar, I wait for Richard to close up while Siddhartha sleeps quietly in her corner spot. I pour two shots of whiskey. "Um, Richard. Can I talk to you?"

He eyes the shots and smiles. "I take it this is going to be a long sit-down kind of talk."

"Um. Probably."

He sits on a stool, leaving the shot untouched on the table. "I'm all ears."

"I've been thinking about a lot of the things you've been telling me and I think I have long-term grief that's triggered a state of agitated depression."

"Why do you think that?"

"Well, because I haven't been able to get over the deaths of Uncle Sam or my friend Tara or my cousin Smitty. I haven't been able to get over the loss of Lights Out, either. I'm consumed in grief…"

"Okay. I'll tell you what we're going to do. I'm going to give you some homework." He disappears into the back room and returns with a giant piece of plain brown wrapping paper, which he lays on the bar. "I want you to make a graph of all the losses in your life starting from birth until now. You can write, you can draw pictures, you can express it any way you want. Take your time and we'll go over it tomorrow night, same time, same place. And let's save the drinks until we're done."

The next night after closing, I sit with Richard and unravel my Loss Graph across the top of the bar. I've created an elaborate diagram complete with drawings, sketches, clipped-out portraits and cut-out landscapes from magazines. An idea starts in one location with arrows sprouting from it, branching to more connected losses.

Richard studies the graph carefully. "I want you to explain for me what the loss was and your feelings around it, then and now."

"Okay, well, um, when I was born I had my first sense of loss—I lost the private womb I grew up in." I point to the next illustration. "Over here, two years later, I lost being an only child when my brother was born.... At six, we moved and I lost the street Stansbury that I grew up on, which had a real sense of community to it.... I lost my first serious boyfriend in junior high to a best friend who decided she wanted him at whatever cost, so I also lost my best friend.... And then I lost my first really successful business in college, which I lost to Derek Rogers who sabotaged me and to this day continues to do so."

"The same Derek Rogers who owns Tribute in a Box?" asks Richard.

I nod. "I keep losing my businesses. White Mondays became Black Tuesdays, Artists International was stolen by Palette Enterprises, Lights Out got snuffed out...." I feel tears clot in my throat. "Then my cousin Smitty died, and a year later a close friend from college, Tara Pintock, died...and then...Uncle Sam. He was my best friend throughout my whole life. He was always there for me. I miss him." I start to weep. "And, um, recently I feel like I've lost my college girlfriend Sierra to her new boyfriend, Milton...and, um, I think my grief is turning people like Victor Winston away from me. I feel like all I do is play the results and the only results I end up with are filled with loss."

"So what I hear you say is that you've had a lot of loss around your career, which ties into your self-esteem...and you've had a lot of loss from deaths in a very short time," says Richard. I nod. "And you feel a sense of abandonment and betrayal by some of your past boyfriends and college classmates," he adds. I nod again. "Can you tell me what results you're playing for?"

My words gush forth between tears. "Well...that my hard work will reward me with a really successful career...and a beautiful home...and a beautiful healthy husband...or partner, and, um, beautiful healthy children, and a beautiful dog…the dog part I now have."

"What I hear you say is that you're playing for perfection," states Richard. I nod again, wiping my eyes with the tissues that he hands me. "Why do you feel you have to have perfection in what you do and in your relationships?"

"So I can have a good life."

"Perfection doesn't exist, Maddy. It's the imperfect that's perfect."

"Is that a conundrum?"

He grins and continues. "Do you think you can have a good life accepting the way things are in the moment?"

"I'm trying to accept myself right now."

"That's great. Can you explain to me just how you are doing that?"

"By not being so critical of myself, and repeating affirmations that I'm good enough as I am right now. Good enough for myself, at least."

"Sounds like you don't believe you're good enough for anyone else."

I nod again.

"Maddy. Love is simply about growing with another person, which just so happens to put the lights on your character defects, so if you're stuck on perfection, you're stuck on stagnation, and that's not growing either alone or with someone else. When you stop growing in a relationship, you're done and you move on so you can continue to grow, whether that's with another person or not. But people like to get attached to people, to things, to concepts. I'll tell you this much—the more attached someone is to those things, the more difficult their death will be."

I nod.

"There's really nothing for you to get, Maddy. You get it. All you have to do is be…and just let life happen."

"But when I *be,* I get *bored.* Is that agitated depression?"

He smiles. "That's *schpilkes,* as your uncle would say." He sighs and gently pats my hand. "I want you to do something for me. I want you to pretend that you have three days left to live and to plan your own funeral. Write down for me every detail you can, who you want to speak, what you want said and by whom, what you want to leave, if you want to be cremated or buried in a casket and anything else you can think of. And I also want you to write a letter to your uncle with your left hand."

"But I'm right-handed."

"That's why I want you to write it with your left. Some folks call it activating the inner child. I call it slowing down the *schpilkes.*"

I smile at that.

"Meet me at the corner of Jefferson and Eagle Point tomorrow, an hour before we open."

"Okay," I say. "What about you, Richard? What's your love story?"

"I was married once for twenty-one years. My wife passed away and, well, I've grown accustomed to the role of loner and it suits me just fine."

"What about now, are you growing?"

"When you're helping others, you're always growing."

And all the way home with Sid by my side, I wonder how Richard Wright got to be so wise—and would I ever be that wise? It was something I wouldn't have to wonder about much longer.

That night, I sit in a hot bubble bath by candlelight thinking about my three remaining days on earth and writing out my own funeral plan, which I title "The Life Celebration of

Madison Banks." Siddhartha lies next to the tub keeping vigil over me.

Later, in front of a warm fireplace and with Siddhartha at my side, I hold up the Ziploc bag with Uncle Sam inside and show it to Sid.

"Sid, meet Uncle Sam. Uncle Sam, this is Sid, short for Siddhartha, and also with an *S* because she was named after you." I place the bag on the coffee table and begin awkwardly writing a letter to Uncle Sam with my left hand. The process is tedious.

Dear Uncle Sam,
I miss you so much…I wish I could talk to you. I am filled with…sadness and regret. I regret not getting married and being able to have you see me walk down the aisle. I regret…not having children so you could be there to enjoy them with me.

Feelings rise to the surface between the words I compose. Suddenly, I start to cry. "Oh my God," I exclaim. "I get it. I get it." I look at the dust of Uncle Sam in the Ziploc bag. An epiphany takes hold, Uncle Sam is all around me. I lift my fingers to gently rub the air in front of my face. "I get it," I repeat. And this time, I weep for joy.

Next day, Sid and I meet Richard at the crossroads. It's a half mile to the bar.

Richard greets me. "Do you have your funeral preparations?" I nod. "And the letter to Sam?" I nod again. "May I have them?" I hand them over. "Okay, Maddy, for the next four hours, you're dead. You can't say a word, you can't make a comment, you certainly can't tend the bar, and you can't pay attention to Sid. Now let's walk to your funeral." Richard starts walking.

I feel funny. I finally take a step forward and follow him, realizing I no longer have the capacity to speak or be heard. Sid walks between the two of us.

Richard turns to the puppy, now approximately seven months old. "So, Sid, how are you doing, sweetness? You miss your mom? I know. She took good care of you, didn't she? We'll find out very soon who she instructed to take care of you." I watch Sid hang by Richard as he talks to her. I feel a pang in my heart. I can't talk or hold Sid, because I'm dead.

When we reach the bar and go inside, Richard pulls a large white sheet out of the back office. He instructs dead me to sit at the bar and then places the cloth over me. Sid can no longer see me and starts to whimper. It breaks my heart but I force myself to remain quiet. I listen as Richard sets the bar up, predicting every one of the customs in his routine. I hear him unlock the refrigerator, followed by the extra liquor bin. I hear him walk to the front door and flip the Open sign around. I hear Sid's paw steps follow Richard around as if Sid knows I'm gone and is looking to see who she is supposed to latch on to. I hear new noises that break away from the routine: sounds of a bottle being opened followed by a quick pouring of liquid.

"I'm going to really miss your mom, Sid," says Richard. Then I hear him swallow some liquid and place a shot glass on the bar. Just then, I hear another person's footsteps. Sounds like Guy. Must be Guy. *But he's early,* I think.

As Guy walks toward the bar he asks, "Where's Maddy?"

I can practically see Richard cock his head toward me and I hear him reply, "She died."

"Oh," says Guy. "I'm gonna miss her." He's bent down to pet Sid. "Who's gonna look after the dog?"

"I'm sure we'll find out at the funeral. It starts in fifteen minutes," says Richard.

"In that case you better only give me half a beer to start. I don't want to be sloshed at her service."

I hear the front door open and close. Feet and paws shuffle against the floor. I can tell it's Wally. "I'm not too late, am I?" he asks.

"No," says Richard.

The door opens and closes again followed by more pitter-patter of Sid's paws.

"Hello, Siddhartha!" says the sweet voice of Mrs. Jones, the librarian. A bar stool scrapes against the floor as she takes a seat. "Hello, Richard, Guy, Wally." Richard must have planned this, I think. Wally and Mrs. Jones never come in this early.

"Everybody, could you please move your bar stools so we're all sitting around the deceased." I listen as the stools squeak along the floor. Richard continues. "We're here this evening to mourn the passing of Madison Banks. I have with me her instructions regarding her passing." Papers rustle. I wonder how on earth he's going to read my writing. Much of what I wrote came in a flush of thoughts. I could not write fast enough to keep up with the ideas that poured out. Had I known he was going to read them, I would have made my instructions legible.

"Okay," says Richard. "It says here that Maddy would like her funeral to be held at Clark Lake at her uncle Sam's cottage. For a two-day…I can't tell, that might say three-day…event. First, she wants her friend Sierra to put together a life bio video, which she would like shown at night outside under the stars against a big screen, weather permitting, she writes. She wants her mother and father to speak about her, her best friend Sierra, and her nephew Andy…if he's up for it—I think that's what that says. She'd like her brother, a poet, to write an original poem about her and read it for everyone. She would like Maurice LeSarde to sing "Fishing Free" live and in person, and then for her mother to lead everyone in telling a story about her around…I think that says scrambled eggs and rye toast, Neshama sausage and some sort of…cookie, I think…."

Neshama sausages, I think to myself. It means "soul," but I forgot to write that down. The thought makes my mouth water for them, but those taste sensations are only memories now in this moment, never to be experienced again.

"She would like everyone to take a sunset ride on a big pontoon boat and have her ashes cast into Clark Lake…while the film score from the movie *To Kill A Mockingbird* plays." I can see in my mind's eye Richard struggling to decipher my writing. "Oh, it says here, she also wants her favorite… Can you read that, Lillian?"

There is a pause and then Mrs. Jones says, "It looks like the word *client*."

"Thanks." Richard continues. "She wants her favorite clients, Arthur Pintock and Norm Pearl, to attend, as well. For the exit song, she wants everyone to walk out with open umbrellas that are to be funeral favors with her initials on them, and—wow, this is hard to read—everyone is to leave…the…party…to the tune of—let's see, what's that say?— Oh, 'Raindrops Keep Falling on My Head,' by Burt Bacharach. She would also like a… I think that says *sculpture* made of her…like the one of Uncle Sam."

I remain still under the sheet feeling more and more awkward. I'm angry at myself for not making the directions more clear and yet there's nothing I can do because I'm dead. And in an even weirder way, getting upset doesn't really matter anymore, because I am…dead. I feel a tremendous sense of frustration that things are not perfect. That my intentions are all messed up. At the same time, I feel a complete and utter relief that the desire to be perfect no longer exists…because I'm dead and, well, what difference does it make? Tempering all of my feelings brings a sense of acceptance for what is right now. It feels unfamiliar, yet oddly peaceful.

"She wants her sculpture to represent a person of ideas. She wants everything she owns to be divided between her family and Sierra. She wants all of her business ideas to go to Victor…Winston…who she believes can turn them into something one day. And she would like Victor Winston and Professor Osaka to start an entrepreneurial think tank in her name with twenty-five percent of whatever she may have left in her estate. She wants her mother Eleanor to take care of Sid, but for Sid to spend part of her time at the Eagle's Nest bar, under the supervision of Richard Wright…and she would like everyone to have drinks on her at the Eagle's Nest."

I can almost see all of them smiling.

"Does that mean free drinks tonight?" asks Wally.

"Is that any way to pay your respects, Wally?" Mrs. Jones chastises.

"Sorry," he says.

"Well, those are her instructions, as best as I can read them. Does anyone have anything they'd like to say about Maddy?"

"I think she was really special," says Guy. "She always made me feel like I mattered."

"Yes," says Richard. "And she had a real sense of justice, didn't she?"

"I think it was very hard for her not to want to take care of people or to help them make their dreams come true," says Mrs. Jones. "To the point where it superseded her taking care of herself."

I shrink inside. Am I that transparent? It feels so strange

to hear people talk about me as if I'm not there, but I am there, only I'm dead-there.

"Even when I was down, which is pretty much all the time, she picked me up with that spark in her eye," says Wally. "And sharing Sid with us has always been a nice thing to do. Ya know…she let me take Sid home one night when I just didn't feel like being alone. And she promised not to tell anyone, cuz I didn't want to look like a wuss or anything."

"That's a lovely story," says Mrs. Jones. "I liked that she liked to offer her opinion about whatever mattered to others and to her."

"What did you think of her opinions?" asks Richard.

"She had strong ones," says Guy. "Good ones. I think if she could have gone back in time, she would have really given it to that groomer who killed Dunlop."

This time, through the sheet, I can see Richard smiling over that one.

"She didn't think lightly about things, did she?" asks Richard.

"No. She was always thinking," says Guy. "You could see it in her eyes."

"Yes, I think you could call her a deep thinker," adds Richard. "Let's all take a moment to think deeply about Maddy in silence."

I sit still under the cloth sheet, not really sure how to feel—after all, feeling dead is a whole new experience for me.

Perhaps a minute passes, then Richard says, "Let's carry her toward the lake."

Suddenly hands and arms grope my sides and legs and back as I am lifted from the bar stool and carried to the waterfront.

Great, I think, wondering if the finale is a toss in the lake. Well, that would surely wake the dead beast in me. Dead beast in me? Do I have a dead beast? What is it? Some part of me that refuses to live in the moment? The part that's on a never-ending quest for perfection before life can be lived? The part that prefers to wallow in some form of self-pity? I feel my body placed gently down upon the docks. I hear the water lap underneath it. I feel Sid paw at my side and hear her whimper. Of everyone, I'll miss Sid the most, I think. Sid is the one who opened my heart, got me out of a workaholic modus operandi because she needed me. To be needed. To love…so you can grieve. Would Sid grieve the most for me? In her own doglike way? What about Victor? Would he miss me? We started to connect but then he sent me away. What was that about?

I feel a light breeze glide over me. I wonder if dead people think the way I am thinking now, only from outside of their bodies. Did Uncle Sam feel that way? What if there were words left unsaid? How would they ever communicate to their loved ones again, or did it just not matter anymore from this altered state. Not to sound cliché, but maybe that's why it's so very important to say what you feel when you feel it, because the opportunity may never come again, at least not in the physical realm.

"Everyone, let's lift the sheet," says Richard. The sheet slides off me. "Madison, you can live again," he says.

To my ears, it's the most beautiful decree I've ever heard. Richard, Guy, Wally and Mrs. Jones all give me compassionate hugs. I bend over and hug Sid, who showers me with a facial licking.

"What was that experience like?" asks Richard.

"That was really powerful. I think that by learning how to die…I just learned how to live."

"That's exactly the point of the exercise. Most people don't get that until they actually experience a simulation like this."

"How do you know how to do this?"

"I used to teach it to funeral directors in mortuary school."

"Well, you should teach it again. Everyone on the planet should go through this…including presidents and dictators! Think about it, it might curtail war and help social programs—"

"I told you she had strong opinions," says Guy.

"That's what we love about her," says Mrs. Jones.

"Does this mean free drinks now?" asks Wally.

"Yes," I declare. "Free drinks for all of you!"

Back inside the bar, Richard and I pour free drinks for Wally, Guy and Mrs. Jones, while a bevy of other regulars enter.

Richard turns to me. "So, what was it like writing the letter to Sam?"

"It was strange writing with my left hand. It forced my thoughts to slow down and between the thoughts these epiphanies kept popping up."

"Like what?"

"Like I realized that if I ever get married, Uncle Sam would still be there. He could still watch me walk down the aisle because…he didn't really die. He's still with me, here, just in a different way." I look at the black ribbon on my black T-shirt. "I realize…I don't have to wear the black ribbon anymore."

Richard smiles. "You got that? Most people don't get that, but when you do get that, it's in the most profound and powerful way."

"Yeah," I agree. "It's powerful. Look, Richard, I've been thinking. Why don't you write this all down? Turn it into a pamphlet or manual on how to grieve and how to create meaningful tributes. You could call it the 'Pamphlet on Grieving & the Nontraditional Personalized Tribute Experience.'"

"I'm not a writer, Maddy," says Richard. "But I'll tell you what. I'll talk it through and you write it up. I'll cover the grief part and you cover the tributes, and we'll co-author it."

I feel the old flame in my eyes flicker to life. "Okay, you're on," I say. We clink glasses.

"Hey, Maddy," says Rocky from the other end of the bar, still in his mailman attire. "I forgot to drop this in your mailbox. From Winston Capital in L.A. Can I give it to you here?" He pulls out a letter for me.

Richard recognizes the name on the envelope. "Go ahead, take five," he says.

Sid and I cross over to the outdoor patio, away from customers. I open the letter. "Now what do you suppose Mr. Winston has to say, Sid?"

Dear Maddy,

Life sounds good on Clark Lake. Sorry not to write sooner. I've been embroiled with a merger-acquisition in biotech. Talk about merging cultures and organizational behavior. A leader who can't bring the two together inherently affects productivity. When goals aren't clear, people's roles in companies aren't, either, resulting in a chaotic clash between personal and corporate objectives. Aside from that, the launch of Designer Tank was a success. Norm Pearl decided to integrate all of our products into his office-apartment-lofts in NYC. Funny how you seem connected to all of this. They all ask about you and I've told them you're on a retreat and doing well. They said if they can help with the resurrection of Lights Out, to let them know. In the meantime, how's the digging? Need an extra hand? I happen to be good with a shovel. Let me know. Perhaps an advisory board meeting is in order. Any local bowling alleys around you?

Yours truly,

Victor Winston

"What do you think, Sid? Want some company?" Sid and I slip into the back office where an antiquated computer sits. I get online and send Victor a quick e-mail: "Dear Victor, Yes…come for advisory board meeting. Digging is all done but polishing the uncovered relics is an option. Come whenever. You can always find Sid and me at the Eagle's Nest. Beers are on me. Yours, Maddy."

I send the e-mail and write a quick one to my lawyer, Todd Lake. "Need you to please trademark 'Pamphlet on Grieving and the Nontraditional Personalized Tribute Experience.' That done, I register a blog Web site for the pamphlet. And suddenly I feel very much alive.

The next few days I spend catching up with family in Ann Arbor. I take Andy to the movies and to the park with Sid where we all romp together. I meet Rebecca and Keating for lunch. I have dinner with Sierra and the ever-elusive and charming Milton, whom I say I approve of when asked in private by Sierra. I try to talk to Daniel, but his doom and gloom overwhelms him. I tell him he should try pseudo-dying sometime, it might help, but I receive only a dumbfounded expression in return. I take my parents to a klezmer concert and bask in enjoying the moments with them, especially the moments when Eleanor dotes on Siddhartha.

When Sid and I return to the Eagle's Nest a few days later, I am devastated to learn that Guy died the night before in his sleep from some sort of undetected heart condition. He had no family, and so Richard and I decide to put a funeral together for him.

Richard and I enter Guy's apartment and discover that he has very little in terms of possessions: a painting by Lillian Jones of him in green overalls standing outside the

Eagle's Nest on the dock at Clark Lake; a box of photos of him as a child and as a teenager, the only hint of family members, frozen in the past; several first-place ribbon awards from high school for most innovative in engineering and design; and several boxes of metal parts and circuit boards.

We load up his possessions and place them in Richard's truck. Then we drive up to Sally's house on three acres of land. Guy's fenced engineering feat glints in the sunlight.

"I've never informed someone of a death before," I say to Richard.

"Just be compassionate and emotionally available," he says. "When a survivor's pain touches your heart, a bond is made. It helps them through the grieving process. But to get there, you have to be willing to be touched." He pauses to reflect as he puts the truck in Park. "When I was a funeral director, I learned that what people really want is to know that you're just doing the best you can."

"*When* you were a funeral director, Richard?" I pose, poignantly. "What makes you think anything's changed just because you're working in a bar?" I smile at him and then open the truck door to step out.

Sally takes the news hardest of all. When she breaks down, I gently hold her in my arms and tell her how much Guy enjoyed doing that for her.

Sally weeps. "I should have done more. I should have told him how much he meant to me after Joe went. I should have had him move in with me. Maybe I could have saved him," she laments over and over.

"Sounds like you guys had a really special relationship, Sally. Please be comforted knowing that Guy was very fond of you. All he ever talked about at the bar was *you,* and how much he enjoyed looking after you."

Her eyes light up for a moment. "Really?"

"Really," I assure her.

"Sally, you know that Guy didn't have any family. You have a lot of property here—how would you feel about burying him on yours?" says Richard.

Sally stops crying and looks at us both. "Why, I would be honored to have him here…but what about a casket? He should have a nice one. Mahogany. He always liked mahogany…but they're well over five thousand at Tribute in a Box," she says. "I remember from when Joe died. And they're the only ones around here. I'll help pay for it, but I won't give a cent to that Tribute in a Box company after the way they took advantage of me."

"I'm sure I have a mahogany casket left in stock at the old funeral home from before Tribute in a Box took over. We can use one of those," offers Richard. "And they're much less expensive."

"Fine," says Sally. "Count me in for five hundred."

Richard and I share a look

"Don't we still need a funeral home?" Sally asks, wiping her eyes with worn-down tissues.

"No. We don't have to, unless we need the space for viewing and a service," explains Richard. "If we have a viewing we most likely have to embalm him. If not, I can make sure his remains are washed and disinfected. Maddy and I thought we'd have a memorial service for him at the bar."

"A memorial service is nice. And the three of us can have a graveside prayer for him. Will you both come to that?"

"Of course," says Richard.

"By the way, what was Guy's favorite food?" I ask Sally.

"Well," she says coyly, "he used to say he lived for my sandwiches and lemonade."

"Was there any kind of music he had a preference for?"

"He liked it when I played Beethoven as he worked, but he always talked about Roy Vernon's singing," she says with fondness. "He asked me to go with him to hear Roy sing on Thursday nights at the bowling alley…but I just haven't been able to leave the house since…you know."

We say our goodbyes and head outside to the truck.

"Isn't a mahogany casket at least three or four grand?" I ask Richard.

"Yep. I've got a thousand I can put in to cover it, but then I'm figuring on another five hundred for all the liquor at the service."

"I can put in five," I say.

There's a look of gratitude in his eyes. "Maybe others will pitch in, too."

"Hey, Richard. Do you mind if I take a run at some ideas for the memorial service?"

He smiles. "Not at all."

I remember the extraordinary painting that Lillian Jones made of Guy fixing Sally's fence. I head over to the library with Sid to have a talk with Mrs. Jones about it.

Later that day, I take Guy's box of photos with me to Ann Arbor. Sid accompanies me. I meet with Sierra, and later with Eleanor and Charlie, and I even get Daniel to sit still and listen to me.

Two days later, Richard closes the bar to the public for the entire night and devotes the time and space to Guy's life celebration ceremony with about twenty townspeople and bar regulars who knew him. A memory board with photos of Guy is erected at the entrance of the bar, along with a donation bucket for the cost of the funeral. The paintings by Lillian Jones sit on easels on either side of the fireplace where a circle of chairs has been placed.

Richard and I start out by serving everyone Guy's favorite draft ale. Siddhartha makes sure no one feels alone, making herself available for instant companionship with a lick on the hand in return for a pat on the head. Once everyone is seated comfortably around the fireplace, my natural inclination to produce the ceremony kicks in, and I ask Eleanor and Charlie, who are there, to help pass out sandwiches to the mourners. My brother Daniel sits quietly in the back of the bar with a pen and pad of paper in hand. Sierra and Milton stand by for support and video assistance. I first invite Sierra to project a life bio video of Guy on the TV monitor. The three-minute video displays a montage of the photos from the box in Guy's apartment, and the paintings of him by Lillian Jones. It all plays to the symphonic strains of Beethoven. Everyone mentions how they never knew he had won awards for his engineering designs.

I get up and explain that usually a life bio video includes interviews of family and friends, but there was no time or budget for that and so instead we're inviting those present to take a turn and tell stories about Guy as the torch is passed. In this case, the torch is one of the metal contraptions that Guy invented. The contraption is first passed to Lillian Jones who starts the storytelling, and then there's Wally, and all the other bar regulars and townspeople who either knew Guy or had hired him in the past. If someone is shy, my mother masterfully puts them at ease with a prompt to get them going, and Charlie humorously reminds them to have another sip of beer.

After everyone's spoken, Mom introduces a surprise mourner, local singer Roy Vernon. Roy stands up in the back of the room. I see the shadow of someone else back there but I'm not sure who it is.

Roy moves toward the fire and stands before everyone. "I didn't know Guy the way you all did. I knew him as the guy who was there every Thursday night to hear me sing, the guy who truly appreciated my gifts, and I came to count on seeing him there. After a while, his presence alone became a source of inspiration for me…and so this one's for Guy."

Roy sings and plays his guitar. Everyone is in awe as Roy nears the end of his song. The entire bar is silent. Suddenly, Sally appears from the shadows and slowly comes forth, holding a pitcher in her hand. Everyone knows this is the first time Sally's left the house in the ten months since Joe passed. Their silent respect for her fills the room. Richard immediately offers Sally a chair. She sits and listens quietly as Roy sings another song. Siddhartha is by her side, as if sensing that she's in need of support. There's a huge round of applause. Sally has tears in her eyes. Then Eleanor asks Sally if she has a story to tell.

"Yes, I do," replies Sally, and she slowly stands up holding the pitcher in her hand. "Guy was an amazing man. After Joe left, I couldn't function, but Guy was always there…to help with chores, to bring me groceries, to fix my fence…and then some…" Everyone smiles, as her fence is the talk of the town. "He got me to laugh again. He used to sit on the porch at the end of each day with a glass of lemonade, just appreciating the sunset. I never saw a man so content with every moment. So I, uh, brought some of his favorite lemonade for everyone." There are tears in her eyes.

"That is so beautiful, Sally," I say.

"Thank you for sharing that," says Richard. He helps her with the pitcher. "Everyone, grab a shot glass for some of this delicious lemonade." Everyone cheers for Sally, recognizing that in a deeply ironic way, Guy's death brought Sally back to life.

Sally smiles at the group and sits down, visibly allowing a weight of regret to lift from her. Daniel signals our mother. Our mother looks at me. "I think Daniel's ready."

"Okay," I say, still moved by Sally's appearance. "Can you introduce him, Mom?" Eleanor nods and announces Daniel as the nephew of Sam Banks and a poet who has something to say about Guy based on everyone's words and sentiments tonight.

Daniel stands next to the fireplace and reads a poem he's just written. It is a masterful work of on-the-spot-interactive-collective-poem-making. Richard asks Daniel for a copy to hang in the bar. Sally asks him for a copy to put in her house. Mrs. Jones asks for a copy to frame in the library. And Roy Vernon asks for a copy to turn into a ballad in memory of Guy. Daniel is more than surprised by the reactions—remarkably his doom and gloom seems to subside.

Eleanor and Charlie share a knowing glance. "Our children are quite a credit to us, aren't they, dear?" says Charlie.

"Yes, sweetie, they are," replies Eleanor, turning to Daniel and me.

Charlie grins at her.

"I know." She smiles.

Everyone mills about continuing to drink and memorialize Guy. A buzz grows through the crowd. They wish they had more funerals like this in town, and not the rip-offs they've been getting from Tribute in a Box. I overhear Donny, who runs the local symphony orchestra, tell Wally, "All the pallbearers are carrying one of these fancy Tribute in a Box caskets to the grave when the bottom drops out! And you know what hit the ground, besides the dead guy? Wadded-up newspaper!"

"Did ya hear about the TIAB branch in Kalamazoo? Cremated the wrong guy. Family sued for emotional damages. They never got to see the body and then found out the ashes were a scam, too. TIAB tried to squirm out of it, saying 'not to view' is not damaging, but guess what? The prosecution handed the jury TIAB's literature about how viewing is 'essential for grief wellness' and they finally had to pay up."

"How was Guy able to pay for this?" Mrs. Jones asks me.

"Well, technically, if there are no heirs or assets, then the state will cover approximately $947 in funeral costs. The rest of it Richard, Sally and I pitched in on."

Rocky, the mailman, stands up on a bar stool and lifts his mug of beer. "Hey, everyone, I have an idea, let's petition our congressman to stop the rip-offs from Tribute in a Box and make room for memorials that mean something, man."

I hesitantly raise my hand. "Uh, excuse me, Rocky, well, actually, excuse me, everyone, but you can all start expressing your concerns and comments right now. I started a blog at www.lightsoutenterprises.blogspot.com. You can let everyone in town or anyone all over the world know what you think. It might help to get it off your chests and put it on the table—I mean, on the screen."

"What's the address again?" asks Mrs. Jones as she pulls a pen and paper out of her purse.

Rocky shouts, "Lightsoutenterprises.com! Great idea, Maddy!"

I take a moment to be alone outside. I watch the moonlight glisten over the serene lake water and I start to cry, sniffling over my own memories of Guy and how beautiful this tribute to him has been.

"Care for a cup of tea?" says a voice in the dark behind me.

I turn around, shocked to see Victor Winston standing in silhouette. "Victor! Hi...what are you doing here?!"

"You did write 'come whenever,' for that advisory board meeting regarding Lights Out, but I have to say, from the looks of it, you're doing just fine."

"I—I had no idea when you were coming. How long have you been here?"

"I've been lurking in the back since Lillian Jones got up to speak. I didn't want to interrupt. I'm sorry about Guy. Sounds like he was truly beloved."

I realize I had mistaken the shadow in the back of the room for Sally, when all along it was Victor.

"Was that your brother Daniel, the poet?" I nod. "He's quite talented. And your mother's quite an emcee. Now I know where you get it."

"So you saw...pretty much everything."

"Pretty much. And I saw you light up. I have to say, you can take the woman out of the sunshine, but you can't take the sunshine out of the woman."

I smile. No one's referred to me as "sunshine" since Uncle Sam passed away. Siddhartha finds me outside, clearly looking to make sure I'm okay.

"This must be Sid," says Victor, bending down to gently pet her and instantly endearing himself to her. "Hello, Sid. She's sweet."

"Yeah, sweet and mischievous at the same time. Siddhartha, say 'hi five' to Victor." Siddhartha lifts her paw in the air. Victor smiles, and Sid licks his face.

"Siddhartha is her full name?"

"Yes. We're on a journey together."

"Any discoveries to report?"

"The joy of unconditional love for starters," I say, giving Siddhartha a warm hug. "So how was your trip?"

"Good," he says. "I checked into the Comfort Inn downtown."

I had wondered about that—where he would stay if he came and if I should offer Uncle Sam's place. I am relieved to hear that he didn't make any assumptions.

The back door swings open and Sierra and Milton appear. Sierra immediately recognizes Victor.

"Victor. Hi. This is Milton. Milton, Victor. What brings you here?"

"I thought it was time for an advisory board meeting with Maddy. Are you still on the board? You're welcome to join us."

"It's at the local bowling alley," I add.

"Oh, darn, I'm going out of town," says Sierra.

"You are?" asks Milton.

"Hmm…I forgot to tell you," she says. "Maddy, it was a very meaningful evening. I'm proud of you. We've got to get back to Ann Arbor now."

"Thanks for all your help."

Sierra camouflages a whisper in my ear with a goodbye hug. "Let your fire shine." She winks at me as they leave, then Eleanor appears.

"Maddy?"

"Mom, over here. I want you to meet someone." Eleanor walks over to where we're standing in the light. "Mom, this is Victor Winston. He's the guy who seconded Uncle Sam on Lights Out. Victor, this is my mom."

"It's a pleasure to meet you. You've got quite a daughter."

"Thank you, I know." She looks him over. "Would you like a sandwich?"

"I'd love one."

For the remainder of the evening, I introduce Victor to my family, to Richard Wright and to bar friends. Richard and

I notice Wally offer to escort Sally home. We share a glance, one that humbly recognizes the ironies of how one event leads to another.

The next day, Victor meets me at Uncle Sam's place. Victor plays Frisbee with Sid outside while I make lemonade. I bring two glasses out.

Victor takes a long sip, staring at the sailboats and jet skiers. "It's beautiful out here. Kind of hard to imagine bowling indoors right about now. What do you say we postpone our meeting and take in the great outdoors of Michigan?"

"I'm game. What do you suggest?"

"Is there somewhere I can teach you the art of the Eskimo roll? It's a powerful negotiating tactic when it comes to kayaking."

"Yeah, and I know just the place. Follow me." I drive us to the Canoe-Kayak Livery on the Huron River, where we rent two sea kayaks with skirts for flipping.

The river moves under a warm breeze. Victor kayaks away from shore and gallantly offers a demo.

"All you have to do is flick your hip to twist it over and then use your waist to swing you through to the surface." I watch him maneuver the apparatus with a quick underwater sideways somersault, returning to the surface on the other side, his lean muscular body arching to bring him back to center gravity above the river's surface. Glistening water drips from his biceps.

I give it a try. At first being upside down underwater freaks me out, but then, I've already died, so this is really nothing. After several attempts and under Victor's coaching prowess, I actually get it. *Another first,* I think to myself. Is it the teacher or the student? Or some willing, ready and able combination of the two?

We take some mild rapids and find ourselves invigorated by the challenge. I realize it is indeed a negotiation with immovable nature as I maneuver through jagged rocks and swirling eddies.

Later, as the sun sets on Clark Lake, Victor and I take Siddhartha for a walk along the water's edge. I wear my Stansbury top hat, explaining to Victor the origins of my entrepreneurship. He smiles at my off-key attempt to sing. Siddhartha jumps for a reprise at a dance with me. Victor's eyes flicker with affection. We decide to go to the bowling alley for our supposed meeting over burgers and ten pins.

Victor bowls a strike, as usual. I pick a ball and remember to keep my vision on the pins. I use the spot technique and the arrows and I roll a strike. I offer Victor a swagger and a smile.

"I see you found a cocky side to yourself during all that digging and excavating," he laughs. "What else did you find, Maddy?"

"Self-acceptance. I'm just polishing it up right now." I grin. "Watch yourself, for I shall soon be a glistening morass of confident energy."

"I look forward to it."

Carl brings us our burgers and we dive in. Then I venture the first business question. "Victor, do you think Lights Out will ever see the light of day again?"

"I do."

"How can you be so sure?"

"Faith."

"So, have I missed anything in the *Journal?* I can't help but hear the local reactions to Tribute in a Box—is there anything in the news on Derek Rogers?"

"If there was, I wouldn't tell you."

"Why not?"

"I'd like to see where you go without his negative influence on you."

"Okay. I'll tell you where I want to go. I started a blog so people in town would have a place to put their anger about Derek's monopoly. But more importantly, it's a place for them to put their feelings about grief and a way to raise money for a Tribute Service Fund for those who can't afford it. Everyone deserves basic rights in life. I think they deserve them in death, too."

"So everyone deserves a tribute like the one Guy had?"

"Yes...because no one deserves to die anonymously. The more a society values their dead, the more they value their living. And because I wonder, are we all the millwright, Victor, or the poet?"

"Maybe we're a little of both, Maddy."

I shake my head and bite into my burger. "Please, no more conundrums."

"Okay, as your adviser, what would you like me to advise?"

"Help me get advertisers for the blog so I have enough funds to run it."

"That sounds like a request for action, not advice," he says.

I stare at him. I feel a long-lost fire inside.

"Okay," he says, "I'll help get advertisers for your blog. Who knows? Maybe Norm Pearl and Arthur Pintock will go for it."

I hold my beer up for him and we clink bottles. "Thanks," I say. "Speaking of Norm Pearl, what do you know about the stars?"

"Very little, but I have a feeling I'm about to learn a lot more."

The sky is black. The stars are out in full force. Victor and I lie on our backs inside the little Sunfish in the middle of

Clark Lake, quietly drinking beer and stargazing. "Did you know that on a really dark night you can see a thousand stars?"

"Only a thousand, huh?" asks Victor.

"I guess that depends on your vision. Did you know farmers used the constellations to know when to plant? Kind of like a mnemonics game of survival and entertainment. Oh, I think I see Sirius. Also known as the Dog Star, part of Orion." I draw the shape with my finger in the sky for him. "See it?"

"I see the rabbit on the moon."

"Doesn't count. If it's not an established constellation, you have to make one up."

"Oh, sorry. I didn't know we were playing the constellation game. In that case, you go first so I can get the hang of it."

"Okay. I see…a giant eighteen-hole golf course in the sky."

"Sure it's not a thousand-hole golf course?"

"That depends on how many beers you have." I giggle. "Your turn."

"Okay, I see…Clark Lake…with a boat in the middle of it and…wait a minute, wow, that is incredible!"

"What?"

"I see a giant bowling ball…and ten pins. See?" He draws the ball and pins in the sky. Sure enough, there it is.

"Victor? Is there anything you can't do?"

"I can't drink more than two beers at a time without needing a restroom. And I'm on my third."

"Copy that," I say and stealthily sail us back in.

We're greeted by Siddhartha, who carries a toy over to us. Victor hits the bathroom and then obliges her with a stint of tug-of-war.

"Would you like something else, Victor? I have water and I have Uncle Sam's stash of whiskey."

"Water's good. But will you show me that famous fishing lure collection of his?"

"Do you fish?"

"Everyone fishes." He smiles. "Just depends on what you're fishing for."

"Oh…really? And what do you fish for, Mr. Winston?" I ask as I lead him to the second bedroom that doubles as a fine-art fishing-lure museum collection.

"Well, let's see. I fish for business opportunities. I fish for consumer opportunities. I fish for——"

"How about fish? Do you fish for fish?"

"I prefer fishing for restaurants that serve them."

"Choosing the right lure depends on the object of your attention." I open the door, revealing my uncle's prize collection. Cases of fishing lures neatly organized, catalogued and identified by date, artist, quality and purpose. "There's a lot of artistry and craftsmanship behind the art of the lure. For example, take a look at this lure, the Trout-a-Tooni, designed to lure only the most beautiful trout ever born—the queen trout, if you will." I see I have Victor's full attention.

"Yes, especially if one is fishing…for love," he says, looking at me intently now.

I gaze back, feeling that this moment is one we've both been secretly moving toward. He takes me in his arms.

"Maddy, I've wondered what it would be like to kiss you for a long time. May I?"

"I—I was hoping you would."

He leans toward me while gently pulling me closer. His mouth touches mine, and we kiss, long and sensuously. He pulls back from me and says, "Now that's a catch."

I laugh. "You're a catch yourself."

He lifts me up and carries me to the bedroom. Our passion increases as our kisses intensify. It feels good to be so connected to the present. Then I feel myself start to squirm, holding back, as the photo of the mysterious woman in Victor's office haunts the moment.

"Is everything okay?" asks Victor, gently removing my blouse.

Sierra's words come forth in my mind. *"Let your fire shine."* I don't want this to end. My curiosity has waited this long. It can wait just a little while longer. I murmur, "Everything's fine. You feel great, Victor. You feel great."

"You, too," he says, burying his face in the crook of my neck to kiss me again.

We make beautiful love, after which I privately rejoice in the awareness that for a while, my workaholic on-button has finally been turned off and a personal one activated instead. We cuddle in the aftermath.

"Are you all right?" he asks, gently stroking my face.

"Oh, yes, that was a beautiful merger." I smile back at him.

"No barriers to entry?" he quips.

"Almost."

He turns on his side to look directly at me. "Almost?"

"I, uh, I need to know something."

"Then ask… I promise to answer."

"Who's the woman in the photo with you, the one in your office? You seem so close to her—I mean, it looks like a lot of love there."

Victor's eyes glaze. For a moment he seems to stop breathing. It's the only time I've seen him remotely trip up.

"That's my sister."

"You told me you didn't have any sibling rivalries."

"I don't…because she died. Five years ago. In a car accident. Her name was Shoshanna. She was twenty-six."

"I'm so sorry." I gently stroke his chest and cheeks. "Were you close?"

"Very."

We are both silent for a while. "Is that why you got involved in Lights Out?"

"No, not consciously at least…though I had experienced grief on that level…and her funeral service was an absolute injustice to her—but then, we were all in shock."

"How are your parents?"

"My parents. My parents are still grieving. I don't believe they'll ever stop. It's one thing to grieve, it's another to allow it to debilitate you."

"Sometimes grief triggers depression," I inform him.

"Yes. It certainly can." A hint of anger drips through his vocal cords.

"Sounds like you're upset about that. Do you want to talk about it?" I ask, realizing the paraphrasing has become second nature now.

He falls on his back and sighs. "Sometimes, yes, I get upset. I think because my parents are so consumed by their grief, there's no room for me. And I'm part of the living."

"So you do have a sibling rivalry, Victor. It's just a post-mortem one."

"You're right." He pauses.

"I've gotten better at listening."

Another idea hits me. "Hey, Victor, what if you could redo the past? I mean, what if you prepared a tribute ceremony for your sister that really did justice to who she was? You know, the way Lights Out would do it. Do you think maybe a life celebration for her now would help bring some closure to your parents' grief?"

"I think your optimism is endearing…but impractical," he says, then takes me in his arms and holds me close to him.

"I don't," I murmur as we both drift to sleep.

In the soft dawn light, we make love again. Victor kisses me on my neck and murmurs, "How come an attractive, complex, beautiful lure like you hasn't caught the fish of your dreams?"

I murmur between kisses. "Because this little lure's been waiting for the right value proposition while foolishly playing the results." Before I can ask the same of him, our mutual passion overwhelms us.

He envelops me in his arms. "God, you feel good, Maddy." He smothers me with more kisses and I melt in his embrace. I'm swept away. Then, exhausted from lovemaking, we fall asleep again.

The clock on the nightstand indicates nine when Sid jumps on the bed offering morning facials. Victor wakes up and sees the time. "Maddy, beautiful. I've got to get going. I need to call a cab. I can't miss my plane."

"You don't need to call a cab. I'll drive you." I hop out of bed and let Siddhartha outside, then I scoot to the closet. Still half asleep, I quickly don some jeans and a black T-shirt. I step into some shoes, but pay no attention to what I've got on. We hop in the car.

Victor glances at my shirt and suddenly clams up, withdrawing his intimacy. Maybe it's a guy thing, maybe he's just nervous about flying, maybe he's got some pending deal on the table or maybe I was just a love opportunity to be fished and cast back to sea. Whatever it was, it hurt.

I drive toward the airport, fidgeting with the radio dial. I turn to him. "Do you always get so quiet before getting on a plane?"

"I have a lot to think about."

"What do you think about…us?"

"I think…we both had a really wonderful time. But I think we're both committed to playing our results."

"I'm done playing my results. I'm ready to play the present, Victor."

"Are you?" he asks, glancing at my T-shirt. "Then I guess I'm not."

A chill runs down my spine as I pull up to the gate. I had let the fire rage and now I felt it quickly extinguished by the words rolling off his tongue. Well, I've come full circle, I suddenly realize. Wasn't it a year and a half ago that Seth dropped me off at the airport for Tara's funeral, and I, too, though less succinctly, carried out the same objective? But this was different, I had thought. Where did I go wrong? And why was I suddenly blaming myself?

"I had a great time. Thanks. We'll be in touch." He pecks me on the cheek and dashes out of the car with his carry-on luggage.

"Victor, wait." He turns around. "You know what? Um, forget about the advertisers for the blog. I'll handle it myself."

"Okay," he says, nodding. "Bye." And he resumes his run inside.

I stare after him, confused, my heart bleeding from yet another wound, this time a wound not from the dead, but from the living.

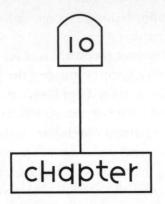

chapter

10

Organizational Strategy: The Resurrection of Lights Out

Richard and I work the bar serving drinks and chitchatting. Close to the register sits a pad of yellow legal paper with notes scribbled all over it under the heading of Table of Contents. I've got a red pen stuck behind one ear and a yellow Magic Marker behind the other ear as I pour Wally his usual. Richard's at the other end of the bar listening to Rocky.

"Did I ever tell you about the time I had to clean out my brother's closet?" asks Rocky. "Picnic it was not. My mom couldn't handle it. Just seeing his old baseball mitt tore her apart. He was the all-star pitcher, ya know, all through college. Did I tell you that? He had such a bright future. My father made sure he had to be out of town when we opened up the closet. He couldn't even come within ten feet of Glenn's bedroom without losing it. It was…an emotional mess."

I pull my pen from behind my ear and thoughtfully jot some notes on the pad.

"Did your parents ever recover?" asks Richard.

"Yeah," says Rocky, then he finishes the last of his beer. "A few years later, they rented out his room to a college kid and they became this sort of minifamily. They all kind of saved each other. Hey, thanks for listening, man. I gotta run." Rocky winks at Richard and starts to head out the door.

I lift a finger toward Rocky. "Um, Rocky, I didn't get any…"

Rocky shakes his head. "Sorry, Maddy. No mail today."

"Okay, thanks. I was just wondering…because sometimes you forget to put the mail in the mailbox and then sometimes you forget to bring it to the bar. But that's cool. It's not like I don't have enough to read here between books on death and blogs on funerals, ya know."

Rocky offers a perfunctory nod. "Right," he says, and leaves.

"You know," says Richard. "Sometimes loss is not about the dead. A lot of times it's about the living."

I stare at him. "Do you see that sign?" I point to a hand-written note on the cash register: "No Conundrums Allowed."

Richard grins. "I forgot. Look, sometimes you have to confront your pain by faking the death of someone who's hurt you in order to move on."

I quickly change the subject because, well, it's too friggin' painful. "Hmm. Thanks. But you know what, Richard? I think we should have a section on how to Confront the Closet. You know, how do you deal with grief when you have to face the articles that represented the very life of the deceased? It was hard enough with Uncle Sam. I can't imagine how it must be for a parent who loses a child or for a couple who loses a spouse, even if it's a couple that only just started to have a life together after bonding over athletic activities like bowling and Eskimo rolls and…other stuff…but then it ended for some unknown reason…"

"Impossible," pipes in Wally. "Grief is a can of worms. And if you can hand me a road map on that one, by golly, bring it on. Could have saved me years. Instead—I let the moths destroy everything in the closet. And now I'm helping Sally through it."

"How are you helping her?" asks Richard.

"I let her talk about every single memory that comes up from every single piece of clothing. Takes a long time. We're just getting through his socks right now." Wally sips his drink. "Joe had a lot of socks…and every one of them tells a story."

I frown, wondering what kind of stories all those socks could tell.

Richard cocks his head toward me. "What are the chapter headings so far?"

I read from our list. "Okay, not in any particular order…here we go—How to Connect with Survivors, Lessons on Paraphrasing, The Role of Experience Design, Criteria for Designing Authentic Customized Tributes, Human Tribute Stories, Pet Tribute Stories, Life Celebration Suggestions for the Soul, Estate Planning, Syndicating Pre-Needs, and…I just added Confronting the Closet…oh, and there's the Directory of Resources."

"I say add it to the list. Closets are dark and scary enough as it is, man," says Carl, who's been listening to the ping-pong conversations at the bar. Carl operates the local bowling alley; he hands me a bowling shirt with my name on it. "Here ya go, Maddy. She's all yours—on the house."

"Thanks," I reply, delighted with the addition to my wardrobe.

Richard ponders this for a moment and then in one swift

motion he hits the mute button on the remote for the television set, lifts a small iron rod and bangs an iron dinner bell. A ring bellows through the restaurant and bar. Everyone stops, frozen in place, and looks up toward the bar where Richard stands.

"All in favor of a chapter on cleaning out the closet of a loved one who's passed, raise your hand."

The entire clientele raise their hands. Richard and I share a look. As everyone drops their arms and goes back to their business, I make a note on the pad. Richard punches the mute button again, allowing the sounds on the television to return to life.

"Okay, we'll work on that chapter tonight," he says.

"Great," I say. Then I see the clock. "Oops, I forgot to roll last call." I hit the mute button on the remote for the television set again, lift the iron rod and tap the dinner bell. No one hears it. I tap again, louder this time. Everyone stops and looks my way.

"Sorry to interrupt again," I announce. "But tonight is last call on handing in those Tribute Stories for Pets, Friends, Lovers, Businesses, Beliefs, and, well, anything that constitutes a loss. Oh, and that includes living and breathing lovers who leave you for no good reason, especially after they've given you the impression that everything is swell…so, um, where was I? Oh, yeah, the most moving and descriptive tales will be in the pamphlet. Pens and paper are in the straw hat at the end of the bar. And don't forget to add your names and the city you're from."

People pull out notebooks, scraps of paper with their already written stories. Some head to the bar for paper and pen. Lana, a girl in her early twenties and part-time college student, hands me her story on lined loose-leaf paper. "I wrote about my horse, Jet, who passed away last year. Thanks for doing this, Maddy. It felt really good to write about him. I hope you use it."

"Hey, thank you, Lana, for participating," I reply. "I'm glad it made you feel better." I add her story to the folder lying next to the register. As Lana exits the bar, I turn around to pull down one of the many books on the sociology and psychology of grieving that now line a shelf next to the liquor bottles. I open the book to where a bookmark rests and start reading where I left off. I pull the yellow Magic Marker from behind my other ear and highlight a passage: "Sharing your grief with others is a crucial and necessary function of healthy grieving." I think about that, and glance over at Richard, then I close the book and start writing on my pad.

Dear Madison,
I must share and mourn the death of my lover with you.
He lost it in an Eskimo roll on the Huron River—no,
scratch that—he was destroyed by an army of giant ten-
pins in a bowling alley—

"Hey, Maddy. Can I have a Hefivisen when you get a chance?"

I look up. The young, strapping Pete Gallagher, a blond, blue-eyed electrical engineer from Grass Valley, smiles at me over the bar. He sits down with his sports section of the *Detroit Free Press* under his arm. I bring him his beer. "How's the log cabin coming, Pete?"

"Good. I'm done with the outer framework and starting on the fireplace now. Hey, you want to go stone hunting with me sometime?"

I think it over. "I'm not ready yet."

"That guy really took it out of you, huh?"

I immediately sit down next to Pete, my obsession with

loss superceding any obligatory bartending duties. "How do you know when it's right?"

"I'm still trying to figure that out. But this book says, when you know you don't have to question it."

"What book?"

Pete opens up his newspaper, a camouflage for his true literary interests. Inside is the latest self-help book on relationships, titled *The Menu of Relationships: How to Order Up What You Want.*

I nod. "Huh. How many of those self-help relationship books have you read?" I ask, peering at its contents.

"I think this is my thirty-seventh one."

I nod. "Fair enough. Let me know if you find any answers."

Donny walks into the bar with a scruffy beard around his face and bad sunburn. Everyone cheers. I look at Richard. "Did I miss something?"

Richard winks at me and raises a shot glass. "To Donny, winner of 'How Long Can You Stay on the Lake?' Answer: Eleven days, twelve hours and thirty-six minutes. To Donny, one martini boat special on the house comin' up—that is after you wipe some of that grime off your face." Richard tosses him a disposable shaver, and the people in the bar cheer again.

Donny smiles, lifting his hands for a moment of quiet. "Thank you, all, for your support. I couldn't have done it without Wally's pontoon boat, Lillian's homemade pies, Sally's homemade lemonade or Eagle's Nest's burgers. Thanks again. And don't forget about Rusty Uzzle's Hermit Crab Race next week. Ten bucks a crab and all the proceeds go to the school. Beers are on me."

After serving a round of beers, I duck into the office to check my e-mails—still nothing from Victor. But I do find an e-mail from Norm Pearl telling me a check is in the mail for five thousand dollars for five months of advertisements on my blog. I smile, muttering, "Yeah, Norm!" I check the Lights Out blog where a banner ad promotes "Pearl Living— affordable work-live spaces from Chicago to New York." Under the Express Yourself category, I find eight more stories about dead pets, twelve stories about funerals and six more opinions about the state of funeral practices in this country. I print them out and then take them behind the bar to show Richard.

"You are not going to believe this," I tell him. "According to Stan Hope in Oklahoma, the Tribute in a Box funeral home down there figured out how not to show their customers the casket price list."

"He has to show the CPL and the general price list, otherwise it's a ten-thousand-dollar fine for every violation," Richard states indignantly.

"Apparently, they get away with it by claiming their caskets are all customized. But they really aren't, according to Stan. Only when a customer buys a casket do they stitch the departed's initials on the interior cloth. On top of that, this guy says TIAB tells their clients they can't guarantee extra care and attention on embalming and cemetery maintenance if caskets are purchased from third-party suppliers. So everyone in the town is too intimidated to go elsewhere when TIAB owns the only cemetery around for miles."

Richard shakes his head.

I continue reading from the printouts. "Check this out. A woman writes from Grass Lake that TIAB insinuated embalming was mandatory under state law. When she found it wasn't, she asked for her money back and they refused. Oh, and here's the clincher. TIAB has created an Executive Memorial Society to give discounts to executives. No wonder he ran me out of business."

"He can't do that," says Richard.

"Apparently, under the 'religious groups and memorial societies' section of the funeral rule, he can…and does."

"That's just not right. People need to know about the FTC's Funeral Rule and what their rights are."

"You're right. I'm going to post the entire Funeral Rule on the blog. And I'm going to highlight 'misrepresentations.' In fact, let's have a topic of the week to bring it to the forefront."

"Yes…like informing people that it's against the law for a funeral home to charge a 'casket handling fee' if you decide to buy a casket from someone other than the funeral home itself."

"And that funeral homes are obligated to show CPLs and GPLs especially when pre-need contracts are modified…before or after a death," I say.

"And we have to make sure people know that caskets are not a requirement when you choose direct cremation," Richard adds.

I write that down. "Anything else off the top of your head?"

"Tribute in a Box cannot go around quoting different costs on the phone and then increasing them at the door. I don't care what they say. That's a monster no-no. We need to inform folks that Derek Rogers's company is an exception. Usually, funeral directors are honest, caring people who work hard to serve their communities."

"Got it," I say, writing that down, too. "I'll do these updates tomorrow morning. In the meantime, let's write this chapter on cleaning out the closet."

For the next three weeks, I spend my mornings jogging with Siddhartha, my days updating the blog and pulling in a few more advertisers to keep it running, my evenings bartending and late nights with Richard working on the pamphlet. Together, we lay the groundwork, fine-tune each chapter and compile the many stories we've received from local residents at the bar and from people all over the country who now use the blog to express their opinions and share their stories about funerals.

Finally, one night at 3:00 a.m. in the bar, I print out the final version. I proudly hold it up for Richard. "Here it is…seventy-five pages."

PAMPHLET ON GRIEF WELLNESS & CREATING PERSONALIZED TRIBUTES
By Richard Wright and Madison Banks

Table of Contents

Part I: How to Grieve
Confronting the Closet
Connecting with Your Grief
Connecting with Survivors
Lessons on Paraphrasing
The Loss Outline
Planning Your Own Funeral

Part II: How to Create a Personalized Tribute Experience
The Role of Experience Design
Criteria for Designing Authentic Customized Tributes: Making It Interactive
Elements of Experience Design
Making It Affordable for Everyone
Resources for Authentic Experience Design: Jackson-Ann Arbor—Candelabra Prod. for Life Bio Videos

Part III: What to Know about Pre-Need Arrangements
Your Rights

Pre-Need Investing as part of Estate Planning &
Syndicated Pre-Needs

Part IV:Tribute Stories for the Soul
Human Tribute Stories
Pet Tribute Stories
Suggestions for the Soul

We take turns holding the pamphlet in our hands, feeling
the physical and spiritual weight of our work and our words.
Richard pours two shots of whiskey. We clink glasses. "To
blogging," I say. We smile and toss the drinks back.

A few nights later, I take time off from work. Sierra comes
over. The two of us along with Siddhartha hang out on the
deck. Dusk settles in and the night air's temperature descends
with the crisp smell of changing seasons.

Sierra occupies one lounge chair. I'm in the other. She
reads through the pamphlet, her other hand free to pick up
a mug of hot tea nearby. Siddhartha snuggles between my
legs as I watch a cool breeze tickle a branch of muted green
leaves. The leaves dance in the wind and it feels as if they
are creating a collective modern-dance performance for my
benefit, entertaining me, amusing me, teasing me. I watch,
mesmerized by their performance. Who needs Broadway, I
think, when I've got the Dance of the Leaves? Then the
music of the wind gusts up and one leaf breaks from the
group, ambitious for a solo performance. I watch the fading
green leaf dismount and flutter in a routine of somersaults,
flips and twisted backbends for a graceful and gentle landing on earth. Fall will soon be upon us.

Sierra signals that she's finished by placing the closed pamphlet on her stomach. She whispers, "This is really great, Maddy. I'm amazed at how much you've learned."

Uncomfortable with compliments, I skip her acknowledgment. "But how's the quality of the writing?"

"It's great. Will you try to get a publisher or self-publish it?"

I shake my head. "Publishing is too expensive, and I don't want to spend the time looking."

"Then how are you going to distribute it?"

"I made an e-version and put it online with PPV."

Sierra nods, impressed. "Clever. How much are you charging for the pay-per-view?"

"Two dollars and ninety-nine cents."

"That's smart. You're making it affordable for everyone. What's your protection strategy?"

"I sent a copy to the Library of Congress to copyright it, and I hired a DRM company."

"Digital rights management is safe now?"

"If it's safe enough for the government, it's safe enough for me. But just to make sure, I used my code based on Roman ciphers."

We watch the stars twinkle. A shooting star goes by. "Quick, Maddy, make a wish."

We both shut our eyes and then pop them open again and smile at each other.

"Still no word from Victor?" asks Sierra.

"Not since I last saw him…six weeks and two days ago."

"Okay, so you've got three to six weeks to go."

"For what?" I ask, looking directly at her.

She stares at me. "They always call in threes, Maddy, and always within twelve weeks. It has to do with oxytocin, the hormone that gets released when you're intimate with someone. You'll be hearing from him in three to six weeks. I promise."

"Where did you come up with this theory?"

"I didn't. It's factual, and as reliable as the setting sun. The question is, what are you going to do when he contacts you?"

"First of all, he can't contact me because…because he died…in my mind, a pseudo-death."

Sierra raises a brow. "That deserves an explanation."

"Nothing to explain. My brain conveniently reported that he lost it in a bowling alley, an attack of the giant bowling pins. Victor no longer exists."

"Oh, boy, sweetie. You must have really fallen for him."

"I let the fire shine and…and now it's out, Sierra. That's all there is to it. I've finally gotten my risk management down to a science. Come on, let's go inside and watch this movie I rented. Hey, Sid, wake up."

The three of us head inside the cottage and cozy up on the couch. I turn the television on and pop the VHS tape into the machine. The film score begins and I join Sid and Sierra on the couch.

"We're watching *Remains of the Day?*" asks Sierra. "This is one of the saddest movies ever made, about a love that never gets consummated. It's heart-wrenching."

"Exactly. I've been watching it because it makes me realize how important it is not to allow the past or the future to hijack the present. It's my risk-management reinforcement program."

"Sounds like emotional torture. Are you sure it helps when you see the characters say goodbye without ever telling one another how they really feel?"

I start to get weepy. "Please don't say that G-word. And I think they handle their loss quite well. They're very dignified about it." Siddhartha licks my tears.

"That's because their characters are trained not to express their feelings."

"It's not their fault. It's because of the era they live in."

"But, Maddy, sweetie, we don't live in that era. So, tell me, what are you going to do when he calls...or e-mails you?"

"I trust my delete button will be working just fine."

A few nights later, Richard and I are working in the bar, listening to everyone's feedback about the blog and how helpful it's been. Rocky walks in and waves.

I nod at him. "The usual?"

"You got it. Oh, here's some mail for you, Maddy." He hands me a few envelopes from his mail sack.

I quickly leaf through it. One letter is from Norm Pearl. I open it. There's the check for five thousand dollars. I shout, "Look, Richard! Our first advertising revenue!"

"I'll be damned," says Richard, staring at the check. "What do we do with it?"

"We cash it. And then I reimburse you and Sally and me for Guy's funeral costs. Pay for the Web site's operational costs. The rest goes into a funeral fund for the town of Jackson."

"You would really do that? Start a funeral fund here?"

"Why not? Corporate philanthropy and stakeholder interests are just as important as profit and loss statements."

Suddenly everyone sitting at the bar listening—Carl, Rocky, Wally, Donny and Mrs. Jones—lift a glass and they shout in unison, "To Madison Banks and the Funeral Fund of Jackson!"

I look at Richard. "Jeez, is that all you have to do to get a toast around here?"

I open another envelope from my digital rights management company. My eyes pop open to discover another check. This one is for twelve grand. I do a major double take. "Whoa! Is this right? We just got another check for twelve thousand dollars for the pamphlet!"

"That means four thousand people bought the pamphlet online in one week," Richard says, thinking out loud.

"That is so friggin' awesome! You guys should write that thing in different languages," hollers Rocky.

"Can you translate it into Russian? I know my grandma would appreciate that," yells Carl.

"My relatives in Mykonos would like to see it in Greek," chimes in Mrs. Jones.

"Maybe you should check the blog," says Richard.

"Right." I turn to where Richard has finally made room for the computer beside the register so I don't have to run back and forth to the office all the time. I log on to the blog. It's clogged with messages from all over the country. But of course, my eye zeroes in on one particular message, a message from Victor Winston. Pain, fear and love all shoot through my heart together like a recipe gone south from the wrong mix of ingredients. I take a deep breath and with all my emotional might hit the delete button, banishing him. I swallow the lump in my throat and focus on the present moment at the Eagle's Nest on Clark Lake in Jackson, Michigan, in the United States of America in the Northern Hemisphere on planet Earth.

"Are there a lot of messages?" asks Richard.

"There're over a thousand," I say, scanning them. "Wow. A lot of people want to know if there are workshops available for personalized tribute training."

"That's a wonderful idea," says Mrs. Jones. "Why not have them right here?"

Richard and I turn to each other. The lights go on behind our eyes.

One week later in the restaurant area of the bar, Richard and I face a group of ten participants sitting on bar stools in a circle. Richard sits calmly and addresses everyone. "Welcome. Welcome to the first three-day workshop here at the Eagle's Nest on how to create nontraditional personalized tribute experiences. Experiences that can be affordable for everyone."

The group claps. That's my cue.

"We thought we'd start by asking all of you to take turns telling us your name, why you're here and what you hope to achieve—personally that is. How about you, would you like to start?" I ask the dark-haired fortysomething woman to my right.

The woman clears her throat. "Hi, everyone. My name is Cheryl. I'm a former mortgage broker turned housewife from Toledo, Ohio, and I'm here because Tribute in a Box feels more like funerals-in-a-box. All they've really managed to do is turn personalization into a mass market, which completely defeats the purpose to begin with. So I'm here to learn about preparing personalized pre-need services for my husband, my dog and myself."

"Hi. I'm Bob. I'm a fireman from Grand Rapids," says a man in his thirties. "I'd like to learn how to put together my own tribute since I'm in a risky profession, but I also want to know how to work it into my estate planning as an investment."

To Bob's right is a twenty-one-year-old. "Hi. I'm Dana. I'm from Detroit and I want to learn how to deal with the loss of my parents and plan a belated tribute for them."

"I'm Leo Darnell. I'm a funeral director at a small funeral home outside of Chicago," says a man in his fifties. "I want to learn how to be a better funeral director, especially because the community I serve is requesting more and more nontraditional services."

And so on and so forth…the workshops multiply. They grow from ten to twenty people at a time, which is the limit that Richard and I can handle. Suddenly the town of Jackson discovers tourism, where there was none before. Now all the local motels, restaurants and shops are experiencing a small boom. And new businesses sprout up, in Clark Lake style of course, like Stargazing Midnight Cruises on pontoon boats. People sign up to learn about the celestial bodies and the mythology of constellations.

The Eagle's Nest remains the local bar at night, but transforms into our workshop headquarters during the day. During breaks, Richard and I serve drinks and food. The workshops become a hot spot where people get to know who they are and what they want as we guide them through grief, pseudodeath and how to create participative experiences.

I go all out in developing the workshops. I include a special speaker hour every night at the bar for both the workshop attendees and the locals. I have my mother Eleanor come to tell "Funeral Tales" and my father Charlie talk about the myths surrounding death across cultures. Sometimes Daniel appears to create and recite an on-the-spot memorial poem from audience members' stories. And sometimes, Roy Vernon shows up and he and Daniel riff together on a customized poem, turning it into an improvised ballad.

At one point, I even bring in a famed financial adviser to discuss pre-need investment planning and how to make those dollars pay for your time of need and still leave a small fortune in your estate, or how to get quarterly dividends and interest from it, and even how to create a "syndicated pre-need investment group," so it's almost like a small town's personal mutual fund. Soon I begin hearing how all financial planners are stressing the importance of pre-need arrangements of your tribute as a fundamental part of estate planning.

I invite Sierra to come and teach people how to make a

life bio video. I follow this up with local artists, sculptors, photographers, weavers and so forth talking about what they can add to a life celebration to make it unique for each individual's passing.

One evening, Eleanor says, "This is kind of like the stone soup of life-celebration-making, dear. Everyone pitches in something they can offer, and suddenly you've fed the whole town with something truly emotionally nurturing."

"And it works because it's authentic," adds Charlie.

Word continues to spread through the blog and through local newspapers. People come from all over the world for our workshops and guest-lecture series. I even invite my artistic cousins from around the globe, including the llama-wool weaver, the violinist and the modern dancer. Richard and I use the money generated by the sale of the online pamphlets to pay for the guest speakers. As for the workshops, we ask for money only on a donation basis and add that to the Funeral Fund, which we leverage to make more money through dollar-cost-averaging investment practices.

One night at the bar, Pete Gallagher approaches me. "My log cabin is all done and, well, I'd like to invite you over for dinner. How about it?"

I blush. "Okay, I'd like that," I say. Richard catches on and orders me to take the night off and leave immediately. "But I need to check the blog and e-mails," I retort.

"That can wait until tomorrow. Go. Have some fun."

"Okay, I'll just take my cell phone in case you need me."

Ten miles down the road, I enter Pete's now-completed log home on several acres of land. I am amazed at what Pete has managed to do with his own bare hands. Every log, every stone in the twenty-foot-high fireplace had been put in place by him. "This is incredible!" I announce. Siddhartha happily runs around.

"Thanks," he replies, pouring me a glass of wine while he stokes a meal of Tex Mex-style chicken with a scrumptious aroma. "It just needs some help on the interior decorating. That's where I kind of fall short."

As I'm about to take a sip of my wine, my cell phone rings. I reach for it, only to discover the caller ID reads "Victor." Under my breath I mutter, "Why now?"

Pete looks at me. "It's that guy, right? I swear it's always like that. One of the books I read said that's to be expected. It's kind of like a test to see if you can move on."

"Well, I already did move on. And he no longer exists, therefore I can't answer it." I close my eyes and turn the phone off.

"Another book I read talked about that, too," Pete informs me. "They call it denial. The author said pretending to move on is not the same thing as really moving on."

"Yeah? Well, what about that phrase 'fake it till you make it'?"

"Doesn't count when it comes to breakups. At least according to twelve out of forty-two authors I read."

"What do *you* think, Pete?" I ask him.

"I'm not sure," he says, thinking it over.

"Well, why aren't you in a relationship?"

"I'm not sure. I keep trying to figure it out."

"Are you sure about anything?"

"Yeah, I'm sure I want a brick-red couch for the living room...but I'm not sure."

I nod at him. "Well...I'm sure you'll figure it out."

"Yeah, I've got about twenty-five books on decorating to read. What do you think? Brick red, forest green...or caramel brown?"

"Hmm. I think some sort of mushy gray might be more

fitting." I don't know if Pete got the metaphor, but it was black-and-white to me that I no longer cared to find out.

I prepare for a small group of seven workshoppers at the bar. I am taking roll call and waiting for Richard to show up when I realize that Grace Pintock, Arthur's estranged wife and Tara's mother, has joined the group. Siddhartha seems to sense some sort of connection and stays close to Grace.

I privately approach her. "It's so good to see you. How are you, Mrs. Pintock?"

"I'm getting along, Madison, getting along. You know, some days are functional and some days aren't. But…call me Grace, will you, please," she says, offering me a warm hug, and then she sits back down.

As I return to finishing the roll, a tall, chunky man in an oversize jacket enters the bar. He sports a thick gray beard, a low-hanging baseball hat and dark sunglasses, making it difficult to see his face.

"Hi, there," I say. "Are you here for the workshop?"

The man nods. I check my paperwork and then look back at him. "You must be Alex Barber. Welcome."

He shuffles a note over to me. The note reads "I'm a high school baseball coach from Cleveland, and unfortunately I've come down with laryngitis but this is the only week I could do this."

"No problem, Alex," I say. "Everybody, this is Alex. He's got laryngitis so he won't be able to give much feedback, at least verbal feedback. Alex, if you want to come back another time to get the full benefit out of this workshop just let me know."

He nods thanks and sits down. "Do I know you?" I ask.

"You seem so familiar." He emphatically shakes his head. "Okay, well, let's get started. Please open your pamphlets to page one. We're going to teach all of you how to confront the closet of a loved one who's passed on, how to create a loss timeline and how to plan your own funeral, because we've discovered that by planning in advance for your time of need you actually re-energize your own life. We'll also show you how to make pre-need investment planning worthwhile. One of the wonderful experiences you'll gain here is to create new ways of honoring our memories, both for others and for ourselves."

During the lunch break, Grace turns to Alex. "Would you like some help ordering from the menu?" Alex nods. He seems so shy and yet so familiar. Grace also brings him some napkins. And it's the napkins that give him away. I can't help but notice when he nervously rubs his hands together on the napkins and then on his pants. Something's not right. I get a twitch in my belly. I check the cars in the parking lot—no Ohio plates. I see Alex do the nervous napkin thing again and my stomach turns.

When Alex stands outside eating a burger by himself, I whisper a command to Siddhartha. Siddhartha runs over to Alex and jumps on him, and in the scuffle his baseball hat and sunglasses are knocked off, causing his beard to hang crooked. Siddhartha proudly holds the hat in her mouth. Alex attempts to regain his balance, but then his "stomach" falls from beneath his shirt, or rather, the padding does.

I realize I'm staring at Jonny Bright. My mouth drops. "I don't believe it. What the hell are you doing here?"

"Now listen to me, Maddy, before you jump to any far-fetched conclusions—"

"Far-fetched conclusions? You sneak into my workshop in disguise and I'm the one who's not supposed to jump to conclusions? Besides your quest for competitive intelligence knowing no boundaries…what is *wrong* with you?"

"Hey, you can't discriminate against me! I have a right to come to this and I knew you wouldn't—"

"Wouldn't want you to be here? Gee, I wonder why. Read the fine print, Jonny. I have the right to turn anyone away. So shoo! You are not welcome here."

"Before you make assumptions, like you tend to do—"

"Whatever idle threats you have to say, keep them to yourself."

"Listen to me, Maddy. Derek's in tight with the cats in D.C. He can shut you down in a heartbeat because you're in violation of the new Funeral Rule and—"

"And what? Our little blogship has no affiliation with any funeral homes. Furthermore, we work on a donation basis only. We don't provide a service nor produce one. We only offer ideas to help others facilitate their own life celebrations. We're simply an information provider, Jonny. Therefore we're exempt from the new Funeral Rule. Tell Derek to take *that* to his attorney!"

Richard, Grace Pintock and the rest of the participants watch me give Jonny Bright the verbal boot.

Richard saunters up to Jonny with a John Wayne swagger and a menacing frown. He stands right over him, his face and posture stern. He says, "You ought to be ashamed of yourself. A man who hides behind a silly costume is no man at all."

Without another word Jonny sheepishly gets in his car and drives off. Siddhartha barks after him, dutifully protecting the bar, the workshoppers and me. I collect myself and return inside.

Grace quietly approaches. "What was that all about, Maddy?"

"That…that's what you call corporate espionage, an occupational hazardous by-product of big business where some competitors will stop at nothing."

"My goodness," says Grace. "I had no idea. Is that in all businesses? Even the mortgage business?"

"Across the board and around the globe," I say flatly. "Most wars these days are waged on corporate battlefields."

On the last night of the workshop when all is said and done, Grace and I sit on the bar stools talking before the bar opens to the public.

"I can't thank you enough," says Grace. "This workshop has given me a whole new outlook on life and a way for me to continue loving Tara in a healthy way."

"I'm so glad, Grace. By the way, is it okay to ask—how's Arthur?"

"We don't talk much. He seems to be moving on with his life. I did send him a copy of your pamphlet because it's time we go through Tara's closet. In fact, I'd like to plan a memorial for her, Lights Out style. Can I write up some ideas and come back to talk to you about it?"

"Of course, Grace. Come in anytime."

"Thank you. But I don't want to be sad anymore tonight, Maddy. I'd like to buy you a drink. How about the Guy Special or Uncle Sam's Favorite?"

I glance at the chalkboard on the wall that is now labeled with drinks in memory of loved ones who frequented the bar or are related to those that do. The list includes Joe's Choice, Glenn's Pitch, Jet's Last Run and Tara's Song. "I'll have Jet's Last Run, lemonade with a shot of iced tea.

Thanks." I start to get up, but Richard winks at me from behind the bar.

"I got it, you sit," he says, and starts fixing me the drink.

From the television that hangs above the bar, CNBN's signature music carries over to the group of us sitting on bar stools. I glance up, only to see Derek Rogers sitting smugly in front of the camera on *James Malek Live*. The caption beneath him reads "The Heartache Handbook for Tributes in a Box."

I feel my pupils dilate and my mouth drop open. "Oh, no, not again!" Richard and Grace and the other workshoppers react and glance up at the screen.

James begins, "We're here with Derek Rogers, wunderkind of Palette Enterprises and now CEO of Tribute in a Box where he's working the same magic." James shifts his attention to Derek. "You turned Palette Enterprises into a gold mine and now you're doing the same in the funeral industry with a chain of mortuaries and funeral homes called Tribute in a Box. Before we get to the book, tell us about these expansion plans you're about to unveil."

"Well, as you know, James, we have over one thousand funeral homes across the country. But now we're in the process of expanding our business tenfold by acquiring an extraordinary number of international, publicly traded and privately owned funeral homes to become the largest conglomerate of mortuaries and funeral homes in the world."

"This has to be an incredibly costly venture."

"Yes, it is, to the tune of two hundred million dollars."

James shakes his head. "Tell me, how do you put together that kind of money?"

"Well, James, we have deals in place with several Fortune 500 companies seeking sound investments for the future, as well as stable mortgage companies like Pintock International who are key to these deals in terms of national and international real estate."

I sit there, stinging in sudden pain, from the implications on-screen.

Grace gently holds my hand. "Maddy, he must not know. That's just not Arthur's style."

"And now you have a book with a major publisher, coming to bookstores nationwide, called *The Heartache Handbook for Tributes in a Box*. I understand this book teaches people how to deal with grief and how to create nontraditional ceremonies that depict the life of the deceased in a celebratory manner. In fact, you even talk about how to get your favorite musician to appear at your funeral for a song or two. For someone who is known to practice an imperialist style of management this is a very heartfelt book. So tell us, Derek, where did you get the idea for it?"

"Well, it was a natural tie-in for our funeral homes, so of course we will be selling them there, as well, but more importantly, James, the book is designed to really help people overcome grief and make a statement about the lives they've lived. It's about creating new ways of honoring our memories."

"You have chapters on how to confront the closet of a loved one who's passed on, as well as a step-by-step plan for your own funeral. I guess that's a kind of do-it-yourself tribute."

"That's right, James. We discovered that by planning in advance for your time of need you actually re-energize your current life."

"And apparently, with this kind of pre-need planning, you've invented a road map for making it a worthwhile investment so it pays for itself when the time of need comes. Is that right?"

"That's right, James. Tribute in a Box provides pre-need investment planning for all of our clients within the guidelines of the FTC's new Funeral Rule. It's really a win–win for everyone—the client, their survivors and us."

"Hey, he's flat-out copycatting you guys," howls one of the workshop participants.

"What are you going to do, Richard?" asks Grace.

Richard just stares at the television.

James Malek wraps up the interview. "Thank you, Derek. Join us tomorrow to…"

Richard clicks off the TV. He looks as numb as I feel, but not too numb to pull a bottle of whiskey off the shelf. "First, I'm going to have an Uncle Sam's Favorite, before I get really mad. Maddy?"

I take a moment to contain my burgeoning anger, then reply void of emotion, "I'm going to meet him on the battlefield." I stare at the blank screen. "And he'll never know what hit him." I turn to Richard. "Can you look after Sid? I'm going to New York first thing tomorrow morning."

chapter 11

Risk & Mitigation: The Stakes Keep Rising

Sierra maneuvers her truck through a mixture of mild rain and congested traffic, following the signs to the Detroit airport. I sit next to her, dressed up in my one really great outfit, picked out by Eve Gardner and paid for by Uncle Sam.

"Are you ready for this?" asks Sierra.

"I've been up all night preparing. But don't worry, my second wind never fails to appear when needed."

Sierra glances at me. "Well, you look great. Very hot for 7:00 a.m. Did you get all the paperwork from your lawyer in L.A.?"

"Yep. I've got the copyright from the Writers Guild and the Library of Congress, the trademark paperwork, original Lights Out business plan and DVDs."

"Is there anything else you need?"

"No. I'm good to go, thanks. The digital rights management company is in New York so I'll pick up that paperwork there. I'll keep you posted. Oh, there's my drop-off."

Sierra pulls over to the curb. "Good luck, Maddy."

"Thanks, Sierra." I hop out of her truck with one carry-on bag. Before I board the plane, though, it's time to reinstate a ritual. I proudly pick up a copy of the *Financial Street Journal*. I touch it fondly. I bring the headlines to my face and inhale the scent of black ink. I look at the words and proudly announce, "Hello, *FSJ*. I'm back."

Back in Tara's Ann Arbor town house, Arthur Pintock makes his move to open the closet of his deceased daughter. Gripped tightly in his hand is the pamphlet that his estranged wife Grace sent him. Neither Arthur nor Grace had taken steps to empty the town house in order to rent it or sell it. Surrounded now by empty boxes, Arthur stands alone beset by Tara's clothes, books, computer, notes, jewelry, shoes, photos, linens, electric piano, microphone...all the articles and possessions of his precious daughter's life.

He stops to sit on the edge of her bed, collect his psychic energy and refer once again to the minichapter on confronting the closet of a loved one. Arthur realizes he should be doing this with Grace. And that she is the only one he could possibly do it with. But it's too late for that now, he thinks.

He takes a deep breath and removes one of Tara's business suits, but then a box on the floor of the closet catches his eye: "Original Songs by Tara Pintock." He opens the box. It's filled with computer disks in protective cases neatly labeled and dated. He sifts through them, smiling at the humor in some of her titles. Then he sees a CD case labeled "He's Got Black Dye Under His Fingernails." Arthur tilts his head. The title is familiar. Didn't Madison Banks use that phrase the last time they had dinner together? Curious, he pops the disk into Tara's CD player on her nightstand. The song plays. Arthur listens as Tara sings a detailed tabloid-esque tale of a shyster named Derek who swindles his classmates and a college town for a prize he didn't deserve. The song depicts how the deceiver poured black dye into his competitor's laundry service business to win, thereby turning Tuesdays in Ann Arbor black forever. The chorus repeats, *"He's got black dye under his fingernails."*

Arthur listens to the song a second time. Then he pulls his cell phone out of his jacket pocket and hits a number. The automatic dial rings through to one of his associates.

"Jake? Arthur. You know that young man Derek Rogers I told you to help find a lender for. I want you to stall on closing his deal. There may be some risks involved that we don't yet know about. Right. I'll get back to you." He hangs up and hits another number. "Anita. Get hold of George Toffler at the *Financial Street Journal*. Tell him I'll give him an exclusive on my next move if he would do a little digging for me on Derek Rogers and the infamous Black Tuesdays of Ann Arbor. And one more thing, Anita. Find out for me where Madison Banks is these days."

In New York City I leave the offices of my digital rights management company and am soon entering the offices of Agam Publishing, the largest imprint of Panda House, the largest publishing company in the country, which is owned by Vertihore Media, one of the three largest media companies in the world, which also happens to own Ubiquitous Music.

I approach the receptionist with a smile. "Hi, I'm Madison Banks. Lights Out Enterprises. What's your name?"

The receptionist cagily responds, "I'm Jennifer."

"Hi, Jennifer. I'm here to see the president of legal affairs. I don't have an appointment but it is an urgent matter."

Jennifer responds by rote. "Mr. Darwen is not available right now."

"Is he in town today?"

"Yes, but he's on the phone. And he only takes meetings from three to five on Fridays. Today is Tuesday. So you'll just have to wait like everyone else."

I continue smiling, having expected the brush-off. I hand Jennifer a legal-size manila envelope. "In that case, please tell Mr. Darwen it's in his best interest to review the enclosed file immediately and that he can find me in the offices of Vertihore Media's chief of legal affairs and corporate communications—that would be Mr. Aidelman, who is both your and Mr. Darwen's ultimate boss—in—" I glance at my watch. It's now 10:30 a.m. "—approximately two hours." Then I pull out my PDA-cell phone-camera, which also captures video. I point and record Jennifer, the receptionist. "For my records, Jennifer, I just want to be clear that *you* are clear and understand the directions attached to the package that you now hold in your hands. So what will you do with it?"

Suddenly, on camera, Jennifer takes a more cordial and accountable tone. She can tell I mean business. Her haughtiness falters.

"I will notify Mr. Darwen that it's in his best interest to, um, review the contents of this right away. That it's urgent, and that you will be in Mr. Aidelman's office at Vertihore Media, in, uh, two hours."

"Excellent, Jennifer. I do appreciate it." I put the PDA-cell phone-camera in my purse and then pull out a small gift-wrapped box and hand it to her. "Here's a token of my thanks. It's perfume. I hope you like it."

Jennifer looks baffled. "Thank you. I'll make sure he gets this right away."

I leave Agam Publishing and step back onto the streets of

New York where I hail a cab to Panda House. This time I get past the receptionist to the secretary, pull the same stunt as before and drop off a duplicate package to Ms. Hadley, head of legal affairs.

On the street, I check my watch. I'm just ahead of schedule as I hop inside another cab for Vertihore Media. En route, I call Adam Berman on his direct line. As his phone rings, I whisper a prayer, "Please be there."

"Hello?"

"Adam," I say, relieved. "Madison Banks. Don't know if you got my e-mail last night, but I need to call in that favor you offered months ago. Can you help me?"

"With all the business we've done from adding Maurice LeSarde to our roster, name it."

I finish outlining my request to Adam as my cab pulls up to the Vertihore building in Times Square. I pay the driver and step out of the cab, only to be pushed around by a crowd gathered near the building next door. Unconcerned, I try to quickly slide past to the main doors of Vertihore. I maneuver through the crowd, uttering a continuous flow of *excuse me's*.

I collide into a spiffy, pressed Armani suit with a familiar scent. I'm about to say *excuse me* for the eighty-seventh time when I hear, "Maddy?"

I turn. It's Victor Winston. I swallow hard, forcing a grin. "Victor. Hi. You're alive and well. Imagine that. So, um, how are you?"

"I'm great. How are you?"

"Great, just great."

"So you got my invitation?"

"What invitation?"

"I sent you e-mails and tried calling you weeks ago. So…you're not in town for the grand opening?"

"Grand opening?"

He points to a mega-banner announcing the grand opening of Pearl Living Apartment-Lofts featuring Designer Tank's Furniture for the Future.

"The apartment-lofts," he says. "Remember?"

"You invited me to this? Did you say anything else?"

"I thought you might like to see how the building turned out and say hello to Norm and Elizabeth."

I nervously check my watch. It's 12:20 p.m. And the little hand is moving fast. I've got nine minutes to be in the office of Vertihore's chief of legal affairs and corporate communications.

Victor reprises his perspicacious once-over of me from when we first met. "You look really good, Maddy. No more black ribbon, I see."

"Oh, that. I haven't worn that in months. Look, I really have to go."

"Months, huh…" he murmurs. "You can't stay and celebrate?"

I think there's a hint of disappointment in his voice but I can't be sure. My mind is elsewhere. Before I can answer, Alyssa Ryan appears, tugging on Victor's arm.

"Quick, Victor, Norm wants a photo with the maddening crowd before we get on his private jet for lunch." She glances at me and then…ignores me.

Victor quietly yet firmly pulls his arm away from Alyssa. "I'll be there in a minute," he says. He turns back to me.

I smirk inside, knowing that an invitation to lunch was never part of the invitation to the opening for me.

"We should talk, Maddy."

"About what? The money we lost, I lost, that I'm still trying to gain back for you, or the results you're playing? Look, I really have to go. Goodbye, Victor."

"Wait a minute," he says, stopping me. "You said 'good-bye.' Not 'see ya later'?"

"Sorry, but I don't have a sixth sense," I say, and start to brush past him.

"Sixth sense? What does that mean?" Victor mumbles half to himself.

"Like the movie. Means she doesn't see dead people," offers someone in the crowd.

Within eight minutes, I'm sitting across the desk of Vertihore's head of legal affairs and corporate communications, Sanford Aidelman. I lay out my paperwork with all of the facts, check my watch and then look straight at Aidelman. "You should be receiving calls from your head of legal affairs at Panda House and Agam Publishing any moment now. I would appreciate it if they hear this on a conference call."

At that moment, Aidelman's intercom buzzes. "Mr. Darwen and Ms. Hadley are both on the line," says the voice of his secretary.

"I'll take them both," he says, staring at me with raised eyebrows. "Darwen, Hadley, welcome to the meeting. Ms. Banks here apparently has something very important for us to know about. Ms. Banks?"

"Thank you for your attention. Mr. Aidelman, Ms. Hadley and Mr. Darwen, the truth is that Derek Rogers of Tribute in a Box stole the pamphlet from our pay-per-view blog to sell you his so-called handbook. You all have copies of the files I dropped off, which contain the trademark, copyright, digital rights watermark and encryption code for the pamphlet. It all proves that the DNA of Derek's handbook was plagiarized from our pamphlet and is hence highly illegal. If you want further proof, compare the business plan of Lights Out Enterprises dated and launched six months prior to Tribute in a Box—also a case of plagiarism. But more importantly with respect to this publication, I can prove it right now with my do-it-yourself backup encryption code."

Aidelman's assistant slips in and out of the office with a cup of hot tea for me.

"Thanks," I say, and I promptly forget about it as I flip open my computer for a PowerPoint presentation. I jump to a slide with two alphabets, one on top of the other. "I used the Roman cipher to protect my intellectual property. In this case, I shifted the bottom alphabet over by three letters, so *A* equals *C*, *B* equals *D*, *C* equals *E* and so forth. Just in case anyone was to try anything. Now compare Derek's handbook on pages 6, 8, 10, 12, 14, 16 and 18 with our pamphlet on pages 7, 9, 11, 13, 15 and 17." I point out the code, which spells "Derek Rogers has black dye under his fingernails." "Everyone see?"

Aidelman lets out a long sigh. "Adam Berman wasn't kidding when he said I should take you seriously. Darwen, Hadley, please get on this right away, and in the meantime, stop all distribution of Mr. Rogers's handbook immediately."

I freeze, having a moment of victory. I finally release a breath. One battle won, or at least one move gained that will keep Derek behind the scrimmage line, but for how much longer? That's one question I'd like to put to rest forever.

Aidelman stares at me. "Madison Banks. Do you have a few minutes to stay and talk about your pamphlet?"

It was a question loaded with a first-and-ten position for me. "Yes, I do," I say, sliding into quarterback mentality.

Approximately twenty-nine hours later, I'm behind the bar at the Eagle's Nest cleaning shot glasses and recounting my New York adventure to Richard, Rocky and Mrs. Jones. Mrs. Jones strokes Siddhartha's head while she listens.

"And then he asked me, 'How many copies of your pamphlet have you sold?' I told him 'fourteen thousand at 2.99

apiece.' He said, 'That's approximately…' and I beat him to it, saying '$41,860.'"

"Damn," says Rocky. "That's awesome!"

"Wait, there's more. Then he says, 'How would you like a book deal with Panda House?' And I told him as long as my co-author and I retain worldwide e-publication rights, I'm open." I turn to Richard. "So, Richard, are you open to a publishing deal?"

"I think I could handle that." He smiles.

"Think you can handle a sequel, too?"

"No kidding."

Just then the door to the bar opens and Arthur Pintock, dressed in casual clothing, saunters toward the bar. It's so out of context for me that it takes me a minute to realize it's him. "Mr. Pintock! Hi! What brings you to Clark Lake?"

"You," he says, as he reaches the bar. "How are you, Maddy?"

"I'm good. This is Richard, and Rocky, and Lillian. Oh, and that's Siddhartha. Everyone, this is Arthur Pintock."

"Of Pintock International?" asks Lillian. "Your company helped my husband and me buy our first home twenty-one years ago. Thank you so much."

Arthur nods. "You're welcome. Nice to meet you all." He looks at Richard. "Richard Wright?"

"That's me."

"You both did a nice job on that pamphlet of yours. Without it, I don't think I would have been able to go through Tara's closet—at least half of it, for starters."

"I'm glad you found it helpful, and I'm sorry for your loss. Can I get you a drink? It's on the house," says Richard.

Arthur scans the specials on the chalkboard and grins. "I'll have Tara's Song. By the way, what's in it?"

"It's on the sweet side. Little Kahlúa, little vodka, little crushed ice, topped with whipped cream," replies Richard.

"Sounds great," says Arthur, who then trains his eyes on me. "Can we talk? In private?"

"Sure, let's go sit by the fire. Come on, Sid." Siddhartha follows us. Arthur and I pull two chairs up to the fire in the main room attached to the bar.

Arthur quietly begins, "While I was going through Tara's things I found her box of songs. One song in particular caught my attention. It prompted me to do some digging…as far back as Black Tuesdays. Why didn't you warn me about Derek Rogers's character?"

"I didn't know you were doing business with him. You told me he didn't need you and that you thought *he* and *I* should meet."

"Yes, well, he came back and worked his charm on me, but he never mentioned tributes, only acquisitions of mortuaries in terms of real-estate holdings."

Richard brings Arthur his drink. "Here ya go, Tara's Song."

Arthur takes a sip. "Excellent, thank you." Richard leaves, and Arthur focuses on our conversation. "What happened to Lights Out Enterprises? And don't hold back, Maddy."

"Basically, the FTC revised the Funeral Rule and adopted a new accreditation program devised by Derek Rogers, also to be officiated by Derek Rogers, with major penalties attached. Under the new rule, Lights Out got shut out."

"Isn't that a conflict of interest?"

"One would think," I say.

Arthur swirls his drink, thinking. "I've instructed my associate to hold off on mortgage lending for his expansion plans until I get to the bottom of his business practices. However, as the lender go-between, I know all the terms of the deal and if you want to see Lights Out get a long-overdue fair shake, I suggest you contact this particular list of funeral homes in Michigan, Ohio, New York and half a dozen other states and see if you can work out a mutually conducive arrangement with them." He pulls a sealed envelope from his pocket. "I can't make any guarantees, Maddy, but it might be worth a try."

"But I don't have the proper accreditation," I say.

"That can change, under different circumstances," replies Arthur as he hands me the envelope. "And I have a feeling it will, soon enough."

This time I hold the envelope in my hand along with the weight of Arthur's actions behind it. This was serious business, and for the first time in my life, I felt equal to the giants. But was the acceptance of this envelope an ethical move? I flashed back to the theme of *The Brothers Karamazov*—that anything is lawful, because everything is not lawful. Victor had been right all along: the game was far from over. But without Victor, I didn't know if I had the strength and wits to carry out this mission on my own. We had been a good team together. And it wasn't Richard's forte to fill Victor's role, nor did I have any intention of calling Victor to discuss it. Even though seeing him in New York had brought to the surface all the feelings I had fought so hard to bury, I would pay him back on his original investment from my share of the proceeds of the pamphlets and be done with him.

As if reading my mind, Arthur says, "You can do this on your own, Maddy, but if you need help, I'll be there. And it's not wrong—it's your turn for a fair opportunity."

"Thanks. I'll think about it."

"Good."

"What about you? I thought you wanted to leave Pintock International."

"When I find the right opportunity, I will," he says. "I've got to get back now."

We stand up and as I walk Arthur toward the door, Grace

Pintock enters. She and Arthur are surprised and shocked to see each other. It's a stiff, awkward moment. I see the love connection between them and then shut down, likely from memories and grief gone awry.

"Hello, Arthur. What are you doing here?" Grace asks innocently.

"I wanted to thank Maddy and Richard for writing that pamphlet. And thank you for sending it to me. It was, uh, most helpful, Grace."

"I'm glad. Well, um, Maddy, if you're busy, I can come back another time."

"You two have business to discuss?" inquires Arthur somewhat curiously.

"Maddy's helping me plan a life celebration for Tara," says Grace. "I want to complete what we didn't have a chance to do before."

"I see," says Arthur. There's an uncomfortable pause. I can feel the brief sting of Arthur's exclusion from his wife's new plan for closure and redemption—redemption to memorialize Tara's life and redemption to honor her own.

"Well, I was just leaving. It was nice…seeing you, Grace." And he walks out the door.

Grace watches him go. "You know, Maddy, I think maybe I should go over this with you at another time."

"Are you sure? You just got here."

Siddhartha nuzzles up to Grace and whimpers. Grace looks down and pets her. "No, I'm not sure."

"Why don't we make a start and then you can come back next week and we'll finish then. And by the way, Grace, you were right. He didn't know."

Grace nods. We sit down by the fire. Siddhartha curls up next to us as we go over Grace's plans.

★ ★ ★

The next day, I take Siddhartha for a long walk along a dirt path through the forest. The day is full of contrasts; large white puffy clouds drift in and out of a bright, crisp blue sky. An exceptionally warm breeze drifts through near-empty tree branches, as colored leaves slip to the ground, announcing the birth of fall.

I pull the sealed envelope out of my pocket and stare at it. I hold it in my hand, thinking as we walk the path. Siddhartha finds an acorn and proudly carries it in her mouth, looking for someone to show it to. We pass a farm where an old thoroughbred named Romeo roams the field. Siddhartha runs up to Romeo and drops the acorn for him and barks as if to make her gift known to him. Then she runs up to me and sits right down at my feet. I pull a carrot from my pocket and give it to Sid. Sid gently takes it in her mouth, carries it over to Romeo and plops it down next to the acorn, then backs up and barks at Romeo again. Romeo bends down and eats the carrot. Satisfied, Siddhartha rejoins me on our walk, taking the lead once again, happy that all is well with her assorted flock.

All the while, I ponder my options. What are the risks, what are the rewards and what does my gut have to say about it? Sid and I reach a small knoll in the woods. Siddhartha leaps on top of the knoll and with a glance, offers me an invitation to join her.

I climb to the top, pet her and look around. "Sid, think Uncle Sam is here?" I ask. Siddhartha barks and a ray of sunshine peeks through drifting clouds to land near my feet and Siddhartha's paws. I smile. "Just checking."

I hold the sealed envelope in the light. "What do you think?" The ray of light disappears for a long moment, and then just as suddenly it reappears even brighter than before. "Hmm. Interesting." I re-pocket the envelope in my jacket.

"Come on, Sid. Let's keep moving." And then I look up at the sun and add, "Thanks, Uncle Sam. That's what I thought."

Richard serves drinks at the Eagle's Nest while I stand engrossed at the computer next to the register, checking the blog for updates and responses. "Hey, Richard, someone from Louisville wants to know about outer burial containers and grave liners. Can you take this one and I'll cover for you?"

"Sure," he says, adding, "fellow at the end of the bar wants a mug of hot tea. Can you take this to him?" Richard hands me the mug.

"Got it," I say as we switch places. I carefully carry the tea to the end of the bar, only to discover Victor Winston quietly sitting there. I nearly drop the mug.

"Hi, Maddy," he says, smiling smugly. "How are you doing?"

"Victor. What…are you doing here?"

"I thought we should talk."

"Well, I can't talk. I'm working."

"I'll wait until you get off."

"That's not a good idea."

"Why not?"

"Because…because I have to work after I finish…working," I blurt out.

"Okay, well, when you have some time, let me know. Maybe during your break or something. I'll be right here."

"That's not a good idea, either."

"Why not?"

"Because…because, I'm not going to have time for a really long time," I sputter, exasperated, trying not to make a scene. "And I'm sure you have more important things to do than hang out in a bar on Clark Lake," I whisper fervently.

"No. I have nowhere to go, so whenever…because, you

know, the dead don't have agendas. Or do they?" Victor turns to Wally sitting next to him. "What do you think? Do the dead have agendas?"

"Hell, yes," says Wally. "You think they just stop being 'n doing cuz their bodies dropped out on 'em? Nah, I think they're comin' and goin' all around us. Not a day goes by I don't feel 'em in the air. Fact is, I think Guy's here right now."

"What do you think is his agenda?" asks Victor.

"To see to it that we appreciate life…the way he did."

"And how would that work?"

Wally thinks about it. "He'd probably want us to have a Guy Special."

"Okay, one round of Guy Specials for this gentleman and me," Victor tells me. "On me," he tells Wally.

"Thank you. Guy would appreciate that," says Wally.

I look up at the ceiling and shake my head, then get their drinks for them. I see Richard crack a smile to himself from behind the computer.

Victor spends the rest of the evening chatting with other customers and playing with Siddhartha. I do my best to ignore him. Rocky walks in and hands me my new subscription to the *Financial Street Journal*. I blatantly make a lot of noise as I snap it wide open to scan the headlines.

When Richard and I finally close up for the night, Victor asks me, "Can I drive you home?"

"No, thanks. Sid and I prefer to walk."

"Can I—"

"Girls only."

"All right," says Victor. He leans down to pet Siddhartha. "See ya later, Sid." He walks out.

The next night, I open up the bar wearing the black ribbon pinned to my shirt. Victor walks in right when the doors open and sits at the end of the bar. He carries with him a copy of the *Pamphlet on Grief Wellness & Creating Personalized Tributes.* He orders another cup of hot tea, which he never takes a sip of, then notices my shirt.

"What's with the black ribbon?" he asks.

He sounds surprised. "I thought you were done mourning your uncle."

"I am. I'm mourning an old lover now," I say, and turn around to ignore him.

"Ouch." He sits there for a moment, then quietly reads from his pamphlet until Lillian Jones enters. "Aren't you the one who painted that remarkable portrait of Guy?" Victor must recognize her from Guy's tribute.

"Yes, that's me, thank you."

"Could I hire you to paint my portrait?"

"Why, of course." She beams. "Do you have a particular location in mind?"

"Yes, right there, by the fireplace."

I pretend not to hear, realizing the fireplace is in my direct line of vision. I sigh to myself and roll my eyes.

Lillian grabs her paints and easels out of her car and spends the next three nights creating an exquisite portrait of Victor beside the fireplace with Siddhartha next to him remaining perfectly still.

Every time I call Siddhartha over to the bar, she refuses to come.

Richard smiles. "I think Sid is bent on having her portrait done, Maddy."

"F-fine," I stammer. "I need to check the e-mails anyway." I read one from Sanford Aidelman telling me to expect the contract for the book deal in two weeks. I send an e-mail to Arthur, letting him know how much I appreciate his intentions, but that I've decided to wait on that envelope he gave me...for now.

After we close shop, Victor asks if he can walk Sid and me home. Again, I refuse.

The next night, while having his portrait completed, Victor asks Lillian, "So tell me, what's the real estate like around here?"

I stare at Victor from across the bar, wondering what he's up to.

"Oh, you can still get some good buys," she says.

Just then, Victor's mobile phone rings. It's on the bar next to his pamphlet. I see it but ignore it.

"Hey, Victor," Richard calls, "your phone's ringing."

"Could you answer it for me? Thanks, Richard," Victor responds.

"Hello?" Richard covers the mouthpiece and calls out to Victor. "George Toffler from the *Financial Street Journal.*"

George Toffler calling Victor? What's that about? I snuff my curiosity by continuing to nonchalantly wipe down the bar.

Victor turns to Lillian. "Do you mind if we take a break?"

"Not at all," she replies.

Victor gets up and takes his cell phone outside with him. I peer after him. Fifteen minutes later he returns, still talking on the phone. He looks at me. "George Toffler would like to speak to you. He's had a difficult time getting a hold of you."

I hesitate. Taking the phone would acknowledge Victor's presence.

He smiles at me. "Just for tonight, we can pretend I've been temporarily resurrected."

I take the phone. "Hello?" Victor returns to his seat next to Siddhartha so Lillian can finish their portrait. I head outside for the conversation as Victor had done.

When I return twenty minutes later, I find Victor back at

the bar next to Lillian. I hand him his cell phone, pretending nothing unusual happened.

"Since we're pretending I'm in the flesh tonight, I'd like you to have something to remember me by," says Victor. He hands me the finished portrait of himself and Siddhartha. Even I feel my breath taken away by the incredible likeness of both man and beast. "Be careful not to touch it until it dries."

"It's remarkable," I comment.

"Thank you," says Lillian. "Now where are your manners?"

"Um, thank you," I say to Victor.

Victor, Lillian and Richard release simultaneous sighs. I look at them, wondering whose side they're on.

"With regard to that phone call we both received," says Victor, "there's something I need to show you and you're just going to have to trust me on this."

I hesitate. Anything to do with the *Financial Street Journal* is my Achilles' heel and he knows it, and I know he knows it. "How long will it take?" I ask.

"Two hours max," he says.

I turn to Richard. Before I can speak, he commands, "Get out of here. Now, please."

I climb inside Victor's rented hybrid. He drives us to the bowling alley.

"We're here," he says, and parks the car.

"The bowling alley? This better be good, Victor."

We enter the building and pass by Sally and Wally in the attached restaurant watching Roy Vernon sing "The Guy Ballad." A few bowling regulars spot me and wave hello. Victor misses it as he greets Carl behind the counter and buys two games and shoe rentals for each of us.

"The burgers still good here?" asks Victor, winking at Carl.

"Second to Eagle's Nest," replies Carl.

"Okay, two burgers and two lemonades. Is that okay with you, Maddy?"

"Whatever," I say, going along for the ride. "But I really don't feel like bowling."

"Is that because Madison Banks is actually afraid to lose?"

"Are you challenging me?"

"Absolutely."

"You're on," I reply.

Carl smiles as we get onto Lane 10.

We pick our bowling balls and start to play. I take aim and quickly claim a strike. Victor follows with one of his own.

"So what does bowling have to do with George Toffler?" I ask.

"Arthur Pintock started out as your front bowling-pin client, right? And I trust Toffler asked you all about Lights Out," he says. I nod, fearing a conundrum is on its way. "Well, it all ends here, Maddy. Because that phone call was instigated by Arthur Pintock. He specifically asked Toffler to investigate Derek Rogers. His fact-checking interviews are just part of a much bigger story. Your turn."

I grab my ball as I try to digest the information. I refocus and get another strike. I'm on fire.

"Nice," says Victor. "You've really improved."

"What kind of story?" I ask.

Victor rolls his ball for a spare. For the first time, I'm ahead of him. He takes it in stride and turns to me. "Tomorrow's *Journal* is going to cause Derek Rogers to implode. Tribute in a Box will soon be Toppled in a Box. And it's going to completely debunk the accreditation program under the new Funeral Rule. Lights Out won't be stymied anymore by Derek's shenanigans."

I sit down, stunned. "Are you serious?"

Carl brings us our burgers and lemonade. "Here ya go." He checks the ball machine, half-grins at Victor and splits.

Victor sits next to me. "Yes. But there's more. A lot more."

"What?"

He hands me an envelope. I open it up and there's a check for $36,876 made out to Lights Out Enterprises. "What's this?"

"Seems your protégée picked up quite a bit from you."

"My protégée?"

"When I asked Eve Gardner to wrap things up for you, she did. She closed a three-way co-branded deal with a client you introduced her to. The deal included repurposing a life bio video into music videos and commercials, and Eve got to promote FT 101 Designs in all of them. She even made sure a percentage of the revenue generated went to Lights Out Enterprises for initiating the relationships."

I scan my shoes. "Wow…she trumped me. I never thought of ancillary markets from the life bio videos."

"Your thought processes rubbed off on her…as did your ethics."

I am impressed by Eve. But Victor had said… "There's more?" I ask.

"It's in your next ball."

I look at him funny, but pick up my ball. Something's stuck in one of the holes. I pull it out. It's a sparkling diamond ring. "What the hell is this?"

"It's my way of asking you to marry me. Please, let me speak before midnight rolls around and you proclaim me history again." He takes a breath, exposing a degree of nervousness I've never seen in him before. "I think playing the results is overrated. I believe we're both missing out on what life is really supposed to be about. And I made a mistake, Maddy. I thought you weren't done grieving over Sam. That's why I left the way I did, which was pretty rotten of me and I'm sorry for that. I didn't realize what I was doing, which was trying not to compete with the dead. I've done that with my sister for my parents' attention for too long now. It was my issue, never yours…and I've resolved it." He pauses, shoring up his resolve. "I confronted my parents. I told them I can't stop living my life because they aren't living theirs or even acknowledging mine. It's not what Shauna would have wanted, either." He takes another breath. "Look, I love you, Maddy. And I'd like to be your husband…if you'll have me. But before you answer, I want you to know I'm real, I'm alive, and I'm not leaving."

Before I know what hit me, Victor takes me in his arms and kisses me. It's an amazing kiss and easily reignites my feelings for him. Finally, he pulls away.

"You think sticking a diamond ring in a bowling ball will make me swoon over you?" I ask.

"Well, that and the fact that I love you," he says. "Please, at least put it on."

I try the ring on. No go. "It doesn't fit. That's a bad sign." I give him a shy smile. "You really love me?"

"Yes. I really do love you."

"Yeah? Well, my love is going to cost you," I goad.

"I'm prepared for whatever that is," he says, catching my meaning.

"Okay, here's the deal, Victor—"

"Wait a minute. You're turning a marriage proposal into a business negotiation?"

"What's the problem with that? We are talking contracts, aren't we? And, well, I have some results that need to be played out before I can take you seriously."

"You're a much better entrepreneur than I gave you credit for. What's the deal?"

I pull out the sealed envelope that Arthur gave me five days ago. "See this?"

12

cHapter

Finale: Playing Maddy's Results—The Pièce de Résistance

Six a.m. the next morning. In the predawn darkness, Sid and I jog to the corner newsstand. I purchase a *Financial Street Journal* and aim my flashlight pen at the front page. The center headline reads, "Mortuary Empire Topples-in-a-Box: Derek Rogers's art of the scandal unravels into view," by George Toffler.

Toffler's lengthy exposé reveals the scandal behind Derek's entire career, concluding with the plagiarism of the business plans developed "by Ms. Madison Banks for Artists International and Lights Out Enterprises, which Mr. Rogers turned into Palette Enterprises (PE) and Tribute in a Box (TIAB)."

In addition, Toffler includes "Mr. Rogers's crime of stealing Ms. Banks's and Mr. Wright's $2.99 online *Pamphlet for Grief Wellness & Creating the Personalized Tribute* and turning it into *The Heartache Handbook for Tributes in a Box* for an advance of $500,000 from Agam Publishing in a first-run distribution deal of 75,000 books that had to be pulled in the eleventh hour when Vertihore Media's legal chief, Mr. Sanford Aidelman, was confronted by Ms. Banks on the issue, at which time Ms. Banks easily proved ownership of her intellectual property."

Toffler goes on to reveal how "Mr. Rogers's leadership of PE leaves the company in financial shambles, exposing not only lavish bonuses paid to himself and his consultant, Mr. Jonny Bright, but mismanagement of funds, embezzlement and bribes committed with analysts to increase stock value."

A great deal more is said of Mr. Rogers's graft with Washington lobbyists and committee members who received TIAB stock in return for making Mr. Rogers the czar of his own accreditation program inside the new Funeral Rule. And that "his lack of compliance with regard to pre-need arrangements and investments in the funeral industry makes him subject to a potential shareholder's derivative case plus major fines with both PE and TIAB. Under the Sarbanes-Oxley Act of 2002, Mr. Rogers must certify company statements as accurate under a threat of perjury subject to criminal penalties of up to twenty years in prison, and investigators intend to prove 'guilty knowledge' and 'intent' on Mr. Rogers's part to swindle shareholders and stakeholders." Toffler makes it clear that this story is not an indictment of the funeral industry, but one crooked white-collar criminal.

The pièce de résistance appears when Toffler concludes, "Ms. Madison Banks is the unsung heroine, and victim of a number of Mr. Rogers's endeavors that under her stewardship might have provided quite a different outcome. How different, we'll find out in the next installment: 'Jackson, MI—Mecca for Personalized Tributes.'"

I do a double take, surprised by the length of the story and its cliffhanger.

Seven-thirty a.m. Showered and comfortably dressed, I pace the deck of Uncle Sam's house overlooking Clark Lake. On this day, I wear a headset to keep my hands and arms free for battle. Siddhartha stays close to me, anticipating the action to come.

I roll up my sleeve, look at my watch; it's now 7:35 a.m. eastern standard time. I dial a number. "Get ready, Sid. It's show time."

I hum the theme song for *Mission: Impossible* until an answering machine comes on. "You've reached Tribute in a Box Corporation. For Derek Rogers, press one. For Jonny Bright, press two—" I hit one. "This is Derek Rogers, please leave a message."

"Hello, Derek. Madison Banks here. Just want you to know that I'm going after your expansion plan. May the best entrepreneur win…and by the way, if you're interested in selling, say, matching your previous offer to me…you know where to find me. Have a good day."

I leave a similar announcement for Jonny Bright, adding that unlike him with his style of subterfuge, I prefer to be up-front.

I continue to pace the deck, then speed-dial a number, leaving the message, "I'm good to go." I hit End, and then punch several more numbers, playing the buttons on the phone like rounds of artillery.

I lay my blueprint of names and numbers on the table and place rocks on the top corners to stabilize it. Beside the blueprint are a standard tape recorder and two brown paper bags. I start pressing corporate office numbers of funeral homes and the extensions of their leaders. As soon as I get voice mail, I launch the tape recorder. "This is Madison Banks, CEO of Lights Out Enterprises. I'm interested in discussing mutually favorable co-ownership and co-revenue sharing opportunities with your organization. If you're interested, please call…"

I do this ten times, then I look at my watch: 8:45 a.m. I hit another button to leave yet another message. "Phase One complete. Check in from the field."

I pick up the two brown paper bags and the tape recorder and then leap into the car with Sid. I drive to a cemetery in Ann Arbor and purposefully walk over to the grave of my cousin Smitty. I hold up my flashlight pen, remove a bottle from one of the brown bags and gently set it next to Smitty's gravestone while reciting the *kaddish*. The label reads "Everlasting Cologne for Men." It was Smitty's trademark. "Here's to you, Smitty," I say. "The coolest cousin I ever had."

I walk over to another grave. It's Tara Pintock's. Sid walks beside me. I remove the second bottle from the second bag. It's Tara's favorite, Lyric Perfume, of course. I hold up the flashlight pen and place the perfume on the grass. "For you, Tara. You will always be in my heart. And I really hope you're seeing just how big a part you still play in my life. Thanks for the song." I close my eyes. "Goodbye to both of you."

Several moments pass. I open my eyes and check my watch: 9:45 a.m. My PDA beeps. I check the e-mail and immediately hop back in the car with Sid and drive to the headquarters of Pintock International.

Ten-fifteen a.m. Sid and I sit on the couch in Arthur's office. "I couldn't do it before this article, Arthur. I wouldn't have had a clear conscience going behind Derek's back, even though he's gone behind mine…many times."

"I respect you for that, Maddy," says Arthur.

Anita's voice enters the room through the intercom. "Mr. Derek Rogers is on the line."

"Put him through," says Arthur. He nods at me. I hit Record on my tape recorder and then ready my fingers on top of my PDA keypad.

"Hey, Arthur, how ya doing today?" says Derek, trying to sound cheerful.

Sid raises her ears at the sound of his voice and lets out a small growl. I quickly shush her.

Arthur cuts to the chase. "Derek. I'm afraid I have some bad news for you. The lender has decided to renege on your expansion plans. After the article in the press today, they feel your credibility as a business leader has been greatly diminished."

"That's ridiculous," states Derek. "It's just a silly article. I've already spoken to Toffler and he's preparing a reprint with an apology. He's well aware that if he doesn't do so, he'll be facing charges for libel."

Arthur looks at me. I shoot a quick e-mail to George Toffler.

"Even if what you say is true, Derek, there's the issue of compliance. The lender can't go through with the deal if charges are brought against you."

"I've taken care of that, Arthur. The right people in the right places know exactly what to do. Trust me, the lender has nothing to worry about."

"What does that mean?" asks Arthur.

I receive an e-mail response from Toffler denying any contact from Derek for a reprint or any mention of legal action. I look at Arthur and shake my head.

"It means there won't be any charges," says Derek. "There's

too much money at stake. Too many people are way too involved to let that happen. And besides, I'm way above that, Arthur."

"Derek. I don't think you realize the seriousness of the implications here. The lender feels the risk is too great and has backed out of the deal."

"That's not possible. We were supposed to sign two weeks ago. They can't just walk away from a two-hundred-million-dollar deal on the table!"

"They can. And they did. It's business, Derek. Sometimes you win, sometimes you lose."

"No, that's not the way I do business. I never lose, Arthur. Never."

"Whatever your game is, Derek, it won't be with Pintock International."

"Listen to me. It's you who doesn't understand the implications involved here. This will be a terrible loss for you, Arthur. I've got other lenders lined up who can't wait to get in. You're going to come back to me begging to be in on this!"

"Is this how you want me to remember you, Derek? Threatening me? You ought to try a pseudo-death sometime. It might be good for your head. Best of luck to you, Derek, you're going to need it. Goodbye." Arthur hangs up. "Talk about true colors. Now let's get that lender on the line." He buzzes Anita. "Anita, please get Jerry Haggerty from Money Manhattan on the line for me."

"Arnie's son?" I ask.

"Yes, do you know him?"

"We met briefly at Arnie Haggerty's tribute. You had referred me to him, remember?"

"Yes, of course. I was out of the country when he passed away but it was the talk of the town. Shortly after that, Jerry took over for his father."

"Jerry Haggerty's on the line," says the voice of Anita.

"Jerry? Arthur. How would you like to put the funeral home consortium deal back on the table, only with a different leader, different company, whole new ball game."

"Who do you have in mind?" asks Jerry.

"Madison Banks of Lights Out Enterprises. I believe you've met."

"I'm interested," says Jerry. "Very interested. But are the funeral homes?"

Just then, my PDA alerts me to another e-mail. It reads, "11:05 a.m. Ohio, Michigan and New York are in."

I speak up. "Hello, Mr. Haggerty. Madison Banks here. And yes, so far all the funeral homes in Ohio, Michigan and New York are in, though the terms have been adjusted to reflect a co-op rather than a hostile takeover, which will actually reduce your risk."

"I'm all for that. Mr. Rogers's terms were much too one-sided for my taste," says Jerry. "Get me the new terms of the deal and count me in."

"Thank you," says Arthur. "We'll be in touch." He hangs up. "Congratulations, Maddy, especially when the rest of the funeral homes sign up—and I'm sure they will."

"Thank you, Arthur. I couldn't have done this without you. But I need your advice on one more matter before wrapping this up. Would you meet me at the Eagle's Nest tonight at seven-thirty?"

"Sure. I'll see you then."

"Great. Before you come, take a look at this DVD." I hand him one labeled "The Designer Tank."

Seven p.m. I'm working the bar at the Eagle's Nest when my cell phone rings. Caller ID says "Unknown." I answer with my speaker on. "This is Madison."

"You bitch! Not one lender will even talk to Jonny or me. You fucked me!" screams Derek Rogers.

I hold the phone away from me and take a deep breath, then calmly reply, "Why don't you look at your initial exposure and expenditures, Derek, and the way you treat people. I think that you'll see…you fucked yourself. Bye-bye." I hang up.

Those sitting at the bar listening—Carl, Rocky, Lillian, Wally and Sally—clap their hands and cheer!

I hold up my hand. "We're not done yet." I look at my watch. 7:10 p.m.

"What do you give it?" asks Richard.

"Any second now." And right on cue, my phone rings again. I keep it on speaker. "This is Madison."

"Madison. Bobby Garelik here. I just fired Derek Rogers and Jonny Bright. I'm putting Tribute in a Box up for sale. Are you interested?"

"You won't get your original investment back," I say.

"As long as I get something."

"All right, meet me at the Eagle's Nest and we'll go over it."

"Okay. What's the address?"

"Eagle Point on Clark Lake in Jackson, Michigan."

There's a pause. "I'll see you in two days."

More cheers from the barflies. I hang up and wink at Richard.

"Boy, am I glad I'm on your team," he says.

Seven-thirty p.m. Arthur Pintock enters. He greets everyone and hands me the DVD. "This design team is excellent, Maddy. Thanks for turning me on to them. If I ever find a need, I'll definitely contact them. So what's our meeting about?"

"Well, it's to gather some advice from both you and Richard."

Richard looks at me. "You want my advice?"

"Yes. Do you mind if we take it to the fireplace? Rocky said he'd take over the bar for us."

Seven forty-five p.m. I sit by the fire with Arthur and Richard. "I've called you both here to ask—" Another e-mail alert hits my PDA. "Excuse me." I glance at the e-mail, look up and smile. "Kentucky, D.C., Maryland and Delaware are in."

"It's getting bigger by the minute, Maddy," says Arthur. "How are you going to handle this?"

"Well, that's the thing. Day-to-day operations on the funeral and cemetery side are going to require not only someone with a degree in mortuary sciences, but someone with a real understanding of how to deal with people fairly and compassionately, and with long-term experience in the field of operations."

"Well, isn't that your forte, Richard?" asks Arthur. "You not only co-wrote the pamphlet, my understanding is that you've owned and ran the Jackson Funeral Home your whole life, until Derek Rogers bought you out."

"Me?" says Richard. "That's a bigger scale than I'm used to."

"I don't see why you can't do it," says Arthur. "All you need is the right support staff. Anyone come to mind?"

I jump in. "I would think maybe some of the locals would be a good place to start and some of the workshoppers like Grace, who's a natural at planning life celebrations. She really gets it." I glance at the bar where Lillian, Carl, Rocky, Wally, Sally, and now Roy, Eleanor, Charlie, Daniel, Rebecca, Andy, Milton and Sierra all crowd around. Sierra winks at me. Richard's and Arthur's gazes follow mine.

"I never thought of it that way," says Richard. At the sight of all of them together he can begin to see the possibilities. "Yeah, I think I could manage," he agrees. A huge smile takes shape on his face.

"But I'm concerned about something else," I say to Arthur and Richard. "All these funeral homes that we're acquiring— I think they're awfully dated in terms of their physical structures. I'm not sure we'll get the maximum benefit out of them for the increase in nontraditional services. They need kitchens and bars and fireplaces, and, well, a whole makeover for a whole new approach. I think we really need someone who brings a fresh sense of design and architecture to the table, to make each building a unique monument, functional and celebration-friendly for today."

"Is that why you had me watch that DVD? You want the Designer Tank to create new designs for tribute centers?" asks Arthur.

"Yes, they would be one element, but there are lots of possibilities. Imagine if other architects and designers got involved... But someone with the right skills and knowledge needs to oversee it." I look directly at Arthur. "Someone like you...someone who's looking for the right opportunity."

Arthur looks stunned. Then he sits back and smiles. "Yes. I do believe this is the right opportunity, Madison Banks. The right opportunity indeed."

Before anyone says another word, Grace Pintock enters the bar. She heads toward me, but as soon as she sees Arthur, she stiffens. "Perhaps I should come back another time."

"No," says Arthur, standing up to greet her. "Stay. Apparently, you and I have a new knack in common."

Grace starts to soften but seems a little unsure.

"Yes. Stay," I implore. "Have a Tara's Song. Then you two can play your results out at the bowling alley. You'd be surprised what knocking down a bunch of pins can do."

Six a.m., two mornings later. An ethereal mist hovers over the lake as I sit inside the Sunfish alone.

I talk quietly into the delicate mist. "And then suddenly all the pieces in the puzzle came together, Uncle Sam. You were right. Patience is key. And one set of ethics to live by." I pause. "I guess it's time I honor your request." I pull out the Ziploc bag with Uncle Sam's remains inside. "I now know that saying goodbye to you in this form just means hello in another. You really did stay by my side. I downloaded this new release for you." I punch a button on my PDA cell phone. Maurice LeSarde's "Fishing Free" plays quietly in the boat.

"Goodbye," I whisper, and slowly release Uncle Sam into Clark Lake. A ray of soft sunshine reaches through the mist to touch the patch of water around me. I see the miracle and smile. "And hello, again."

I hear a bark. In the distance. I make out the shape of a floating object stealthily approaching. As dawn gently breaks through the fog, I make out the form of a dog on top of a kayak.

Victor and a tail-wagging Siddhartha paddle up beside me.

"Good morning." Victor smiles.

"Good morning to you. How did you find me?"

"I have a GPS, remember? Out here it's called Sid."

"Well, in that case, what took you so long?"

"Norm Pearl's private jet had to make an unexpected stop in Los Angeles. So while we were there I pulled a few things out of storage, like my kayak."

"Is that how you covered so many states so quickly?"

"You seem to forget that I can be almost as resourceful as you can." He looks at my sailboat resting in a dead calm. "There's no wind. How were you planning on getting back to shore?"

"Patience…that the universe would provide." I smile.

"A man and a dog in a kayak?"

"Exactly."

"Lucky for you, I come prepared." He ties a rope from the back of his kayak onto the bow of my boat. Siddhartha jumps into the Sunfish with me.

I pet Sid. "Yes, we're quite lucky," I tell her. "What other goodies do you have?"

He tosses a Ziploc bag into the boat. Inside is the morning edition of the *Financial Street Journal.* "Page one, front and center," he says with confidence.

As Victor paddles us back to shore, I read the latest installment by George Toffler, titled "Jackson, MI—Mecca for Personalized Tributes: How a Small Town Became Proof of Concept." He outlines my arduous, grassroots journey to build a company with a little town of artists and heroes known for creating memorable events that celebrate the life of its people (and its pets), how a small town created a Funeral Fund from pamphlets and workshops on grief counseling and experience design, including the role of Richard Wright and the Eagle's Nest. And he breaks the news of Arthur Pintock's resignation from Pintock International to join Lights Out Enterprises as chief design officer. He adds that Arthur Pintock has declared a mandatory action for every viable candidate who wishes to succeed him at Pintock International. The action? The intended successor must go through the Lights Out pre-need program. Pintock believes that the results played out by this action will reveal the successor, because how a successor plans to die will tell him how they plan to live—and how they plan to live will tell him how they plan to lead. Toffler ends on Lights Out's expansion plans with Madison Banks, Richard Wright, Arthur Pintock and Victor Winston at its helm.

I feel a bump and turn around. We've reached land. Sid leaps into the shallow water. Victor glides his kayak onto shore. I toss the paper down and jump out to help pull the sailboat in.

"What do you think?" he asks.

"I think it's great. Don't you?"

"I'm not sure if it should face north or west."

"What are you talking about?"

He glances toward the other side of the property. I look up to see the patina sculpture of Uncle Sam standing between the deck and the shoreline. My mouth drops open. "Oh my goodness! How did you...get this here?"

"I told you. I had to pull a few things out of storage."

I run up to the sculpture. I run my hand along its contours. "Did I ever tell you the story of when Uncle Sam and—" I stop. There inside the memento holder is the ill-fitting wedding ring Victor tried to give me in the bowling alley. I look up at him.

"Now will you marry me?" he asks.

I put the ring on my finger. It's a perfect fit. "Yes, I'd love to marry you." I beam.

"How about a kiss to seal the deal?"

"I can't wait," I reply. He takes me in his arms.

"Where would you like to get married, Maddy?"

"Right here."

"I'm not surprised."

"Victor? You know what? With or without Lights Out, and with or without this ring...I'm the richest girl in the world."

"Why is that?"

"My self-worth has finally capped my net worth."

He smiles at me. "What took you so long?"

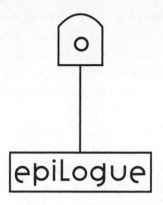

Everyone's Exit Strategy

The Lights Out expansion plan goes through and prospers, including the acquisition of Tribute in a Box at a highly reduced rate.

Richard Wright and the town of Jackson run the operations from the newly remodeled Jackson Funeral Home, its striking renovation delivered under the guidance of Arthur Pintock.

Maddy, Victor, Arthur and Norm start The Tribute Network, a cable network dedicated to life celebrations, informative programming on care for the dying, grief counseling, diversity of social customs surrounding death, as well as available options for pre-need and time-of-need experiences. Some of the program titles we develop include *Lights Out Around the World Tour* (a show about customized tributes in different cultures); *Designer Funeral Homes* (Arthur

Pintock's works-in-progress); *DIY—Do It Yourself Funerals* (where to get customized gravestones, what to know about cremation, casket-buying, green burial opportunities, et cetera); *Pet Tribute Stories; What to Know about Pre-Need; Grief Wellness, Life Celebration Fashions* and more.

Daniel Banks gets a book deal on *Authentic Tribute Poems* from Agam Publishing. Andy convinces Daniel to let him take some of the profits and invest it. He invests in products he likes and makes the money multiply…apparently Maddy's talk on dollar cost averaging left a mark on Andy.

Eve Gardner's FT 101 takes off and wins the Challenge a Vision Prize in school. She no longer searches for an MBA husband to support her. Instead she takes the boy from the bizarro student film she made and turns him into her vice president of operations.

Maurice LeSarde records a cult-favorite CD of Tara's songs, and launches a successful comeback in the youth market.

The List of Happily-Ever-Afters

Arthur & Grace Pintock reunite with a second wedding at the Jackson Bowling Lanes and produce an anniversary tribute fitting for Tara à la Lights Out style.

Daniel & Rebecca fall in love again and forgo all plans for divorce.

Sierra & Milton become engaged.

Norm & Elizabeth Pearl happily raise an adopted baby girl from China and continue to expand the Golf Camp Academies.

Alyssa Ryan & Davide elope.

Wally & Sally move in together.

Maddy & Victor have their wedding on Clark Lake—a

two-day event filled with stories, emceed by Eleanor and Charlie, with customized poems by Daniel, scrambled eggs, Neshama sausages and a live concert by Roy Vernon and Maurice LeSarde. FT 101 Designs handles all the wedding attire. Maddy and Victor soon after buy the house next door to Uncle Sam's and make their home together on Clark Lake.

Victor's parents have a celebratory tribute for Shoshanna and love Victor in the present.

<u>Unhappily-Ever-Afters</u>

Bobby Garelik loses most of his investment in TIAB, save for the small amount he makes back on the sale to Lights Out. The good news is, he becomes a primary investor in the Tribute Network, which saves Shepherd Venture Capital from going under.

Jonny Bright goes to prison for five years for investor fraud.

Derek Rogers is sued in a shareholders derivative case. His "veil of ignorance" defense strategy fails and he goes to jail for twelve years. In prison, he receives a gift from Maddy— a copy of *The Canterbury Tales*—and highlighted in yellow marker is "The Reeve's Tale"—with Cliffs Notes declaring the deceiver is finally deceived.

For this dyed-in-the-wool city mom,
life in the country is no walk in the park…

Wonderboy
Fiona Gibson
On sale September 2005

Urbanite parents Ro and Marcus are trading in life in
London's fast lane for a quiet country life in Chetsley.
As Ro struggles to adjust to the "simple life" though,
she learns that her husband's reasons for moving may
not have been so simple, and Ro must make a decision
that may change her and her son's life for good.

**Available wherever
trade paperbacks
are sold.**

RED
DRESS
INK
TM

www.RedDressInk.com

RDIFG532TR

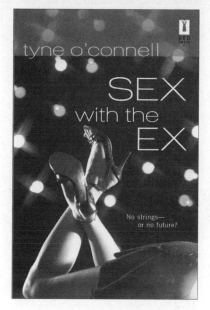